OIL FOR THE LAMPS
OF
CHINA

Oil *for the* Lamps
of
China

ALICE TISDALE HOBART

BANTAM BOOKS
NEW YORK

A BANTAM BOOK *published by arrangement with*
The Bobbs-Merrill Company

Bantam Edition Published
November, 1945

Second Printing January, 1946

To

MY HUSBAND

None of the characters in this book is a portrait from life. All are creatures of the imagination. Neither is any institution described an actual one. The oil business was chosen because light is symbolic of progress. Likewise, the events related are not history. The whole is a composite of my experiences, observations and reflections during a life spent in China and elsewhere.

I have endeavored to simplify the complicated Romanization of Chinese words in order to help the reader in their pronunciation.

A. T. H.

OIL FOR THE LAMPS
OF
CHINA

PART ONE

I

To THE north where the red plains of Manchuria draw near to Siberia the light of the September dawn lay along the horizon. But inside the inn there was no suggestion of day. The paper window-panes, coated with dust, were not brightened by that faint glow, and the wooden door was shut. But some hint of morning must have touched Stephen Chase's mind, for he turned over on the brick platform, the common bed of the inn, and reaching under his pillow drew forth his electric torch, centering its beam full on his watch. The hands pointed to three o'clock.

The ray from his flash shining through the bars of his mosquito net and along the *k'ang* showed him the other wayfarers lying in a row, wrapped in their blankets, only their stiff black hair visible. As he switched off his torch and the inn dropped back into darkness his body grew heavy with sleep. There was plenty of time . . . the carters said they could make the town by early afternoon . . . besides the mules would not be done eating . . . it was only a little while ago he'd heard the carters go out to give them their midnight feeding . . . sleep, how good.

To the surface of his mind rose an image of Lucy, a far-off shining presence. Half-dreaming, half-thinking, he saw a long road of endeavor over which he trudged

1

toward her. Two-thirds of it behind him, another year and he could go back to America for Lucy. A hurdle ahead of him—his mind moved up upon it—an important piece of work, his first opportunity to do something on his own. Success . . . defeat—he jerked himself wide awake. Better not to rely on the Oriental to estimate the time of arrival. He must be on his way by four if he were to be certain of making his destination by sundown.

"Kin, a candle," he called, "and get the carters started." The voice of a Chinese farther along on the *k'ang* grunted in response.

Stephen, within the dark and tiny house the four walls of his mosquito net made around him, attempted to dress, fumbling for his clothes which the night before he had placed carefully under the corner of his mattress. "Too dark. Mustn't use my flash. Kin will be along after a while with a candle." But although he sat quietly waiting, his feet out before him, the palms of his hands flat down on his thin mattress to support him, his slight young body was full of suppressed energy.

Ignoring the rustling of travelers stirring on the *k'ang*, their coughing and spitting, his mind went busily tracing the pattern of his work through the two years that he had been in Manchuria for this American oil company. Two years of rigorous training: first in the Company's main office listening to the "boss," as the men affectionately called the local manager of Manchuria, while he talked over important business matters with the Chinese agents; going on short trips to settle small matters of business, an interpreter to aid him; later made the inspector of Manchuria, investigating opportunities for expansion; now, for the first time, entrusted with the difficult and delicate undertaking of choosing a Chinese agent for a new territory.

He had no interpreter because the boss felt that any Chinese would feel it his inalienable right to arrange a

2

commission for himself out of the deal. Therefore, with his limited knowledge of the language, he must handle the arrangements alone. He must be careful not to fail in the nice etiquette demanded; if he did, he might lose a good agent for the Company. On the other hand, in his care to maintain the "face" of the would-be agent, there was the danger of stumbling into a trap the man might shrewdly set for him, thus in some adroit way gaining undue advantage. He felt a glow of pride—the boss had confidence in him. He'd done pretty well for a "griffin."

Suddenly his mind gave a leap backward. He was in New York, sitting in the classroom high up in the oil company's great building. It was the morning the appointments were made. The instructor of the class in foreign trade stood at the blackboard, drawing a rough map of the world. Stephen could feel the old tightening of his heart. Would he stand the last test? Three months before there had been one hundred young men in this class. Now there were but twenty. Then his name and his station were read out.

He had work to do! His sense of self-respect sharpened. After his graduation from the College of Mines two years earlier he had sought futilely for a position. With the country caught in the depression of 1908, the mining profession was glutted with men. Then he had felt the humiliation of the jobless. But now he had his place in the work of this great corporation.

The corporation. After the assignments had been made, a director of the Company had spoken to them of what the corporation wanted. Cooperation, emphasis on the whole and not the individual, hard work and loyalty.

"From my own experience," he had ended. "If you give these things—you know the reputation of the Company—it takes care of its men." In the two years of his service, Stephen had learned something of the import of those words.

Ah, there was Kin! Stephen watched the face of a middle-aged Chinese appear out of the murky background of the room and move toward him. Illuminated by a burning candle the man held in his hand, his smooth yellow skin, high cheek-bones and calm black eyes struck Stephen anew with their racial peculiarity. With an interest which never seemed to lessen, although he had seen him do the same things many times before, Stephen observed his servant let the wax run from the candle making a little mound on the foot-high table beside him. Just before the wax hardened, Kin placed the candle with delicate precision in its center; then, with one flick of his hand, he released the mosquito net from under the mattress and tossed its folds over the beam to which it was fastened.

Stephen dressed quickly, sitting on the edge of the *k'ang* to draw on his trousers, careful not to touch his feet to the earth of the floor until he had his shoes on. At the end of the *k'ang* a flame leaped out of the flue of the brick stove which in winter heated the platform and in all seasons heated the cauldron placed over it. The inn-keeper pulled back the wooden bolt and opened the door, letting in the morning.

"Chow, master." Kin put a plate of eggs and a pot of coffee on the *k'ang* table and dropped the net around it to keep off the flies. Stephen, looking at the food, felt the stale night air of the inn filling his lungs almost to the point of nausea and, walking to the door, stepped over its threshold into the morning.

The clear tonic air ran into his lungs like wine into the stomach. The sun, just showing over the high red plumes of the giant sorghum which grew close to the brushwood fence of the inn, touched his imagination into life. He saw the three hundred thousand square miles of Manchuria spread out before him—virgin forests, great rivers,

4

arc of hills encircling its immense red plain. For two years he had been traveling over these stretches by rail, by junk, by mule-cart; always each trip a new destination, something new to see. Now he wanted to start the day's journey for its own sake.

He went back into the inn, resolutely eating his breakfast, helping down the not too fresh eggs with an abundance of mustard pickles, in turn washing the pickles down with strong black coffee.

As once more he came forth the sun had risen clear of the horizon and the tall grain. The courtyard was filled with the bustle of many journeys. All the carts were faced toward the gate of departure; mules and ponies and horses were being forced into the shafts, donkeys were braying, men were shouting and gesticulating.

"I'll walk," Stephen said to his servant as together they lashed his food basket and traveling kit to a platform at the back of the cart. Kin sprang to the right shaft, the driver to the left, letting his long whip sing and crack about the eyes of the shaft mule and the lead mules. The cart bumped its way over the high sill of the gate into the rutted road.

All was silent in the fields except for the creak of the cart. In the golden light of the morning, across a field of low-growing beans, Stephen's shadow, moving black and enormous, brought him some special sense of importance. Now time stretched shining and unbroken from sunup to sundown. So it had been for three weeks.

Hour after hour he went forward, never breaking his rhythmic slog, slog, never lessening, never increasing the space between himself and his plodding equipage. Two years had trained his mind and muscles to the slow even rhythm of primitive travel across gigantic distances. He kept his eyes on the road unwinding under the cart, flowing toward him, a rough red band of tangled hoof-

5

marks between the deep ruts which heavy wheels had made. The modern world lay far, far away. He was lost to all but the vagabond days, the life of the inns, the rumbling cart.

For a long time he did not look up, but he knew by the pull on his muscles that the road was gradually but steadily mounting. An hour, two; the black shadows of the cart, the mule, himself, became less attenuated, grew stocky. Abruptly the red band stopped unwinding as the mules stood still, panting from the climb. Stephen looked up to see a plain, vast, rolling, set above the vaster plain of all Manchuria spread out before him. The *kaoliang* reached its red-gold heads of grain toward the blue sky. In large fields the soya-bean stood rank and vigorous. The oats and the wheat and an occasional field of beans had already been harvested, leaving red-brown patches. Clouds, like bags stuffed with foam, floated free between the sky and the earth, now and then passing before the sun and throwing shadows over the plain. Here and there the tiny figures of men bent to their sickles cutting the grain, and women in bright red trousers and blue top garments gathered it into bundles. An occasional brown hut nestled to a curve in the earth's surface. Stephen stood enthralled in this spacious outer room of China as yet so little tenanted.

He thought as he had so often, "A new land like our West." Enterprise brought these frontiersmen here. Progress should follow fast. Already railroads had been built—to be sure by Russia and Japan, not China, but they were the beginning. The telegraph tied together a few cities. Soon the country would be well lighted, too. Light had become Stephen's fixed idea of progress.

The cart began rumbling, the road unrolling beneath it, narrowing, threading its way through the *kaoliang,* an eight-foot-high forest of slender stalks. Above Stephen's head the blade-shaped leaves made tiny clashing sounds

6

like toy swords. On through the lower-growing beans, a waist-high growth, on, on.

As the hours and the silence accumulated, he thought of the talk of other men. The Company had no right to send them off on these long journeys, they complained. The trips should be shorter. It was too much to be isolated among the Chinese for weeks at a time; it made men queer. In proof of it, always the same old tales were brought forward: a man living alone in a remote station carrying on lively conversation with himself each evening at dinner; a man returning after a long absence wearing a sparse mustache, a few straggling hairs that drooped to his chest. "A Chinaman's mustache," they said meaningly. Stephen wondered at these vagaries. He had found a kind of solitude living among the Chinese and he had no objection to solitude. There was something within him that responded to this dispeopled world. Around him was the shining air, ahead the open road. He wanted little, he felt no haste.

Days like this brought his desire for Lucy back again to a gentle thing. He and Lucy going off into such sweet freedom as this, walking hand in hand all day, lying close together under the hood of the car in the inn inclosure all the night. Alone he would be with his mate, the animals munching near. . . .

The reality of dark inns, closely shuttered through the night against robbers, did not enter into his dream. Neither did the words from his mother's last letter. She had seen Lucy. "She has grown up. Are you growing up, Stephen?"

Last night how the words had torn at his heart; in the darkness he was caught in the anguish of uncertainty and his inability to end it. But not to-day! The bright thin air lightening his body, this brilliant northern sunlight beating through his khaki coat, seeming at times to penetrate even his sun helmet, making his head throb, pitched

7

him to some high ecstatic mood. Only his dreams seemed real.

The ruts of the road became deeper as it led down the street of the village, all but empty now. Men, women, children in the harvest-fields, only a few old women in the town washing clothes in a stone trough. Stephen stopped for the noonday meal for man and mule. Almost the stillness of the plain lay in the village, broken only by the pat of wooden paddles on wet clothes, and from the distance, the high singing chant of plenty, *"Ih bai ih, ih bai erh,"* one hundred and one, one hundred and two, the count of the measure of the harvest, the hard running of the beans into the matting grain towers.

Again the long road. Again in time he and his cart cast attenuated shadows. It was far past the hour when they should have reached their destination, but there was still no sign of the town rising out of the plain. Although his feet were sore from the hot uneven road, Stephen did not hurry the carter. Now that the moment of his testing was upon him, he drew back.

At last the road curved westward. Dazzling his eyes was the setting sun. Against its fiery depths, he saw silhouetted the heavy red-brown heads of the *kaoliang*. As they passed out of the grain, beyond a field of beans, he caught sight of the rounded mud roofs of the village. He strode forward. "Kin!" he called.

Kin emerged from the cart, blinking with the light and his long sleep, and stood deferentially as Stephen hoisted himself to the high shaft, wriggling into a half-reclining position within. Thus, in accordance with custom, he would enter the town not displaying uncouth energy by walking. It pleased him in that in these small matters he knew the custom.

Through the arched doorway of the cart he caught glimpses of an uncovered tunnel six feet in depth—the road worn away by the travel of the centuries and

8

crowded full of the "long carts" piled high with beans and *kaoliang*. The noise rose to a roar. The blue-turbaned drivers, urging on their animals, shouted and cursed. The six-foot lashes of their whips swished through the air, the cart wheels creaked and above all rose the triumphant chant of harvest numbers, *"Ih wan, ih wan ling ling ih,"* ten thousand, ten thousand and one. A thrill of excitement shot through Stephen as out of his days of dreams he came thus suddenly into the hubbub of the market-place.

The cart stopped. He wriggled out of it, walked along the shaft, and by resting one hand on the back of the mule hoisted himself to the hard-trodden earth path above. "This the shop?" he asked Kin.

The merchant lifted the reed curtain which hung before the doorway of his inner office. So this was the great oil king's representative—this boy! And an albino at that! Heavy boots like a coolie's on his feet! Quietly he ushered Stephen within.

"Oh, Prior-born," he addressed him, "take the highest seat which I, the humblest merchant of this miserable town, have to offer you."

On the right and the left of a square table they sat—Stephen, correct in his well-cut riding breeches, neatly wrapped puttees and leather shoes, unconscious that the dust of the road upon them betrayed the fact of his uncouth energy; Merchant Yang, clothed in a long blue cotton gown, protecting the silk one beneath from the dirt of the shop—short, sleeveless silk jacket and black satin, narrow-toed slippers adding touches of elegance to his costume. In his left hand, then his right, Yang held two walnuts which he passed constantly back and forth over each other. Stephen felt his gaze held by the supple beauty of the merchant's moving fingers.

The slow Eastern politeness began. Sons, ancestors were discussed.

"Is the most honorable merchant a native of this new and rich province?" asked Stephen, following the custom of the country in asking many questions.

"I, a most miserable and humble man, am a native of Shansi."

Ah, then, Merchant Yang must be a banker also. Bankers came from Shansi. That at least he had learned, thought Stephen, as he addressed Yang again.

"Ah, a newcomer then, like my most miserable self? How long has the honorable one been here?"

"Two hundred years."

Silence between them, a long Eastern silence. The reed curtain rose and fell. Apprentices entered bringing the water-pipe, lighting it with a paper spill, bringing tea, bringing sweetmeats.

"Two hundred years!" thought Stephen. "And I have been thinking of Manchuria as new country and these men as pioneers!" Some door of perception in his mind opened and he saw Yang a thousand, two thousand years old, so identified with his clan that he did not distinguish his residence in Manchuria from that of his ancestors. Two thousand years of memory—the accumulated wisdom of Yang's merchant ancestors was his. A staggering total of banking and merchant experience which Stephen, in his inexperience, must cope with! He nursed the core of manhood so recently acquired and wished he looked older.

As they sat on, the smoke drifting up to them from two stick of incense stuck upright in a round pot filled with the ashes from countless incense sticks, the long northern day waned. At last Kin came, announcing Stephen's evening meal. Now with decorum he could leave the presence of Yang.

When he stepped into the passage between the merchant's private room and the high-countered shop opposite, the night was being hastened by two men who were

10

sliding into place shutters that reached from floor to ceiling along the front of the building, filling the interior with darkness. Heavy shadows lay along the counters and in the corners and among the rafters. "Why do they put up the shutters so early?" Stephen thought impatiently. "They haven't any light but their smoky candles."

With fatigue moving in upon him like another blackness, he walked heavily toward the opposite end of the passage. Not lifting his feet high enough, he stumbled over the threshold, its height an acquired knowledge which in his weariness he forgot. The cool night air of the courtyard revived him and he walked with quickened steps across the packed dry earth, following Kin into a room on the other side, stepping free this time of the threshold.

"*Ai*, their shop is so full that this cake kitchen was the only place where master could be alone," said Kin. "Only in the day is it used and then only for great affairs." Stephen could just make out the sieves for flour and sugar hanging in rows, and a great table jutting out from the wall.

"They feed a great many mouths?" he asked.

"Yes, master, a hundred assistants and then the head men."

"No women?"

"No women, master. Once in two years the men return within the Wall, as do I." As he spoke Kin straightened himself, conveying to Stephen his disdain for Manchuria. Then he bent to light a candle.

Stephen saw beneath the window the brick bed, his mattress upon it, his net hung from the rafters above. On a low table, inclosed also within the net, stood his coffee-pot, cracker-box and aluminum plate, filled with eggs. Eggs! He could not eat eggs again. To-morrow surely Kin could find him a bit of beef, maybe some vegetables. He wondered what they had here.

11

"Get water for a bath," he commanded. "But first give me the coffee."

He seated himself on the edge of the *k'ang*, drinking quickly, then threw off his coat, his puttees. When Kin had placed near him a brass basin in its four-legged stool, Stephen motioned him away. "No, I don't want any help, Kin. There are no more affairs. Shut the door as you go out."

Swiftly he finished undressing and dipped his sponge into the hot water. Lifting it, dripping, he scrubbed his chest, his arms, his legs, taking delight in the freshness of his skin. For several days he had had to sleep in the common room of the inn; there had been no small inner apartment where he could bathe.

Beneath the staccato counting of money and the clicking accompaniment of the abacus balls as the head men itemized the day's receipts, Stephen detected a soft rustling as of many moles moving. Then he heard a sound like the popping of a cork and looking at the window he saw the newly frayed edges of a hole in one of the paper panes. The ever-curious crowd, intent on seeing the white man. If he were at an inn he'd shout for Kin to drive the intruders away, but here in this shop where he wished to do business . . . He looked about for some other means of privacy, saw the kimono he had adopted as sleeping apparel since he came to Manchuria and with two safety-pins fastened it to his bed net, making a curtain behind which he could not be seen.

In the candle's dim flame, how white his body looked! "Because my hands are so tanned. The tan's better." Then the thought suddenly struck him, "Why, I don't believe the Chinese would be white if they could." Finishing his bathing he crawled carefully under the net.

Again the soft rustling outside his window and the sound of the tough paper of the panes giving away. All

12

his powers of attention were fastened in nervous irritation on those staring eyes at the peep-holes and he pulled the sheet up under his chin. Then he was conscious of his fingers clutching the sheet. He had always been proud of them because his father, once an expert surgeon, had had hands like his. Square hands, with short fingers, strong, sensitive. But lying there with the sense of many eyes watching him, his fingers seemed to have no sensitiveness. He could see the long slim fingers of Yang moving the walnuts. Panic seized him over the coming negotiations. He tried to think what he would say, and no word of the Chinese language came to him. He would fail.

The court and the shop in front were quiet now. He took a bundle of letters from under his pillow. They were folded so that he could read quickly what he wished most to read. His electric torch illumined the words, "Stephen, I want you." Then he looked at Lucy's picture; her head like a miniature set in the circle of light, her large gray eyes, the odd indecisive curve of her mouth, the whiteness of her skin—her black hair enhancing the whiteness of her forehead and neck. Now his white body seemed beautiful—white, like Lucy's.

The rustlings outside his window began again and he snapped off his flash, still seeing the face of Lucy in the darkness, remembering her words. But along this line of thought there lay no peace. The unaccustomed bath had made acute his physical sensibilities. Night was a terrible thing out here where the darkness could not be illumined. If only it were day so he could flee from himself!

How easily he had made the promise that the Company expected. It had not seemed a sacrifice then to give his word that he would not marry for three years. Even after his engagement to Lucy, with his work bulking so large in interest, his love had held no mastering desire for immediate fulfillment. He supposed his mother was right.

It had taken him a long time to grow up. Passionate love had been slow in awakening within him. But now a man's hunger for union gripped him.

At last he slept.

II

STEPHEN had been in conference with Yang an hour before the merchant reached the end of formal conversation and came to the matter that had brought them together.

"I hear that your excellent Company wishes to find an agent here to sell the new light. I would like to recommend my friend, Wen Hou. He is a big merchant. My miserable business is small."

This was a situation Stephen had not foreseen. The information which had come over the grapevine Chinese telegraph had been that Yang wanted to be agent, and such information Stephen had understood was more accurate than the written or spoken word. What lay behind Yang's refusal? Was it only Eastern politeness? Should he urge him, or should he set about dealing with Wen? It would be necessary to take the responsibility upon himself of deciding about Wen's fitness. If Yang were the man, no such decision was involved because Yang, the office had learned before Stephen left, was sound.

While he was trying to decide what to do, Yang rose, ushering him into the passageway where Stephen saw to his surprise four square tables in a row stretching from the open front of the building back to the door leading into the court. Chop-sticks, porcelain spoons, saucers with watermelon seeds and little flat cakes were on each table, and men, dressed in silk without the protecting cotton gown, were coming in between the rows of onlookers gathered outside.

14

"A feast this early in the day! What is the purpose?" said Stephen to himself, as he met them all, the Lings, Yangs, Wens and Hos. "I must be on my guard," he thought, looking at Yang sitting opposite him, splitting watermelon seeds with his teeth and spitting out the husks.

He pulled his stool well in toward the table for the passage was congested. Servants were trying to get by him with their small pewter teapots. One leaned over his shoulder, filling the thimble-sized porcelain bowl at his place with warm *kaoliang* wine. A man with a brown paper package hanging suspended by a string from his finger came from the shop into the passage, and leaned over to look full into Stephen's face. *"Ai yah!"* he ejaculated. Then a beggar wriggled through the onlookers who had inched slowly in from the street. He was dressed in old sacking, his black hair was matted and his skin was encrusted with dirt. When he plucked at the sleeve of a guest, whining, "Do good, do good," the man took from his inner girdle a few *cash* and tossed them into the beggar's bowl, but Stephen hastened to make his offering before the beggar touched him.

The hot steaming dishes of food began to appear. Yang arose and with his chop-sticks lifted a choice bit of meat, placing it in the saucer before Stephen, other choice morsels before the other guests. Stephen watched as, with polite sucking sounds of satisfaction, the heavy lips of the men closed over the morsels. The sense of his difference from them increased.

Then, as he began eating, dipping again and again into the large bowls as did those around him, he found the well-cooked foods good and soon he was sharing the gluttonous pleasure of the other diners. It was not long, however, before the unwonted dishes and the feast palled on him. His back ached from the backless chair and he found it difficult not to let his interest waver as he gave the

15

same polite answers to the same polite questions, while one guest after another came and sat beside him, eating a course or two, then moving away. Only one thing interested him—each man told him of the good points of Wen, but even this information failed, finally, to make its impression.

The scene grew confused; all the yellow faces fused into the one astute, middle-aged countenance of Yang. He remembered that Wen had sat beside him at the beginning and that he was a little man, but of his character he had no inkling. The distinguishing lines of the faces of men of his own race were not in these faces. He was baffled by the strange sameness: the secrecy of the agate eyes, the lineless skins, the serene mouths. "They all look alike," he said to himself in despair, "how shall I judge?"

As the elaborate feast moved endlessly forward, the servants taking away the bowls of food, bringing others, bringing hot towels, the guests wiping their faces, their hands, a band of golden light between the heads of the crowd and the overhanging eaves of the shop pulled at his attention. If only he could get out beyond the town, be on the road! On the fringe of his mind, threatening to dominate it, hovered his own affairs. When he reached Harbin there'd be letters from Lucy; they were there even now awaiting him.

It was not until mid-afternoon that white rice piled high in individual bowls was served—the customary sign that the feast was over. But even this brought no release. Pots of fresh wine were set on the tables, the cups were filled, and Stephen realized that the men were settling down to the wine game. This pastime had been carried on only in desultory fashion throughout the hours of feasting, but now the drinking began in earnest. The men set their feet squarely on the floor, knees apart, the skirts of their silk gowns carefully gathered around their waists. Each turned toward his neighbor, his partner in

16

the game. Every man's right fist was raised, then brought down sharply as from the closed fist one or more fingers shot out and each man shouted his guess of the number of fingers his opponent had thrust forth. If he lost, he must drink. The game was to see who could remain sober the longest.

In the beginning Stephen was merely an onlooker, for his neighbor, already overcome by wine, had gone to sleep. Yang played with the man at his right. The fists opened and shut with lightning rapidity; numbers were called *erh, ih, ssu*—two, one, four. To Stephen the air seemed full of slender yellow fingers. Now Yang's partner was drinking; Yang quickly filled the man's tiny bowl as soon as it was emptied.

The game grew to a wild fury. The clipped numerals beat upon Stephen's ears; the delicate flying fingers flickered before his eyes. At last Yang's partner slept, his head on the table. At once Yang turned to Stephen. Desperately he tried to throw out his fingers with that lightning speed but he was no match for Yang, and the drinking fell to him continually. Was there some special desire to get him drunk? Would it serve Yang's purpose in their negotiations? "I don't know," he said wearily to himself, "I just don't know."

He braced himself for the ordeal. He simply must keep sober. He had some advantage in that Yang had been drinking more than he and that the Chinese do not carry their wine well. If only he could get a breath of fresh air, he thought desperately as the crowd pressed close. The smell of their unwashed bodies, the garlic on their breath sickened him each time he drank that unaccustomed tepid wine. Once, twice, Yang had to drink but Stephen many times. He could not hold out much longer.

At last Yang got unsteadily to his feet and passed into his own room. Stephen rose. A sudden exasperation took hold of him. He could scarcely keep himself from hitting

17

out at the crowd, flaying the guffawing, leering louts with his fists. He stumbled on across the threshold and laid himself down on his mattress in the cake kitchen.

Whatever the purpose of this feast, it stood to Stephen as the waste of a day. It still remained for him to find out what the real Wen was like; it still remained for him to try in every way he could to persuade Yang to take the agency.

Never before had business kept him more than a day or two in a town, the rest of his time had been occupied with the activity of travel. Now the long slow days stretched out before him, filled with the necessity to conduct himself according to a code, old and rigid, its motives an enigma to him. By this code called "face" must he live out his days. Otherwise he would become the victim of a passive resistance that would make his work of no avail.

In his heretofore short periods of intercourse with the Chinese this idea that life was a game played behind a mask had amused him. But now as he sought to break his racial habit of coming to grips immediately with an issue, instead of spending days carefully preserving the face of Banker Yang, something within him seemed to quiver under the strain. Adroitly by word and deed he must convey to Yang that it was enough the great Yang had said Wen was a good man, and yet continually he tried to discover whether this was true. When he was not sitting with Yang or Wen he went about the town, playing his unaccustomed rôle of indifference. He schooled himself to watch with blank eyes into whose courtyard beans were carried, into whose shop men went most often to buy, attempting to show no interest in the comparative business of Wen and Yang.

Although he tried in many a conversation with peasant, shop-apprentice and loafer in the crowd which trailed

18

him everywhere to catch some one off guard and thus pick up the town's true rating of Wen, he learned nothing new of either merchant. Had he raised against himself that passive boycott which he dreaded? He thought not, for Kin attended him carefully. He had learned to gauge the amount of prestige accruing to him at any one time by his servant's attitude. Kin was respectful these days, although he did not aid his master with even the slenderest clue.

Little by little Stephen realized that no man in this town, not even Yang, was interested in any mechanical device the Western world had to offer. It was not the foreign lamps they wanted, but the oil sold in tins, a good medium of barter. Sugar and oil to be paid for in beans when the peasants had harvested their crop. To Stephen's enthusiastic accounts of lamps, and even electricity, Yang remained apathetic. "I have seen," he said, "in the city of Chefoo as I have gone to and fro to my home." And there was that in his tone which implied that he regarded such things as of no more importance than a woman's trinkets. Stephen wondered if Yang would be stirred even by the big lamp he had brought as a present. He could not understand the mind that did not desire light.

The boredom of dwelling among alien minds now threatened to engulf him. He had to fight back the temptation to close a bargain with Wen and get away, recognizing his growing weariness as a dangerous weapon in Yang's hands.

"I'll have a day to myself," he said, "and then settle down again to waiting. I'll have Kin get me a pony and I'll ride north to the new land."

The hours on the plain with no eyes watching him, and the pleasure he got from the sight of the rough strong grass awaiting the plow, broke the boredom and he settled again to his task.

If only it were possible to read in the evenings! In desperation he had had Kin put a candle on the low table within his net. It was one of the native candles, his own had given out. The flame was feeble, the hard wick of bamboo smoked and flakes of soot fell from it on the pages of his book. Crawling from under his net he went out into the court. It was empty. He strolled into the court beyond. A door stood open and he saw faint light within. Idly he drew near. There was the customary long brick platform and on it lay sleeping in a row, their heads toward him, the small apprentices of the shop. Then something unusual caught his eye. At the other end of the *k'ang,* a boy bent over a Chinese book, and on the table at his side stood a crude lamp! Through a tin stopper in the neck of a bottle filled with bean oil protruded a wad of waste, lighted.

"I, too, have been reading and I saw your light," said Stephen, speaking softly, hoping not to frighten the boy. The child was frightened, nevertheless, as all the children were of Stephen's strange appearance, but the mask of his indifference was complete.

"*Ai,* Prior-born."

"Where did you get your lamp?" Stephen asked.

"It is nothing," answered the boy.

"Did you make it?"

"No, no, I bought it in the great city of the coast when I came to this outer land."

But Stephen knew the boy had made it for the glass bottle was one of his own empty pickle jars, the label still on it. "He masks his facts instinctively, as his elders do," thought Stephen. Then, suddenly, the boy's reply did not matter. The youngster had created a lamp, however crude! Here was an impulse toward change such as actuated Stephen's own countrymen.

With energetic tread Stephen walked back to his own quarters, full again of the desire for action. Well, he wouldn't bother any more about Yang. He'd take Wen.

20

And this night when he blew out his candle there was no torment for Lucy. He lay happily thinking of his plans. He'd close the bargain quickly now and get away. He felt confidence in himself again. He felt his old vigor coming back; he believed now it was inertia that was his danger.

That Yang had worn him down, he did not know. It was on some such impetuous move that the merchant had gambled to get the agency for Wen—a member of his clan. It was when he had first seen Stephen enter his shop that he had decided not to take the agency. He had observed his quick unmeasured step and his features filled with the flaw of impatience. He knew he had only to wait until haste betrayed the barbarian into action.

The next morning as Stephen dressed, he hummed like a bumblebee, glad at last he could act. "I'll call on Wen to-day," he said to himself as he looked in his traveling mirror, surveying his features, finding his mask of indifference well in place. But Kin, hearing his satisfied humming, reported to Yang that his master would see Wen to-day.

In the shop of Wen the apprentices of the establishment had found duties near the manager's inner room; on Stephen's arrival they were leaning over the counters, each industriously clicking his abacus; the coolies, their blue trousers rolled to their groins, stood in the passageway busily restacking piles of piece goods. All had heard of the profits, legitimate and illegitimate, that could be made from selling the Foreign Light.

Graciously was Stephen ushered in. There before him were the square tables spread for a feast. Did they have a suspicion then that he would come to-day? But how could they? He had taken the precaution to tell no one, not even Kin.

It was not until late in the afternoon that an opportunity was given Stephen to broach the subject of his visit.

"Would Mr. Wen consider taking the agency of such a miserable Company?" Wen replied that the extra care and worry entailed in the business of the honorable Oil King made him hesitate. Still the matter might be discussed. They went to an inner room far back in the dim recesses of the shop.

Stephen found relief in making clean-cut, businesslike statements, telling Wen exactly how much money must be deposited as cash guarantee before he would be given the precious oil, how much the Company would allow him as commission, and how much for leakage. "The Company knows," he said, "that the seams of the tins often spring apart, bumped along as they must be in the carts." He ended, "And once in thirty days you must pay for the oil you sell."

Merchant Wen was secretly pleased. Aloud he said, "*Ai*, if the Oil King cannot be more liberal, it is impossible to do business except at a loss."

The bargaining began. Presently the room grew dusky. One final shout from the tower-building bean counters, "*Ih wan*," ten thousand. The harsh pouring of the last measure of beans fell away. Stephen, exhausted after the hours of feasting, the many thimblefuls of warm wine, perceived that it would take more time than he had thought. He postponed further palaver until the next day.

It was four days later that every item was settled. The money guarantee and the land deeds had been arranged. Only the agreement remained to be signed. Wen clapped his hands. The apprentices came bringing wax for the seal. As Wen took it, he said, "There are a few little matters." Once more he opened the discussion. The commission was too small, the carters would not carry the cumbersome tins for the small amount allowed for freight, he would lose heavily on the leakage allowed. Finally he told Stephen he must be given longer credit.

Stephen yielded a little here, Wen a little there. At last the merchant took his ring, pressing its seal into the thick red ink. Then he stamped the contract.

Stephen wrote his name as witness to Wen's signing. He thought, "Surely my moment has come at last to show this Oriental the adventurous spirit of big business." His energy, held back for so many days, flung itself forward, charging into the inertia of the subtle astute merchant. He set Wen a high figure of sales for the winter, and was gratified with his attention.

After a long silence, the merchant spoke.

"Most honorable one, mine is a poor and miserable shop, not worthy to house the Oil King's business. A king would lose face if it did not appear that his affairs were important enough to be housed in a separate shop."

From his pleasant relaxed contemplation of Wen's interest Stephen awoke to gird himself for another struggle. No, no extra shop would be provided. Refused, Wen with blandness suggested that the Company paint his most miserable building, thus making it more worthy. It cannot be done? Then the Oil King would surely pay a little rent for the use of his shop. It cannot be done? In patient voice Wen mentioned the fact of how poorly staffed his shop was.

Stephen, proud of his self-control, forebore to call attention to the hundred men and boys moving languidly about. But, instead, with a suavity equal to Wen's own, he spoke of the Company's inability to secure young men as fine as these apprentices. Any others would be inferior quality.

"Ah, well, since Prior-born values them so highly," answered the merchant, "would it not be well to make them an allowance? Such men must entertain the country dealers handsomely. It is the custom of the country."

There were times in the discussion which followed when Stephen felt that he could hold out no longer.

23

Only because he had reached the limit of the concessions the boss had authorized did he manage to withstand the persistence of Wen. At last all was arranged, though etiquette made it necessary for Stephen to wait another day and give a feast in the name of the Company.

The feast was served in the passageway of Wen's shop. At its close, Stephen ordered Kin to bring in the present the Oil King had sent to his new agent. The box was opened by two stalwart coolies. Then Stephen pushed away the excelsior and took out chains, pulleys, a great bowl that gleamed like silver, and something the like of which many there had never seen. It resembled a horn lantern only it was so clear you could see through it—a glass chimney. Yang, sitting next to Wen, felt it with his fine thin fingers.

"This Western lamp hangs from the ceiling," said Stephen. "Where shall it be put?"

There was a stir through the front shop among the apprentices and the bystanders who had gathered to watch the feast. *Ai yah, ai yah,* they exclaimed, crowding close, fingering the round wick, smelling the kerosene which Kin was pouring into the nickel bowl. A few dipped their long sleeves in it, using it as perfume.

"Hang it to the beam in the middle passage," Wen ordered his coolies. Then Stephen took a paper spill, lighted it in the charcoal brazier and held it to the wick. He let the flame travel slowly around until it made a complete circle before he placed the chimney over it— the first chimney that ever in this town had guarded a lamp's flame.

"Stand back," he cried to the crowd. He had a sudden desire to see unbroken the circle of light that the great lamp would throw on the floor.

For one moment it lay in its perfection on the packed dirt of the passageway. Then merchants, coolies, beggars

24

from the street pushed in, stamping out the circle of light, gesticulating. Their voices had the sound of an angry mob. All evening the crowd surged under the lamp, staring up, seeing it as some magic thing with no relation to their humble lives. *"Ai yah."* Setting the Merchant-Banker Yang apart in a class of his own. "Merchant Yang has arranged it nicely. He, the silent partner, will not have to be bothered with supervision from this young barbarian. It would be beneath him to be thus directed. That is for this younger member of his clan. But when the barbarian leaves, the great light will be taken to Yang's shop."

Even the beggars knew this; only Stephen did not know it.

III

ACROSS the northern plains Stephen pushed his little cavalcade. He was happy; his difficult task was completed. The roads were good—thirty miles a day they made. Stephen sat inside the cart fingering Lucy's letters, frayed with much handling. At last they came to the Sungari River. The cart bumped its way down the one street of the river town and under three hoops with their dangling red fringe hanging over the gate of the inn courtyard. He must wait here for the stern-wheel paddle-boat that would take him to Harbin. Down the steel line of the Russian, the Japanese railways, the length of Manchuria, he would then travel to the main office of the Company.

Once within the inn, he sat cross-legged on the brick platform before the *k'ang* table writing his reports, paying no heed to Kin hanging his mosquito net from the smoky ceiling. As the transparent white walls of the net fell around him they were filigreed with bluebottle flies darkening the space within. Stephen leaned closer over his work. Scarcely raising his eyes, he took the plate of food which Kin thrust under the net, ate it quickly, then lighted his pipe.

Daylight failed. Stephen sat staring at a table at the other end of the long room. A wick burning in a saucer of oil flickered on the faces of a half-dozen travelers, the innkeeper and Kin. Their eyes gleamed above their rice bowls as with their chop-sticks they shoveled in their food. In the stillness of the great plain the grunting of a pig under the table and the clucking of a hen in the rafters were loud and distinct.

The minutes dragged on. No whistle of the stern-wheel paddle-boat. Out of the accumulated monotony of such evenings, Stephen's mind turned to its habitual contemplation, his eyes staring at the smoky flame. Gradually the fluttering light took on familiar shape, the tiny lamp of his childhood, the night-lamp that stood by his bed. Suddenly he felt the electric shock of inspiration. Why had no one thought of such a lamp—to be exported with the oil? A tiny chimney, tiny bowl that would hold a few coppers' worth of oil! A lamp that peasants and coolies could afford to buy! Stephen smiled to himself, seeing their childish delight, remembering the pleasure they took in examining his watch, his flash-light. How the boy with the pickle-bottle device would enjoy such a lamp! His dream expanded. In time the Company could put a lamp in every inn, every hut in Manchuria, in China! Four hundred million people, millions of lamps. He saw himself famed for the little lamps, important in the Company. Lucy and him married. All the things he'd do for Lucy.

The night wore on. His dream became old; he had contemplated it from every angle. It afforded his mind no more occupation and even the thought of Lucy did not evoke her presence. Somehow, to-night, his mind was playing him a trick, refusing to conjure the woman Lucy out of the shadows.

Sitting on the brick *k'ang*, his back against the discolored wall, his brows drawn together as he tried to find Lucy, Stephen slept. Then she came and lay down beside him. He felt her young body there against him. He put out his arm to draw her closer—closer than he had ever held her. Then a shriek, a strident whistle, filling the inn.

In a panic, he jumped up. He must not miss the boat. He followed Kin down to the black river. With a terrible hunger he wanted Lucy, the anguish of that interrupted embrace was upon him.

In the prow of the boat a little away from the huddled figures that crowded the deck, he stood straight and stern, the cold wind off the steppes blowing against him, trying to cool the fever that raged in his veins—for yet another year.

The boat was late in reaching Harbin. He had just time before his train left to get his mail from the Company's branch office. "You'll wire the main office I'm back!" he said to the man in charge as he stuffed his pack of letters into his pocket. How strange it seemed to be speaking to a white man.

On the train he took out Lucy's letters—forty of them, one for each day of his absence. He placed them in order, according to the date of their postmarks, and began to read. The plain rushed away behind him; his heart was warm with the new words of Lucy's that made her vivid again.

Sitting there, Lucy's love surrounding him, happiness filled him. He read on and on, folding the last letter with a sigh. If only there were no end, if only he could go on reading new letters, living in her like this!

His dream when he put his arm out to draw Lucy into

27

that closest of embraces and the anguish of its interruption was again upon him. He sat very still, a sensation of coldness creeping around his heart. With the plain flying by, now gray in the dusk, for the first time he realized that it might never again be the same with Lucy and him as it was in that first wonder of their loving. Fear of changes within themselves possessed him—changes they were powerless to prevent.

The car was suddenly illuminated. Stephen shook himself. What was wrong with him? He and Lucy loved each other too much to have anything matter. The train came to a stop. Chang Chun—he must change to the Japanese line here. Rushing along the platform as if he were in America, he felt his spirits rising.

Elation and lassitude alternately possessed him as he journeyed. Elation, how this train rushed across the plains; passivity that seemed to have been communicated to him from Kin and the agent in whose shop he had spent so many days. Elation—eagerly he paced up and down in the aisle. He wanted to get back to his friends. He wanted to speak English—"great gobs of English," he said excitedly to himself. He walked through the train. There must be an American or an Englishman on it. But he found none, only Russians talking their language, Japanese talking theirs, Chinese, theirs.

Mukden at last. A Japanese, in the garb of the railway hotel, came through the train holding a telegram. He was calling out a name that sounded like gibberish, but it gave Stephen the thrilling sense of being in the world once more. The man came near, stopped. Why, it was "Chase" he was calling! Stephen tore open the white envelope. The telegram was from the boss, telling him to attend to some business with the Mukden agent.

He gathered together his belongings, went in search of Kin in the third class. As he entered the hotel, he looked delightedly at the Western furnishings. But still no white man's face greeted him. It was late and only the Japanese attendants were standing about.

The next afternoon Stephen was again on the train, moving once more over the great plain. Here and there he saw barracks, eloquent of the Russian advance; here and there cemeteries, eloquent of the Russian retreat. In the midst of this Buddhist plain the Greek crosses on the huddled graves looked lonely and exiled. And this railway, belonging to the Japanese, how it seemed to defeat itself, struggling with the plain.

Late in the afternoon, he alighted at his station. He urged his ricksha-man along the wide dusty street. Above the huddled dwellings of the Chinese and Japanese, he caught sight of the taller foreign buildings. Like a conqueror he was returning, throwing down the armor with which he had combated the mind of the Chinese. No need for armor now. It was with a quickening of his pulse that he turned from the dust of the road into the alley leading to his own dwelling. "Open," called the ricksha-man. The black gate swung back. How pleasant the crunch of the gravel on the path leading to the door of his house. "Hey, Jim!" he called as he took the steps of the veranda at a bound.

"Well, hello, Galahad!"

The man with whom he lived, the number two in the Company office, met him in the hall. "Glad to get you back. You've been gone an ungodly long time."

How good were the words to Stephen's ears, even Jim's bantering nickname.

"Let's have a drink to celebrate your return. Say when." Jim poured from a bottle of whisky on a table by his side, added the soda, passed the glass to Stephen. "Well, here's glad to have you aboard," and he lifted his own glass in welcome.

"We're proud of your work," he went on, lowering his too heavy frame into an easy chair. "Thought it was a bit

29

hard on you, keeping you out so long, but I've got no sympathy for you now." His eyes, showing the weariness of dissipation, regarded Stephen's lean frame with a hint of envy. "This travel business seems to set you up."

Stephen, with his legs neatly wrapped in puttees sticking out in front of him, sat contentedly listening as his friend recounted the happenings of the town, the office.

Then he, too, felt impelled to talk, and when he began to put into speech the things he had done and seen they took on color and vivacity. He told Jim of the bumper crops, of the unusually early moving of the beans, of the great northern plain, and as he recounted his dealings with Wen and Yang he took keen pleasure in describing their struggle of wits.

"I never quite got the hang of it," he ended, "why Yang wouldn't take the agency."

"Well, the chances are," answered Jim, "that Yang is the silent partner. He wanted to dodge the responsibility. In fact, we gathered as much from the Chinese after your telegram came telling of the contract with Wen."

Stephen looked crestfallen. After all, then, he had been outwitted.

"Probably no one could have found it out until after the contract had been signed," added Jim. "Not a Chinaman would have peeped before. And you did a master stroke when you got Yang as one of Wen's guarantors."

"Say, Jim," Stephen said suddenly, "the other night while I was waiting for the boat I had an idea. You know as long as the people use those saucers of oil for light our sales won't go up very much. You know as well as I do we'll never sell many of our big lamps. They're too expensive; even the merchants don't buy them often. Well, I got to thinking—saw a boy one night with a lamp made out of a bottle——"

"Come on with the big idea," encouraged Jim. "Spill it."

"Well," said Stephen, "I thought if we could make a little lamp that would hold just a cup of oil, a lamp a coolie could afford to buy, something like the night-lamps our mothers put by our beds when we were kids . . . I've worked it all out. We might make the bowl of colored glass. The Chinese would like that. Do you think there is anything good in the idea?"

"Good?" Jim sat straight in his chair, the look of the waster gone from his face. "Good? It's grand! A tricky little thing like that would take hold with the Chinese. It ought to set us ahead of the British in the business. We'll put the idea up to the boss in the morning. He may not see it at first, he's almost as bad as the Chinese when it comes to new ideas. But yes, yes, he's sure to see it after he's thought about it a little. It's too good for the boss not to. Let me tell you, if there's anything really sound in the idea the boss will work for it, put it up to New York, fight for it."

"Jim, I thought this lamp might bring me recognition from the Company. I'd be known for those lamps. You see, Lucy——"

The older man looked at his watch. "There's a big stag dinner at Tim's to-night and here we sit like two fools talking about Company business. We'd better be getting into our togs."

"Am I wanted?"

"It's for all the bachelors, so come along."

"Bleak old burg," said Stephen, but he really did not mean it to-night. The treeless tide-washed town looked good to him as he walked with his friend down the dirt path, hugged on one side by the compound walls of the white men's houses, bordered on the other by a ditch, muddy and brackish with the residue of the ocean left by the outgoing tide. Ahead the towers of "Tim's palace" rose above the monotonous banks of the river.

Stephen's pleasure heightened as he passed into Tim's compound between two lines of giant tripods from which dangled red paper lanterns. An unaccustomed sound reached his ears—white men's singing, white men's laughter.

On a raised platform at the farther end of the banquet-room behind the *zakuski* table stood Tim, a small, middle-aged Russian aristocrat. The hanging lamps cast a kindly light over the shabbiness of the room and the master—both done originally in the grand style. The tarnished gilt of the chairs, the mirrors in their garlanded gold frames, the marble-topped tables, the red brocade curtains to-night took back their lost grandeur, gave the room a faint semblance of the Russia that Tim and his compatriots had dreamed of planting in this outer province of China. To-night the smudged look that dissipation had given the master's face was erased. The counterfeit homage these men paid Tim for his wines and his food brought back to him a feeling of old power, redrawing in clear line his once handsome features.

Stephen plunged into the crowd around the table. All at once he felt remote and out of it. His return proved each time a more difficult adjustment. He stepped aside and stood leaning against a window. As he took in the scene around him, he observed Jim coming toward him, carrying cocktail glasses.

"Limber up a bit. I didn't bring you here to be so confounded removed," Jim said, half under his breath. "Everybody's got to do his part in this God-forsaken hole, I say."

Stephen realized that Jim was tight, or he would not have spoken as he did. But he also realized that the white man's town spoke through Jim tight. Solidarity. An unbroken front. He knew the town's secret. Stalking each man was the unacknowledged fear that he might submerge his identity in that of this other race. He took the second cocktail, added his voice to the others shouting down the voice of the East coming in at the windows—the insistent cling, cling of the bells of the ricksha-men as they trotted docilely between shafts, the high whine of the beggar at Tim's gate.

The men began making bets on their prowess. Tim, a whiplash of excitement, flung himself at the crowd, inciting them to abandonment. Twice he motioned back the house-boys as they came from the pantry with the hot soup. Not yet. Soup was too sobering. "Who'll take the bet? Ride Daredevil up the stairs in the central hall!"

For a moment Stephen saw his father's house, its ordered life, his father's disdain for excess, for wasting of courage. Then the precious sense of being one of the crowd blotted out the picture. The crowd's desire fell on the soft soil of solitude, meeting no resistance. He had been shaping his will and his intelligence to combat the unspoken but unyielding will of the Chinese; his guards were down now before the outspoken will of white men.

"I'll take the bet," he cried.

"Hurrah for Chase!" The men stood at the top of the stairs as Stephen rode the Mongol pony through the door. Daredevil's flanks quivered. He cast a baleful look at the stairs when Stephen brought him to the foot. The crowd grew tense.

"Didn't know the kid had it in him," whispered the man next to Jim. "Thought he was too refined to have any guts."

"Well, now you know," said Jim, moving away with distaste. He thought angrily, "What's he taking such a risk for? Why does he let a beastly crowd like this have its way with him?" But in spite of his anger he was proud of his friend.

There was a nice balance between caution and daring in Stephen's horsemanship. Now he was beginning to ascend, and Daredevil was calmer. If nothing frightened

33

the pony, he'd make it. No one seemed to breathe. Beneath the clatter of hoofs on polished step after polished step could be heard Stephen's whisper, "There, Daredevil, it's 'most over. Now the last step. Take it, Daredevil." He turned to start down.

"Fool!" Jim ground between his teeth, "no one can ride a pony *down* the stairs." He grabbed the bridle, shouting above the din of voices, "Carry the hero!"

"Carry the hero down!" echoed the men, as they crowded round, raising Stephen to their shoulders, chanting as they descended, seating him at last at Tim's right hand. Abandonment seized him. It was Stephen now, not Tim, who lashed the men into hilarity, feeling himself gay, witty and sought after.

White wine with the fish, red wine with the joint, champagne with the fowl. The bond of friendship around the long table grew. English, German, Russian, French and American were brothers, secret homesick longings forgotten, national jealousies and superiorities, holding them apart in the daytime, gone. Safe now to banter one another.

"How's the Russian Bear?" a stout German called to Tim. "What you going to do with him, now you can't wash his paws in warm water?"

"We'll get him to warm water yet," answered Tim.

"Might get him through the Open Door," cried Stephen, feeling that he'd said something witty.

"Yes, Big America, hold your door open," shouted a blond Englishman.

Stephen's attention was drawn to the luxurious beauty of the table—the gold brocade table-cloth, the silver plates, the glass catching the light from the crystal chandelier. Tonight he could believe all the tales he had heard of the extravagance of his host in the days of Russia's power. The best from every country he had

34

brought to his house. A Satsuma plate was placed before Stephen, and he thought suddenly of the weeks he had eaten in primitive inns from an aluminum plate. Great to be here with his own people.

The lanterns stood dark in their tripods when the men, Tim at their head, passed out to a line of waiting rickshas.

A man walking at Stephen's side spoke to him with easy familiarity. "Never liked you before, but you've got guts. Told Jim so to-night. Damn fine, riding that pony. Never afraid to say so when I'm wrong. Always thought you squeamish, but I see you're not. Great stuff these geisha girls."

They walked together, leaning on each other, to the rickshas. No barriers to-night for Stephen. "Like all these men damn well, like this common chap too," he told himself.

The rickshas trailed themselves along the dusty road, going toward Japanese town. As Stephen's ricksha came to the alley that led to his house, the coolie, without command, swung from the line, turned in.

"Hi! what are you doing!" shouted Stephen, forcing him back in line.

Another ricksha bumped his. "Don't be a fool," hissed Jim. "Go home, Galahad."

"Cut it out!" Stephen answered angrily. Jim was insulting, calling him that name. He wouldn't be patronized. With the clarity of drink, he saw how the men had despised him.

The paper panes were alight in the low building which housed the geisha girls. At the sound of the rickshas, a *shoji* was pushed open, one here, another there. Stephen saw a girl in bright kimono and broad bright sash. The fires of wine and of his abstinence from women burned

35

in his veins. He stepped from the ricksha and entered the house, demanding the prettiest girl.

As Stephen and Jim finished their breakfast the next morning the older man pushed back his chair and meditatively packed his pipe with tobacco. "Now as to that idea of yours, Steve, of the lamps . . ."

When there was no response, Jim for the first time noticed the bleak despair in Stephen's eyes. "Umph! So that's the way the land lies," he said to himself. "Look here, kid, give you a tip. Don't take yourself too damn seriously."

IV

THE thermometer dropped to zero, to ten below, to twenty. The white man's town, Stephen's headquarters, looked of little consequence, shrunken and isolated, pushed in upon itself by the frozen plain, the frozen river and the Chinese city, to the wall of which it clung like a barnacle. Across the vast plain from Siberia to the Yellow Sea, from the Great Wall to Korea, over the fields and roads now hard as iron, over the rivers, now silver roads, the carts creaked and groaned, hauling the huge bean crop to the towns, the cities.

On the way to the Sungari River, Stephen, clad in goatskin garments lined with fur, his feet incased in Mongol felt boots, plodded after his cart, or sat inside it squeezed between the grain sacks. Once he had watched with interest the long carts moving toward him laden with the produce of the interior, wondering in what far-away city of Europe the round bean cakes, large as cart wheels, would land; into what rich man's house in China the huge twig baskets lined with waterproof paper and containing wine made from grain would find their way. Once he had caught the onrush of economic forces behind these moving carts, pushing peoples forward, changing cultures as the giant winds moving mysteriously from out the Gobi Desert picked up the red powdered dust, flung it forward in swirling clouds and dropped it at will in ridges or drifts, changing the contour of the plain. But now with unseeing eyes he looked at the plain slipping past, absorbed in chaotic thought over the happenings of that night at the geisha house: his own fastidious recoil, his uncertainty as to what bearing that act might have on his relationship to Lucy, his realization that she would regard it as the supreme treason, his conviction that the essense of his love lay in some spiritual intensification of himself that transcended the physical. He tried to see what had happened as Jim saw it. He did when he discussed it with himself coldly. Strange and confusing was the lightness with which Jim regarded his act and the significance Lucy would attach to it.

Strange and confusing to him, too, was the knowledge that through this door of humiliation to himself he had at last come to stand erect before Kin. He was impatient that his position with his servant should matter to him. But it did matter. The esteem in which Kin held himself made it impossible for Stephen to be indifferent to the fact that he had not gained Kin's full respect. There was punctilious service but no devotion such as he had been told he might expect from the Chinese servant. In the two years there had been times when he had felt uncertain whether Kin would be there to attend him in the morning. But Kin seemed now to have identified himself with his master.

Stephen could not know that he had been to Kin a man under the spell of enchantment. The disposition of the master was good, *lao-shih,* very gentle, but Kin sometimes believed him to be bewitched. That picture which stood in the place of dignity where the master's ancestral tablet should stand? Once, when dusting Stephen's room, Kin had dared to take the thing from the golden frame to see if there were more, but there was not—just the head and shoulders of a woman which held his master enthralled. *"Ai!"* But now the picture had been taken away. His master had become as other men. He had escaped from the evil spell of the enchantress.

As the days passed, unable to come to any decision, Stephen drifted into lethargy of spirit, inertia from which he made no effort to rouse himself. He failed to write Lucy, though it was his custom to send her a letter daily.

In this self-indulgent languor, he returned to the town. It was late when he reached his house. By way of welcome, a scribbled note from Jim, saying that Stephen would find his mail in his desk. On top of the pile of mail lay a letter from Lucy. It was in answer to his of the late summer, and it reflected his mood of pride and confidence in the steady advancement of his work. Lucy was radiant with the prospect of their now not far distant marriage, assured, it seemed to her, by his making good in the Company.

The refuge in passivity Stephen had built crumbled, leaving revealed to him his conviction that concealment of his disloyalty to Lucy might, in its own time, take revenge upon their happiness. Even before he was engaged, he had thought out a scheme for his own marriage, as most men do, wherein, he believed, lay its best chance for success. The open road of frankness, and the same code for both of them. Two years he had kept his pact with himself, in spite of other men's chaffing, in spite of that objectionable nickname, "Galahad," Jim called him. That he had destroyed one of the fundamentals of his scheme of marriage was no reason for losing the other.

He must write to Lucy. No, he could not. It was a

thing impossible. Inconceivable to shock her with such ugly truth. When he saw her . . . but that would be upon the eve of their marriage. It would not be fair to her to wait until there was no time left for drawing back, for freedom of choice. It might make her feel she had been tricked into marriage with him. It might spoil everything just as concealment might.

He sat before his desk, his mouth set in a fine line of pain and determination. He must write. At this distance, there was no other way to safeguard their happiness. His decision was the supreme evidence of his faith in Lucy's understanding. He staked all on her compassion. To Lucy the mother he addressed himself, not to Lucy the sweetheart.

The night was far spent when the letter was finished. The rumbling of the carts had died away, and the last deep toning cart bell. Only the barking of the dogs broke the silence of the plain. Lucy seemed very far away. Two months must pass before he could receive her answer.

The business trips dragged themselves out, a succession of solitary days and more solitary nights when he lay on the *k'ang* in inn or agent's shop, hugged into the darkness by the low roof, the close-pressing mud walls, the dirt floor, tracing in his mind the slow journey of his letter. As the time of its arrival drew near, apprehension grew in him.

In shuttered darkness, he lay asleep among the other wayfarers on the warm *k'ang*, only his clothes box and food basket making a space separating him from them. With a start, he awoke. Knowledge was upon him. Twenty-four days since he had written her. He threw the beam of his flash on his watch. This hour of the night was midmorning in New York. He was as certain as if he saw her that Lucy was reading his letter at this moment, that he had lost Lucy. Even in the darkness he was exposed to her fastidious recoil. How could he have written such a letter? He must have been mad.

After that night more and more Stephen turned to his work, traveling harder than he had ever traveled before. He failed to remember the warning experiences of other men. There was danger to one's personality in isolation among the Chinese for any length of time. He was caught in the snare of his own isolation. In a slow seepage, inertia again entered his spirit. Longing for release from the pain over his loss of Lucy which he felt his letter had brought him, he opened his mind to the Chinese fatalistic acceptance of calamity. Still through the sleepless hours of the night, the image of Lucy tormented him. But during the days, when he was in contact with the Chinese, their acquiescence seemed to pass into him, giving him the sense of shelter from his own act.

Now, bit by bit, the Chinese seemed to communicate their disdain of his world to him. In the first months out from America, he had been invited to a dinner where the conversation had turned on the discussion of Western materialism, Eastern freedom from it, the glorification of peasant simplicity and the primitive. Filled then with belief in himself and his country, he had scarcely listened. The peculiar genius of his race in the cunning of their brains, that produced railways, discovered light in kerosene, electricity, had seemed to him a great gift. Now such things were suddenly robbed of their worth. His ardor for progress left him. What was progress? Could he be sure that these trinkets his country set so much store by were really progress?

After a little that sensitive consciousness of his difference, experienced in realization of his white skin, his blunt fingers, grew into a sense of inferiority. And with that sense, grew his admiration for the Chinese.

One thing puzzled him. As he became more and more willing to accept the Chinese belief in their own superiority, it became increasingly difficult for him to secure good results in his work. He paid high prices, but got poor mules, carts, attention in the inns. At times he felt that Kin served him with a kind of insolent protectiveness. He did not know that the Chinese, with a sure and uncanny instinct, sensed the weakness within him in the loss of his self-esteem.

Twice he failed on a bit of investigation. No longer did his mind cut through the suave evasions of the Chinese. Now he called these evasions finesse and the agents found it easy to pull the wool over his eyes. The second time he returned without the desired information the boss told him sharply he had better wake up if he wished to do business with the Chinese. "I tell you, Chase, a lot of men go to pieces in their work with the Chinese. Can't stand the gaff. There comes a time . . . something happens to them personally, doesn't matter just what. . . . Let me tell you, Chase, there's nothing in going Chinese, take it from me! You've had more than beginner's luck. Don't waste it. Now," he continued, "I'm sending you to find out about some rebating—I'm sure it's going on. Lin claims the British agent is rebating and so gets all the sales. It's my opinion Lin is rebating, too. He's pretending he isn't. Don't let him fool you."

Stephen sat with Lin in his private room. He was maneuvering for an opportunity to ask Lin to show the account books. The boss had said that was the only way to check up on the man. Although the agent had talked with the usual politeness, so thinly veiled was his contempt that Stephen could not be unaware of it. He laid it, however, to the treatment the man had received from the boss. The boss had not handled the matter adroitly, offending the sensitively tuned Oriental. Stephen set himself to remedy the mistake. Delicately, he apologized for the boss. At last, with some reticence, he asked to see the

41

acount books. He implied that he, himself, felt it unnecessary.

The afternoon grew into the early winter darkness.
Without impatience he waited. At last the demands of
his body, weary and cold from the day's ride, would no
longer be denied. He excused himself, going in search of
Kin and his supper.

But there was no food. And Kin was in that state of
emotional excitement which often resulted, among the
Chinese, in fever. Under such circumstances their flesh
"put forth fire," they said, and the occurrence never
failed to surprise Stephen. Now, resting as he was on
their passivity, it startled him.

"I have eaten bitterness," exclaimed Kin. "While I
prepared the master's food, the servants of this agent set
my food on the back of the stove where it grew cold. And
when I made ready to eat, they had gone out! Not one
of them was there, not the lowest coolie, to serve the
master's servant! Master must go to the inn to save his
honorable face."

Leave the shop at this hour of the night? It was absurd.
Kin thought himself too important. "Nonsense, Kin,"
said Stephen. Then he paused, a vague suspicion in his
mind. Suppose in the servants' treatment of Kin, there
was some subtle insult to himself? On the other hand, suppose his leaving would simply minister to Kin's conceit?

Stephen scrutinized Kin. But he was as much in the
dark as when he had scrutinized the agent. Which
Oriental was with him, or was neither? Suddenly, he
knew Kin was right. He remembered the thinly veiled
contempt of the agent, and he remembered a matter he
had paid no attention to as he crossed the court—little
leering faces of the younger apprentices, peeping from
every doorway. The whispered epithet, "Foreign devil,"
before they had scuttled away. Now he no longer thought

42

of this as a boyish prank. Yes, the treatment of Kin was the indirect insult of the Oriental, insult meant for him. He picked up his hat and walked from the room, calling loudly for Kin to follow.

"Unbar the way," he commanded sharply when none of the many assistants made a move to open the front shutters.

A rustle in the inner room, and the merchant lifted the bamboo curtain.

"All is not as you wish?"

"I fear I cause you too much trouble," said Stephen.

"Tell me, and it shall be done."

"Your house is too full for hospitality. I, perhaps, but my servant—it is asking too much."

"*Ai yah.*" The agent raised his voice in anger. "My good-for-nothing dogs of servants cannot be trusted. I will go myself and see that all is right." Behind the man's glossy black eyes Stephen saw respect.

The next morning he began to question Lin, taking it as a matter of course that he should see the account books. When they were brought, he refused them. "It is the other I wish—the one Mr. Lin uses himself." Stephen spoke without apology now. All day he worked over the involved bookkeeping; by night he had proof of the rebating.

When he had finished his dinner, Stephen went out, walking along the street, pitch black except where candle or floating wick sent a small glow through the cracks of some shuttered shop-front. He walked on into the countryside, losing the road, stumbling over the frozen furrows of the fields. There was no comfort to him in his triumph over the agent; it was not because he understood the Chinese, as he had liked to believe, that he had got the necessary information, but simply because Kin had

43

bestowed on him a kind of contemptuous fathering. It had awakened him to the fact that the Chinese despised him.

Now he was robbed of the illusion which had passed into him from the fatalism of the Chinese, and without its anesthesia, he must face the pain of his conviction that he had lost Lucy.

There was a sniff at his heels. One of the half-starved dogs of the town had left off prowling in the refuse heaps of the village and was following him. He raised his walking stick and drove off the animal. But soon the ugly cur was back again. Stephen thought he felt him nipping at his heels, then saw his eyes shining out of the darkness ahead, saw other eyes, and realized that not one but many dogs were moving in upon him. He was near the Mongolian border, these Mongol dogs were mean brutes.

"Chuba, chuba!" he shouted. "Be off, be off!" But they closed in on him, snarling.

"Chuba, chuba!" It was the familiar voice of Kin. At once the dogs slunk away into the darkness.

"Master," admonished Kin, "the foreign one is strange."

Stephen felt himself standing in an outer room. This race with whom he had sought to be friends had no use for him. Even the dogs knew he did not belong.

The day Stephen returned, an urgent need developed to investigate the towns along the Korean border. The manager eyed Stephen critically, considering his physical fitness for the task.

"Little rough on you, to send you out again so soon, but the work is there to be done. It won't hurt you, if you're as well as you look," he said. "Anyway it's your job."

"I'll start this afternoon."

Stephen stood erect, determined. He would make no

44

plea for himself, although he felt he could hardly endure it to go out again so soon. That afternoon he was on the train, innumerable days of solitude stretching ahead, loneliness given its final poignancy, for there had been no letter from Lucy. The time for the reply was overdue. Evidently silence was to be her answer. He stared from the window at the plain thinly covered with snow, the *kaoliang* stubble ragged and uneven, sticking through. Night settled down.

In the lack-luster twilight of early morning he awoke and raised the blind in the sleeping compartment. They were in the hills. A hint of New England was in the landscape—a hint of home. These hills let his mind go slack and rest itself in their beautiful familiarity. The train was pulling out of a small town; he noticed the station master, a middle-aged Japanese, tuck his red signal flags under his arm and move off across the empty platform. Shriveled with the cold, he showed he was not used to this rigorous northern winter. The wind blew his gray cotton kimono flat against his body, disclosing the chapped calves of the legs above his ankle-high black-cloth stockings. About his neck he wore the skin of an otter, unmounted, the tail thrust through the slit where one of the eyes had been, to draw it close around the throat, giving him the appearance of being throttled by this wild creature, native of Manchuria. The sight of this man, so ill-adapted to his surroundings, made Stephen's mind again tighten with its own strain of adaptation. He lowered the blind.

At the Korean border, after a great deal of negotiation, he got his carts and his pack-mules for the long journey over the frozen river. He followed each detail with suspicion. The inroads into his resources, the commission taken by Kin on every transaction, he had until now accepted with a certain tolerance. He had been told it was the only way to get along. But since he had found that

45

Lin respected him less because he could trick him, Stephen had been fiercely exacting in all his dealings with the Chinese, insisting on knowing each detail in Kin's arrangements with carter, innkeeper and shopman, determined that they should put nothing over on him. It roused opposition such as he had not encountered before, but in those moments of combat he was eased of his trouble.

When he visited an agent, his inherent sense of workmanship made him hold in control his now definite dislike of the Chinese. But toward Kin, the carters, the muleteers, he used less and less control, letting his dislike leap out in withering sarcasm. He had incurred the thing he had been warned against—the Chinese passive resistance—the "go slow strike." He began to have a surprising number of petty annoyances.

The full power of the boycott would have been invoked against him, had it not been for Kin. Fortunately, Stephen's natural gentleness had kept him from pressing Kin too far; he had never made his servant lose face before his fellows. Kin permitted the daily annoyances, but he would not allow complete defiance of his master. That would mean the journey would have to be given up—defeat for Stephen, resulting in such loss of face that Kin, to save his own face, would have to leave. He did not wish to do this. The revenue was good with this master.

"Kin is a poor servant, with no control over men," was Stephen's disgusted conclusion.

Stephen sat in his allotted place on the *k'ang,* his knees drawn up under his chin, his spirit withdrawn into its now habitual contempt and isolation, eyeing cynically the innkeeper who was soaking the grain for the animals before he measured it for sale.

His attention was attracted by the feeling of a cold nose against his hand where it lay on the warm *k'ang.*

46

He looked down into the face of a tiny, short-haired Pekinese. He loved dogs and with delight he gathered this smallest specimen into his arms. As he did so, in the leaping light of the boughs thrust under the cooking pot, he noticed the black eyes of a little girl gazing at him with the fear Chinese children felt for his light hair and eyes. He could never get them to play with him.

"Li Tsu, Li Tsu," the child called.

The brown thing in Stephen's arms raised his ears. So Little Chestnut belonged to the child, probably her one possession, thought Stephen, looking at her worn padded garments, the rags around her bound feet.

"He's a very fine dog," he said to her in Chinese.

In her pride, the child forgot her fear and came close to him, commanding her pet to sit up and rub his eyes with his paws. Then Kin joined them. It was a charming disarming moment: the wind beating the trees crazily against the wooden shingles, but unable to get in, gave Stephen the good sense of shelter shared with Kin and the little girl, the three of them laughing and talking together, admiring the dog. For one moment he stood within some common humanity which loosened the loneliness clasped so tightly around his heart. Though he did not suspect it, he held for the first time the key to real companionship with this alien people.

When, later, the travelers slept, the innkeeper came to Stephen.

"Honorable one, your servant says you of the West can cure. You hear the cough of the little one. She disturbs the guests of the inn."

Listening, Stephen heard, above the sighs and the groans of the sleeping travelers, the racking cough of the child. He got up and went to her. When he saw her lying with her knees drawn up, her arms clasping them round, shutting off the blood from her bound feet, he was filled with pity and indignation. In her padded garments he

47

had thought she was a stout little girl but, when he gently loosened the neck of her coat, he saw the sunken chest, the arms little more than bones. With delicate touch he felt the tense muscles of the pain-racked body.

"She will be more comfortable if you will unbind her feet, though the cough has gone too long."

The innkeeper murmured, "*Ai yah,* it is the custom. *Mei yu fatsu,* there is no other way."

Stephen was sickened by the man's cruelty, angry with his stupidity. But when he looked at his simple puzzled face, he stood again within their common humanity—a man this was, like himself, and in need. He must do what he could for the child.

Then he knew that he dared not ease the child's suffering even by so simple a thing as a poultice. It might be pneumonia, it might be tuberculosis, a common complaint among the Chinese, from which they often die suddenly without warning.

Suppose the little girl should die? Then this superstitious peasant would believe he, the foreign devil, had killed her with an evil charm. Gently, Stephen laid Li Tsu within the folds of the child's garments where he had found him. "It cannot be helped," he said, using the expression of the Chinese, and went back to his place on the *k'ang*.

In the morning when he asked about the little girl, Kin told him she was dead.

Stephen bought Li Tsu and went away. How small the little dog was; he mustn't let him get cold; he opened his many garments and Li Tsu crawled within, nestling with a sigh of satisfaction against Stephen's breast. A low crooning, guttural and unmusical, jarred in its rhythm by the bumping of the cart, escaped Stephen.

Suddenly he was shot through with the consciousness of Lucy.

* * * * *

48

In this mood he returned to the town. Lucy's answer had come. He should have known it would. It was doubting her to think otherwise. There was the old endearing heading but, as he read, he felt his confidence, his theories of marriage, his hope for their happiness crumbling. How had he failed to take into consideration her Puritan upbringing? It had been his, too. In this so different environment he had failed to reckon on the force of its power over the woman's mind. What to him had seemed above all an act of disloyalty to Lucy, set right by his frankness, was to her above all an act of sin, which had no atonement in confession. Yet disloyalty bulked larger in her mind than in his. He had thought that complete frankness would reestablish between them that precious thing, trust. But he saw now that his frankness had only served to plant suspicion in Lucy. Pervading her protestations of love, was an unexpressed doubt of his future faithfulness. Love, disappointment, suspicion, warred in her, making it impossible for her to come to any decision.

He sat for a long time, helpless before the tangle. At this distance, how could they come to understanding? Their love was too big a thing to be destroyed by misunderstanding. At rock-bottom, love and confidence were there. He must see Lucy, it was his only hope. But his leave was still six months away. By that time, the tangle would be hopeless.

He had had no vacation since he came out. Would it be legitimate to ask for leave this spring? He hated to speak to the boss about it, his fastidiousness drawing back from the suggestion of asking a favor. Besides, his native reticence had grown this winter until it had become all but impossible to break. At last, he managed to speak of the matter to Jim. They had gone out beyond the town into the stubbled *kaoliang* fields which for the winter had been made into a crude golf-course.

49

"Jim," he said, as they were about to begin their game, "how'll I go about getting my leave? It's due this summer . . . my three years are up. I've been traveling pretty steadily with no vacation. . . . I'd rather counted on going back to America this spring. . . ."

"What's the use, Steve? You're making good with him" —Jim pointed to the sturdy figure of the manager ahead —"why upset it by going home? You know what he thinks. A man who hasn't been back himself to America for forty years isn't going to see much in your wanting to go after three years. He believes in a kind of molding against return, if you're to do good business out here."

"It isn't that I want a vacation," explained Stephen. "You know that. I want to get married."

"That makes it worse." Jim carefully built into a tee a bit of the red-brown clay of the plain. Then he went on, "The boss thinks it makes men soft to have vacations. And the general manager in Shanghai is sure it makes them soft to get married. Besides, you're asking a favor in going before your three years are quite up. Better think twice, kid. It's a harsh régime out here. Men are harder than they would be if they were on their own. Every man is soft in spots where his own brand of kindness is concerned—some of them would do a favor even against their own interest, if it were not for the exactions of some other man. You see, each knocks out of the other his particular pet kindness. That's what gives big business power. . . ."

"Yes, yes," broke in Stephen, "what I want to know is how I'm to manage so that I can get married. I've kept my half of the bargain; it's only fair the Company should keep theirs."

The last of Stephen's sentence was broken off, torn from him by a great gust of wind. Both men turned their back to get their breath.

"It's a God-forsaken place for a woman, Steve. Why

don't you quit when your three years are up? There'd still be time to get a start at home. Take me. There'd be no use of my going home, too old to get a start. And I'm shaped now for this life."

"So am I," answered Stephen. "It's got hold of me, and what would be the use of all the grilling I've had, if I quit now? But I've got to get married soon, if I'm going to. At this distance, too much chance for misunderstanding."

"Well, if you're determined, we might wangle it. But why don't you get your girl to meet you in Japan? Then you won't have the boss against you—only the Shanghai manager, who will probably see to it that Lucy proves up. He once sent a man who got married to live on a native boat away from all white people. Girl couldn't stick it . . . he said she wouldn't. Do something like that to you. But you've got a good friend in the boss, if you just nip over to Japan and back. He's all for you. Says you're the best traveler he's ever had."

All at once they were in the midst of a howling dust-storm, its coming unnoticed, so absorbed had they been in their conversation.

"Come," said Jim, "we've got to get out of this."

As they charged forward, Jim saw Stephen's face for an instant through the swirling red-brown clouds of dust. His fur cap buttoned under his chin framed it close. He was startled by lines of suffering which he had not noticed before.

"Go along, Steve, and get married," he said suddenly. "I'll help you. Better wire your girl. See if she'll meet you in Japan this summer. If a girl's backing and filling—and yours evidently is—the thing to do is to sweep her off her feet. If she says yes, I'll put the matter up to the boss."

As they entered the house, Jim went on, "I'll clear out and let you have our diggings. Might go in with the

51

boss. He's just had word that his wife's spending another year in Europe."

"Thanks," answered Stephen. He wanted to say more, but could not.

Two days . . . and the storm still hurled its brown particles at the house. Stephen sat looking out of the window, thinking of the fight before him to prove himself with the general manager in Shanghai if he got married. He thought of the many men above him through whose hands his work passed, diluting it of any personal value. How was it possible ever to rise to any individual expression? An intense individuality, developed in the three years he had spent mostly by himself, made him sharply conscious now of the forces that held him to inconspicuous service. Like a drowning man, he clung to his idea of the little lamp to keep him from being submerged in the organization.

"Say, Jim," Stephen tried to speak in an offhand way, "was anything ever heard about those lamps?"

"No. The boss put the scheme up to New York, but they've never answered."

The storm thickened. Stephen wandered restlessly from room to room. Desolate and meaningless this house in its masculinity; Jim sprawled out in a chair asleep, a pile of old newspapers on a table in the corner of the room, Jim's houseboy setting the table for luncheon. The table-cloth was spotted from previous use, a vinegar cruet was the table's sole decoration, the cold remainder of last evening's roast of mutton stood before Jim's place. A barren unlovely scene.

Kin came with the white envelope of the telegraph station. He opened it: "Japan in August, Lucy."

V

THE long northern winter drew to its end. The grain towers grew lower and lower as their spiral matting walls were uncoiled and the last of the beans taken by junk down the rivers, swollen by the spring freshets. Patiently, slowly, with crooked sticks made into plows, the peasants cultivated the almost incredibly vast fields. Over the red plain lay a green shimmer of young *kaoliang* and beans.

July came. The *kaoliang* stood ten feet tall. Pods heavy as money weighted the bean vines down, and Stephen had returned from his last trip before going to Japan to meet Lucy. As he came into the Company building, he was surprised to see the desks deserted. He glanced into the boss's private office, and there, crowded around the doorway to the storeroom, was the entire office force— the boss, Jim, the new classman recently arrived from New York.

"Look what's here!" cried the boss, turning as he heard Stephen's step.

As the men made a place for him among them, Stephen saw the coolies taking hundreds of little lamps from a great packing box. Rows of them stood on the floor, along the wall.

"What do you know," said the boss, "they've never said a word about my letter, telling them of your idea. But they didn't let the grass grow under their feet. Been perfecting it, I see."

Stephen picked up one of the lamps wonderingly. Very different from his conception and better, he had to own. Yes, better.

"They hit on a good thing when they made that broad base," he heard Jim saying. "It's really like a Chinese tea-bowl inverted. Solid as the devil. Won't upset."

"The red color's good," the boss broke in. "Good

Chinese red—that'll please 'em. Somebody was smart to think of that. And making it of tin was a clever scheme too. Chinese will be making them out of old oil tins as soon as the Company begins charging for them. . . . Circular letter in the mail to-day says they're going to give the lamps away all over China—for three months. That'll stimulate business."

"Umph!" said Jim. "Suppose they've done so many things to the idea they've forgotten it came out of our office."

"Teamwork, that lamp." The boss carried one to his desk.

The other men went back to their work, but Stephen stood with a lamp in his hand. How he had dreamed of it—the Chase lamp—the honor, the individuality it would bring him. Anger flamed within him. It was his idea . . . he should profit by it. Lucy should profit by it. The Company was exploiting him in not acknowledging his rights in the lamp. Then, suddenly, his anger was gone. Let him be honest with himself, others had contributed. With a sigh, he set the lamp among its fellows, relinquishing his bright dream of personal aggrandizement, sinking his personality in the organization.

That afternoon as Stephen left the office Jim fell into step at his side. "After all, it's the little old pay check that counts," he said. "That's the thing that talks. You'll learn to keep your eyes on that. I know the boss recommended you for a good increase this year. Suppose you found the letter about it in your mail. The rest of us got ours two weeks ago."

At the corner Jim left him—he had already moved in with the boss—and Stephen went on alone. Never mind the lamp; he'd do as Jim told him, think only of his increase. It was a good one. He had not told Jim how much; that would be against Company etiquette. Each man's salary was a secret, not even the boss knew the increases given his staff. The Company said it made for better feeling if there were no comparisons. Stephen had respected the Company's wish, not realizing how it strengthened the power of the organization to handle each man separately.

On the day of Stephen's departure, after he had started for the train, he turned back, making a pretense of having forgotten something. He wanted to see the house once more. He was proud of it. He'd spent more than he intended, but it was worth it. He was glad now that he had the increase, the extra money instead of the hoped-for recognition.

At last he closed the door for the final time. Nothing was to be touched until he and Lucy entered together. Kin was going to visit his ancestral home in Shantung and would bring back an *amah* to attend the master's first wife. He had insisted upon this. Stephen did not see just what Lucy would do with a personal maid, but he had consented. He wanted everything to be right for her.

When Stephen reached Yokohama he saw that he could not meet Lucy in the clothes he had brought from Manchuria. At the Company office he asked about a good native tailor, the kind that could make a suit between a steamer's arrival and departure. He bought silk shirts and ties; and then there were the things he had often dreamed of getting for Lucy. He had sent her a kimono when he came through three years ago, but he had in mind a far lovelier one. There was the wedding-ring to buy, the minister to see, and the American consul who must be a witness to the ceremony. He had three days in which to do all. Though he was busy, these three days seemed interminable.

On the fourth morning there was no suggestion of

light when he awoke at the habitual hour of the road. Because it was his wedding-day, he had no drowsiness to overcome. With fastidious care he bathed and dressed. The new pongee suit fitted him perfectly, but it worried him a little. Looked too new, he thought, though the silk shirt gave him the sense of fine raiment, such as would make him acceptable to Lucy. He picked up his sun helmet, newly whitened for the occasion, and went down to the hotel lobby to await the first news of the incoming steamer.

Six days Stephen had been tramping in the mountains, trying to sink the pain of his loss of Lucy in physical weariness, in the accustomed slog, slog on foot. It was like taking away part of himself to take Lucy out of his life. Love for Lucy was the basis of his being.

Back and forth his mind moved over their meeting, each detail vividly remembered: the empty hotel lobby as he waited for some news of the steamer bringing Lucy, the minutes dragging themselves out into an hour, the lobby filling. He remembered going out on the veranda of the hotel and seeing the shipping company's house flag run up. The ship was sighted. In little excited groups people were gathering, talking of friends they were going to meet. In happy silence he had joined the crowd going to the dock.

The steamer was a white speck in the distance; a larger one. Finally, looming high above him it slowly moved in to its dock. Then suddenly the faces of the crowd on the deck grew clear and the people around him were calling out to friends and relatives but still he could see no one that resembled Lucy. Then the gangplank was put down and he went forward with the crowd on to the deck. As he passed through the lines of passengers a man addressed him:

"Are you Chase? Thought you answered the general

56

description Lucy gave me. She told me to tell you you would find her in her cabin. She traveled out in our party."

"Thanks," said Stephen, moving off, so happy that their meeting was to be private, happy that Lucy wished it to be. He hurried below to find her.

"Lucy!" he had cried, flinging open her cabin door.

"Stephen." Only her faint whisper in answer to his joyous cry.

He paused there at the door, the distance of the cabin between them, checked suddenly in his eagerness, for she was motioning him back with an appealing gesture. Thus they stood on opposite sides of the cabin as if in a trance while that impetuous first moment he had imagined so often slipped away, leaving him exposed to her gaze.

Until that moment he had been entirely unconscious of himself, all the unhappy broodings of the past year forgotten, his life of travel and isolation put aside. Lucy and he picking up their lives where they had left them three years ago. But now Lucy suddenly seemed a stranger to him, not the familiar girl of those last days together, days relived a thousand times along the out trails of Manchuria. She was older, more finished in appearance. All the superficial external changes seemed not superficial but real changes in Lucy herself. Even her clothes, different from anything he had been accustomed to in out-of-the-way Manchuria, made her a part of the outside world, lost to him. Thrust into it suddenly, he felt an uncertainty that made him unable to take the lead, sweeping Lucy forward into a new consent. So he had stood waiting, too submissive to her mood he thought now. Suddenly he had felt a little gauche despite his correct attire.

Into this growing uncertainty of himself her words had fallen with finality: "Stephen, I can't. I'm afraid. I'm

57

sorry. I thought I could go through with it. When your cable came, everything seemed all right again. And then I was excited, getting ready. But as I have lain here night after night in my bunk, I've known really—though I kept thinking maybe when you came . . . But, Stephen, I know now I don't love you."

"Don't you think," he had managed to say, "it would be different after a little? If I gave you time? If we waited a few days for our marriage?"

"Please, Stephen, don't. I can't stay over. My friends are going on. Stephen, I don't love you. I haven't since . . ." She had not finished, but he had understood what she meant, that suspicion of him lay at the core of her love.

Well, he had freed her.

He had managed to speak naturally, he guessed, though his voice felt dry in his throat. He didn't want her to be unhappy over him. He mustn't let her know his hurt. "I won't hold you," he had said. "You're free." Then for a moment his heart had leaped; she seemed to be looking at him in the old way—love for him in her eyes. Just for one instant he had thought maybe she still loved him. Was she speaking, hardly detected, drowned in the happy greeting of people in the corridor outside? They moved on. The cabin was very quiet. There had been no sound from Lucy. Without looking back he had plunged forward while he had strength to go.

Now he had stopped at a little Japanese hotel high in the mountains. How he had got here he hardly knew. Tramped most of the way he guessed. It was like tearing away living flesh to take Lucy out of his life. Since childhood, once affection was established in Stephen it seemed ineradicable. Affection was not the flower of his spirit but its rootage. To lose her at the moment of taking her into his arms—if only he could have kissed her good-by.

As he stared at a calendar hanging on the wall of the

Japanese hotel where he had stopped, it came over him what day of the month it was, and that his leave was over. He tried to wrench his mind free from Lucy, so that he might think of his return.

Suddenly he saw that return in its reality. The little white man's town, with its ingrowing interests, its prying eyes! The women over their teacups, whispering. The men at the club, smiling. He saw himself standing alone at the door of the house he had prepared against Lucy's coming. Kin greeting him . . . Kin who had that terrifying intuition of the Chinese to sense a man's weakest moments, his blackest hours, his defeat. And he saw the house as it had been that day of the dust-storm, bare of the feminine. He could not face it.

What should he do? It never occurred to him to take Jim's advice to return to America. Work, like love, was rooted deep in him. He would go back to his work, but he would go back married. As Jim said, no one out here married the woman he would have if he'd stayed at home. It seemed Jim was right. Love was finished. He would make the marriage of convenience. Coldly he made his decision.

He had no doubt but that he could arrange such a marriage within the next few days. It was done too often in the East. In Harbin it would be the easiest thing in the world. Americans had the reputation among the Russians of making good husbands. He could pick up a Russian wife very quickly there. For a moment he entertained the idea of going to Harbin; then he knew that wouldn't do—the news would get around Manchuria. But undoubtedly it could be done in Yokohama, too. The adventurous among women the world over knew that men coming into the port cities from the interior of China and Japan longed for white women's companionship. Often a man married a girl a few days after meeting her.

With sudden self-assertiveness he wired the boss that he had been unavoidably delayed. Then he set off for Yokohama.

VI

The next morning, sitting at breakfast in the city's biggest hotel, he looked over the room to see if there was a girl here of the kind he sought. He noticed a number of family groups, tourists seeing the world. It would take too long to become acquainted with the daughters in these groups.

The dining-room was filling up. Just leaving her seat at a table next to his, was a young girl, an American evidently, an inconspicuous little person in black. His eye roved past her. At a corner table was a girl of the type he sought. He wrote her down for an adventuress the moment he saw her. Rising, he went toward her.

"If you are not waiting for any one, may I join you?"

For a moment the girl did not speak, looking into his eyes, weighing him to see if he were worth her while. He saw he had won, as a calculating smile parted her lips. "Well, I'm just as calculating," he thought, and sat down.

"Been in Yokohama long?" she asked him.

"Not very."

"From the interior?"

"Yes."

"My name is Mamie," the girl said. "And yours——?" She reached over, pulling his card-case from his inner pocket. "Stephen Chase? I'll call you Charlie. Stephen's too fancy."

All day they roamed about the city, but when evening came he had not asked her to marry him.

"I'll be ready for dinner about seven," she said, as they entered the hotel.

"Awfully sorry. I've got a business engagement and I doubt if I can get back in time," he answered, not realizing until he had spoken that he was going to refuse to have dinner with her. When she left him, he looked at his watch. It was already six o'clock and he went into the dining-room. He'd eat and get away before she came down.

At the table next to him sat the girl in black. "She's not the kind to be traveling alone," he mused, observing her more closely than he had in the morning. He watched her hands moving among the array of dishes which the Japanese maid placed before her. Delicate, expressive hands. A man would find rest under their touch. He felt his nerves relaxing.

He wondered again how it happened that the girl was traveling by herself. "It's no more unnatural than that Lucy should," he said to himself. "Odd, and she's evidently in mourning."

An American family just entering the room greeted the girl, and when she smiled back, he was surprised to see beauty come upon her. Then he noticed that at each human contact, some light seemed to kindle within her. "Why, she is lovely," he said to himself. "Almost as lovely as Lucy." But as soon as he made the comparison, he could see no one but Lucy. Only by exerting his will could he see this other girl, her shapely head set off by her heavy black braids bound around it like a coronet, the sensitive lift of her short upper lip, the fine nose, the long straight eyebrows, the deep-set blue eyes with their look of sincerity.

"I could marry her," he said to himself, "and not be ashamed." With the detachment he used in business he now studied the girl. She met every requirement except that she did not stir him to love. But that was not necessary. Love was dead within him. He could respect this woman. Perhaps she would make a good companion—she

61

looked as though she would. Anyway, she would be beautiful to look at, and to show Jim and the prying eyes of the port.

He rose and went to her, so absorbed that he forgot she might resent his coming without an introduction.

But she did not. When he asked if he might join her she said, "Yes," very simply.

"Perhaps we could do some sightseeing together?" he went on. "Stephen Chase is my name. I'll give you my credentials. I live in Manchuria where I work for an oil company. I'm here on my vacation."

"I'm Hester Wentworth." She hesitated. "Can you tell me anything about Nikko? My father and I had planned to go there. He died at sea," she added hurriedly.

"I'm sorry."

"Do you think," she spoke rapidly, "we could go there —to Nikko, I mean? Father wanted me to see the temples."

"I think we could," he said, and glancing up he saw Mamie eyeing him as she passed. She shrugged her shoulders and went on. "Perhaps some of your friends are going up, and we might join them," he continued. "We ought to take several days to do it properly."

He saw she had not known it was more than a day's trip when she proposed that they go to Nikko.

Stephen and Hester Wentworth had left Nikko and their party, going off by themselves for a long day's mountain climb. They were passing out of the mists which so often in Japan hang low on the ranges. Finished and stylized the scene: sharply etched above the draperies of fog, one craggy peak; below them the mists, parting, framed in gossamer shreds the rimmed rice-terraces which descended in rhythmic yellow of ripening grain to a cluster of thatched houses at the mountain's base.

High, on a rock ledge, they found a small temple. The

priests gave them tea and invited them to rest in the guest-room. Stephen stretched himself on the matting floor at Hester's feet. From the temple came the low-toned chanting of the priests. "That intoning!" murmured Hester. "I don't understand it—its rhythm is so different from ours."

"Is it?" said Stephen. "I didn't know, I'm not musical."

"I play the violin," said the girl.

He looked at her with new interest. "I've often wished I did since I came out here. Being away on such long trips—inns too dark to read—it would have been company."

He saw compassion in her gaze. Did she sense that he was in trouble? It broke up his difficult reserve. As sometimes happens to the sensitively reticent, once released his feeling poured itself out in a torrent. He told Hester that he had come to Japan to marry a girl he had known all his life, that it had not come off. He told her of the days afterward alone in the mountains and his reckless determination to go back married. He even told her of Mamie, holding nothing back, except that act of his which had brought him to such misery. That was a closed book now, a thing that concerned only himself and Lucy.

"You don't suppose . . ." he said as he ended. "It isn't the same—but you do understand, don't you? It would be sweet to take care of you."

There was silence between them. Well, he'd done the wrong thing again. Women . . .

She was speaking now, her voice gentle. "I do understand . . . Perhaps not all . . . but enough . . . I must think."

Without further speech, hand in hand they went down the mountainside, Hester letting Stephen lead her, too absorbed in her thoughts to watch her footing. To her own amazement, she loved him. She was aghast at the strength of her love, aghast that she could love so easily.

She had known this man only three days and a new well-being had come upon her, healing the raw edges of her grief over her father's death. The outpouring of protective care, so essential to her nature, held back since the death of her father, threatened to break bounds. She longed to heal the wound that other girl had inflicted upon him. That girl had been given so much of this man's love. What was there left for her? Wistful regret filled her. And something else—her need of him. She was alone in the world now that her father had gone. Then she drew herself up with proud reserve. Yes, she needed him. She needed him too much.

"I think it must be no," she said at last. "It's not that I don't understand. . . . I love you, I think. But there are reasons I can't explain."

She saw the stricken look in his face. All her inhibitions were swept away. She loved him, he needed her.

Three days later, they were married.

After their marriage, they returned to the temple. It was evening and they opened the sliding front wall of the guest-room to the moon, a huge orange disk, thin as tissue, riding level with their high-perched shelter. Behind, in the temple, the stocking-footed priests moved noiselessly across the matting-covered floor. Only the sound of their midnight chant reached the guest-room, and the deep tone of a gong.

With the moon for light, they undressed. Hester stood for a long moment looking out. She raised her arms and let down her hair, her braids hanging down like black ribbons over her white gown. Like laying aside her crown, Stephen thought. But his heart cried brokenly for Lucy, for the touch of her hands, her lips. Then remorse touched him. What right had he to take this beautiful proud girl, giving her the outer husk of affection? Yet his quiet regard for her made it possible for him to be very

64

gentle. So he had planned his first night with Lucy, holding his passion in abeyance.

They reached the border of Korea, spending the night in the Japanese hotel. To-morrow they would enter Manchuria. Long after Stephen slept, Hester lay awake. An aloofness which made her belong essentially to herself was shattered. There was bondage in love; no one had told her that love took away freedom. In some mysterious way, her life to-night had been welded to Stephen's. Why should the physical take upon itself such ominous spiritual force, a force which she did not understand, inimical to the self that loved beauty, that could create beauty? Now that secret self must be cold and unillumined, the flame of her music gone out, if it were necessary to make Stephen happy. Along what alien path did his happiness lie? Love then was not freedom but bondage. Some terrible submission had come upon her.

But in the morning, looking at Stephen in his young beauty, she forgot.

They sat side by side in the train passing over the long bridge into Manchuria. Japan, Korea and now Manchuria, with their mountains, their narrow valleys. So beautiful, thought Hester. Her marriage, except for that secret hour last night, so beautiful, too . . . After a time the hills were gone. The train seemed to push itself forward with infinitesimal progress over a flat earth toward a far-off horizon which never came nearer through the long hours of the day.

"This is really Manchuria, this plain," said Stephen, and then fell into silence. Hester was silent also.

At last she spoke. "I never felt like this before, as if I had the strength of a giant. What is it?"

"It's the climate," Stephen answered.

"You're very matter-of-fact about a thing so godlike," said Hester, looking first out of the window at the shocks of *kaoliang* touched to red glory by the sun, then back at her husband.

"Yes, too godlike for ordinary men." A swift passage of pain crossed his face. Hester wondered if the Stephen she knew was the whole Stephen.

They pulled into the station at Mukden, where they were to stop for the night.

Often, the next day, as the train moved across the plain, Hester felt that she and Stephen, instead of being giants, were tiny things, without any armor to meet the great country that stretched around them and this corporation of which Stephen talked more and more as the days passed. She could see only its hands, working tirelessly— the director in New York, the manager in Shanghai, another man styled "the boss," a man named Jim, one named Kendall, and Stephen himself. But the face was hid. Was it good, or was it evil? As they came near their destination, Stephen seemed less himself, more as if he were merely a part of something. Even his thoughts seemed to be presided over by that mysterious face she could not see. It made him seem a stranger. Stephen, glancing at her, saw that there were tears in her eyes.

"You're not troubled, are you? There's nothing to fear in this country, if that is what's the matter," he assured her. "There might be if we were out here on our own. There is something about this country, about this race that does swamp one alone. . . . But we're backed by the biggest thing in America, men united in a corporation. We're safe." Stephen hesitated. "But, Hester, we'll be tested."

"What do you mean—tested? Haven't you proved your worth? Wasn't that what the three years you've told me about were for?"

"Yes, but you see the manager in Shanghai has funny notions. He thinks this is a man's country. He has it in for men that marry. He claims it makes them soft, so he tests the wives to see if he can break them. A kind of idea about a chain being no stronger than its weakest link, you know."

"Then, in this man's country, I've got to be as strong as a man in endurance?"

Where his arm encircled Hester, Stephen felt the slightness of her body, delicately made for delicate purposes. For a moment his heart stood still; the manager in Shanghai had power to bend her to his own particular prejudice, and he could not protect her. Then he felt the vigorous reaction against such thoughts that a healthy man feels toward imagined fears.

"Sweet, we're all right. We mustn't let the manager in Shanghai get us buffaloed. We can always resign."

But Hester was not listening, hardening her spirit into steel to be strong as a man's. She had turned away from him. In that moment she felt her violin in her hand, her cheek resting on its wood, a long sustained note drawing along its strings.

Stephen took her chin in his hand, turning her head so that he could look into her eyes, intending to reassure her. But he saw with surprise that there was no need. Her blue eyes looked out at his undaunted. He was thankful.

"We'll be there in half an hour."

"Oh!"

Stephen did not speak again, beset now with his daydream, lived with through three years—coming home with Lucy. No, he must not think of her. He must turn his face sternly away from the past.

Kin, in a blue gown, met them at the train. As they walked through a turnstile at the side of the clapboard station, a dozen ricksha-men ran toward them, coming to a sudden halt like fencers arrested in the moment of action, the shafts of their rickshas pointed upward like an array of swords hemming them in. At the loud command of Kin the swords were withdrawn.

Hester found herself in a ricksha of Kin's choice, pulled along behind Stephen's out of the station inclosure on to a wide street. Dust rose in clouds, stirred up by the flying feet of ricksha-men, by the hoofs of mules, by heavy wheels of carts. Tall yellow men clad in coarse garments of faded blue, wearing on their feet grass-lined moccasins, plodded beside the carts, swinging long whips with the strength and vigor of cowboys throwing their lassos. Water in the ditches alongside the road, lying even with its surface; shanties beyond, men before them stripped to their waists, squatting over anvils, hammering out crude tin kettles, axes, farm implements. No women's things.

A turn down a rut-scarred alley, refuse heaps cast up againts the walls that bordered it, Stephen's ricksha-man pushing open the halves of a tall black gate. Hers following, the ricksha-men running carefully now, zigzagging from side to side so as not to upset the little vehicles into the ditches bordering the path. Bare brown earth beyond, flecked with white; here and there beds of coxcomb rearing red wattles; straight ahead a one-story house, its curtainless windows shining like black agate. Stephen jumped from his ricksha and helped her out.

She walked along a short hall, then along another, crossing it, making a T in the heart of the house. Flanking the short hall on each side was a room. Behind the long hall, running from end to end of the rectangular house, three more rooms. The furniture! Where did Stephen get it? To Hester, sensitive, fastidious, the chairs, the tables seemed to have been touched by too many people, like worn furniture in old hotels. She drew away from them.

Stephen, watching her anxiously, explained. "You see, it's a Company house and Company stuff." He was a trifle crestfallen that she did not appreciate his efforts.

She could not live without beauty and there was none here. Yes, there was. There was Stephen. It was to his beauty, not to his love, she clung to steady herself.

But in the night when Stephen lay sleeping, she woke in panic, sitting up in bed. It must have been late, for the moon was up, that moon that had risen early on her wedding-night. It was shining into the room and across the little patch of garden at the back of the house. It was unearthly, this moonlight, in it the same strange luminous quality of the sunshine that all day had held her both entranced and apprehensive.

Like the sunlight, it keyed her to some high pitch of excitement, sharpening her every sense. As she pulled the blanket closer around her, her finger-tips seemed touched to the quick by its harsh surface. She felt assailed by some curious scent that she took in with every breath, no matter how lightly drawn, a scent filling her with vague uneasiness. She felt that for long hours she had been played upon by undertones of sound and rhythms that jarred the accustomed rhythms of her being, leaving her with a residue of fear.

Why was she here? She looked at Stephen. Even he seemed a stranger to her. Only her violin was left of the old life of assured and ordered living. How had she come to leave her precious instrument to the care of Kin? She slipped out of bed and along the hall where their baggage stood. The violin case was easily distinguishable in the bright moonlight. She placed it on a chair by the bed and lay down far from Stephen.

On the night air, filtering into the room, lay the scent of incense, the sweet fumes of opium, mingling with the odors of dust and garlic. Now and then the one-stringed violin accompanying the voice of a singer set the quiet room to vibrating. In the hard-packed courts behind the shops many a tall northerner, stirred by the moon, had pitched his voice to a conventional high falsetto and was singing the songs of his people dwelling within the Great Wall of China. Sometimes loud, sometimes faint, beat the monotonous drum, drum of a tom-tom.

There was no longer any movement in the room. These two slept the quiet sleep of the young. . . . Just once Stephen turned, threw out his arm as if searching, murmured, "Lucy." The moon, hanging low in the sky, shone on a tiny brass plate on the end of the bureau, making it blink like a bright eye, showing the number which was registered in the great files of the Company, where Stephen also was docketed.

Toward morning there was the sound of pigeons circling over the house. The whistles which the rich merchant living across the way had fastened to their tails made a sweet singing sound; and as dawn approached there was the rumble of the studded cart wheels beyond the compound wall.

It was this familiar sound belonging to his work that awakened Stephen. When he discovered Hester lying at the edge of the bed, her violin on a chair beside her, in a flash of intuition he envisioned her night vigil and knew that she would not want him to know. Very gently, so as not to disturb her, he drew her to him; she did not waken.

Holding her, there came to him again, as on the train, the realization of how delicately she was made. Here in this room where he had dreamed of Lucy, his passion for the frail and small on whom he could lavish care broke up the coldness round his heart. Hester should be his child to guard. Then a new conception of Hester came to him.—Hester, not merely an object of his attention but a distinct personality, a mysterious lovely personality that he did not know. What did music mean to Hester? He wished he were musical. Could he give her what she needed?

VII

THE afternoon following their arrival, Stephen brought Jim home with him. Jim had not wanted to accept the invitation, but knowing that he'd have to meet Stephen's wife some time, he decided that he might as well get it over with. He supposed that Steve had picked up some poor sort of creature in Japan, and that he would have to pretend otherwise. He had thought Stephen was going to do the natural thing in marriage, which so few did. But Galahad, like the rest, was running true to Eastern form. He married in a hurry, and would repent at his leisure. He wished now he hadn't made it so easy for Steve to marry. As they turned down the alley to the house they had once occupied together, he wondered for the hundredth time what had happened to Lucy. Stephen had given him only the bare statement that he had married some one else.

Hester rose to welcome them. "By gad, Steve has done well by himself! She lifts her head like a pedigreed filly. She'll make the goal or drop in her tracks." So thought Jim, the ardent lover of beautiful horses and beautiful women. "Well, I'll have to hand it to Steve. He certainly has good taste." He asked Hester what she thought of the town.

"Oh, I like it."

He saw he'd get no complaint from her. . . . "We're a gay little village. We ice-boat, skate, dance and play cards; and we go to bed at three in the morning."

"Does Stephen?" Hester looked up with interest, as she handed Kin Jim's cup of tea.

"Not me, I don't get a chance." It was Stephen who spoke, turning to Jim. "How about it, when do I go out again?"

"She deserves an even break," thought Jim, "I'll have to manage the boss, make him keep Steve at home for a

71

time." He was about to answer the question when Kin entered. "Master comes."

"Ask him," said Jim with a grin. Hester turned to behold a middle-aged, thick-set man coming toward her with a shake of his shoulders, like a bashful boy throwing off a detaining hand. He held a great bunch of chrysanthemums which, with the utmost discomfiture, he thrust into her hand.

"Oh, how lovely!" she exclaimed.

"You can get all the chrysanthemums you want a little later," Jim explained, noticing how eager had been her response to the flowers. "Just tell your coolie to go out and buy you a lot."

"But surely not so fine as these." Hester turned with a smile for the boss. "You have had something to do with the growing of these."

"My own greenhouses," he answered. He liked this girl young Chase had chosen; and he acquiesced gruffly, when Jim proposed they give Steve a month to settle down.

"A whole month," thought Hester. She turned first to one, then the other, watching their faces as they talked of business, of conditions in the country. They seemed to have forgotten her. She tried to make her way into the labyrinth of new impressions.

What was this talk of a lamp that was going to light all of Asia? And of a market of four hundred million people? Four hundred million! "Backward people," they called them. But where was the China her father had loved?

"Not very interesting for you, this talk," said the boss, turning to her. "How do you like the town?"

"Oh, very much," answered Hester, wondering if every one was going to ask her this question. These people seemed to have the same local pride that Americans at home had.

"We're proud of this town," said the boss, as if reading her thoughts. "And the natives like us now. I've seen the

72

day when it wasn't too safe. A mere handful of us went out to meet the Boxers. We're in a new era now," he hastened to add, remembering she was going to be left alone in this house.

Then the men forgot her again, talking of treaties and the Open Door Policy. "I've looked over your reports about Kirin Province," said the boss, turning to Stephen. "We've got to give it up. About half a case of oil would leak out before we got it in there."

"If we had roads! The Chinese may do what the Japanese have done in their area and build roads; they could shorten the distance; change their trade routes . . ."

"Hm," grunted the boss, "try to get them. Besides, roads wouldn't do any good, so long as they haul with the carts. Those studded wheels would cut roads to pieces in no time. As for changing anything . . . the whole thing goes together, you know that. You've seen enough in three years."

"I suppose so," answered Stephen, "but I can't give up the idea that if the merchants would join together, they could change this country in no time . . . they've got the money."

"And the sense," Jim broke in.

"Sense, yes. They've got cunning to drive a good bargain. They know how to make money. But what I can't knock into you fellows is that they're traders, damn clever bargainers, not merchants. They've not got the spirit of adventure, bold enterprise such as our business men have. Perhaps three years isn't enough to knock the difference into Steve's head, but Jim here is old enough, been here long enough, to know that. They've not got the energy, either. Why, what do I keep Chase here on their trails all the time for? He's their dynamo."

"Well, what do you expect?" Jim was nettled by the boss's uncomplimentary reference to him. "They've been browbeaten for centuries by their officials. Republic's too new yet to show what they can do. You're too skeptical, boss."

"Have it your own way, but we'll not waste our money in Kirin Province. That's final. As for changing trade routes, might as well try to change the course of the blood."

Suddenly the boss realized he was not in his office, that there was a woman in the room, and his shyness returned. He rose awkwardly, saying good-by.

After Jim had gone, too, Hester came and sat on the arm of Stephen's chair.

"The boss likes you," said Stephen with pride. "Nice of him to arrange this month, wasn't it? But, Hester dear, you aren't going to mind too much next winter, are you? Once the boss sent me out again in the afternoon, when I'd only got in that morning."

Hester sighed. "The boss loves this business, doesn't he? He'd sacrifice you for it, or me, or even himself for that matter, wouldn't he?"

Through Hester, Stephen was brought to the realization that the boss would do just that, and it seemed to him startling in so kind a man. Stephen sought to justify him.

"Well, it's natural. He came up here years ago when the business was nothing. He's made it. It's his creation. He knows how to choose good Chinese and make them work, he has the faculty of being hard-boiled and still make them like him, and he's a wizard on exchange."

"What is exchange?" asked Hester.

"The different moneys. We deal in six major kinds, and that isn't all. Even inns in some towns issue their own notes. The men have a bet that if you take a dollar and start out over Manchuria, changing it at every night's stopping place, in the end you wouldn't have anything left. And the boss manages all this and makes money for the Company."

74

"Do you handle exchange when you travel?"

"Yes, but that's not the point."

"Well, what is it? Why, Stephen, I think you're wonderful."

"Seriously, Hester, the boss is great."

"I should think if he's so great the Company would take him to Shanghai."

"That doesn't follow," answered her young husband. "They need him here. And besides, he says he wouldn't live anywhere except in this town. He's lived here for years and he'd rather live here than in New York. He's never taken a vacation, and it's been twenty years since he's seen America."

"What nonsense! You all talk about not going back," cried Hester. "Why, America is our country. At least we can go home when we retire."

"Well," said Stephen, "I can't retire probably until I'm entitled to a pension, and that's not until I'm fifty. Even you may not want to go then. We may be like the boss. This is his home-town now. He's a great personage here. He can't afford to leave either, he's land poor. He bought a lot of property when the port was flourishing—that was when the Russians were in power. He meant to sell it for a good sum when it became more valuable. He does rent a little of it to the Company for storage purposes, but that doesn't bring him in much, in fact not enough to pay him for the risk. It seems he didn't want to rent to them. Somebody might accuse him of using the Company for his own purposes, he says. The boss is darned independent and so honest he leans backward. Anyway, he did rent it to them, finally, when they couldn't get hold of any other good spot."

"Well, when the land does become valuable, he can sell," said Hester.

"It's never going to go up," replied Stephen. "The port's dying. The Japanese have succeeded in shifting the trade from here to Dalny. Now there it is!" He sat up straight, excited by his new idea. "The Japanese are shifting trade routes! If the Japs can do it, the Chinese can! Jim and I weren't so wrong after all. I've thought a lot about it. I guess I never told you I was trained for an engineer, and I've worked it all out. A system of roads—key roads. It's not so impossible as the boss thinks. Gosh! The undevelopment out here stirs you!"

He fell silent, absorbed in his dream of progress, only a little conscious that Hester had spread his hand out on her knee, murmuring, "A musician's hand. This reach between thumb and fingers." . . . He was absorbed in his thoughts.

"Stephen, I've been talking to you and you didn't hear. You are an artist; only artists dream."

"I?"

As Hester twined her slim fingers in his, he felt himself taking off from the flatness which life had assumed of late. Hester's faith in him wrought an act of faith in himself. It pushed his spirit upward past his numbing despair over Lucy, past the dulling of his interest since the lamp episode. He was again a mystic of work.

So now they had this month in which to get acquainted. Then big business would begin grinding out Stephen married, making him smooth as a ball-bearing, or jagged as a gear-wheel, according to the need on this frontier in capturing the oil trade.

The short-lived northern autumn gave Stephen and Hester time only to skim the surface of their union. After office hours, Stephen showed his wife the town, its few straggling streets running almost immediately into the three hundred and fifty thousand square miles of the great Manchurian plain, the Company's potential market, every city, every town known to Stephen after long arduous travel. He took her to the recreation ground where the white inhabitants gathered for tennis. In the matting shed, around the tea-table, he introduced her to the women. They were idly polite, secretly avid in their inspection of her. As he had foreseen, he could take pride in showing the town his wife.

After breakfast, when he went to his office, it was pleasant to have her walk with him along the bund as far as the custom house. At noon, he enjoyed being led about by Hester, Li Tsu and Kin at their heels, to see what she had done to the house. He praised and admired and thought humbly of his own masculine efforts in preparation for Lucy. As he watched the rooms take on comfort and grace, he began to feel the delicate beauty he associated with women pervading the house. In no way did she disappoint him. He felt even gay and light-hearted the day that Hester drew him down beside her on the sofa. Cunningly placed, it was, opposite the hall, so that you could see a corner of Tim's palace, framed in the doorway.

"Wait," said Hester. And in a moment across the space moved the brown sail of a junk. No sign of the junk, only the sail above the compound wall, like a huge butterfly floating past. Stephen slipped his arm around her. Li Tsu barked furiously, jumping on Stephen's lap, licking his face.

"Jealous, old chap?" Stephen held Hester closer in order to tease the little dog. Then she rose and moved away, not because of Li Tsu's protestations, but because of Kin's hostile eyes.

It was only in the night when she crept into his arms, that Stephen dipped below the surface of his being, groping for some way to rend asunder his heart's closure.

But to Hester this union brought completion. The solitude of her spirit, even the deep and radiant solitude of music, had heretofore held for her its moments of loneliness. Now when she was alone in the low brick house behind the mud wall she stood, violin under her chin, her small head bent lovingly above it, playing with verve, with abandon, her inadequate self perfected in union.

The month was gone and once more there was a moon. Out of the Manchurian night, it hung high above the tide-washed town, transforming into things of romance the mud walls of compounds, the black gates with their brass dragon knockers, the refuse heaps, and Tim's rococo palace alike.

Hester stood at the window, gazing out at the hoarfrost of salt left by the tide, which spread its ghostly blight over the garden. It was beautiful in the moonlight. She reached her hands out, locking her fingers in ecstasy. Wife of Stephen, number three in one of the hundreds of offices of the great oil corporation, filled with the mysterious significance of herself!

"See, Stephen, I've put on my wedding-nightgown." Her voice had a new quality, not quite the voice of her maidenhood. Still, though, a fragile child in a child's shift, he thought, folding her in his arms. Never must he let anything harm Hester. He felt his energies doubling to work for her. . . . And something more . . . a faint sense of bondage to his job. He needed it in order to give Hester all she should have. He knew she wanted a piano. Could he manage it? The freight alone. . . . And then his mother. He must send her money this winter. Exchange was against him. Chinese silver would buy so little American gold.

The next morning they walked as usual along the path toward the office, unheeding the tide lying slow and brackish in the ditches, unheeding the bleak and dusty square. But when they came out on the bund where the river flowed between its monotonous banks, they heeded the touch of the wind on their cheeks. From somewhere out of the still air it came, startling them, for it felt cold as if it had passed over ice.

Stephen held up his hand. "The wind's shifted. Winter will come quickly. This is a winter country."

That evening as they sat at dinner the wind rose into the sound of a hurricane, shrieking in the chimney, swinging in through the butler's window where Kin's immobile countenance kept watch over the dining-room. A brown powder of dust lay along the window-sills and, at each new gust, it piled itself up in miniature dunes. Dust hung in the room and settled over the table. There was a gritty substance in the food.

All night the wind rattled the tiles on the roof.

In the morning Kin superintended the coolie in stuffing cotton into the cracks around the windows. Then with his delicate tapering fingers, he pasted narrow strips of rice paper along the cotton-stuffed cracks. That afternoon he packed the master's winter clothes for a trip, and the next day Hester was left in the care of the cook, the coolie and Kin's wife, appointed by Kin to be her *amah*.

VIII

STEPHEN was back in the accustomed groove of travel. Although the dust-storm had spent itself, the sun, still veiled in a bronze sky, looked out at him like a dulled moon. The land seemed remote and hostile. In the last two months he had lost the knack of riding in the springless cart. He shifted uneasily, trying to adjust his body to the continuous jar, and his mind to the patient attitude that primitive travel entailed.

Also he had not that sense of snapped communication which before had made it possible for him to work with such singleness of purpose. He could not release his

79

thoughts from Hester. Hester alone at night . . . their house not so far from the king of the robbers. Paid to protect them, the robber chief, but suppose he did not. Stephen realized that he should have taught Hester to use a revolver. It was too soon anyway tot leave her alone. She didn't know a half-dozen words of the language. Why, even the men were given a longer time to get adjusted. The Company was asking too much.

Never before had he questioned the discipline under which he worked. No matter how difficult things had been, he had never turned back from a trip. Whatever the conditions, he had met them in silence, proud that he functioned so well for the Company. Stephen loved machinery, and the idea of the Company as an intricate machine, dependent on perfect coordination of its members, had always stirred his imagination. But now no fervor of efficiency made the possible suffering of Hester inspiring.

What before he had not trusted himself to decide, he now decided. Not all of these inspection trips on which the boss sent him were vitally necessary, and this was one of them. Three years of experience had given him the knowledge, he believed, which justified this conclusion. The boss was too keen not to know this. Why then had he sent him? Testing him, perhaps, to see if initiative, individual judgment, had developed in him. Perhaps beginning to think he had none.

Decision swept over Stephen in a vitalizing wave. He commanded the carter to turn from the way, make the nearest telegraph station. He'd wire the boss that he had collected the desired information and was returning. As a matter of fact, he had it all in his note-book. A smile played about Stephen's mouth. The boss had lived so much with the Chinese that he would appreciate this indirect way of telling him that the trip was a wild-goose chase. For the rest of the day he was filled with a proud sense of self-esteem.

The next morning in the cold gray light of four o'clock Stephen drank hastily the coffee Kin brought and then helped with the bedding roll and the packing of the food-box in order to hasten their start. He intended to make the railway town by evening. He'd be home by midnight.

He had wriggled into his place in the cart between the grain sacks; the carter was ready. Where was Kin? He leaned forward peering around the side of the cart. He could just discern Kin in conversation with some one. Hang it all! There was always so much palaver to get through with before starting.

"Come, come, hurry!" he called.

"*Lai, lai,* coming, coming," answered Kin. "An electric letter for the master."

Stephen read the telegram in the light of his flash. There was but one word, "Proceed." Moodily he reversed his orders. Never before had he felt as he did at that moment. When the Company ignored his part in the lamps, there still had been a certain personal satisfaction in the fact that his handiwork had proved itself. But this contempt for his judgment was another thing; this futile journey prostituted his intelligence. Jim was right. The little old pay check was the only thing. That day the way was long, life reduced to an aimless performance of duty.

Some time during the day it came to him what the motive was for sending him on this trip. The boss was testing him, but not testing his initiative as he had at first thought. The actual purpose of the trip was to find out if the Company's best traveling man in Manchuria had been spoiled by marriage. A hot flush rose to the roots of Stephen's hair as he thought of the telegram he had sent. It was the first time he had dodged work. The

81

boss had seen through it, knew that he wanted to get home. Stephen was ashamed.

Then anger filled him. He had been tricked into mistaking his own motives. If the boss had made the test a real piece of work, he was certain he would have gone through with it, regardless of his desire to get home. Through the thin glove of the useless trip he felt the iron hand of Company discipline. Fear flicked his heart. Would the boss report him for insubordination? Now he planned eagerly to make the trip in some way yield returns for the Company. Throughout the rest of the day, his mind worked at fever heat. At nightfall he had made nothing out of the barren trip; but he would, he was determined he would. The stimulus of fear was never again quite absent from Stephen's service.

It was nine o'clock when they reached the night's stopping-place. The long street of the town was deserted and dark, except in front of two shops where spears of light, shining through the cracks of the shutters, fell across the rutted road. The first year Stephen had been in Manchuria, he had sold these merchants hanging lamps. The rest of the town lived as before, content with wicks floating in bean or peanut oil.

Now, above the rumble of his cart, Stephen heard the voice of a child seeking admittance to the shop. "We need foreign light," the voice was crying. *"Kai mun, kai mun. Open, open."*

The iron bar ground in its socket, a shutter was removed, and in the shaft of light a little girl stood revealed—grotesque and awkward, the graceful lines of childhood lost in the layer upon layer of quilted coats she wore, for the night was cold.

Jumping from the cart, Stephen stood in the shadow of the next shop to watch. The child came out, carrying one of his little red lamps, lighted. It was a windless night and the flame burned steadily, protected by the chimney.

Stephen followed the child. Down the street she went, with her light, turning in at the door of a hovel.

Stephen went on to the inn. There, too, he found his lamp, standing on a rough table where wayfarers were eating. They were discussing the lamp. "It gives forth small light," said his own carter.

The innkeeper defended his new possession: "You turned the wick too high. You know nothing of these foreign delights."

"The old is better," the unconvinced carter reiterated.

Stephen stepped to the table. "In my country," he began, removing the chimney, "we pinch the wick—so—and then the flame burns high, like this."

"Au, au," grunted the crowd. Wonderful! Wonderful! An old man bent forward and with clawlike hand turned the wick up and down. *"Au, au,"* was all he could manage to say in his absorption in the task.

"With a rice-bowlful of oil, they will give you the little lamp," said Stephen.

The innkeeper walked away in disgust. He had not told the wayfarers this. He had had great face in their presence until this barbarian had spoken. But perhaps they still thought he had bought the treasure, for they shook their heads incredulously. "No one would be such a fool as to give away this costly light. It is worth many coppers," they said.

"Go to the big shop on the Long Street and you will know that my lips speak truly," Stephen continued.

Ai! Give away the glass bowl with no bottom or top wherein the fire sits? That alone would be worth much. They went back to their places on the *k'ang*.

At last a man, wearing the dress of a well-to-do farmer, rose and went out. Stephen followed, disappointed when he saw the man fumbling about his cart. He had hoped he was on the way to get one of the lamps. Then the peasant left the inn courtyard, walking down the Long

Street to the big shop, Stephen not far behind him. Now again the shutter came down and the farmer stepping within placed on the counter a can such as swings from the bottom of every cart for holding axle grease.

Lifting the skirt of his gown he drew his money pouch from his belt and counted out a few coppers. "Foreign oil and the light that is a gift."

"One copper more, and we give you the lamp," said the assistant behind the counter.

"The barbarian said his lips spoke truly, the lamp is a gift."

Then beside the can of oil, the lamp was placed. Carefully the peasant stowed it away in the folds of his padded coat and went out, the can of oil in his hand.

When he was once more in the inn, Stephen sat in his usual attitude on the *k'ang*, lighting and relighting his pipe, for he forgot to puff and it went out often. Just as he had foreseen on that long-ago night when he had had his inspiration—the little lamps were going to make their way into every nook and corner of Manchuria. This evening he had seen them enter hut, inn and farmhouse. . . . In Europe and America, the lamp which burned coal-oil, as it was then called, had been the forerunner of the machine age. Might it not be so out here?

Stephen regained his pride in the lamps. Nothing could make the lamp other than his contribution to the awakening that was to come to these men who lay around him, rolled up in their quilted comforters.

The boom had come at last to the oil business, the boom so long deferred that the men had despaired of it. The immediate and spectacular cause, Stephen could not fail to see, was his little lamp. Even those who earned but a few coppers a day skimped on their coarse fare of millet until they had saved enough to buy the cupfuls of oil which would give them the precious lamps.

84

But success, Stephen had to own, was not due entirely to that. The giving of the lamps would have profited nothing, had it not been for the splendid organization built up by such men as Stephen's boss and the manager in Shanghai, an organization sound in every detail. With Occidental ability they had built this business structure, but as no man without experience of the Orient could have done. This knowledge they had gained through long years in China in business for themselves. Failure had engulfed their enterprises, for their capital had been unequal to the struggle. But before they gave up, they had come to know good from bad Chinese. Because of such insight, every agent in Manchuria was sound, and the organization built around them was sound, resting on the ethics of China. Through this perfectly constructed conduit flowed the energy of such men as Stephen.

It was the coldest winter for many years. The animals' coats were frozen white as they traveled. Stephen's breath, rising and settling under the visor of his fur cap, frosted his eyelashes. It was impossible to hold a handkerchief to his suffering face, for when he tried, his hands, even in fur-lined gloves, became so cold that he had to tear the gloves off with his teeth and thrust his hands beneath his many layers of clothing that they might gain warmth from his body. His feet stretched out before him, in spite of the heavy Mongol boots stuffed with straw, grew numb until he learned the trick of slipping them under the carter.

But he hardly considered the discomforts. His love of the open road came back to him: the brilliant shining distance, the "long carts," loaded with beans, pulled by mules and ponies, crawling slowly south; other "long carts" loaded with neat wooden boxes, each holding two tins of oil, crawling slowly north, a dark streak of oil marking their trail.

For Stephen the Chinese world receded. The Chinese,

no longer impinging upon his consciousness as friend or enemy, became for him once more, as in his first days in Manchuria, actors in a play. The long-robed merchants merely a cloud of witnesses testifying that the streak of oil on the road was a great, great stream, draining away their profits. He knew it was a little stream of oil, the agents also knew it was a little stream, but neither said so. That would be to take away the mask of decorum. It was an amusing play to the gallery in which Stephen, with a comfortable sense of superiority, humored the merchants, always taking time for the theatrical masks to be donned.

Ground between the upper and nether millstones, two money-making millstones—the Chinese merchant and the great corporation—he came to think of little but the battle over money. The great corporation in the name of efficiency demanded its final cent in profit; the Chinese merchant, with his medieval outlook, believing that cunning was a part of shrewdness, took as much "squeeze" as he could. If the oil were diluted a trifle, the profits were greater. Besides, you had proved yourself a good trader, more cunning than the customer. If, also, you could manage to convince the Company that the leakage was greater than the amount allowed you, you had honorably won a victory over the barbarian. In the scheme of ancestral life, the man outside the clan was fair prey.

From Mongolia to Korea, from Siberia to the Yellow Sea, up and down and across Manchuria, Stephen traveled by train, by cart, by muleback. No notice was sent to an agent of his coming. He arrived suddenly, weighed the tins of oil to see if they were as light as the agents contended, watchful of the Company's interests, tested a tin here and there in the stacks in the godowns to make sure there was no dilution, watchful that the Chinese peasant was given oil without a brown residue of water which would make the flame of his lamp sputter and flare. The great increase in sales made this inspection arduous work. But Stephen exulted in the toil.

Often as he neared home after a long journey, he awoke with a sense of guilt to the realization that he had not thought for days whether Hester was happy. How would she spend her time while he was gone? He sensed that her music would contribute to her happiness. "Something to do," he put it. That she was deprived of a world of music where her spirit lived, naturally, he did not realize; nor did Hester at first.

IX

HESTER was in fact happy in the town hugged in between the ice-bound river and the iron earth of the winter plain from which the high wind flaked off bits, sifting them over the snow like rust. The bleak mottled expanse of brown earth and old snow, pierced by the stubble of the *kaoliang,* out of which an occasional village of mud huts rose like gopher mounds, seemed but to intensify her sense of snugness in her house, where she was nestled in heat and care. The air-tight stove in the passageway glowed red. In her sitting-room, in her bedroom, the fires with their coals beautifully arranged in rows seemed never to die; the hand of the coolie built them perfectly, so that when the coal turned to ash the structure of ash stood as the structure of coal had stood.

Amah, speaking no English, hovered about Hester. Her soft black eyes spoke only of one thing, service. Gently her fingers moved over Hester's hair; with butterfly touch she powdered Hester's shoulders, her arms. She did all she could to make her lady beautiful, as Kin had commanded her: keep her in idle enervating ease, flawless for the master, she, the possession of the master.

Hester did not guess out of what threads her soft cocoon of comfort was woven.

The first night she had spent alone was a strange and memorable experience. So long as Stephen was there she had held at bay the nameless fears which had lain in the unexplored recesses of her mind. She had gone to the station with her husband in order to hold off until the last moment the coming to grips with her fears. She did not tell him this. No word of protest passed her lips. The Company should find no weakness in her to lessen the strength of Stephen.

When the train had disappeared into the brown haze of the spent dust-storm she walked from the station, facing alone the array of ricksha shafts raised like the swords of fencers, hemming her in, the men's unwashed bodies exuding the odor of garlic and the unrecognized sweet odor of opium. Then her "funk," as she called her terror, had closed in upon her. But she managed to choose a ricksha, seat herself in it. She was running clear of whatever menace was in the crowd when a new danger assailed her. She could not speak to her puller, direct him; he was running away with her straight to his own lair in the Chinese city. Somehow, by taps on the side of the ricksha, by the Chinese words for "Go! Wait!" spoken rather too loudly, she had managed to direct him until the house-door closed at last behind her.

The cook who was in charge in Kin's place had slipped away after paying the ricksha-man. The *amah,* taking Hester's hat and gloves, had stumped off on her bound feet like a little club-footed animal. All at once the Chinese seemed natural to Hester, a race serving her, guarding her. She had examined the fear which had looked darkly in on her ever since her coming, and thus could dismiss it.

Hester walked slowly along the hall into the living-room, sitting for a moment in Stephen's chair, then into the bedroom, moving lightly back and forth, her spirit seeking its home within this house. The month of happy days and nights spent here seemed no longer to inform it.

"This is a Company house," she said to herself. "We make it ours, only as we pay for it in service."

She took out needle and thread and began mending a hole in the rug, taking pleasure in the long needle going in and out, stitching her service into the Company house. The coolie, seeing her thus, knelt by her side, "Please, missie, I do," and he took the needle gently from her. Hester got up, remembering what Stephen had told her about "face."

The afternoon moved slowly, each minute spinning itself into nothingness. When the hour arrived that before had brought Stephen from his office, the coolie came with the lamp and the cook with tea. At seven dinner was announced, and she sat alone at the table.

At last the servants went to their quarters and she lay down in her bed. It was the first time that she had ever spent the night completely alone in a house. Lying straight and still in the dark, her heart searched out the mysteries of her new submission, this union with Stephen.

When the windows became gray squares and the first rumble of the carts could be heard, Hester's thoughts turned to this white man's town, unknown, and unrelated to her as yet. To-day she must make her calls. It seemed officious, a newcomer, calling on women she had never met. But Stephen had said this was the custom.

That afternoon she started forth, admiring her own calmness as she sat in the ricksha, her hands in their white gloves lying in her lap lightly clasping her card-case. Adroitly she negotiated the first, the second stop. No one at home. The word "Out" filled the little space above the slit where cards could be dropped into the neat boxes fastened to the gate posts. With some disappointment she deposited her cards, wishing she might

89

know what the houses and the people hidden behind the high walls were like.

At the third stop, "Missie have got," said the gateman when he came in response to her knock. What did he mean? Well, evidently that his mistress was at home as the word "In" was clearly displayed above the card-box.

Through the half-open gate, Hester saw a vista of walk bordered by the pompomed heads of a thousand chrysanthemums rising proudly from blue and green glazed pots. She all but brushed them as she walked toward the house-door standing open, for some sudden warmth had come into the air with the passing of the dust-storm. The patterned path of round stones, the beauty, the extravagant gorgeousness of the garden touched her with a subtle abandonment. Straight down the long hall the white-robed house-boy led her. The braid of his queue hung like a glossy black rope almost to the hem of his snow-white robe. Hester made a mental note that she would have Kin dress like this. Kin's gowns were of dark blue and usually unironed, simply stretched into shape by hanging on a bamboo pole thrust through the sleeves.

Now they had passed into another garden. With surprise, Hester saw three tennis courts shut in by the house and the compound wall, a hotly contested tournament in progress. Then the club courts were not the only ones in the town! She caught immediately an air of exclusiveness here. It was difficult to cross the space to the benches where the onlookers sat, transferring their gaze from the game to her.

She had the startled sensation that she was outré with this group. This was an official party: the consuls of three countries—France, England and America—the port doctor, customs officials.

The commissioner's wife, reclining in a long wicker chair, languidly stretched forth her hand, after glancing at Hester's card the house-boy presented on a lacquer tray.

"Ah, Mrs. Chase." Then turning to a tall youth, "Be a darling, Billy, and get Mrs. Chase some tea. Billy's our new railway engineer."

"Ah," spoke Hester eagerly, wondering afterward why her eagerness, "my husband's a mining engineer."

"How quaint," said the commissioner's wife. "A professional man and in trade."

Presently, Hester took her departure, approaching her next stop with a little diffidence. A retired sea-captain and his wife lived in this house, a large square structure, clearly to be seen behind its fence of narrow iron palings, the only house in the town not surrounded by high mud walls. Its American owner's insistence upon "seeing out," Hester already knew, furnished amusement for the English in the town. Strange place for a sea-captain, even a retired one, she thought, picking her way along the twisting paths.

The captain's wife, a stout, pouter-pigeon English-woman, in great contrast to the angular, aristocratic wife of the commissioner of customs, was bustling about, superintending the moving of pots of chrysanthemums from the veranda into the house.

"So you're the new bride?" she said, clasping Hester's hand.

Hester felt this woman's inclusion as clearly as she had felt the other's exclusion.

The dining-room into which she was led, with its pots of chrysanthemums, bronze, pink, yellow, magenta in un-assorted colors, oppressed her with their indiscriminate profusion. "If it weren't for the flowers, I'd like the room," she thought. "I'd believe I was in a ship." Heavy chairs, that looked as if a storm could not move them, stood around a green baize-covered table, a square of white cloth ineffectually covering it; a ship's clock ticked

91

on the wall. Her hostess served her with plum cake and tea as strong as lye. As they sipped it, the captain's wife spun an endless tale of drab and gorgeous threads— beauty and ugliness indiscriminately mixed together like the chrysanthemums.

"I've had eleven children," she told Hester. "Most of them born at sea. The captain took care of me when they came. They've all left me now. All but one is in America. Doesn't seem as if they're mine any more. That one I lost . . . sometimes seems as if I have him. Our sailing ship was wrecked and he was drowned. . . . Just as I was dressing him. I've got his little shoe I was putting on at the time. And afterward it was in my hand. I'll show it to you some time. They're nice when they're babies."

Her fat little hands ceased for a moment their hovering over the tea-things and she leaned close to Hester, whispering a question.

"Oh, no, not yet," said Hester, flushing.

"Well, now, you don't need to be embarrassed with me. When you need a friend come to me. I've had eleven."

"Thank you," said Hester. "No, I really can't stay." But she was a long time getting down the twisted paths to the gate, the captain's wife leading the way, turning often to talk.

She found three other women at home. There are not many calls left for to-morrow, she was thinking, as she consulted the list Stephen had given her. Only twenty men in the town who have wives. Now she realized that, in the afternoons Stephen had taken her to the tennis courts and in her calls to-day, she had seen them all. "Why, I'm the only young woman in the place. Where shall I find a woman friend? It seems a little lonely. I wish Stephen were here."

When she entered her house she found Jim seated by the fire.

"I've come," he said, "to see if you'll be a kind of mascot for me this winter. Ride on my ice-boat in the Saturday races."

"I, only, among the women am young," thought Hester and she felt proud, as if she had achieved this distinction by her own effort.

X

THE months passed, and Hester spent them almost entirely without Stephen. At ten o'clock, day after day, the sun reached her windows. She would not let the servants close the blinds, as was the custom in the town, for she wanted the sun to wake her, streaming across the gray painted floor, across the counterpane. Before she was dressed she would hear the first low tones of the wind beginning far off, drawing nearer, soughing in the chimney like organ music. Steadily the wind mounted and with it came to Hester an unfamiliar excitability, a futile energy.

Strange new land, a rough frontier offering enervating ease and at the same time holding to her lips that stinging raw stimulant compounded of dry thin air, crystal-clear sunlight, never-ending wind. It brought her to no happy achievement, only to nervous activity.

There were times when her desire to play her violin left her completely. Then she was distraught, certain that never again would life render itself for her in the beauties of sound, forgetting, in the blackness of the moment, that the ecstatic mood of creation had always before returned.

And sometimes lassitude controlled her, absorbing the very core of her vitality. Hour after hour, she would sit curled in the corner of the mammoth Russian couch Stephen had bought from Tim, one foot under her, the other loosely suspended over the side. Where was Stephen? Out somewhere traveling in a cart like those which she heard creaking above the wind, iron-studded wheels complaining, the deep-toned cart bells tolling. How far away he seemed from this snug room.

At five o'clock she began holding her court; sometimes before, for a few left their offices early to see her alone. Delight in her beauty looked out at her from Jim's eyes, from many a griffin's, from an old Frenchman's.

They vied with one another for the privilege of being her escort.

"My luck's good," said Jim as he crossed hands with her skating out over the ice, the night of the carnival.

"Jim, isn't it lovely!"

Hester looked with delight about the matting shed which protected the flooded tennis courts. It was a glittering scene of shimmering ice, flags of many nations, colored lanterns, men and women in fancy dress.

"You're the loveliest thing about it in that Priscilla costume. That white kerchief against your throat sets off your color."

Pleased with Jim's discriminating praise, Hester was a proud and graceful figure, enjoying to the full her youth, when the commissioner's wife entered. She did not know that the haughty glance which the older woman threw over her shoulder as she skated past was because of Jim.

The door opened to admit a short figure clad in the white gown and baggy trousers of a Korean, a black buckram hat perched jauntily on top of the head.

"Why, it's the boss!" she exclaimed.

Smoking his long Korean pipe, the boss strolled up to her as she stood resting for a moment. She had never known him to be so friendly. The costume seemed to set him at his ease. "Why, I've never thought of him as human before, only as Stephen's boss." She wondered

94

what his life was like, his wife still away in England. Was he ever lonely?

It was three o'clock when, with the ice so powdery that it was impossible to skate longer, Hester consented to sit down and let Jim take off her skates. As they went out, with a sigh of regret she looked back at the great shed, the hundreds of lanterns, one by one going out, the tables with their clutter of coffee-cups and plates half-full of sandwiches. She wished she didn't have to go home to her empty house.

But when she reached the door, it was Kin who let her in. She gave a cry. Stephen must be at home. There he was waiting for her, asleep in his chair. As she sank down beside him, he opened his eyes. But in the instant before he had wakened she saw Stephen as she had never seen him before, off guard, lines of patience and resignation in his face. How odd he looked, as if the mask of an older man had been let down over his youth. Youth! Could it be so easily destroyed?

"Have you had a good time, sweet?" he asked gently after he had kissed her. "I'm so glad."

"But, Stephen," she demanded, "how did you come to be home? And why didn't you come to the party?"

"Oh, well, I was late," he said.

The suspicion crossed her mind that he had been here all the evening. She felt worried about him. After each trip he seemed less able to mingle light-heartedly in the doings of the town. Sometimes even on the defensive, she thought.

"See what I've brought you," he said, speaking a little shyly as he always did when he made her a present. She noticed by his chair a bundle tied in a square of blue cloth, the corners knotted together.

"Open it quick," she cried, forgetting her concern of him, sinking back on her heels, the wide skirt of her gray gown spreading around her.

95

Without haste Stephen untied the knots; at last he shook out the soft folds of a fur garment.

"Oh, Stephen, what I've always wanted! A fur coat! Why, Stephen, it's sable!"

"Slip it on. I thought it would suit you. You should have had a fur coat before now. Your cloth one isn't warm enough for Manchuria."

The long Chinese garment fell to her heels and the sleeves hung down below her hands.

"It'll make me a lovely coat. I'll get the Chinese tailor to-morrow. I can have it ready for the ice races."

"It's Russian sable," said Stephen. "It's better than the Chinese."

"My dear, you're very good to me!" cried Hester.

Only ten days and Stephen was gone again. Hester was busy making the coat after the pattern of one brought from America. In despair, first because it would not fit, then at the slowness of the tailor, fearful it would not be ready for the races.

But when the night came she walked beside Jim, wearing her sable coat and a close little cap made from the left-over pieces.

"Lord, you're pretty!" exclaimed Jim. "Those cunning black curls round your cap. I ought to win with anything as pretty as you on my boat. Steve's missing a lot."

They were on the sled now, Jim lying flat, the rope of the sail in his hand. Hester threw herself down beside him, feeling like a little girl again clasping the side of her sled in the New England hills. Lifting her head she could see the other boats in a row to the right.

The moon shone down on them, making their sails gleam. The town, Tim's palace, the custom-house, the curved roofs of native buildings seemed cut out of black cardboard. Then they were beyond the ugly sheds of the Japanese railway and the shore lay a level band of black. For one instant, as they flew past, Hester saw silhouetted

96

against the ice a Chinese, heavy as a bear in his padded garments, standing on his rude sled, pole in hand, pushing it forward. Then she forgot everything but the thrill of the boat skimming along. She and the boat and Jim, one harmonizing whole, answering the wind. The boat leaped wildly as it struck ridged ice that the tide and wind had whipped to roughness as it froze. Jim swerved around a pile of jagged ice like great rocks, white in the moonlight. Hester, her eyes almost level with the river, saw two boats shoot out ahead of them.

"Hold tight," Jim said. "I'm going to let out full sail."

She felt the jerk of his body as the sail, caught by the savage wind, yanked at the rope in his hand. They shot forward. There was no other boat to be seen on the river.

They had won. There was the goal—the great gray tanks of the Company.

Suddenly the wind caught the sail and flung the boat this way and that. It was like riding a wild horse trying to free itself of its rider. Jim's fur coat yanked itself from her hand, the boat shot from under her and she gasped, her breath knocked out by the hard impact of the ice. She saw the boat, its sail snow-white in the moonlight, she saw two shards of steel, moving down upon her. . . . Then Jim's voice shaken with fear.

"Speak to me, Hester."

She rose, standing dazed before him. Too dazed to resist his arms, his lips pressed against hers in a kiss that seemed to draw the very life out of her. Then he let her go, talking raggedly.

"Hester, I thought I was going to kill you. I . . . kill you. . . . I saw the boat going straight for your head. Then something happened. . . . It was the wind. It shot the boat right over you. You lay between the runners. Even the wind loves you."

There was a pause. . . . Jim spoke again, naturally now.

"Well, you're safe. Suppose I'd killed Steve's wife. I'll take better care in the future." And Hester almost believed what had happened between them had been a dream.

Soberly now they made their way to the sled. Jim furled the sail until the wind had little surface against which to push. So they crept back to receive the medal of honor.

Mechanically Hester saw Jim taking into his hands the silver trophy. . . . That burning kiss. Never had Stephen kissed her like that. A realization of inadequacy in his love reached her. If only it had been Stephen, not Jim . . . She did not love Jim.

The day after the ice races, Hester needed her old world of harmonious sound to reestablish her. But there was no music anywhere. At first, when she came here, she had thought there was. "Several of the women have pianos," Jim had told her. "The wife of one of the pilots has the best one. She's English."

This Englishwoman played accompaniments. "Of an evening when we all do our bit, I play if any one sings," she had told Hester. "Some of the men have nice voices." With eagerness Hester had entered this Englishwoman's house, but she never went again. Her delicate ear still remembered that untuned piano and the long-drawn-out horror of the afternoon. The other pianos were as bad— or worse. Who was there to tune them? There was no music anywhere.

Now, sitting idly by the fire, she looked out at the blank brown surface of her compound wall. Suddenly there reached her over the wind the Chinese high wailing dirge for the dead, gusts of feeling, elemental emotions filled with the mystery of something that the old know but the young do not.

Hurriedly she caught up her cloak, ran out along the path, the cold tearing at her lungs, and threw open the gate. There was the meager white man's town fading into the plain, and strident against it the brilliant, exotic procession of the dead—the great catafalque in red trappings suspended between red poles, the beggars who carried it, their rags flapping below the green garments of ceremony. Ahead in sackcloth walked the mourners, still farther ahead, the musicians. The wind flung fragments of the dirge back to her. It set her spirit jangling.

She hurried into the house, away from the disturbing death wail. As she sat, her hands clasped tensely together, apprehensive of its repetition, she heard the tinkle of the gate bell, the shuffle of the coolie's feet along the passage, a man's quick step on the veranda.

"Hello, there. May the griffin come in?"

Hester jumped up. "Oh, I'm glad to see you." With an eagerness the situation did not seem to call for, she advanced to meet a blond young man, frankly American in voice, manner and dress.

Then the door opened as a servant brought the tea-tray, and with it came the scraping sound of a one-string violin, the high falsetto of a man's voice, singing.

Hester spoke sharply. "Shut the door." Her voice was shrill with irritation. "I won't have the cook playing. He's got to stop it this instant."

"Here, I'll take a hand," said the young man, "I've learned enough Chinese to do that." He strode along the passage to the servants' quarters. The music stopped abruptly.

Hester was half-laughing, half-crying, when he returned. "Oh, thanks," she said eagerly, "I can't *stand* their music. It does something to me. It makes me into a madwoman."

"Can't stand the *racket,* you mean," he said scornfully,

sinking into a chair. "Well, I've settled them. I guess they won't bother you again for a while. I suppose they've been imposing on you because you're a woman."

Hester looked at him with amusement, her poise restored. How full of male superiority he was. However, it was nice to have a man take a hand. But how quickly this boy had acquired the lofty tone toward the Chinese that was habitual to so many of the people of the town. Stephen never spoke like that. She wondered why. It was all an enigma to her.

Walter Cheatham got up, moving restlessly about the room. "How do you stand it here?" he asked, as he sat down beside her. "It's indescribably dreary, this town. To think I'd pictured China as something like a Maxfield Parrish drawing."

"Poor dear," murmured Hester, patting his hand lightly. "There's nothing on this afternoon that we could do, is there?"

"No. Wind too high for ice-boating. The skating rink's no good, too much dust has got in through the cracks of the shed. Ice is spoiled, flag's up at the entrance, saying so. . . . I wish the boss would let me travel. I wonder when he'll think I know enough. I know enough now if he only thought so. I understand these Chinks. Didn't I tend to 'em in the kitchen just now? I'd push them, American business drive—that's the stuff."

"Yes?" Hester knew how Stephen would hate such talk. "Let's dance." She jumped up, swept into one of the unaccountable restless moods that came upon her here. She put a record on Stephen's victrola. After a few moments of dancing, she left the young man.

"Wait a minute," she called over her shoulder, "it's too dark here."

In answer to her ring, the coolie came bringing a lamp.

"Look," cried Hester, "isn't it funny? See, he's got cotton stuffed in his ears." Her laughter rang through the room. "And look at poor little Li Tsu. He's going to howl in a minute. He never likes the victrola."

"It's an insult to you." Cheatham's face darkened as he strode toward the coolie.

"Don't, Walter." Hester laid a detaining hand on his arm. "The coolie and Li Tsu are just like me. It's not their music, so they don't like it."

It was after Cheatham had gone that the echo of her laughter came back to her and the voice in which she had spoken to the servant—the hysteria of her voice, the rasp of her laughter, thin tinkling hilarity. She no longer understood herself.

The next morning, turning again to sleep, cuddling into the soft nest of her bed, Hester heard the clatter of Stephen's hobnailed shoes on the floor of the passageway. She sprang out of bed, now for the first time realizing how lonely she had been without him. He held her in his arms. Oh, his embrace, the shelter of his protective substantial self—Stephen not played upon as she was with conflicting emotions. Through her silk nightgown the icy cold of Stephen's greatcoat penetrated to her body. She felt it chilling her flesh, and vigor and poise returned to her. Suddenly Stephen realized how thinly clad she was.

"Hester, you'll catch your death of cold. Into bed this minute."

She lay again in her warm bed, watching Stephen pull off his great boots.

"My, it's good to get home. What have you been doing, Hester?"

"Nothing much. What have you? You look so, so, so . . . I can't explain it." She remembered his look in that moment she had caught him off-guard the night of the carnival. "Well, certainly not as if you'd ever lived in New York—kind of stripped of city sleekness, kind of rubbed down like a nice clean blade."

"Hester, you're funny. You've got such an imagination. You look awfully cared-for. You're the sleek one. Like a kitten that has been stroked the right way."

"Oh, Stephen," said Hester, reproachfully.

Thus their spirits, moving a moment before with such intensity on such different planes, sought to regain each other.

XI

HESTER went about her house filled with the vitalizing presence of Stephen. But there was more than the presence of Stephen changing the atmosphere of her home. There was Kin. At night after he had brought the coffee, he stood by his master's chair ignoring her, telling Stephen the transactions of the day. This was the relationship of servant to master when the servant's personality took on dignity. Hester felt herself shut out. Only now and then did she catch a Chinese word that she understood, and the long-flowing incomprehensible conversations annoyed her.

"What does he say?"

"I can't seem to tell you." Stephen was listening intently to Kin. Although he had talked the language for several years, he still had to give careful attention in order to understand.

"Don't you know what he's saying?"

"Yes, I know in Chinese, but it's not easy to translate."

Hester felt hurt. Stephen did not want to let her into the discussion. She did not comprehend that he was thinking in Chinese, and the English words were not ready to his mind.

Kin waited patiently for his opportunity to go on.

"Why do you let him take up our evenings like this?"

she demanded one night. "It seems to me it's out of place in a servant."

Stephen looked troubled. "I can't explain. I don't know. He does it on the road and somehow I can't put it in words—but Kin thinks it's the proper thing. And I've learned when the Chinese expect a thing, that you get along better if you hold to their standard."

Hester looked at her husband curiously. Was Kin the master of Stephen, or Stephen the master of Kin? She felt uneasy. They were terribly in Kin's hands. Was he good?

"Stephen," she said, when Kin had gone out, "what do you know about Kin? Is he a good man to have around the house?"

"What do you mean!"

"Why, what's his character like?"

"How do I know," her husband replied.

"He's been with you all these years!"

"Well, but how should I know about his personal life? How could I?" he replied helplessly. Reading character in a Chinese face was still impossible for him.

To Hester, Kin's personality seemed to pervade the house. Silently, perfectly he served her when Stephen was at home; silently, imperfectly when Stephen was at the office; and penny by penny, in amounts so small that it would be undignified for her to argue with him, he increased the household expenses.

To-day, a week after Stephen's return, at the third ring of her bell, Kin appeared before her to take accounts. He was without his long gown of respect. In panic at reprimanding this man twice her age and filled with his own superiority, she thought at first to ignore the matter. But Stephen had said Kin must never appear before her like that. After she had sent him for the gown, she sat nervously drumming on the desk, looking out at the frozen garden, watching the dry stalks of last season's sunflowers blowing disconsolately in the wind. When Kin returned, she must challenge every item of expense— Stephen had said the bills must come down: His salary would not stand it.

Again Kin stood before her, now clad in correct long blue gown, looking very neat with his queue wound around his head. Hester felt somehow, in the presence of this middle-aged servant, ridiculous in her youth.

"We could not eat two dozen bananas in three days." Those precious bananas that only now and then appeared in the compradore's store—the few that were not frozen in transit.

Kin waited. No word passed his lips. At last, Hester entered in the book the two dozen bananas. Kin passed on to the next item. Coffee, a pound in two days. Stephen drank a great deal, she knew, but surely not that much.

"I shall not pay it."

Silent, without change of expression, Kin waited. Hester nervously entered the amount, went on to the next and the next item until the accounts were finished. Kin closed his book.

"Coal." He spoke but the one word, disdaining to explain why twice as much coal had been used since his return as before.

Hester felt angrier than she had ever been in her life. How dared he demand coal so soon? She jumped up, knocking over a vase on the desk, caring not at all, and flew down the passageway to the kitchen. Kin righted the vase, then quietly followed. In the kitchen sat the cook, idle, the fire out.

"Why are you not getting the master's tiffin?" demanded Hester in a shrill voice.

The cook motioned toward the empty coal-box. Tears struggled in Hester's throat. She felt a burst of fireworks in her brain as red-hot primitive anger flamed within her. She heard herself shouting, glad that she was shouting, as she pounded on the table until the dishes rattled.

Kin stood in the door, the cook sat at the table. Neither moved, neither gave the slightest indication that they heard her outburst.

Suddenly, Hester's anger collapsed in humiliation. She threw down the coal money and fled to her room. Distraught, she moved about, lifting Stephen's personal belongings, his brushes, his mirror, with some vague feeling that they might impart to her something which would command the respect of the servants, respect showed to the master, but never to her. Whence had come such devastating anger? She longed to forget the undignified scene.

All at once she felt herself tired. Her muscles ached as if she had been in physical combat. She lay face down on her bed, dropping off to sleep, only to be roused again by her anger—futile anger, impotent before some not-understood strength. She burst into tears. Thus Stephen found her on his return at noon.

"You mustn't let Kin win over you like this. I'll talk to him. My salary won't stand it," he told her, sitting beside her on the bed.

He summoned Kin to the living-room, sitting where Hester had sat that morning to talk to him. The servant's face was stony.

"Prior-born," he spoke in the measured phrases of his own language, "it is necessary to leave the honorable one. The lady's custom is not good. She pounds upon the table."

"But *I* pound on the table when you are wrong," Stephen exclaimed in astonishment, "and you have never threatened to leave me!"

"It is different," replied Kin.

Patiently Stephen went over each detail of Kin's duty toward his head lady, of the head lady's duty toward

Kin, and at last when peace was established between them, he went to Hester.

"It is all right now," he told her. "There were certain forms which you broke this morning and Kin was going to leave, but I've explained to him that you did not know them."

Hester sat up, staring at him. "So you took Kin's part? After telling me not to let him get the best of me, you let him get the best of you?"

"Well, not exactly. You don't understand, Hester."

"Evidently I don't."

They had their first quarrel. And over Kin.

Afterward, Hester was quiet and Stephen uneasy. She was different from the serene girl he thought he had married—this magnifying of Kin's importance, for instance.

They gave their first dinner-party that evening. Looking at Stephen at the other end of the dining-table, Hester found her soreness of heart disappearing: no longer was she able to recapture her grievance. As she talked to the manager of the English steamship company sitting on her right, she caught fragments of conversation between an elderly Britisher on her left and the Frenchwoman sitting next him.

"Talbott, you know Talbott?" the Britisher was saying. "Too bad he's turned out so badly. His Company is sending him home."

"*Mon Dieu!*" exclaimed the Frenchwoman. "Such a nice young man. I knew him when he first came out. A little, what shall I say . . . ? But so gay, so childlike."

"Too much for him," the man answered her, "his love of women." He looked at the Frenchwoman with an expression of satisfaction, as if he had made a good thrust. "This latest escapade of his was too much even for his Company. Couldn't ignore it."

Suddenly Hester realized how abnormal was the

life of these men forced into years of celibacy by their organizations. And for the first time she was really curious about Stephen's past in this town. He did not seem to be specially interested in women. Now she was startled into observation of him. Women must have loved him. And that girl who had hurt him so. He never spoke of her. Had he forgotten her? Was he beginning to love her, Hester, as she loved him? Her heart see-sawed back and forth—he did, he didn't. As the women left the dining-room she managed for one instant to squeeze his hand.

When the guests had gone, eagerly she made the first advances. "Stephen, dear," she said, swallowing hard for she was proud, "you were right about Kin." And then, saying at random the first thing that came into her head, "Why don't we have Kin wear his queue around his head all the time, especially when he serves? It seems so much neater."

Stephen looked at her curiously. "Just when has Kin worn it so in your presence?"

"Why, this morning when he came in after I sent him out for his long gown."

"Why didn't you tell me this before, Hester? Oh, well," he added hastily, "it doesn't matter. But don't ever let him do it—it's bad custom."

He wasn't going to stir Hester up again by explaining that the queue was only wound about the head when it was necessary to get it out of the way. It was as disrespectful for Kin to come before Hester thus as it would have been for one of her guests to have come to her dinner-party with his coat off. Stephen felt a strong desire to kick Kin. The man had won, got away with an insult to his wife—and he'd let him do it. Idiot! He stood in absent-minded silence, wondering if he would ever learn to understand this race.

Wistfully, Hester watched him, feeling herself shut

107

out by his preoccupation. This husband of hers—that kiss of Jim's. She missed something in Stephen's love. From some heretofore unknown depth of loneliness, she cried, "Stephen, love me."

"In the eyes of the Chinese." Now that Stephen was home, it seemed to Hester that they lived always in the eyes of the Chinese.

Muffled in fur coats, they hurried along the path. The hobnails on Stephen's shoes resounded against the frozen earth as if one metal was being struck against another. Hester wished they had not had to come. Really it was too cold. But it was the boss's fiftieth birthday. Stephen had explained to her that they must not fail to show respect to him to-day; in the eyes of the Chinese it would be discourteous if they did not. The eyes of the Chinese.

They were walking straight into the wind now. Hester tried to speak but could only gasp as the ice-cold air cut into her lungs. Even though Stephen stepped ahead to shield her from the wind's mighty drive, she had to pause in the sheltered garden to get her breath before going in to meet the boss.

Stephen said "sir" when he addressed the boss. She divined it was not because of deference for him as a power in the Company, but because he cared for him, and wanted to show him respect. So did Jim, who had just entered. Hester, an onlooker in their man's world, understood better now the boss's utter contentment in this town; he was respected, loved. She watched with sensitive sympathy his gruff pleasure in the friendship of the two younger men.

As the three stood talking, the door was flung wide open by the house-boy, and into the room filed such a company as Hester had never seen.

"Who are they?" she whispered to Stephen.

"They're the agents. Jiminy, they're certainly doing the old boss honor!" Stephen whispered back. "They're all here—from all over Manchuria. You don't know what that means. Even Liu from up the Sungari. He's had to travel days in a cart, and he hates travel. All Chinese hate travel the way a cat hates water. I wouldn't believe they were here, if I didn't see them with my own eyes."

Hester was nudging his elbow. He saw mirth beginning to break over her.

"Don't laugh," he whispered almost fiercely. Suppose Hester should laugh and make these agents lose face!

But surely the compradore was a sight to betray any one into mirth. Stephen had not noticed him until now. He was clad in satin, as were his fellow-countrymen, not the conventional gown reaching to his heels, but satin trousers cut like the white man's, cuff and all, a purple satin swallow-tail coat and, encircling his thin neck, a starched white collar with wide bat-wings of pink.

"Progress!" whispered Jim with a cynically raised eyebrow.

Led by the odd figure of the compradore the agents advanced. Three times they saluted the boss, shaking their own hands, murmuring *"Kon shi, kon shi."* In silence receding. Alone, the compradore came forward, presenting the boss with two scrolls. Then with dignity so great that it was unimperiled by his strange garb, once more he stepped forth bearing something very heavy, wrapped in red paper. With his two hands he presented it to the boss who, embarrassed, deposited the parcel on the table behind him.

Jim tore off the wrappings. The last red paper fell away. A great incense burner, and of pure gold! No one could mistake that soft gleam. These old-time Chinese knew nothing of alloys.

109

Hester felt ashamed of her mirth. She sensed something big in the moment: the wind and dust whirling by the windows, the purple-clad throng making genuflections before the shy, insignificant-looking man of her own race. But Stephen knew that only to a person very great among them would the merchants make such a gift, one whose power they had felt, one whose business acumen they greatly respected, one who had outwitted them in many a closely contested battle.

The house-boy, with an air of deference matching the total respect accruing to the boss on this occasion, entered with glasses of sherry. Austerely, the agents sipped the unaccustomed foreign wine and then, as solemnly as they had entered, folding their hands in their sleeves, they filed out. Jim, Stephen and Hester broke into excited exclamation, but the boss himself showed only discomfiture.

"What will a simple old fellow like me do with a gold incense burner? I'll have to put it in the vault at the bank. My payment to the king of the robbers wouldn't protect me now."

"He was pleased, wasn't he?" said Hester, as she and Stephen walked home arm in arm, the wind at their backs.

"Yes, he couldn't help but be. It places him very high in their regard. Only a few white men ever attain it."

They fell silent, Stephen oppressed a little with the thought of those agents, in the mass a formidable foe, his old uncertainty returning and the sense of his youth—how had he ever had the effrontery to accuse them of misdeeds?

Was this the China Stephen lived in? Hester was thinking. How different it was from hers! Bit by bit the incisive ancient pattern was being pressed into her, making her spirit quiver. Let her hide herself in this stout little town, its gaiety, its frivolity.

110

XII

I⊤ was a spring morning. As Hester and Stephen walked toward the office soft air touched their faces. When they reached the bund, out on the river in the direct line of their vision, a rusty old tramper had just dropped anchor.

"Look," said Stephen, "the first steamer! Winter is really over. The river is open!"

Hester stood transfixed, watching the human mass packed on the desks of the tramper, seething up and down, spilling over the sides of the ship. Scrambling like rats, men dropped into the flat-bottom scows beneath. The scows, soon packed as the decks of the steamer had been packed, pushed off, landed their human freight on the pontoons, on the ice-floes jammed against the bunding wall, and hurried back for other loads. Soon Hester saw swarming up the ramps that led to the bund a multitude of abject creatures—poverty-stricken, dirty past all belief, the marks of disease upon them.

"Where did they come from? What does it mean?" Hester plied Stephen with questions.

"A lot of peasants from China come to plant the crops."

"From China? Is this China?"

"Hurry home, where it's clean," said Stephen, kissing her. Why should Hester know that out of the oldest province of China, where the race had been conceived thousands of years before, out of the valley of the river called "China's Sorrow," this surfeit of humanity came each spring to this rich outer country to work in the fertile fields, returning in the autumn to their clans to live meagerly on the hoarded pittance until the next spring? Why should Hester know anything about it?

But when Stephen had left her, Hester lingered within the shadow of the two walls that bounded the lane lead-

111

ing to the bund. These women with their hoof-like feet, hobbling forward, leaning on their staffs, babes lying within their blue top-garments, next to their sagging breasts! What was it that was written in their faces? Men, and women and children—such children! What was it stalking behind their eyes? As she walked slowly home, something half comprehended moved like a shadow before her, falling over her house, her comfort, her security. Something that the spirit denied.

Stephen, too, was held by the sight. During the morning he went often to the window of his office to stare at China's glut of humanity moving toward the great stretches of fertile plain. Like swarms of locusts they seemed, devouring Manchuria's plenty. How many thousands, millions, of such people as these were there hidden behind the Great Wall of China?

He tried to imagine what life must be like for any of the Chinese—the life of men like Kin, well paid, compared to most. His wages, twelve Mexican, six American dollars a month. Twenty cents a day for Kin and his family to live on. He thought of the look in Kin's eyes as he maneuvered for every extra *cash* of squeeze in the day's expenditures. A little he began to comprehend.

And yet here was Kin, when he had given him his choice of obeying Hester or of leaving, choosing to give up his security. What was it in the relationship with Hester that made Kin refuse to obey her? Stephen gave it up. Well, Kin had had to go. He wished Hester could have managed him. He was going to miss him. Kin was like a part of himself, his China self.

As the morning wore on, Stephen forgot about Kin, even about that throng, although another ship had come in and the dense mass of humanity pressed close up to the low windows, darkening the room.

There was an undertow in the office that pulled at his thoughts. All through the winter, each time he came

112

back, he had felt a growing excitement; talk of the foreign director who was traveling over China and would be here some time soon; talk of the pioneer days of the Company being over. A new note. Change of spirit. Expansion. The next step forward. Many new classmen had been sent out. Two had arrived at the office that morning. From what they said Stephen gained a curiously vivid impression of the Company, self-perpetuating, ever renewing itself with young men eager for success, crowding men like himself forward, men like himself crowding upon men like Jim, the boss. What was going to happen if there was to be room at the top? Wasn't the class in New York always told there *was* room at the top?

As he and Jim walked toward the club at noon, his friend said, "Likely to be fireworks around here when the director comes."

"What's his plan, anyway?" asked Stephen.

"Expand the organization. Open substations with white men in charge. It's the highly developed type of organization which they use in America. But the boss contends it's only a waste of money—and it isolates the men. Harder on them than it needs to be. He can manage with a simpler organization, he claims."

"So," was Stephen's laconic response. "Do you think the boss is right?" he asked after a short silence.

"Sure," answered Jim. "He understands the Chinese merchant and the director from New York does not."

"Will the boss get himself in wrong?"

"Probably. The director won't like difference of opinion, however obediently the boss may execute his orders."

"Where are you going to stand, Jim?"

"With the boss, of course, if I'm asked. But I'm only the number two, you know. I probably won't be asked."

"Only the number two," said Stephen. "It sounds near the top to me."

*　　*　　*　　*　　*

When her front door shut out the shadow of the trek, Hester moved about her house in a mood of fierce pleasure. Hers, she felt, for the first time. Free, finally, of something Kin had brought to it. She knew Stephen hadn't wanted him to go, but she didn't care. Something that was rightly hers had been given back to her.

Never mind the confusion. She did not gloss over the fact that there *was* confusion, for Kin had taken the other servants with him when he went. Until now Hester hadn't realized how man-made her household, or how perfect had been the mechanism that Kin had created. Stephen had brought a coolie home with him from the office the evening before, but he was as clumsy as a polar bear. The breakfast had been a failure.

By noon, from that inexhaustible supply of China's millions, she had selected a cook. He said that he would get a house-boy for her. She felt proud of her initiative. But after a tiffin of sodden bread and a custard made from bad eggs, and the cook's disappearance immediately afterward with the advance money for marketing, Hester had to acknowledge that she could not read Chinese character, and so could not choose her servants. Still there remained to her a sweet sense of activity. Now all her creative energies were awakening. In the midst of a thousand things to do, suddenly she wanted to play her violin. But when she took it from its case a string had snapped. As she hunted through her things for another, she realized that for a long time she had not played. She had been living without music and had not missed it!

A note came from Stephen. Could she manage to entertain the director and his wife? They were coming in late that afternoon. The boss had asked if Hester would look after them as his wife was away. Stephen didn't like to say "no." He hadn't told the boss of Kin's leaving, and it would seem like an excuse to tell him now. Hester looked at the clock. Four hours before the train was due. They'd

114

have to have Stephen's and her room. And there was dinner to get for five of them, including the boss. Well, she had the coolie from the office, and he had a friend who would cook dinner. She could get the boss's boy to serve to-night. She mustn't let Stephen down.

At five o'clock the house was clean and fresh as soap and water could make it. But Hester's brows drew together in concern when she thought of the dinner. The cook did not promise too well. She, herself, had made the mayonnaise for the salad. She was a little fearful that it had curdled. It was all right so long as she stirred it, but when she left it——— Still, she had charged the cook to beat it the very last minute.

She was ready now to join the others at the office. They were all going to the station to meet the director's train. The floors—those painted gray floors—how had Kin kept them shining? If only Kin had not taken the old coolie with him. Well, she had charged the office coolie to wipe his cloth-soled shoes before he entered the house, placing a mat for such use in the passageway. She stood in the front door and looked back. The coolie had forgotten! There, in dust on the floor, was the pattern of his huge cloth-soled shoe. Hester looked around, and seeing no one, wiped the mark away with her handkerchief, then closed the front door.

The cold spring wind blew through the town. She drew the collar of her fur coat closer round her, as her ricksha-man swung into the line of rickshas before the office. How tired she was, and how puffy and heavy her hands felt inside her white gloves! But she was happy. The memory of the house, all hers now, enfolded her like a blessing. And the road, this long brown road to the station, ruts, dust, ruts, mud. In heat and cold for six months she had traveled this long brown road. Anticipation, fulfillment—yes, and renunciation—all came to her over this road. So often going to meet Stephen when he returned, so often going

115

home alone after seeing him off. The ricksha jarred and shook, wrenching her slight shoulders as it slid in and out of the ruts. . . . Not going to meet Stephen to-day. He was by her side.

Darkness had settled over the station, the wind going with the daylight. At last the toot of the engine, the train grinding to a stop, the boss going forward with that characteristic shake of his shoulders, the coolies' lanterns thrust forward and up. For a moment Hester envisioned New York, city of the successful, as she glimpsed a perfectly attired masculine figure, absorbed in helping a woman alight from the train. And such a woman! Hester, at Stephen's side, gave a gasp, almost a sob.

"I'm a frump beside her."

"What do you care? You're prettier than she is," Stephen stoutly affirmed in a whisper. He had his own thoughts. With the sight of the director he was whisked back to that spring morning four years ago, the classroom, the map of the world with its twenty crosses, the director —this very man—coming in after the instructor had given out the appointments, speaking to them of hard work, of loyalty. . . . Suddenly, the vision of Lucy. Stephen straightened his shoulders. Well, he'd kept faith with the Company. Then through his mind shot the thought, "Does he know I had anything to do with the little lamps?" And another, "If he does, I'll never find it out." Out of what experience was that conviction born?

The moment of appraisal before the two groups mingled was over. Toward Stephen and Hester Jim led a short stocky man with a large paunch, over which a watch chain gleamed. "He looks surly, like a bully," thought Hester.

"Mr. Cobb, this is Stephen Chase and his wife."

The Shanghai manager whom they all feared! Hester suddenly realized she was a bride, not yet approved.

116

"So you're Chase and you're married?" he was saying to Stephen.

"Yes, sir," answered Stephen, looking him straight in the eye. He could look him straight in the eye—Hester had never slowed him up.

"I suppose it's congratulations."

"Yes, sir," said Stephen again.

"Well, you got 'em!" pronounced the Shanghai manager and turned on his heel, leaving them oddly disconcerted.

Then Director Swaley pushed past Cobb's heavy figure, ignoring the boss and Jim, and came toward them, shaking Stephen's hand, giving Hester's gloved one a pat.

"It's to you younger men we have to take off our hats. How many days up-country this last winter? I saw your record in Shanghai." A warm glow passed through Stephen. So his work was appreciated after all. With great suavity the director introduced the finished lady to Hester. Then in businesslike fashion he turned his attention to the baggage. "Now, we won't bother you with all our luggage," he began. "Chase, will you get my wife's jewel-box and hand-bag?"

"Right, sir."

Hester saw Stephen moving toward the heap of baggage dimly discernible in the station light shining across the platform. How would Stephen know *which* in all that pile to bring? In spite of the director's large kindness, she felt he would not brook the smallest mistake.

"Is this right, sir?" Stephen had returned.

"Fine. Put it in my wife's ricksha."

As Stephen helped Hester into hers, she whispered excitedly, "How'd you know?"

"Sh, they'll hear you. Asked his valet, of course. You didn't think they'd leave jewels around loose, did you, silly? Where's your rug?"

It was Hester's turn to say "Sh." "The director took it for his wife. Said one wasn't enough for her. He didn't notice he was taking mine. But did you say a valet? Where shall we put him?" Hester was utterly demoralized now. "Oh, Stephen, why did we let Kin go?"

Again the brown road, the line of rickshas, longer now, the lanterns hanging from the shafts, the pullers' legs twinkling in the light. Just ahead of Hester, the director's wife nestled cozily in her fur coat and two rugs. Hester drew her feet under her for warmth, vainly trying to fasten her mind on her duties as hostess. But all she could think of was the coolie's large dusty footprint and the director's buttoned, highly polished shoes, gleaming in the lantern light as he stepped off the train. No more of him, just those perfectly polished shoes.

The alley, the path, the rickshas zigzagging their slow approach, and then the house-door flung wide and a glare of light almost blinding them.

On tables, along both sides of the hall, were rows of the Company's little lamps. And there, in a purple silk gown and short, sleeveless, filigreed black silk top-garment, stood Kin. Between anger and relief, Hester entered her house. Stephen was angry, too, but not over Kin's return. Over his officiousness, as he termed it. Confound Kin! He was sure it was Kin who had put the lamps there. Would the director think he was trying to call attention to them?

After dinner, when the boss and the manager from Shanghai had gone, the four sat for a time with their chairs drawn close around the open fire, a nicely molded structure beginning to turn to ash.

"How unusual to have such service here in the wilderness," said the director's wife. "Your boy would grace a diplomat's table. What culture these people have! How much more poise that boy of yours has than we have, for instance. I simply *adore* their culture. No wonder sometimes they are a little rude to us."

"Tut, tut," said the director. "What do you know about this culture, except for the trinkets you're collecting?"

Stephen was fidgeting. He always hated conversation like this. What right has the director's wife to talk so glibly? What does she know, he thought, about the stress and strain of our slow understanding? He got up hastily, and passed the cigars to the director.

Hester, seeing Stephen's look of irritation, knowing that because of his growing lack of social awareness, he was apt to break out and show scorn of Mrs. Swaley's opinions, hurriedly said the first thing that came into her head. "Do take one, Stephen got them especially for you."

The director laughed, a mellow warm laugh. How naïve, how unworldly was this couple. Telling him the cigars were especially for him. Or was there more to it? Those two rows of the Company's lamps down the hall. Was the young fellow trying to remind him of his part in those lamps? More designing, perhaps, than he thought. Aloud he said:

"My dear young woman. Of course I'll take one of your Stephen's cigars. He's a fine fellow. I'm going to give him a chance to show what he's made of. Mustn't let us old fellows have all the plums." Inwardly, he congratulated himself on his penetration.

He'd been right about Chase—that idealism of his had certainly proved usable. Thought it would, in a place like Manchuria where a man has to check up on himself. Chase had traveled almost incessantly and without complaint. He thought with amusement of the discussion he and the instructor of the class had had back in New York before the appointments were made, the instructor arguing that Chase's idealism might make him finicky in business; he himself arguing that it was valuable in opening up a new territory like Manchuria. The instructor had said idealism would grow on a man; he had answered

119

that the time to deal with that was when it proved to be annoying. The corporation didn't necessarily take a man on for life, he had finally said, and ended the argument. Chase had proved even more valuable than he had expected. That idea of little lamps had brought the Company a lot of money.

Well, it took all kinds of men to do the work of Big Business. That hard-boiled Kendall the instructor had liked so much was doing his stuff too. Great fellow, Kendall, for a special type of work. That shut look of his very usable when it came to a certain kind of negotiation with rival business houses. Director Swaley was well pleased with himself, as he smoked his cigar.

It was in excited hope that Hester and Stephen went to bed, lying very close together on Stephen's traveling cot placed before the living-room fire.

"Going to give you a chance," was what Mr. Swaley had said. "What do you suppose it will be, Stephen, dear?"

"Have to wait and see, I guess," Stephen answered, but he was inwardly wondering.

Now bewilderment absorbed their thoughts. When they had rung for Kin to lock up, they found he had gone as mysteriously as he had come, and the new cook had gone, also. How should they manage in the morning? What were they to do? They slept fitfully—the bath water, the breakfast for the Swaleys, filling their dreams. Suppose the office coolie should fail to start the fire?

At four, the house dark and cold, Stephen slipped out of bed to see if the water was being heated. No, the coolie had overslept, and so Stephen lifted to the top of the stove the heavy pails made of old oil tins and filled with water for the director's bath. At six, Hester, heavy-eyed but valiant, put the cereal on to boil. There was no Kin, no cook.

"Stephen, what shall we do when it's time to serve

120

breakfast? How shall we explain? Oh, why did I send Kin away?"

"I'll never take him back! The cheek of him acting like this!" Stephen was indignantly setting the table.

"I hear them coming down the stairs," whispered Hester excitedly. They stood in the dining-room, held by a kind of paralysis. And then, Kin walked gravely in through the door at the back of the hall, and they heard him say to the Swaleys, "Breakfast ready."

The director's party left at noon; the valet, the private secretary, the Shanghai manager, Director Swaley and his wife. A shortened line of rickshas returned from the station. Elation and trouble sat on Stephen's brow.

"Hester," he began, as soon as they were alone, "I've got my chance."

"Not really!" cried Hester.

"Yes, but I'm afraid it's going to be hard on you. Shall you mind? I'm to open one of the new sub-stations. We shan't be in a white man's town, as we are here. But if I make good, the director says———"

"*If* you make good! What does making good mean? I thought you'd done it already."

"Well, he made no definite statements, but he implied I'd be in the run for big things."

"Why did you say, would I mind? I'm as glad as you are that you've got your chance." For a moment Stephen held her close, then he hurried away to the office.

It was only after he had gone that there came back to her that first impression of the Company. She had seen so many of the tireless hands, but the face, the face was still hidden.

Late that afternoon, the boss called Stephen into his office.

"It's all against my recommendation," he burst out. "I advised them to send you to Harbin. Pretty big sub-

121

station, but you're up to it. I didn't tell them so, but there'd be music in Harbin for that wife of yours. Russians always have music. They're sending your friend, Kendall, that we're always hearing about, to Harbin instead. This place you're going to . . . kind of lonesome for your wife, but anyway she'll have you at home. Guess she's resented the travel a little lately. Well, you'd better get off as soon as you can."

And Stephen, knowing he and Hester would need Kin in a new town, was glad Hester had said nothing about dismissing him.

XIII

THEY were going north to their new station. Hour after hour as the plain stamped its extent on Hester's mind, her thoughts ran back, trying to knit themselves into the local interests of the town they had just left, but Stephen's mind ran ahead of him, trying to drag Hester's with it.

"I've got something of a problem on my hands," he told her. "The agent in this territory isn't going to like it to have a white man over him, and that's what it amounts to. I've got to handle it so he won't lose face. It's delicate business."

"But you like it, don't you?" demanded Hester, patting him on the shoulder.

"Yes," said Stephen. "Something a little my own, and it's nice to think I'll be at home."

"I wonder what our house will be like."

"You mustn't expect much," he answered hastily. "It was originally built for the construction man's use while he was putting up the tanks."

"I'm not expecting much. I'm only wondering. I'm prepared for anything." Hester spoke proudly, feeling herself equal to any test.

122

"The most important thing I have to do is to increase the percentage of our business," Stephen went on. "There's a free lance there, a man named Blodgett, who buys his oil from the British Company, selling it as he can. He's taken a great deal of business away from the Company. He's half British, half Chinese, and he understands the tactics of both. I'll have to work hard to win over him."

So they came to the city. As their train, the last link with their own people, moved on without them, they felt themselves drawn together in a new companionship.

"Here comes Kin," said Stephen. "By heck, he's got a big family. I didn't know it. He'd always kept it dark. He asked permission to bring his son, but he said nothing of the others. They're girls—of course, he doesn't count them."

He felt again that Kin had put something over on him, but there was nothing to do about it. They could not afford to lose him. Anyway, nothing seemed an obstacle just now.

"Get in," he cried gaily, leading Hester to the cleanest of the droshkies, and motioning Kin into another.

"Where did it come from?" exclaimed Hester, looking in wonder at the ghost of a grand turnout before her, the curved and imposing arch over the horse's head all that was left of the old grandeur, padding protruding from the cushions, and from the quilted garments of the driver.

"It's a relic of Russian days, like Tim," explained Stephen.

"Hail, the conqueror!" Hester murmured, seating herself on the sloping seat.

"We're off!" cried Stephen, and the decrepit equipage, by a series of starts and stops, advanced through the Japanese city. "The Chinese city is back farther, you can't see it from here," he explained with a wave of his hand,

123

taking pleasure in showing his wife things new to her, familiar to him.

"These look like Chinese buildings," said Hester.

"Yes, they're the bean godowns. They're here in the Japanese city next the railroad. See the siding running along behind? The beans have all been shipped for this year, but in the winter you should see the place—the matting bean towers and the carts, the dust rising in clouds. You'd like to hear them counting the measures of beans. This is the way it sounds, *Ih wan, ih wan ling ling ehr.*"

"Why, it's like music."

"Listen to the bean mills—hear them?"

Hester could hear the pound, pound as the hand presses came down, squeezing the oil from the beans. "It would make a wonderful symphony," she said. Her eyes shone.

Soon they were out on the plain. "Is our house very far away?" she asked. She had thought, until now, that the house was in the city.

"Two miles or more. I supposed you knew that, when I told you it was in the compound with the tanks. Tanks are always off away from the cities."

Hester looked at the brown earth, unrelieved as yet with the spring shimmer of young green *kaoliang* and beans. The vast treeless surface lay unbroken, except where the squat city behind them hugged the earth. At last, she could see two round oil tanks, half concealed behind a brown mud wall. Like the city, they were dwarfed by the immensity of the plain. But when the droshky drew up at the corrugated iron gate, tanks and wall grew large, dwarfing everything near them.

At Kin's call a caretaker opened to them, thrusting into Stephen's hands bills of lading that brought vividly to his mind the immediacy of his duties. The oil had arrived to fill the new tanks. Even now cars were being shunted on to the siding at the back of the compound, the caretaker told him.

"Hester, I'll go with you around the house, then I've got to get busy. They're waiting now to pump."

"What a funny house!" said Hester. "It's like a canary's cage with its four-sided roof, and its verandas. It's just about as big, too."

Together they entered the house, passing through the four rooms, each of the same size, each a quarter of the tiny dwelling.

"What's this pillar in the center?"

"The Russian stove. It will heat the whole house," said Stephen. "See the door here at the bottom?"

"I wish we had a fireplace," Hester spoke a little wistfully.

"Fireplaces wouldn't do. It's very cold here."

"The furniture is as decrepit as that carriage we rode in," Hester called from the living-room. "Look, the leg of this chair is tied up with string."

"I suppose they sent up a lot of stuff that had been discarded from some main station," Stephen explained.

"Oh, it's all right," she answered hastily, "I can use it. It will be fun fixing it up."

"You're fine, Hester. I'm sure you'll make it cozy. And, you know, I think we could manufacture some kind of fireplace on that wall across from the stove."

He was grateful for her pluck. The house was pretty awful.

"Now I'll go see about the oil." He kissed her.

"I'll come, too," said Hester. "Look, here's a covered passageway." They went together along it.

"Evidently it's the office. See, here's where the construction man worked. Now, I'll have to go." Stephen kissed her again.

Hester walked slowly back through the rooms, planning what she would do. "The paint is chipped from the beds; they'll have to be painted. Chairs recovered. How odd," she thought, "when it's finished, there'll be no one

125

ever coming to see it. Just ourselves. How strange it seems!"

She could hear Stephen directing the men, and she went to the side of the house that faced the tanks. The Chinese coolies had the pipe lines down and had begun to pump the oil.

"Anyway, Stephen will be here. It's going to be nice," she said to herself.

It was six months since Hester and Stephen had alighted from the droshky and crossed the threshold of this house; the threshold of opportunity it had seemed to Hester then, eager to prove herself equal to the test the corporation was putting her to. She had spent the first weeks settling the house, working with eager haste, outraging Kin, who saw all haste as defect. And then for a time she had enjoyed her handiwork. A secret triumph possessed her. She was learning how to subordinate the Company stamp to the stamp of the individual. She thought this, as she walked through her four rooms— living-room, dining-room, their room, guest-room, never occupied—around the Russian stove, like a pillar, set in the middle of the house.

Often, with her violin under her chin, she stood between fireplace and Russian stove, playing the fire-music motif from *The Valkyrie*. She and fire-music, she and fire-pillar in league against the conformity of chairs, tables, bookcases done in the Company pattern, against the tanks leaning over her, shadowing her, shadowing Stephen, as they shadowed her house.

But one day, suddenly, all this ceased to interest her. Even the satisfaction she had had at first in her courage to accept such a life lost its zest. Gradually, monotony reached out its gray hand, stealthily stealing away her high spirits. As day followed day, one exactly like another, indifference settled over her. Nothing seemed worth doing.

For six months, for twenty-six weeks, for one hundred and eighty-two days, she had watched the sun march across the metallic sky; in the morning throwing the shadow of the tanks to the right over the compound wall; in the afternoon throwing it to the left over her house.

Not to be escaped for one moment, the thought of these tanks. Stephen was the guardian of their precious, inflammable fluid. For six months—twenty-six weeks— they had never been away from the compound for more than a few hours. Even then, Stephen worried. If business took him away for a longer period he left Hester at home to watch, so great was his fear of fire. And ever since that day they had returned to find the number one Chinese knocking out his pipe on a half-filled barrel of oil, Stephen had made excuses to leave her at home, even on his short trips into the city.

All day a watchman stood at the gate, challenging each person who entered. All night a watchman paced the compound, striking his hollow bamboo gong as he went his rounds. For six months, for twenty-six weeks, each night she had gone to sleep to that hollow tattoo and waked if it ceased, feeling Stephen stealthily slipping out of bed to see if the watchman slept at his post.

For six months, for twenty-six weeks, she had listened to the wind blow without shift of direction, with no place in the clumsily built house to escape from its jar of the shutters, its whine in the screens of the veranda, its suck through the door latches. One hundred and eighty-two days, when she had felt something urging her to go and bury her head in the brown earth outside the brown house. Surely, there was no wind far down in the earth.

One hundred and eighty-two days when, after tea, she and Stephen had played solitaire, she on one side of the

127

table, he on the other. Snap, her card down; snap, his card down. Snap, the King here. Shuffle. Snap, the Jack there.

To-day, suddenly she hurled her cards into the dull coals of the grate. "I'm through," she exclaimed. "It makes me sick even to think of solitaire. As long as I live I'll never play it again." She hated herself for making a scene, for being melodramatic, but she hated Stephen more for paying no heed to what she was doing. His silence condemned her in a way she could not bear, driving her to frenzy. She'd make him notice her! She dropped on her knees by the fire, reaching into the live coals for her cards.

"Are you crazy!" Stephen shouted at her, jumping up from the table, snatching her arm back. Then in a moment the tension of weeks had broken and she was crying, her head on his shoulder.

"Oh, Stephen, Stephen, I want to go home." Stephen's heart almost stood still. This was the sickness of nostalgia. It attacked people in dreadful ways out here. In this strange beautiful north with its high winds and its unbroken sunshine, homesickness had been known to drive people mad, especially women who were pregnant, though that was not the matter with Hester, surely. But suppose she broke under the strain.

Such disaster he had never contemplated, absorbed as he had been in his work. This was only a sub-station, to be sure, but it had many difficult problems to hold his attention. Still, he reproached himself, he should have taken better care of Hester . . . but she was always so valiant, so full of high courage, so gay. He thought that she had been wholly content because of the increasing depth of their companionship—and all the time she had been suffering like this!

As he knelt beside her, trying to soothe her, he felt completely baffled by the privacy of her spirit. Was this the

128

real Hester who was pouring her words out so incoherently, not that other buoyant person with whom he thought he had been living all these days?

"It's so bright here all day, always the same. And that shadow of the tanks, falling over the house. And the nights are so dark. It was never dark at home. There was a street-lamp on the corner of the street where our house stood . . . even in the night . . . squares of light on the walls."

"I know, sweet, the first two years I was out here the darkness of the nights got me too," Stephen broke in on her recital.

She had pulled away from him, her hands clasped, dropped between her knees, her eyes peering out as if trying to pierce the distance. She went on in a monotonous voice.

"There were people walking along the streets, happy people. Laughter. And the noises of the town all night long, dying a little, then beginning again. Stephen! I can't bear the day, and I am afraid to have night come, it is so dark."

But she couldn't tell him of the void of silence around her. She was secretive about that.

"Look at me, Hester," Stephen tried to speak lightly. "This isn't anything but homesickness. Everybody has it some time. I did. When I was traveling once . . ." He stopped. He was secretive, too, about that suffering the winter before she came, hiding it now even from himself. "But you'll get over it. After a time you won't want to go home. You'll prefer living out here."

"Get over wanting to go home!"

He saw that he had said the wrong thing. "Dear, is Kin bothering you?" He'd hit on the subject at random, and he was surprised at the response from Hester.

"I can't manage him," she explained. "The minute you are in your office, he defies me in little ways. At first I didn't know what they meant, but I'm learning. Kin makes me feel as if I'm not here."

"What do you mean?"

"I can't express it. As if . . . well, as if I'm really not here . . . as if my spirit were dead in me."

Stephen wondered. The Chinese did not believe that women had souls. Was it possible that Kin, with such a belief, could annihilate that delicate, intricate personality that was Hester?

"I'll send him away if he bothers you."

"But I want to go home."

Stephen felt a knell sounding in this return of Hester to her first cry. How could he distract her?

"Where's your violin?"

"No, no. Not that!"

If only they could get away for a while! He thought wildly of catching the night train for Harbin. But he could not leave the tanks—not without permission. He might wire the boss asking leave for a day or two. He remembered that first trip after his marriage, when he had broken through his orders and wired the boss he was returning. How fearful he had been that the boss might report him for insubordination, and how grateful when he found that the boss did not intend ever to mention the matter to him, let alone to any one higher up. He had made the resolve then that he would never take advantage of the boss's friendship. No, he could not ask to go now.—Yes, he must for Hester's sake.

"Sweet, I'll ask the boss to send some one up here and give us a little vacation!"

"No, no, not that. It would ruin you, for them to know that I was weak. A chain no stronger than its weakest link . . ."

"Oh, I don't think so," answered Stephen, but there was no conviction in his tone. "The boss would understand . . . but if you'd rather not . . ."

What diversion was there here? He had an idea. They could go shooting. For several evenings he had seen ducks flying. He'd get his gun without telling Kin. They'd slip out the side door.

Hand in hand, they moved across the prairie, tiny specks on the plain. Ducks flew over. Stephen was a good marksman, his first shot brought one down. Hester saw it fall like a bit of brown mud.

"There it is on that hummock of *kaoliang* stubble," she cried and ran off after it.

Miraculously free of the depression which for weeks had weighed her down, she ran this way and that. Stephen watched her tenderly. She looked childlike in her knickers, her legs so straight and strong flung out in a funny puppyish fashion because of her boots, which made her feet heavy and unwieldly. Suddenly she stopped, puzzled. Among the thousands of brown hummocks of *kaoliang* stubble, she had lost the particular one where the duck had fallen. Stephen shouted at her and waved to the right. She shook her head. It wasn't there. She came back defeated by the immense brown sameness.

Time after time Stephen shot and the bird fell, but when the light went from the plain without warning of twilight, as it did here, they had bagged only two ducks.

"We've got enough for dinner anyway," said Stephen cheerfully. "I guess at home we couldn't step outside our door and shoot our dinner like this."

"Not in New York anyway," she said with a half sob.

"When we get in, I'll insist Kin have them cooked." Stephen sounded like a child bragging of the way he would command his father, Hester thought. They walked on in silence. After a time they stopped, bewildered. They had lost the house as they had the ducks. The plain had sucked up all distinctions. They swerved to the right, the left. Hester began to laugh. To her overwrought nerves her laughter sounded impudent in the

131

vastness of this silent brown manifestation of nature.

She only half heard Stephen mumbling, "I should have told Kin where we were going. We may wander round half the night." At the same moment, they both saw a light. Stephen shouted, and Hester felt the wind swooping at his shout, pushing it down into the plain. Then the light was lifted high, and they saw it was a lantern. It shone down on Kin, wraps over his arm.

"Here, what's this?" demanded Stephen, taking from Kin his greatcoat and Hester's thin cloak. "You know better than this." But Hester understood that Kin had not intended to bring her warm coat.

As they followed the light, the girl felt her fright and her little freedom collapse. She was like Kin's bird which hopped from its perch the length of the string on its leg. By Kin's grace and his meager English, she lived. Silently he served her; gently, relentlessly he brought her to submission. She felt herself his prisoner with invisible humiliations heaped upon her. Despite Stephen's assurances, she knew nothing would be changed; and as she passed into the house, Kin's shadow, black and long, fell across the threshold.

At breakfast the next morning, the common things, the coffee-pot, the eggshell white cups with their sprays of bamboo, reassured Stephen. Yesterday was unreal. Hester seemed herself again and he let it go at that, eager to forget that glimpse he had had of the white-hot core of her being. His own inner self had been for a long time well hidden under the cool soil of his companionship with Hester and every-day happenings of his work. Even as he awoke that morning, his mind had immediately taken up the problems of the day. Soon the ground would be frozen. Past their compound would be the steady procession of the carts bound for the city, loaded with beans. When the carts returned, many would be filled with barrels of oil from his tanks, or tins from the godown in the agent's compound. The tins of oil were still stored there, despite the complaints of the officials. They did not like oil stored in the city, but for the time the Company, through him, had arranged to leave it there, in order to save the face of the agent. If Stephen took all the stores from the agent, it would look as if the Company didn't trust him.

That afternoon, walking across the plain on his return from the city, Stephen felt only contentment. At last the final arrangements had been made. A set of sub-agents, wholly acceptable to the Company, had been chosen by the agent—men who had shops in various towns in the territory. This was part of the new scheme the Company had adopted. For him to have failed would have been serious. He felt satisfaction with the day's work. Under the pressure of these delicate arrangements, Hester's suffering had been pushed to the back of his mind. Only when he picked up his cards for a game of solitaire, was he reminded of the events of the evening before. He heard Hester sigh.

"You all right?" he asked.

"Yes, Stephen."

"I love you, Hester, and try to make you happy."

"Yes, I know."

She sat opposite, her chin resting in the cup of her palms. For a time, at least, her rebellion had spent itself. Presently Stephen put aside his playing cards, taking in their place a pile of white cards with Chinese characters written on them. He muttered the meaning of each to himself, then turned the card over, to see if he was right, drawing the character in the air with his finger so as not to forget its formation. As she watched him, Hester realized beyond a chance of fooling herself, that the self-respect written in his sensitive face was bound up with his work. Touch his work and you touched his self-respect. She might hate this way of life; it was Stephen's necessity. How singular that trade had become her life's business, she who had wanted only to play the violin. But for Stephen's sake the Company could have its way with her.

Into a world of half-tones Hester now entered. That fierce suffering of the last weeks seemed to have sapped her strength and often, for hours, she lay on her bed, feeling weak and languid. There were mornings when she let Stephen think she was asleep and he would go softly out, leaving her. It gave her a chance not to eat any breakfast, a thing impossible if Stephen were about. All her former rebellion against the wind and the silence and the darkness seemed concentrated now against the food. It was a heavy monotonous diet that Kin provided. He gave them meat three times a day, usually pork. And sweet potatoes, the native vegetables were few up here, so he said; there were no fruits except the puckery persimmon, and an odd Japanese fruit, something like an orange, but sourer than a lemon. Stephen ate them, but she could not. There were days when it seemed to her that she would not mind anything else if she could only have an orange. In her dreams, a stand where she had bought fruit as a child often appeared to her. The oranges piled in a mound upon it were so real that, after she waked, she could feel their lovely rounded skins in the palm of her hand.

She was alone one morning, exhausted after a struggle with Kin over the accounts. For days she had put off the task, dreading it. Now it was finished and she had shut the door of her room. Perhaps she was going to be ill. If she were couldn't she ask Stephen to resign? Then she was ashamed of the subterfuge. She lay on her bed, appalled before the weakness that possessed her.

Suddenly she sat up, startled with a new idea. Strange

she had not thought of it before. It would explain so many moods, so many feelings of the last weeks. Yes, she was sure.

She must be wholly obedient to the Company now. Indeed, she would not entertain the idea of asking Stephen to resign. The instinct to protect her young had been born in her. For the first time in her life Hester felt material insecurity as a danger, not an adventure, felt the inexorable economic pressure. This, before delight entered every cranny of her being.

XIV

WINTER came, and with each advancing month, north, always farther north, moved the oil. In brown huts clinging to the rocky hillsides, in brown huts crouching on the plain, the three-cent lamps, with their red bowls and miraculous chimneys, were placed carefully on low *k'ang* tables. The tiny flames pierced a little the gloom in the dusty rafters where rested coffins, awaiting burial back in the ancestral homes in China, safe within the Great Wall. The wind hurled itself against the huts, as behind the bed curtains on the brick beds the peasants and their families lay sleeping together, protected from evil spirits by the lamps burning on throughout the night.

Winter, and with it for Hester, peace, her spirits subdued to the service of her body. And, as Stephen had predicted, no longer the desire to go home. She shrank from society, as once she had sought it. Only when she had to see the doctor, could Stephen coax her across the city where one or two white women lived. Danish women, speaking little English, they seemed as foreign to Hester as the Chinese.

The long letters which she had written to her friends in America when she first came to this place of isolation, she ceased to write; her panic that annihilation would engulf her, if her friends forgot her, vanished. Instead, the more she isolated herself the more intense grew the sense of her own personality mirrored in Stephen's concern for her. And Kin's, too. She did not know why, but she had become of importance in Kin's eyes.

Stephen did not worry about her any more. She was a brick. He was coming to have great confidence in her. She was not going to let him down. He was winning through now, beginning to find that he could rely on his own judgment in doing business with the Chinese. Funny about that . . . a kind of sixth sense, something as yet not understandable but successful. It was exciting, like venturing from hummock to hummock in swampy land. Those sub-agents were doing good work, and the agent was cooperating.

Slowly the sales in his territory were growing. Slowly, too, he swung the balance of business in favor of the Company, and away from Blodgett. Stephen and his rival had become very good friends, each promising to give the other a fair chance. Then one day Stephen was authorized by his Company to drop prices. He notified Blodgett before he put the reduction into effect. It was on Saturday, when he returned from making his weekly deposit in the Russian bank, that he found Liu, the agent, waiting in his office.

Excitedly Liu demanded that Stephen reduce the price again, "to meet Blodgett." So Blodgett had cut without telling him. At once Stephen saw the plan. Blodgett had waited until Saturday to drop prices below those of the Company, knowing that Stephen could not follow without the consent of his organization, and that Saturday noon was too late to get it. But he'd be ready for him next week-end.

He wrote the boss, asking that he be allowed, up to a certain limit, to use his own judgment about the price cut, both as to amount and to time. That the boss would have to take up the matter with the Shanghai office, Stephen knew. All the week he waited. Early Saturday morning the telegram came, authorizing him to follow Blodgett's price drop of the previous week. Stephen was disappointed and humiliated, for all the week he had been soothing the irate agent by the promise of meeting the cut.

Week after week it went on, Stephen in the dark as to the policy of the Company. In his little universe, where each small phenomenon was of importance, this act of the Company became a major tragedy to him. He thought of little else; he talked of little else, especially over the week-end when his office was closed.

"Let's sleep late," said Hester on the third Sunday, "then we shan't have so much time to think."

But Stephen woke earlier than usual. He had been dozing when a new phase of the matter aroused him. He woke Hester before he thought.

"It's damned unfair. Look, I'm held responsible for the amount of business in this territory, but I'm given no responsibility in the method of getting it. Suppose it goes down to nothing, shall I lose my job?"

Now Hester was wide awake, "Why, Stephen, what would we do?"

"I'm a brute to worry you," he said, and put forth all his efforts to reassure her.

At last the greater resources of the big corporation wore Blodgett down; but long before, Stephen had ceased to feel any responsibility, other than to report accurately what happened. He had become the perfect instrument, the hand, delving, working, but not asking the brain to explain why—a good Company man.

* * * * *

It was after coolness had grown up between Blodgett and himself over this cutthroat competition that Stephen became interested in the visits of Liu. The agent dropped in often for a chat, and Stephen began to think again of friendship with the Chinese.

One day, on an impulse, Stephen asked Liu to come to the house and meet his wife. Hester was delighted at the idea; now she was going to know the Chinese. Aided by Kin she had tea and cakes ready, when Stephen and the agent entered the house. The little social event had passed off in all correctness. Stephen congratulated himself, although Kin, unaccountably, had not stayed to serve tea. But Hester had risen nobly to the occasion, remembering to hold the cup in two hands when she gave it to Liu. She had played the scene well, lowering her eyes demurely, even when she served Stephen himself, following the canons of good taste among the Chinese. He was certain of the success of the venture, when at the end of the call Liu had invited them to feast with him.

Hester felt shy, going into the great bare restaurant filled with men, where the feast of Liu was held. In the short distance to the stairway, almost as straight up as a ladder, she felt the eyes of all upon her. Even the slatternly boy standing by the great brass water-kettle gazed at her in such a way that she flushed. Stephen knew that Chinese ladies do not go out publicly with their husbands, but he walked proudly beside Hester to show how he honored her, not realizing that in exposing her to their gaze, like a sing-song girl, he had given the men cause to believe that he held her lightly. Nor did he realize that Liu believed her to be a favorite concubine; only such women did a man display. Had not Stephen gone out of his way to let Liu see her?

To the second feast, the agent brought his wife, so he said. In reality she was a concubine, bought from a house of prostitution in Chefoo. Liu was secretly pleased

138.

that Stephen had made it possible to bring her to the feast. She sat next to Hester, the first Chinese woman Stephen's wife had ever met, seemingly too busy splitting watermelon seeds with her even white teeth, spitting the husks on the floor, to take any notice of Hester. From time to time she looked up boldly through her long black bangs at the five men at the table—the agent, his partners and Stephen. Occasionally she threw into their conversation sharp terse remarks that each time brought the appreciation of laughter from the Chinese men. As the concubine of Liu spoke in another dialect from the one Stephen had learned, he did not understand her.

There were sing-song girls that evening, who came through the door back of Hester, mincing round the table on their bound feet, leaning over the men's shoulders, pouring out their wine.

"The agent certainly spared no pains this evening, evidently wants to be friendly," said Stephen when they were at home again. "We must invite him and his wife here to our house."

But before Stephen arranged this, Liu had invited them to a third feast. On the afternoon of the day, the merchant called on a matter of business. In their long conversation, the question of leakage came up and Stephen gathered, he did not know how, so adroitly did Liu convey his meaning, that if he would falsify the amount of the leakage, the profits might be divided. He was angry and curtly refused. Too curtly, he realized after he had spoken. Fortunately, the agent accepted his defeat gracefully, bowing himself out, clasping his own hands according to the best Chinese custom.

"The most miserable one will call in person for the honorable one and his great lady at the hour for the feast."

That hour passed and a second. "Liu's evidently been detained and thinks it wouldn't be polite to send any one else. Time doesn't mean anything to them," Stephen explained for the hundredth time to Hester.

"I'm hungry, let's eat something," was Hester's answer.

"We couldn't do that," said Stephen, "we'd make him lose face. He'd be sure to find out from the servants."

But at nine, he rang for Kin. "Get dinner."

"There is nothing prepared," answered Kin, unconcealed contempt in his manner.

Now, in a flash, Stephen knew that the agent had never intended to come for them, that this was retaliation for what had taken place that afternoon. For a second time he had let himself in for an insult—and this time his wife, too. He writhed inwardly when he thought of the exquisite pleasure Liu was enjoying at this moment, he and his fellows, at Stephen's expense. With what zest contempt and revenge were masked in propriety! But what had made Liu think he could do this and get away with it?

Well, to-morrow the agent should know that he was not so stupid. He would handle the matter with the approved indirectness of this country's custom.

Throughout the next day Stephen waited patiently, believing that Liu would come to make his apologies, thus completing the proprieties. He was not disappointed. At four, Liu appeared, a dignified satin-clad figure, the hauteur of race in his bearing.

Stephen rose, bowed, motioned the agent to a chair.

"I have come," said Liu, "the first moment that I have been able. At the hour of the feast last evening, my body put forth such fire that I was unable to come. Now if the honorable one will accept my humble hospitality, we will begin feasting."

"It is with great concern that I learn of the sickness of the honorable one," answered Stephen, tipping back in his swivel chair, conveying a subtle insult by his sprawl-

140

ing attitude. "Which is not escaping Liu," he said to himself. And aloud, "I could not think of asking a sick man to endure the hardship of long feasting."

"*Ai*," responded Liu, with a deep sigh. "My miserable self is not to be considered."

Stephen felt his anger rising. He'd puncture the man's self-complacency.

"Could the injury by any chance be in the honorable one's leg?" Eyeing Liu closely, he noticed a lessening of his composure. "He knows that I have seen through him," thought Stephen, with no little satisfaction. "Once he told me himself of Yuan Shih Kai's excuse of a lame leg when the Prince Regent, who had forced him into retirement, summoned him to the palace to help put down the revolution. Yuan wished the prince to know he was strong enough to give the veiled insult."

Now Liu began sincerely to urge Stephen to feast with him.

"I could not cause the great Liu trouble," the white man insisted.

The agent's disdainful pride fell away. "Come, Prior-born," he begged, "or I lose such face that I must give up the business."

Failing to move Stephen by these entreaties, he went away. The next day emissaries came as go-betweens in the matter. After three days it was arranged. Stephen would go once with Liu to the restaurant, so that he might get back his face. But never after that.

Afterward the proprieties were kept. Liu occasionally invited the Chases to a feast, and Stephen found some reason which made it impossible for them to go.

And now Stephen and Hester had no one to break their isolation. Alone on the plain, for days hearing no Western voices other than their own, the mass thought engendered by the drop-by-drop suggestions emanating

141

from the constantly working will of the Company pervaded their minds. Their days came to be peopled with men and women, many of whom they had never met, employees of the Company scattered over China. For some they felt the hot flare of unreasoned enthusiasm, how engendered they never stopped to think; for others equally unreasoned dislikes and suspicions. A little praise, the faintest censure, of this or that person, spoken by Director Swaley, by this or that man in the Company, were remembered now.

As they sat by the fire at night, the wind howling outside, Stephen spoke to Hester of his friend Kendall, recently transferred from Harbin to Vladivostok. "A coming man," he told her.

"I don't see that he does anything more than you do," Hester protested. "You're too modest."

"I'm a plodder," answered Stephen. "Kendall is aggressive. You should see him, Hester. He's great."

Through the agent a rumor reached Stephen that Jim was drinking too much. He did not say anything of this to Hester, but he thought a great deal about it. Jim had always taken too much, but he had never let it interfere with his work. Must be now, if the agent had heard about it.

The snow fell as it had not fallen for years in Manchuria—particles that bit like steel whirled through the air with high-powered velocity. After the snow, two or three days of bitter cold, glittering quiet, the thermometer falling to twenty, to thirty below zero; then another and another storm of wind and snow. Out of the storm, the tanks looming darkly.

Between Stephen and Hester, shut away from the world, grew an exquisite dependence. Often Stephen left his work, throwing on his greatcoat to hurry through the cold passageway connecting office and house, that he might look at Hester sitting in a low chair, a work-basket by her side, her sewing dropped in her lap, for always she heard his footsteps and looked up to welcome him. It seemed to Stephen that her delicate spirit all but burned through the thin mask of her features, illumining them with incredible beauty.

Through the long evenings they sat side by side on the couch, their fingers intertwined, exchanging intimate bits of their life in America, jealous of the years each had lived without the other. Stephen, especially, had a lively curiosity about every act of Hester's before he had known her. He asked endless questions about her father, the house they had lived in, the children she had played with. Hester told him everything with almost childlike frankness, except of the precious experience of her music; of this she did not speak, and he came to believe that music had been only a small part of her life, not guessing that she was hiding something. Music was gone now . . . he was not a musician . . . these were the reasons for her secretiveness.

And now at last Stephen's satisfaction in Hester's looks and bearing, his contentment in her companionship, flamed up into love. All night he held her in his arms, waking at her every movement, his senses afire as he adjusted his body to her comfort. Sometimes his lips caressed the thick masses of her hair, the now full curves of her breasts. He had not loved her when he married her, but that made no difference to Hester now. Only this ecstasy mattered. She lay in his arms, relaxed, intensifying her helplessness so that she might know to the uttermost the strength of his vigorous body.

Opening the door softly before he knocked in the morning, Kin would find them clasped in each other's arms. He was well pleased. Now had his moment come. The missie would pay little attention. The mouths of his family would be well filled for a time.

143

A new sense of privacy came to Hester and Stephen. All day the rumble of the long carts, passing unseen just outside the compound wall, gave them the excited pleasure of being in hiding together; and at night, hearing in the still air the far-off whistle of the Siberian Express, they drew closer, the world forgotten and undesired.

So the months slipped by, and Hester's time of travail was not far away. In his heart Stephen felt that she should have more expert care than the Danish doctor, who had been here many years, could give her. But when he thought of parting from her, he felt maimed and helpless, and the vision of Hester traveling alone out into the world, the world that now seemed abnormal to him in its activities, its dangers, disturbed him.

"Hester, do you feel that you should go?"

"Oh, no, Stephen. No. I couldn't, I couldn't go alone." She broke into frightened sobbing.

"There, there," he hushed her. "I couldn't bear to have you go, but I thought maybe you'd have better care."

In the morning they confessed they had been foolish. Nothing need take Hester away. The Danish doctor was good, and he was very kind. Once again Hester began to feel that she was in sanctuary, in the little house shut off from the world by the rumble of the long carts.

XV

The winter broke. One day it seemed unending; the next, as they sat at lunch, they heard the drip of the melting snow from the eaves of the house. There was a knock at the door and Kin ushered Jim into the room.

"Well, where'd you drop from?" shouted Stephen, delighted.

"Just asked the boss if I could take a run up to see you."

Stephen eyed his friend with pleasure, realizing how he had missed the comradeship of men. But Hester felt Jim's coming an intrusion, jarring her chrysalis of delight.

That night the two men sat talking together after Hester had gone to bed. Stephen couldn't stop talking. So much to ask about. Good old Jim. He certainly looked fit enough. But, hang it all, he didn't want Jim to lose out now when the big chance was coming.

"Say," he blurted, "why don't you cut the drink out? With all this new organization coming on, you'll get a big place if you don't play the fool."

"Do I look any less fit than I ever have? As for business —you know my work."

"Well, what's all this talk drifting around? I even hear it from the agent. I'd like to get hold of the fellow that started it."

"Steady there, Steve. You'll only hurt yourself with the Company, if you start defending me. And anyway it doesn't matter," Jim went on. "I've decided to chuck the whole thing. That's why I'm up here really—to tell you. I've had a little money left me. Not much, just enough to give me a start."

In the dusk of the next afternoon, as the two men were leaving the office, Jim rested his hand on Stephen's shoulder. "Say, old chap, you won't mind my mentioning it, will you? Hester and you ought to get out of here. Somewhere, anywhere, just to have a change. As soon as the kid comes, you'd better ask for a vacation. You two have been great. Stuck it out up here without any fuss. This new organization which seems to have got all you young fellows by the ear ought to do something for you. They might give you my place." Stephen felt his heart leap.

"You know there's a rumor they're going to move the

offices to Mukden?" Jim went on. "Bean trade all pulled away from our little diggings now, of course. With Dalny the coming port, Mukden will be the center of the province."

"That'd break the old boss's heart, wouldn't it?" asked Stephen.

"I don't mind telling you, Steve, the boss is in a bad jam over that godown he rented the Company. Company seems to have got its back up about the lease. The talk is that he wished a lemon on them."

"But I always understood he didn't want to lease to them?"

"Exactly, but they seem to have got him tangled up. Hate to go off and leave him. Wish you were there. These young chaps harass him over new methods. You know the old boss—all you have to do is to jolly him along a bit, and you can keep the office as modern as it needs to be. And my word, he certainly knows how to increase business. Returns soaring!"

Jim broke off suddenly, changing the subject back to Stephen. "I've got an idea. Suppose I stay and take charge of the business for a while, look after the tanks? Two or three days, I mean. I'll wire the boss. You and Hester take a run up to Harbin. Couldn't? On account of Hester? How about going to my diggings? Good doctor there. Train ride too much? As soon as the kid comes, you do it."

After Jim's visit, Stephen found it difficult to settle back into the monotonous slog, slog, the humdrum routine. Then the desire for initiative passed, as did the desire for companionship. He and Hester lived as before.

The last vestige of old snow was gone. The windows stood open, hardly a cart passed, the spring had indeed come. The dust of the plains again filtered into the house,

146

the shrieking wind set the shutters rattling, the screens whining. But Hester did not notice.

, It was the hour in the afternoon when the tanks cast their shadows over the house. The day's work was done and Stephen and Hester paced back and forth outside the compound wall, on the path which hung like a shelf above the sunken rutted road.

Hester felt her time was near, and Stephen hurried Kin off for the doctor. The sun sank. Gripped more and more by pain, she became fearful that the doctor would not arrive in time.

"There he is," cried Stephen. In the last faint light, he discerned the great Scandinavian plodding toward them. No one could mistake him, with his ill-fitting trousers flapping against his legs, his red beard, nearly to his waist, blowing in the wind.

Often Stephen had met the doctor so, striding about on foot to save the expense of a cart, visiting the sick in the meanest alleys of the city. For ten years, he had labored without returning to his own country. Of peasant stock, vigorous in his strength and his remedies, Stephen once had questioned his ability. Now he felt only relief that into the doctor's strong hands he could put the responsibility of Hester.

"It is not for many hours yet," said the doctor. Then he told how Kin had traced him through the city. "Very fine servant. What is his name?"

Hester was at a loss. "Why, Kin, that's all I know."

The doctor frowned. "This is not the way, Mrs. Chase. He has identified himself with your family."

"Now I shall ask a blessing from the dear Father," he said, as they sat down to the dinner table.

After dinner, they walked with the doctor about the compound, pausing for a moment at the gate, looking off over the plain. All at once Stephen realized that smoke was hanging over that part of the city where the agent had his oil godown. This was not the wraithlike smoke of the evening cooking fires. This smoke bellied up like a giant puffball. Then a tongue of flame shot up into the air.

"Kin!" he shouted.

The three men talked rapidly together in Chinese. Hester could only half make out what they were saying. "What does Kin say? What does he say?" she asked.

Stephen, with an effort, pulled his mind back to give attention to her. "It's a fire, Kin says, not very near the godowns yet, but the wind is in that direction. A lot of thatch roofs in there. If the fire reaches them, the godown is in danger!"

They looked into each other's eyes. They were as one person with no need of speech. Stephen must go. The oil was his responsibility. If anything should happen, and he was not there———

Now that they had decided, Stephen ran back into the house, reappearing almost instantly.

"Kin is here, Hester. You can send him for me, if . . . But the doctor says it won't be before morning."

Gently Stephen kissed her, but not once did he look back as he strode from the compound. Hester watched him, a slight figure, hurrying away. A fierce pain gripped her and she knew her hour had come. The iron gates clanged to behind him, shutting him from her sight.

Under the sharp necessity of gathering together her own forces to meet her travail, she felt a sudden sundering of her identity with Stephen's. During the hours of the night, with their demands of struggle and pain, this separate identity grew more definite until she had lost all sense of relationship with him. She, alone, struggling to give birth to the life within her.

When Stephen entered the city, the crowds of fleeing people he had met in the plain grew denser, congested

148

in the narrow alleys. Suddenly Kin appeared. Stephen, so used to his presence, forgot he had told Kin to stay behind, thankful he was there to thrust himself into the mass, parting the crowds for his master. As they drew nearer the fire, smoke filled their lungs. Coughing, half-strangling, at last the two men came out by the compound, the gray godown roof just showing above the wall. The gates were fast barred. To their loud cries of "Open, Open," there was no answer. For one moment Stephen was terrified. Had the keepers deserted! Then something told him that he could rely on their loyalty.

Kin had got hold of a great timber and together they drove it against the gate like a battering-ram. It made a loud boom and the iron gates shook under the impact. At last the voice of the agent himself cried, "Who is without?"

"Open," commanded Kin, "the *tai-pan*."

A crack, and an eye at the crack. Then, as those inside the compound saw that Kin spoke truly, the gate opened wide enough to admit them. In the flare of the fire, Stephen saw dark creeping figures on the steep slant of the godown roof, clinging precariously as they drew up buckets of water. "They can't save the godown that way," he thought. "Sparks are falling in showers at every puff of wind."

It was a good thing he had come. Now his anxiety over Hester, sharp within him as he crossed the plain, receded into the back of his mind, hanging there like a black curtain of apprehension.

He saw immediately that the godown could be saved, if a space were cleared between the wall and the fire. Should he have it cleared? If he did the Company must pay for all the huts he tore down. There was no time now for the long Oriental bargaining, and the house owners would have the Company at their mercy when the time came for the settlement. He would have to prove that he had not acted too hastily, or he would be censured for such an expenditure. A man's initiative, Stephen knew from the winter's experience, was not desired. Suppose he waited a little, took a chance on the wind changing, or dying down as it often did at night? But suppose neither happened? As he sifted his problem, it resolved itself into spending a relatively small amount of money, in order to obviate the risk of losing the oil and damaging the city; or into taking the larger risk in the hope of avoiding the expenditure. Also, if the oil took fire, the Company would incur the hate of the city. His mind seesawed back and forth unable to make any decision.

As he stepped outside the gate to have a closer look at the fire, the flames leaped into a near-by street, consuming the thatched roofs as if they had been tinder, consuming Stephen's indecision also. He felt a sudden exhilaration as he stood between the fire and the godown. For this night, he, Stephen Chase, *was* the Company! He, the brain! Choose and shoulder the consequences!

He ran into the street with Kin in front, crying, "The *tai-pan* commands the houses to be torn down! The *tai-pan* promises the Keepers of Light will pay!" At his heels followed the agent's little band of faithful coolies.

As the crowbars crunched into the heavy matted thatch, a low and ominous murmur, like the angry hum of many bees, came from the people. But Kin went among them saying over and over, "The *tai-pan* makes himself responsible!" and the angry sound changed to one of satisfaction. "The Keepers of Light Company is rich, rich enough to buy the whole city. The price shall be high, in order that we and our children may live."

Stephen was everywhere supervising his men, himself working. It was like destroying giant ant-hills. The dust of the falling thatch was in his mouth, his throat. Pouring forth from the huts, men, women, children, ants carrying

150

their loads—pathetic possessions, a crude stool, a board with bits of rag pasted to it.

At last the space between the godown and the fire was a heap of rubbish too wide for the flames to leap. But Stephen was aghast when Kin handed him a list of the huts destroyed, destroyed without the Company's authorization. And then the fire, behaving like the demon the people conceived it to be, now that it had frightened Stephen into the destruction of the houses, retreated. The wind dropped suddenly and the flames began to die down. Weary to the point of exhaustion, Stephen's elation over the acceptance of responsibility left him.

The black curtain at the back of his brain suddenly moved forward. Suppose something had happened to Hester in his absence? He was no longer a Company man, but an individual, who would have sacrificed any interest of his own, rather than leave Hester this night to face the birth of their child without him. Looking at his watch, he was startled to find it was past midnight. As quickly as he could, he made his way through the city, over the plain crowded now with those who had been made homeless, denied shelter until the evil spirit of the fire had left them. Stephen used his flash-light to avoid stumbling over them, seeing each for an instant, a succession of pictures, set in the glowing circle of his electric torch: an old man sitting on his haunches, staring straight ahead of him; a young man, knees drawn up under his chin, head on knees like some fantastic Oriental god, asleep; a woman with matted black hair lying as an animal lies, making a half-circle of her body to shelter her young, a brown hand stretched out relaxed, inert, there on the trampled dirt of the plain under Stephen's advancing foot.

His tired brain did not retain the impression of a single face. Instead, as he strode along, hastening to Hester, only countless crouching forms resigned to their calamity. No lamentation, no complaining even before this visitation of great evil. These crouching acquiescent figures seemed to cling around his feet, retarding his progress. But at last he was free, running now toward the compound wall and the corrugated iron gate, stumbling along in the old cart ruts.

Exhausted, panting for breath, he came in through the door that led into the living-room, almost falling over Li Tsu who whined and licked at his boots. The coolie carrying a pail of hot water was coming in from the kitchen, *"Tai-pan, tai-pan,"* ("Master, master,") he said in his soft voice, looking pityingly at Stephen.

Hardly noticing, he stumbled on into the bedroom. He saw the *amah* leaning over Hester. He saw her pass a wet cloth over Hester's face. He heard Hester's moan.

"Sweet, sweet, I'm here. What is it?"

He was about to drop on his knees by her side when a voice, harsh and commanding, spoke. "Here, help me. Thank God, you've come."

Hester lay with eyes closed, only the trembling of her lips giving any indication that she lived. Stephen moved reluctantly to the foot of the bed where the baby lay. But the baby meant nothing to him. Only Hester mattered.

"He does not breathe. Here, beat him like this. I must look after your wife." As the doctor spoke, he placed a towel in Stephen's hand. Mechanically, Stephen obeyed.

Again the doctor commanded him, "Breathe into his lungs."

As Stephen felt the wafer-like lips against his own he suddenly realized that this tiny male creature was his son. He cried out in anguish, for the lips were cold and he could not force his breath between them.

The doctor was shaking him, commanding him sternly to resign himself to the will of God, and to take the child away so that the mother should not know. "She must sleep, see, she yields now to the medicine."

Stephen, carrying the child, who had the semblance of cuddling to him with his hands drawn up on his chest, walked into the spare room and locked the door. Here he examined the beauty of his son, held the diminutive feet in his hand, those feet so like his own; the narrow Chase heel, so hard to fit to a shoe, and the hands, replicas of his own, square hands with short fingers, the kind of hands that like work. But the beautifully rounded chin, the sensitive mouth, Hester's; and the black hair, curiously abundant, lying in damp curls at the nape of the baby's neck. With infinite care he bathed and dressed the child, taking from the drawer of the dresser the clothes Hester had made during the winter. He laid him on the cold white spread of the bed and walked from the room dazed, as if he had awakened in a strange land. Why was he here on this great plain with his dead baby? In the midst of a people among whom he had not one friend—unless Kin was his friend.

He took Hester's low chair and sat down by her door, waiting for some stir within, longing for Hester, longing to let her comfort him, longing to comfort her.

The assistant manager from Shanghai was sent up to give his opinion whether clearing the space had been necessary. The situation had become more serious in the eyes of the Company, since the city had decided it would have nothing but tiled roofs. Stephen hardly heard what the man said. He had been over-cautious, according to the manager—might have waited a little longer. But what did he care, whether Shanghai liked what he had done, or not? Maybe he'd sacrificed his baby to do it. Maybe his son would have lived, if he had been there to help earlier in the evening. He was sure Hester thought so. She was as coldly separated from him as if he were a stranger,

153

taking no notice of him, sitting for hours without speaking, and at night she lay straight and rigid on the edge of the bed.

All Stephen wanted was to get away. Now that it was too late to save the baby, he strained every energy to bring about a transfer, as if, somehow, it would straighten out the past.

"It doesn't do any good to be asking for transfers," the assistant manager said, speaking in the name of the Company. But looking on Hester, he was moved. Chase hadn't told him, but he understood they had lost a child recently. "When's your home leave due, Chase? Overdue, is it? Well, you fellows get kind of buried in these places. Suppose I put your home leave up to Shanghai?"

They had talked it over again in the droshky on the way to the train, Stephen trying desperately to exact a promise. It seemed to him the assistant manager was avoiding any definite statement, as if, after all, he didn't want to take the responsibility of suggesting the matter of home leave in Shanghai.

Hester was scarcely conscious that Stephen and the assistant manager had gone out, even as she had scarcely realized their presence, preoccupied as she was with the dream-beset world where she had dwelt since the doctor had told her about the baby. In that dreaming state, she was happy. Her baby was not dead, but in the dark safety of her womb. Sitting in the same low chair in which she had sat so much during the winter, wearing the same dress, she sought to feel the fulness of her body, the precious dragging weight of her child. It troubled her now that it lay so still. Why was there no sudden thrust of life? Her mind took shelter behind its fabrication, shielding itself.

But reality could no longer be denied. The unfamiliar lightness of her body. There was no weight within her!

She stood up. Slowly she passed her hands down the length of her slim hips. Her untenanted body!

With restless indirection, she wandered from room to room, out to the veranda where the moonlight lay in metallic brilliance. Back into the house again. Her child's tiny but tenacious hold of her loosened. Her husband— since the night of the fire she had been separated from him. Freedom. With swift and certain direction, she reached for her violin, thin ecstasy of life in and for herself possessing her. Ecstasy playing itself into frenzy, becoming disordered, stopping abruptly.

As Stephen came around the side of the house, he heard her. He stood transfixed. Hester's music, usually an unknown medium to him, was not so to-night. It broke his heart.

He went on to the house, rattling the door-knob to prepare her for his coming. She was again sitting in her low chair, listless and silent, as he had left her. All at once fear struck at his heart. This far north with its high winds, its stinging air pitching the most phlegmatic of white people to a high tension, had been known to drive women mad. What had he been thinking of to let Hester stay during the strain of her pregnancy? He dared wait no longer. She must get away immediately, even if she had to go alone.

"Hester," he asked, "would you like to go home?"

"Yes," she answered, and this time she did not cling to him. He was relieved at that, for she must go and he could not go with her. He did not sleep that night, longing to take her in his arms, but she lay as far from him as possible.

It took all Stephen's fortitude to meet the days after Hester had gone. It was summer, and there was almost nothing to do in the office. No oil could be sent out over

155

the roads made impassable by the rains; little supervision of the agents and sub-agents was necessary; the peasants did not buy the precious light at this season, saving their coppers for the long dark winter ahead.

Stephen had received word that the question of his leave had been taken up with New York. Two months of days must intervene before he could expect to hear, two months of days filled with the idle occupation of guarding the tanks. He tried to keep his thoughts from Hester, but he could not. He worried about her on the long trip. She seemed so remote; would she be able to make friends, would her heart forget its trouble? Her letters told him nothing. He could not have believed that a letter could say so little. Was it because she still held herself apart from him, or was this kind of letter natural to her? He could not say, for he had never received a letter from her before.

The house seemed like the cage Hester had first called it, the routine of his days and nights confined within it. The dining-room: three meals to be got through each day with the empty expanse of table before him. The living-room: long noon hours, longer evenings, when everything brought to him the memory of Hester, and yet nothing conveyed association with her. When she went, she seemed completely to have taken herself out of his life. He wondered how she had managed to leave the house so bare of her presence, when once she had seemed to pervade every crevice of it. The bedroom: mechanically dressing and undressing; lying for hours staring into the darkness, wondering how he and Hester, bound in a union so close, could in one night have become as strangers to each other. There was a moment each night when at last he gave up wondering and fell asleep, Li Tsu curled between his shoulders.

After a time, he walked the treadmill of his days numb to any deep feeling. Then his release came. A letter arrived granting him leave, and on the next morning's train, appeared Walter Cheatham, to relieve him.

Cheatham was the bearer of exciting news. The director had dropped down suddenly on China and was making drastic changes in the organization.

"A classy organization, I'll tell you," said Cheatham. "Some of the men are getting regular plums. Director doesn't give much for this talk about learning the Chinese way of business. Teach the Chinese our ways. Modern business methods. No more of this pioneer stuff, either. Says he likes to have the men get married, so he has shortened the probation time to two years. That means me in another year. Cute little house, cozy for two. But perhaps I'll be promoted before then." He strolled over to a mirror hanging between the windows, surveyed himself, straightened his tie as if getting ready to go somewhere.

"Any club around here?" he asked.

"No," said Stephen.

Cheatham sat down.

"There's to be a new manager in Shanghai," he went on. "They say he's fine. Different sort . . . college man, some one who can really represent the Company. Skinflint's retiring on a jolly fine pension I guess, from all I hear. Wonder what the director will do to Manchuria when he gets here? Stir it up, I'll bet."

XVI

Two days later, when Stephen reached the main office, already the stir had begun. The director had come in on the train from Tientsin only a few hours earlier. All the men had been called in from the sub-stations, and Kendall from Vladivostok, although it was an independent station. Stephen had understood the business in Vladivostok had been a kind of sub rosa affair, in which his friend had had to pose as a free lance.

"Wonder why Kendall is here," he thought. "Good to see him, though. Haven't set eyes on him since that day in New York when we were green classmen. Neater, trimmer than he used to be. Has a confident air of having succeeded."

But he had only a few moments to talk with Kendall, for almost immediately he was called into conference with the director, who had turned the outer room into a private office for himself. He began questioning Stephen about the fire. In the eyes of the Company, Stephen saw it was simply a matter of proving whether or not he had acted hastily; it wasn't a question of Hester and the baby, that was the personal side which did not enter into it. Strange, he thought, the old boss isn't called in. He'd have backed me up. But there wasn't much time to think about it—he must make good on his own if that something big the director talked about a year ago was to come through.

After the conference, he went across the hall to the boss's office. "Come in," called the familiar gruff voice in response to his knock.

"I'm here to report, sir," said Stephen, a little discomfited, however, that his superior officer had been sitting here, while he himself had been discussing with the director business pertaining to the boss's territory.

"Well," said the boss, "it doesn't seem to count around here what I think, but I'll tell you anyway—here's congratulations over the way you handled that fire. As a matter of fact, you've done damn well on the whole winter's business."

"Thank you, sir," said Stephen. "It means a lot to me to know I've satisfied you."

"Humph," said the boss. "It won't help you much. But

I hope you get something good out of all this new scheme. If I had any say, you would."

After a moment he spoke again, "Sorry about the wife. Never did approve of sending you there. But you're young. Lots of time yet for a family."

At the club a little later the director, no longer the ruthless inquisitor of the afternoon, chatted with Stephen in a fine spirit of comradeship. Stephen felt a surge of excitement, evidently he had come through all right in his explanation of the fire. When the director asked about Hester, in a burst of confidence, he spoke of his anxiety. "The doctor said she couldn't live in this climate any longer and I had to send her home ahead of me," said Stephen.

"I am sorry," said Swaley. "Nice woman, your wife. We had thought—well, there are going to be some good opportunities in Manchuria. You seem to understand this exchange. Probably (this is, of course, confidential) we're going to bring in some one here who understands the new organization. He'll need a strong right hand. You don't think if you put it up to her, that wife of yours—she seemed a plucky person and interested in your career—you don't think she'd feel she could meet it for your sake?"

"It isn't a question of her willingness," Stephen spoke eagerly, anxious to justify Hester. "It's her health."

Swaley tried to fathom Chase. If it was really his wife's health that held him back, he could not afford to force his demands. Chase was too valuable for that. At the time of the fire, he had shown admirable balance between caution and decision. But if the real reason for his hesitation was his friendship for this backwoods manager, why that was a different matter. It was annoying, the way that old fellow made the men loyal to him. That man who had left the Company, Jim something or other. It seemed he had insisted that "the boss," as he absurdly called him, had been straight in this godown business. Director Swaley felt hot under the collar as he thought of it. A man no more than a clerk, telling the Company the right and wrong of a thing. Good idea, his chucking his job, saved a lot of trouble getting rid of him.

He'd have no nonsense from Chase, either. If he was squeamish about being put over the old codger he called friend, he should be made to take the job, sick wife or not. But as he looked at Stephen's sensitive face, he decided it would be better not to force the issue. "I don't want to buck him now, don't want to lose him. Better maneuver a little."

The next day Kendall joined Stephen as he left the office. "Wanted a little talk with you, Steve," he said. "Keep this under your hat, but I'm to be manager when the office goes to Mukden. Of course, I don't know whether I could get it through, but how about being my number two?"

Stephen looked at him sharply. Kendall wasn't speaking for himself. "When Swaley suggested you ask me, didn't he say anything about my wife's health?" he asked, disgusted to think Swaley would sacrifice Hester if she would consent. He added, "If I stay with the Company, it's got to be somewhere else than in Manchuria."

Kendall was secretly more desirous of him than ever. Steve was keen, just the man he wanted. "And he knows Manchuria better than I do. I'll need his knowledge." Aloud he said, "Better think it over. It doesn't pay to turn the Company down on a proposition."

As Kendall urged him, there flowed into Stephen's mind the knowledge that he was valuable to the Company, and that he had handled the fire business to their satisfaction.

But what about the man who had trained him? If Kendall was to be manager, they must mean to retire the boss. It was two years before his time, to be sure, but

160

two years' extra pension would mean nothing to so rich a Company.

"Your old boss," went on Kendall, as if he had read Stephen's thoughts, "is to be sub-manager here in town." He said it abruptly, glancing at Stephen to see his reaction. There was none. Well, Steve knew how to keep his own counsel. He wanted him more than ever.

"The Company couldn't move him, for he says he wouldn't live anywhere else but here," Kendall added.

"Is that their justification?" Stephen spoke coldly, thinking with distaste of the way the boss's words had been turned to suit the purpose of the Company. Now he remembered the boss on his fiftieth birthday, receiving the homage of the agents. Think of him, sub-station manager here where he had been so honored, all these agents witnessing his demotion! It was such loss of face, he mused to himself, as would wreck a man before the Chinese. Stephen felt disgust for the Company, that it should bring such humiliation on any of its men, and on the boss of all men.

"Anyway, I don't know that I'll come back," he said to Kendall.

That night, the last night of his stay in the town, Stephen had dinner with the boss. Until then he had felt for him nothing except sympathy and the greatest respect but, before the evening was over, he began to wonder if he had overvalued this garrulous old man. He had remembered the boss as reserved, but here he was divulging all sorts of personal matters in an effort to explain the godown affair. And then he boasted that he wouldn't give the Company the satisfaction it would get if he resigned. "That's what they're trying to force me to do," he said. "But they'll pay my pension. I'll show them they can't get the best of me like that."

Try as he would, Stephen felt reaction in favor of the

161

Company, and a withdrawal of his spirit from this bragging old man—for old the boss suddenly seemed. Still he could not have stood it to have the boss under him. He was glad that it was impossible for him to come back to Manchuria.

The train was pulling out from the town that for five years had been the center of Stephen's interests. In a few hours now Manchuria would be for him a thing of the past. He knew that he would be given something good in another part of China if he wished it; and he had kept his man's right to choose where he should go, and he had not allowed them to put him over the boss. Hang it all! Why hadn't the boss kept step with the Company?

The town had faded into the plain; now the lights of the express blotted out the plain. Five years, and yet no single relationship with this country remained. Kin had decided not to come back to him if he returned to China. Even Li Tsu was no longer his. He had given the little dog to Kin.

XVII

As THE steamer sailed out of the harbor at Yokohama the steady strong vibration of machinery that five years ago had been too commonplace for Stephen to notice, now excited him incredibly. When he went below for dinner and saw fresh green things to eat, he felt like a boy in a fairy tale sitting down to a banquet brought by rubbing Aladdin's lamp. The starved cells of his body cried out for this green food after the monotonous diet of the winter plains, and he ate ravenously, wolfing the celery and the lettuce. Then, suddenly conscious of the others at the table, tourists, he felt humiliated that the poverty of

162

his exile had betrayed him into this greedy hunger.

He found himself talking, the starved cells of his mind crying out for companionship. Then, suddenly conscious, he retreated into stiff silence. He seemed never able to be casual. But bit by bit, as Western civilization took shape before him, he accommodated himself to it, although many of the ways of his own people were still strange to him when the ship drew into San Francisco three weeks later. All the long journey across the continent his brain held tenaciously the image of the ancient civilization, into which for five years he had been trying to fit himself, in order that he might change it.

The train pulled into the terminal at New York, its network of tracks stretching away on every side, not just one thin track as in the stations of Manchuria. He was the first on the platform, the first hurrying toward the exit. Beyond the iron grill of the gate stood Hester. Was it only her modish apparel that was different? Was she still the aloof gray Hester of their last days together?

The great station vaulted above them. Sunshine fell in a pattern over the marble floor. As in a trance Stephen felt himself, Hester clinging to his arm, caught up into the stream of well-dressed men and women, moving forward toward the entrance. He was fascinated with the sound of many feet, with the silken swish of the swinging door as they passed through to the street. In sudden assault, the triumphant roar of the city burst upon his ears, and without warning, his brain seemed to turn over. The plains of Manchuria, the stark little house at the mercy of the sun and the wind and the dust, the hovering tanks, even the small grave in the corner of the doctor's compound, were gone. In this city of power, of exultant prosperity, only the impression of his success remained. Glamourous, it waited for him. Until now he had been uncertain whether he should return.

Then at last they were in their room at the hotel, and

he was clasping Hester in a long embrace, trying to bind himself into that intimacy so suddenly snapped the night of their mutual grief.

But Hester broke the embrace. "Your mother is very frail," she said. "You'll see when you get home."

He did see. His mother old and delicate, constantly importuning him to remain in America. Hester, still not wholly recovered, silently waging the same battle. He felt himself intimidated by their imperious frailty.

"It isn't just that I *want* to go back," he told himself. "Suppose I do stay here, how shall I take care of them? Mother's extravagant, and Hester's used now to the ease of the rich. Kin and *amah* have taken care of her so long, she's forgotten how much you have to do for yourself in America."

He would have to start in at the bottom here. When he had said to one or two old friends that he was thinking of staying at home, immediately he had lost standing with them. They discounted the value of his foreign experience, so far as business in America was concerned; made him feel that he would be at a disadvantage starting in now. But when he mentioned his position abroad, then he had prestige among them. "You're lucky, Steve," they said. "Look how we slave."

And then, when in his pleasure in their companionship, he forgot and began to tell them in detail of his experiences they grew impatient, wanting to get back to their work. They hadn't time for an idler like himself. It made him crave the dignity his own work gave him. In that lack of integral participation in his country, a sudden nostalgia for the East swept him. He remembered an early morning, with the sun rising over the *kaoliang,* and his own shadow as he had seen it, fabulous and enormous in the golden light, silhouetted on a harvested field. In remembrance he felt big with importance, having

164

Manchuria as his background. He loved Manchuria, but that at least must be given up for Hester.

On their return to New York, Mr. Swaley asked to see Stephen's wife. Passing through the door of the great building Hester whispered:

"I feel so small. As if nothing that happened to us could be of any real importance; the way you'd feel—well —if you jumped into Niagara."

Stephen hardly noticed what she was saying, wondering why the director had asked him to bring Hester.

To come into the director's office was like being taken up on to a high mountain—the riches of the world spread out at their feet. "See," said Mr. Swaley, leading Hester to the window, "the sun's going down, but it never sets on our business. Well, now, over in China," there was a flourish of his white manicured hands, "why, there's the sun and our business." There was also a flourish in his voice. "Doesn't it stir your patriotism, Mrs. Chase, America's economic empire? A rich empire. New citizenship of the world. Fine, isn't it?" he added.

Stephen, standing at the next window with the instructor, who had given him his first lessons in foreign trade, thrilled to the words. But Hester stared intently at the city.

"I was trying to locate the opera-house," she said finally. "You can't tell me where it is, can you, Mr. Swaley?"

"Well, no, I can't." Confound her, was she too cold to be moved by riches?

"Look," he said, "there's the last of the sun. Don't you like to think it's rising now over your little home in Manchuria?"

He heard the sharp intake of Hester's breath. When he looked at her, her mouth was set in a studied smile.

Proudly, it seemed, she tried to conceal the anguish which her eyes betrayed.

"Umph." So this is why Chase has been dodging a final commitment to return. Manchuria will have to be given up, if we get him. A lot of fuss over a still-born baby. Heard she was a musician. They're an emotional lot.

He drew closer now, a note of appreciation in his voice.

"Mrs. Chase, we are not ignorant of the part you've played in your husband's work. We're not forgetting it. Your kind of woman would never wreck her husband's career. And Chase has a great opportunity. He's considered one of our most promising men.—I wish we could tell you where you are to be stationed when you go back, but it's against the policy of the Company. You see we have to be something like a standing army, each one ready to sacrifice for the good of the whole. However, I promise you one thing, Mrs. Chase," his voice carried a delicate note of sympathy, "I will personally guarantee that you won't be sent to Manchuria. That, we wouldn't ask of you. It's lovely in southern China, Mrs. Chase."

Stephen, trying to catch the drift of their conversation, felt a warm glow. How kind the director was. He was actually asking Hester where, if she could choose, she would most like to live in China. But suppose she should refuse right here to go back? What a relief that, before Hester could speak, Director Swaley should remember his wife's message.

"Why, I nearly forgot, Mrs. Chase," he said suddenly. "I don't know what my wife would have done to me if I had. She told me to be sure and remember her to you. She's so sorry that she is sailing to-morrow for Europe, for she wanted to see you."

Then the interview was over, and Hester and Stephen found themselves passing out through the door of Director Swaley's office.

"Well, what do you say?" Stephen began eagerly the

166

minute they were out of ear-shot. "You know, Hester, I've looked around a bit and it wouldn't be easy to start here at home. Five years out of my profession. Not much chance of getting in again there. Business abroad doesn't count here as experience, they all say." He went on, "The day the director took me out to lunch, some of the men were talking about the fellows who had left the Company. It seems the director likes to keep track of them. Hardly a one of them doing as well as if he had stayed with the Company. And, Hester, I guess they're going to give us insurance. It would be a great relief to me. I've never told you, but I haven't any insurance, it costs so much out there. And of course we'll get a pension if we stick. Seems a pity to throw it all away. All we went through, gone for nothing, just as we're making good."

Hester could hardly think, Stephen talked so much, the director had talked so much. Until now her course had been crystal clear to her. In all the days since the baby's death, Stephen's happiness had not concerned her; her separateness remained through the long weeks in the hospital on her return to America, and through the period of convalescence when she had lived only in music, submerging herself in the beauty of sound. Remote and hostile were her husband's interests.

But now as he pleaded with her, the intention of following her own desires was gone. If she opposed Stephen, he might stop loving her. Once more her life fused with his, and his happiness became her necessity.

Stephen walked at her side, anxiously watching her face for some sign of encouragement. But she had turned away from him. Suddenly she stepped eagerly forward.

"Hester, the traffic! Remember you are on Fifth Avenue." He drew her back.

The lights changed. Hester plunged forward again, he following, dragged along in her impetuous progress. "I won't stop you, Stephen, just as you are making good."

He had an actual physical sensation of release as if a rope at which he strained had given away. Freedom to follow his career, unhampered. An inflooding of love claimed him—and trust. Sometimes, since his return, he had suspected that Hester was using her frailty unfairly to coerce him. He had wronged her. He felt remorseful and tender and gay.

"Let's take a bus," he cried, "and ride all night."

Although it was not morning, it was late when they came back, alone on the top of the bus. He put his arm around Hester as the bus rocked and tipped, plunging along the lighted way. Hester felt the old bliss and safety in resting against him. Mysterious union was again hers. It did not matter at this moment, even if the physician's darkest prophecy came true and she had no other children. Or even that she must be deprived of music.

"Hester," said Stephen, breaking his difficult reserve, "it's my work really, why I want to go back, not the other things I said. There isn't anything very heroic about business. Yet sometimes I feel it's the stone the builders rejected. It stands at the head of the corner of so many things—at least in China. Like the little lamps the Company sells that I thought of."

"They ought to have put your name on the bottom of the lamps, like a Chinese chop," said Hester.

"Well, no," answered her husband, "not in a corporation. You learn to take pride in just fitting in. But sometimes," he added, a little shyly, "it gives me an awful kick to know I thought of them. I can't quite explain, but once I came into town at night and saw a little girl walking down a dark street carrying one of the lamps. And, well, I don't know—it made me feel useful and—I like to keep on introducing them."

The next morning Stephen felt invulnerable, and of importance in the scheme of things until his return to the

168

office, where he didn't seem to be half so important as he had been the afternoon before. Swaley took most casually his going back, as if he had known it all the time. "We're sending you to the Central China district. Let's see. The date of your sailing . . . your three months at home are up on the tenth. Ah, there are two ships sailing around that time from San Francisco. One the first, one the eleventh. Well, how's the first? Get you to China, let's see, about the beginning of April. That suit you all right? When you reach Shanghai, they'll tell you where you're to be stationed."

PART TWO

I

IT WAS spring when Hester and Stephen first came to the rich valley of the Yangtse—China's storehouse of food.

"Oh, look! It's like walking in green pastures beside still waters," cried Hester, as they sat on the deck of the comfortable British steamer which was taking them part-way up the great river to their station. "Such quiet! I didn't know a landscape could be so quiet." Fascinated, she gazed out over the valley which, after thousands of years of cultivation, had lost all the wildness of nature and become man's intimate dwelling-place. Level as a floor, it lay under its bright green carpet of rice, pat-terned into squares by the straight lines of the dike paths bordering the paddies. Gnarled and stunted mulberry trees and lacy bamboos stood in studied groups, furnish-ing it. Mountains shorn of trees, clipped to even smooth-ness, hemmed it in. Crossing the flat surface, long still canals—water without movement lying between flat even banks.

Hester touched Stephen's arm. "Stephen, I feel that if we move, we'll shatter it. It looks as if the earth had been brought to its fulfillment. Everything is perfected. There isn't a weed, as far as you can see. There isn't an inch of land that does not seem to have some purpose. Does it make you feel that way, Stephen?"

"A little," answered Stephen, "since you speak of it, or perhaps because I know how full the valley is of people. They say two hundred millions live in what's called The Valley—more than in all America. It makes me feel if you put another person into it, it would be like throwing a monkey-wrench into a machine."

"But they do, all the time, don't they?" asked Hester.

Stephen smiled. "Rather! Having sons is their obsession.

"The new manager's good, isn't he?" he added, abruptly changing the subject. "Not much like old Skinflint. The men call him 'The Gentleman.' He told me the reason they are giving me this particular station is because the territory is all run down. They expect me to build it up —make the people buy oil. It's a compliment."

"Yes, and I'm proud of you."

"Well, hello there! So this is where you are, tucked up into a corner by yourselves."

"Join us, Look," said Stephen to the stout man who had addressed them.

"Couldn't do that," Look replied. "I'm for having a little get-together of all of us before I leave. Coming to my station pretty soon now. We're all in the smoking-room. Come along.

"Seems like old times to see you around, Steve," he went on as they walked together down the deck. "It certainly is a good idea, this new scheme to get the managers together once a year, isn't it? Improve the spirit among us all right, all right. Too bad you didn't

170

get in in time for the conference. What time did you two get aboard last night? Didn't see you. I was out on a party. Pretty late myself."

They had come to the door of the smoking-room and Stephen had not yet found an opportunity to speak.

"Suppose you two haven't met them all, have you?" said Look. "Girls and boys, meet Steve Chase and his wife. And you two—this is the Yangtse bunch. This is Mrs. Look. Here's Burnham and his new bride. Brave man, Burnham, taking a girl to Chungking. Hawley's boats only run in the summer. Never expected an old-timer like Burnham to do a thing like that. May happen to any one now. Over there in the corner are the Chestertons. Going to Hankow—the metropolis-dwellers they are—and the three little Chestertons. Those fellows at that table drinking at this hour of the morning are the bachelors. The rest of you can introduce yourselves. Steve, here, and I are the new ones. We ought to be seen not heard, but I'm not that kind."

Stephen was silent, feeling more and more the honor of being a manager. The rest were all men much older in the Company. He, Look and Kendall, the only younger men who had main stations. For a moment he thought of Kendall starting this morning for Manchuria.

"Listen to them," said Mrs. Chesterton, pointing to the men, "they are already talking business."

"We've got to get after those interior points," Hester heard Chesterton say. "Look at the richness of this valley. Biggest potential market in the world. That was the whole tone of the conference."

"You'd think they'd get your husband or Joe·Burnham to tell them about America." Mrs. Chesterton turned with a smile to Hester. "But they're all the same. They eat, sleep with the business. Perhaps it's natural," she added thoughtfully. "The Company keeps them on their toes every minute."

Hester looked at these men, known to her only by reputation. Chesterton seemed to fit his part—sound, cautious, conscientious. Look she had thought of as a gay human kind of person. Instead he seemed to her merely noisy. Burnham—she wasn't altogether certain what she thought of him, but she knew she liked his wife.

Suddenly it struck Hester that most of these men were married and doing well with the Company. Always before she had felt that Stephen was a little handicapped because of her. A sweet sense of belonging to this group filled her. She had her place! As the women chatted together, she began to realize that Stephen's position endowed her with honor. She was a bit of a personage in the Company—a manager's wife.

"We're getting in," said Mrs. Look. "I'll have to get our things together."

Every one rose now, going out to the deck.

"I always think this valley looks like the Garden of the Lord," said Mrs. Chesterton. "Just look at it—as if no one could ever want."

As she spoke the steamer turned down-stream, making its dock. Stepping between Hester and Elsie Burnham, taking an arm of each, Chesterton said, "Come along, I want to show you something I'll bet you've never seen." He hurried them to the deck below.

"Look at the crowd over there on the landing," cried Elsie Burnham.

Clinging to every stanchion, hanging to every available beam and cross-beam, and to the railings of the covered pontoon, were men.

"It's like a forest of monkeys," she added. "What does it mean?"

"Carrying coolies after a few coppers," explained Chesterton. "Better stand back out of their way."

A few feet of water was still swirling between the pon-

toon and the ship, when figures shot out from the clinging, struggling human mass, hurtling through the air,
catching at the deck railing, dropping on the deck. Up on
their feet in a minute, struggling with one another,
snatching at the passengers' luggage.

"*Ai yah*," a woman screamed.

"Ease her off a bit," came the voice of an officer. "A
confounded coolie's missed his jump."

"Here, take that, you brute," some one called out.

A Chinese soldier raised the butt of his gun and hit a
man who tried to yank a bundle from him. The half-
naked yellow men crowded around Hester and Elsie.
Elsie gave a little scream. Hester stifled one.

"Here, let's make the stairs—get on the top deck again,"
said Chesterton. "Just wanted you to see it."

"What does it mean?" persisted Elsie, as they reached
the order of the first class.

"The surplus of the valley," said Chesterton, drawing
them into a group of their own people, Look's assistants
and their wives who had come aboard to greet them.

"The boat's stopping an hour," said a young woman,
whose clothes Hester recognized were as much out of style
as those she had worn before she went to America. "Do
show us what you brought from home. I've brought the
local tailor, so he can copy your things."

The women were sitting on the couch and the bed in
Hester's cabin when a Chinese in a soiled silk gown
opened the door and walked in.

"Tailor, you b'long listen at door," the girl accused
him.

"No b'long, missie. Always b'long look see key-hole.
S'pose all right. Enter!"

"Oh, what a pet!" she cried as Hester took from her
steamer trunk an afternoon dress she had bought in New
York. "May I try it on?" Grasping the dress eagerly, she

173

had it on almost before Hester had given her consent.

"Why, she's pretty!" thought Elsie Burnham. "I hadn't realized it before, she looked such a frump in those dreadful clothes. Poor thing!" She rushed away, returning with an armful of her own dresses.

"There," she cried, dumping them into the young woman's lap. "I'm your size. Put these on."

The girl's cheeks flushed. She tried on one after the other, getting more excited, thrusting the tailor out into the passage while she changed, then back again to study another gown.

"Now, look see, tailor. Can do?"

"I savee, missie. B'long number one tailor." He took a dirty fashion-plate from a bundle. "Have got this side, all same."

"Let me see," said Mrs. Chesterton skeptically. "It's a year old," she said to him. "You mustn't make them like that!"

"Oh, tailor!" all the women cried in unison.

"I do ploper," responded the little man, undismayed by the feminine reproach.

"He'll never get them right!" The girl's eyes were wistful as she surveyed herself in a clinging chiffon. "What wouldn't I give to get into a shop again!" She slowly let the dress slip to the floor.

Elsie Burnham stood silent for a moment. Then she thrust the coveted dress into the girl's arms.

"Tell you what you do," she said impulsively. "Take it along with you, then he'll get it right. When you're through, you can send it to me."

"Really?" The girl gave a delighted squeal. "Well, I shouldn't, but I'm going to. Wait until you've been in the interior for a while and you'll have no conscience about such things. But I promise I'll get it to you before there's any chance of summer floods, and the boats can't get up to your station."

"Come, girls, the steamer's leaving," called Look from the deck. "We've got to get off."

An hour later, as they steamed through the smiling valley, Elsie Burnham and Hester paced the deck together.

"Tell me honestly," said Elsie, slipping her arm through Hester's, "shall I be all right up there? I think I'm going to have a baby. I haven't told Joe. I'm sure he wouldn't take me with him, if he knew. He doesn't think a woman can stand things, but I can. Though there's the baby to think of."

Hester squeezed her hand, for a moment unable to speak. It was too sudden—this old ache of her breasts, her arms. Afterward she reproached herself. She had told the girl that she would be all right, that there would be a mission doctor there. Did it mean that if she had it to do over, she would have stayed with Stephen last winter? Surely not.

Farther and farther, into the very heart of the green valley, the steamer took them; at every big city their group grew smaller, as this and that one went away to his station. At last Stephen and Hester were alone. At Hankow they had changed to a smaller steamer which went up the branch of the Great River to the city that was to be their station. Deeper, deeper into the heart of China they went.

At the end of the second day, to the left of them, standing on ground built high above the green sea of rice, they saw in the fading light the shadowy forms of oil tanks. Stephen could not hide his excitement—four tanks giving mute but eloquent testimony to the great business of which he was to take charge. His was a vast domain. Now at last, a disciplined mature man nearing thirty, he had his own territory, could use his pent-up power of initiative.

Nearer came the steamer. A pontoon, used in the high-

175

water season as a landing-place for unloading oil tankers, now lay useless on a sand-spit. Under a bridge connecting the sand-spit with a gate in the wall surrounding the tanks ran a tiny arm of the river. Like a moat and drawbridge they appeared, enhancing the look of strength of this fortress of big business.

Hester drew close to Stephen. "Stephen, aren't you glad we don't have to live there?" she asked, pointing to the house under the shadow of the tanks.

"Well, I'm responsible for them just the same," he answered.

Darkness came quickly, like a pall let down from the gray sky. Drawing nearer, on a level with their eyes, was the low-lying dim gleam of the capital city of the province. The steamer swung round, making dock. Out of the shadows of the lighted pontoon, like bats suddenly disturbed, shot the flying forms of the coolies to the bright decks of the steamer.

"Keep close to me, Hester, so the coolies can't separate us."

As they paused at the gangplank, he noticed in the medley a northerner, bigger of build than these southerners—a little dog in his arms. Why, it was Li Tsu! It was Kin!

Kin thrust the dog into his arms and Li Tsu barked, almost shaking himself out of Stephen's hold in his eagerness to lick his master's face.

For a moment the crowd stopped its jostling. "*Ai yah,*" they cried.

Why had Kin come back? He had said he would not. What had struck the old fellow? Was it "friend pidgin"? Suddenly it occurred to Stephen as strange that Kin should have known where to find him.

"How did you know you would find me here?" he asked.

"Two moons I have known," answered Kin.

The grapevine telegraph, of course, Stephen said to himself. But two moons—two months? Then, the Company had known before he left New York that he was to come here. Swaley had deliberately withheld the information from him. The unnecessary discipline irked him, the tap on the shoulder, reminding him that, managership or no managership, he had no will of his own in the Company.

They had stepped from the gangplank now and two young men came toward them. "I'm Boynton," said the older of the two. He turned to his companion, "And this is Fenton."

These then were his assistants. He had power over these men, even as the boss had had power over him. The thought eased Stephen of his resentment over Swaley's withholding from him his destination, treating him as if he were a bit of inanimate Company equipment without will or individual needs.

"Hope you don't mind a Chinese city," said Fenton, taking Hester's arm. "We've only got to go through a couple of streets. The *hong* is right on the edge. Not quite used to it myself. Just out from home."

"I'm an old hand," Hester assured him. But she was not prepared for that city. Nor was Stephen. Familiar only with the cities spread out on the great plain, with their wide dusty streets, he had not conceived of a city so close pressed with humanity. Single file, the four went through the narrow alleys, the huts so near on either side that the white people felt themselves walking in a corridor between two lines of stalls which spilled their crowded life into the passageway. The air hardly seemed air, so laden was it with ancient odors, never quite blown away. Over candles, over chimneyless lamps, over lamps with chimneys, men leaned, stitching shoes, stitching clothes, weaving mats, weaving cloth. Women helped, or sat in low chairs in the débris of the work, or on the edge of the

177

street, babies at their breasts. Children pushing the babies away, pulling at the breasts, children everywhere like flotsam cast up by the feet of men. Men toiling like animals, carrying heavy loads, carrying men in chairs, trotting between shafts.

As they came to a halt before an iron-studded gate, Fenton spoke to Stephen.

"Look at that lamp of ours on that fruit vender's stand! Couldn't be more Western, could it? And yet it looks Eastern here, doesn't it?"

Stephen glanced at the lamp burning dimly like a candle, the wick crusted over so that it flamed only at one point. It *was* Eastern. The boy straight from home was right. How strange to him, its creator, to whom it had always been an instrument wherewith to alter the East. Of course, all the lamp needed was cleaning, but Fenton's fancy stuck in his mind.

Some one from inside unbarred the gate, and they filed into the compound. Across a hard-packed, clean-swept space of earth stood the hong—the House of Business.

"What a curious building," exclaimed Hester.

"Yes," said Boynton cheerfully. "It's a Chinaman's conception of a foreign house. It turned out a hybrid. His whole idea seemed to have been height. He just took a Chinese ancestral home and piled the rooms from the four sides of a court one on top of the other, called it a foreign hong, and we rented it. 'The Narrow House' I believe the Chinese call it."

From where they stood the length of the hong was enhanced, its width narrowed. Lights shone from the windows, showing the galleries encircling every floor, stairs ascending from gallery to gallery. They entered the hall that ran the length of the building. It, like the galleries, had stairs leading straight up to the next story. Down them now came the outgoing manager, Jenkins.

"At your service," he said laconically to Stephen. "Your office," and he led them into a room on the right of the hall, then out again and up the bare stairway. The sound of their steps echoed and reechoed in the great building.

"Junior apartments here," he went on, as they reached the long hall on the second floor. "Fenton's at one end, Boynton the other, and you've got the whole top floor. I'm staying with Fenton until I turn over the business to you. Now you know it all," he ended with bored indifference.

"Thanks a lot," said Stephen. "Don't bother to come up. Kin here seems to know the way. Good night."

"There's a party going on over at the consulate," Boynton called after them, "in honor of Jenkins. You're invited. It's just next door."

"Give us ten minutes," Hester answered, leaning over the banister, seeing his upturned face. How strangely intimate it seemed; these men so near, all of them in the same house, with their work and their personal desires. She supposed she was still held in the grip of that isolation of the house on the plain.

Hand in hand, Stephen and Hester made a quick tour through the high narrow rooms in their apartment. Oddly familiar, the chairs and the tables, identical in shape and design with those in the low brick house, their first home, identical with those in the house on the plain, their second home. Big and unwieldly in those houses; small and shrunken in these high-ceilinged rooms.

From the living-room windows at the narrow end of the house, they looked into the lighted windows of the consulate. Across the space between came white voices singing.

"Listen! There aren't many women here, are there?"

"How do you know?"

"Don't you hear how the men's voices predominate?"

"Well, maybe so," Stephen answered, moving about the room, humming like an unmusical bumblebee in his contentment.

Hester wandered from window to window, looking down on the city which hemmed them in at the back, crossing the room, looking down on the river filled with junks which hemmed them in at the front.

"It's like two cities and they creep right up to us. Stephen, what's that? That hollow beat, beat? I've never heard it before."

Stephen came and stood at her side.

"Haven't you? It's a part of every Chinese city. But, of course, you've never lived in one. It's men beating out paper money for the dead. Often they work all night."

"In a city like this, I should think there would be no money for the dead unless they robbed the living."

The crowd was still singing when they entered the dining-room of the consulate. As the house-boy swung the door wide, ushering them within, with one accord the thirty-odd people seated around the table jumped to their feet, raised their glasses, singing:

"For he's a jolly good fellow, for he's a jolly good fellow!"

"Who's a jolly good fellow?" some one shouted into the din.

It was Fenton, flushed with wine, evidently thinking he was the cheer leader at a college football game. With a sweeping movement of his hands, he led them into a cheer:

"Chase, Chase, rah, rah!"

Hester looked at Stephen anxiously. Had those years apart crippled his spirit, making it impossible for him to be one with a crowd? Had they crippled her too? Oh, no, she would not have it so.

They all began singing, "Mrs. Chase is a jolly good

180

fellow!" Again that sensation she had had on the steamer as she sat among the wives of the managers. She was important, she had her place. The commotion subsided and Hester was seated at the right hand of the host. How nice to be a member of a community once more. How nice they all looked.

II

AT THE first glimmer of daylight men and boys moved over the valley floor. Not a moment could be wasted, if three crops were to be harvested in the year. A few weeks ago, these men and boys had stood in the black ooze of the paddies, transplanting each blade of rice from the seed-beds. Forty, fifty days thus saved. Now kneeling in the slush of the flooded paddies, painstakingly the peasants weeded the young rice.

Women and girls who had carried in the warm resting-place of their bosoms the eggs of the silkworms, now that they were hatched laid them on trays, and went into the gloom of the mulberry groves, gathering leaves to feed them. Others went to the narrow valleys which lay like long rooms between the mountains, picking the tender new leaves of the tea shrubs. Painstaking and slow was the labor. Each green tea shoot carefully detached, adding its minute trifle to the tons of tea needed.

The toil of the city began—a city of no beasts or machines. In all the valley floor, only a few animals remained, animals needed for plowing the fields. In the cities there were no beasts of burden—beasts of burden eat too much; grass is needed for the fires of man, grain for his food. Even then there is not enough.

This morning from thousands of huts, the men poured. Long lines of them, poles across their shoulders, buckets suspended from the poles' ends, carried to the green valley the night-soil of the city. Conserved in vats the night-soil, later to be used to fit the land for its excessive fruition, in order that it be not exhausted in this, the fortieth century of its use.

Out toward the river, then back into the city, moved another long line of men carrying water. Water is precious, portion it out meagerly. Be not guilty of the sin of using too much. Otherwise, after death penance must be done. The woman who washes her clothes, tipping her tub so that a little water suffices, attains merit. Only the barbarians are wasteful of it. Even those who talk the Western religion, are guilty in the matter. *Ai yah,* they say they are not rich, but how shall we believe them? They wash their clothes before they are soiled, wasting water! *Ai yah!* Wash their bodies every day, wasting water! Sixty carries of water daily to the poorest of them! Poor!

In the water-shops men thrust a few twigs into the clay stoves under the water-kettles. Now the customers began trickling in. Two *cash'* worth of boiling water to fill the teapot, a *cash* for a steaming cloth to wipe the face. In the tea-shops, too, customers were appearing, many buying bowls of hot water, with a few tea-leaves, others only the hot water.

The early morning sun touched the Narrow House, making it glow like a long bar of silver. Charged like a magnet it was for all the city—charged with buying power. It was important news that a new master had come to it last night. The going-away master had not the *dauli.* Was this new and fabulously rich master a keeper of custom?

A coolie from the near-by chair hong stopped at the shop of the seller of hot water. He snuffed out his cigarette, placing the butt behind his ear for future use.

182

"I bring a little news. I have talked with his servant. For five years he has served him. He says he is gentle."

Stephen was awakened by a bugle call—the spirited Western taps, only slow and languid as the East, itself, the notes slipping one into the other, slurring, blurring. It seemed to have gone on for a very long time before Stephen awoke to full realization that just outside the hong some one with untrained lips was attempting to play a foreign bugle. He went to the window. On the bund, a Chinese soldier walked back and forth in his cloth shoes, strutting like a small boy proud of his uniform, proud of his horn.

Stephen looked at Hester. She stirred in her sleep, drawing her brows together as she always did when any sound disturbed her. Slipping into his clothes, he tiptoed from the room and down to his new office.

Jenkins, who had sat at his window the few remaining hours of the night after he had returned from the dinner-party, heard Stephen's step, and sneered cynically. "Fool, thinks he is somebody in the Company." Well, he supposed he'd made a fool of himself, too. He put out his hand; here, almost in his youth, he could not hold it steady. Perhaps if it hadn't been for those months marooned in that launch. . . . This damn country had done for him. He flung his hatred against it for destroying him.

The hong awoke. First the coolie of Fenton, the number three master, the least in importance, arose, lighted the fire in the three masters' stoves, put the kettles on for morning tea, serving Boynton's and Jenkins' coolies when they appeared in the inverse order of their importance. Then all three, their cloth shoes kicked off at the heel flip-flopping as they walked, carried pots of tea to their masters, the house-boys.

183

"Ai," the house-boys sucked in the hot tea. "This servant of the new master. He is an outside man. It is not good that he stay among us, taking our rice."

"We bring you news," said the number three master's coolie, "the new master sits thus early in his office."

"Ai yah!" exclaimed the house-boys.

They put on their long gowns over their short inner coats, tied their trousers neatly around their ankles with black bands, and went to their duties about the hong. For such a master, all must be in order. *Ai yah, mei yu fatsu,* it cannot be helped.

Breakfast was over. The gate at the back of the compound opened and shut. Three cooks, baskets upon their arms, sauntered leisurely forth toward the market-place. Each went alone, except the number one master's cook. Because of his importance, a little "learn pidgin cook," a mere child, trotted docilely at his heels carrying the market basket. Long was the market hour—the fish vender, the keeper of foreign goods, the fruit vender, all must ask, "What of the *dauli* of the new master?"

The door to the offices now began opening and shutting. The shipping men came, the accountants, the interpreters; dressed in long silk gowns, some of them; dressed in long cotton gowns, others of them. Short fragile-looking southerners with faces like Dante. As they sat on high stools before their desks in the back office, the curve of their shoulders beneath their smooth-fitting gowns was as uniform as the curve of a grove of young willows under a strong wind—the scholar's stoop, mark of breeding in China. One by one, on some pretext they made excuse to enter the office of the manager.

Then for a little the door into Stephen's new office ceased to open and shut. Stephen glanced at the wall clock opposite his desk. Ten o'clock.

"You'll find my report on the territory all here," said

Jenkins, throwing a bundle of closely written pages down on the desk. "As to Adviser Ho—you'll have to pretend to use him. He knows the Company's business from *a* to *z*— an agent once. The Company doesn't let him go, because the British Company would grab him if they did. But he doesn't know a thing about present business conditions in the province."

Without a heralding knock, the door opened and a Chinese entered, of necessity stooping, for he was tall— amazingly so for a Chinese. Six feet two at least, was Stephen's silent estimate. The heavy dove-gray silk gown falling to his heels did not suit him as it did his more delicately built countrymen. Indeed, it increased his masculinity, as the habit sometimes increases a monk's.

"I like that man," was Stephen's next reaction.

"Oh, hello, Ho!" Jenkins addressed the tall man in a careless tone, not bothering to rise.

"So this is Ho," thought Stephen with surprise, as he rose giving the eastern salutation. To his further astonishment, the visitor continued to stand, as if he were accustomed to do so in this office. Thoughtfully the new manager watched the little drama between the two men— Jenkins with his insolent superiority, Ho returning his insolence, although Jenkins was not aware of it. They were talking through an interpreter, who was carefully deleting the Chinese epithets and the familiar "you" from Adviser Ho's remarks.

"Tell that outside barbarian whose mother was a turtle, that I know nothing of the activities of the august merchants of the province," said Ho.

"Ah hem!" The Chinese interpreter settled his horn-rimmed eye-glasses more securely on his bridgeless nose. Stephen caught a glint of joy in the man's eyes as he sweetly interpreted. "He say, tell the honorable manager that he know nothing of Chinese merchant beesness. Each man veree close with his beesness."

185

Jenkins had brought this upon himself, but it made Stephen realize how necessary it was that his own first acts with the men of this province be correct. He knew too well that sudden stiffening of the Chinese into contempt. "They may not like me, but I intend they shall respect me," he determined, not knowing that Ho had already judged him.

When Ho went away, he had the knowledge he had come to gain. "This fair one with his strange yellow-brown eyes has the inner control. I shall not leave the employ of the Keepers of Light just yet, as I had thought. With this man, I can honorably contend."

At the top of the Narrow House, Hester moved about, her spirit feeling out its new abode. In this ramshackle building where the floors shook a little even at her light step, and each badly fitted window shut and opened with its own particular protestation, the many activities of the hong were manifested to her in continuous bits of sound. Doors shutting, opening, far down at the bottom of the well of the stairs; the cling, cling of a bell; *"Whei, whei?* —Who, who?" shouted into the telephone receiver; the voices of the Chinese; the voice of Stephen. Through every window, the city intruded its presence: stones tumbling about in a wooden box heralded the approach of a traveling food vender, the high squeak of wheelbarrows, a thousand tumultuous sounds.

Now she could hear the cadence of white women's voices . . . her neighbors, gathered in a knot below on the bund. Presently they would come to see her, taking the gallery stairs to avoid the offices. Last night they had told her they would come. Friendship.

Her neighbors were drawing near, crossing the floor of the second gallery. Now they were walking up the last flight of stairs; the thin soles of their pumps, gritty with the dust of the bund, rasped on the wooden treads.

186

Passing through the French window that gave on the gallery, Hester went to the top of the stairs, looking into the uplifted faces.

"Hello!" the women called up to her in chorus.

"We're 'most dead with the climb. You should have a lift," wheezed the comfortable wife of the customs commissioner.

"It's lovely to have another woman here. Lovely!" The consul's wife ran up the last steps, and put her arms around Hester.

They advanced, talking and laughing, Hester in their midst. She tried eagerly to give herself to them, telling them everything they asked, letting the intimacies of the tiny community pluck at her privacy. But she felt herself shut away—something held her aloof. "Because of my habits of solitude," she said to herself. "I'll learn how to mingle with them."

All day the word passed over the city. "The new master is worthy. He is a keeper of custom. An honorable adversary."

The seller of curios picked out a precious piece or two, added a few spurious ones, packed them carefully, tying them up in a dirty white cloth. To-morrow he would visit the new mistress. So did the seller of ancient embroideries. Junkmen, chair-bearers, petty merchants, had heard the news. Good people had come among them.

Early in the afternoon the great Ho went to see the city agent of the Keepers of Light. The two sat in the agent's inner office, while to the broad cracks in the thin partition many an apprentice's eye and ear were pressed. "He talks the custom," said Ho. Immediately the agent considered what old grievances against the Company he might present to this good manager. The apprentices slipped out to the tea-houses, carrying the news, "The great Ho says a keeper of custom has come among us."

At evening the accountants, the shipping clerks, the coolies of the hong, returning to their homes, were the last bearers of the good news.

In the fading light Kin sat on the top gallery outside the number one master's kitchen—his master's kitchen. This morning he had feared that the other servants would raise against him their resistance, driving him out, but now that the great Ho had made his master a worthy man in the eyes of the city, he, Kin, was too important for these underlings to send away. They were obsequious now, fearing he would bring in his own men. *"Ai,"* these servants should each pay him well, if he permitted them to stay. He could look down the flights of outside stairs, see any one who went into the number two, number three masters' kitchens. Nothing in the hong should be purchased without a good per cent. being paid to him.

"My teaching the master as we would our little children has brought reward; no longer has he the bare and uninteresting mind of the barbarian. Even the great Ho has found him worthy. It is well that I came again into his service. When no big position came to him in Manchuria, I left him. But now he is a big man. As for the missie, a woman, and thus stupid, unteachable, I must rule her before she grows too old. Old women are powerful. If only she would grow fat with well-being!"

A narrow alleyway separated the hong from the garden of Ho, beyond which lay the courts of the ancestral dwelling. From his vantage point, Kin could see the tile roofs and a glint of white walls. A little to one side, far back, the branches of a sweet olive tree stood above a roof line. Here, he had already learned, was the court of the old *tai-tai*, Ho's mother, ruler of Ho. Yes, old women were powerful. *Ai,* immediately he must plan the affairs of this household before missie gained too much control.

* * * * *

188

At eleven the next morning, the ority agent entered Stephen's office. His furled fan stuck out from the collar of his satin gown, rising like the end of a sword just behind his left ear. The day was exceedingly warm for early spring and, if the discussion became heated, he might need it before the encounter with this yellow-eyed, short-fingered one was over. All the way, with satisfaction, he had considered this visit. *Ai,* a keeper of the custom, was he? *Ting hao,* very good. A good game with a good man. But he had no doubt he could hoodwink the new manager. When had there ever been an outside barbarian equal to a man of the Flowery Kingdom in the matter of finesse, the rock upon which business is built? He had decided to take up that loss of last month.

Two hours later, as he walked away from the office fanning himself, he had respect for the new master. In this first skirmish of wits he had found that the pale washed-out-looking one had not a pale washed-out mind!

Deep and dark, it was. Ah, velvety, too, in its texture. He continued to enjoy the good points of Stephen's game. Not only had this new manager not torn away the mask of his adversary, he had worn a mask himself. *Ting hao,* very good. None of that shocking intimacy of most barbarians. *Ai yah!* Patience he has, too. Two hours, and I could not wear him down. Ah, well, another time. After others have contended with him, when he is a little discouraged.

With measured step, he passed over the hard-beaten earth floor of his shop into his inner room. He lay down behind the drawn curtains of his bed and slept. Enough had been done for to-day.

One by one, the agents from over the province came to the hong to do battle with Stephen. Bit by bit, they worked upon him, trying to wear him down, to find how good an adversary he really was.

189

Stephen was not always so successful as he had been with the city agent, but as the days went by, he found that those years on the plain had brought him knowledge, accumulated unconsciously, lying fallow in his mind during his stay in America, guiding him now through the maze of his testing.

And now an important thing began happening to him. Whenever he shut his eyes, whenever he let his mind idle for a moment, when he was dropping off to sleep, faces would appear before him—Chinese faces, all different. That sameness of agate eyes, folded eyelids, which had so bewildered him all the time he was in Manchuria, making him unable to distinguish character, was no longer there. Just as his reaction to Ho had been, "I like that man," not "I like that Chinese," his reaction to these faces appearing on the curtain of his eyelids was to character, not to cast of features. That agent from the south of the province—Lin, his name was. As Stephen lounged in his chair one evening after dinner, the man's character was suddenly revealed to him. In the afternoon, when he had talked with Lin, Stephen had not realized it, but now he knew that Lin was sly. He could not analyze his knowledge. Some subtle quality in Lin's lineless face made it furtive, not fearless like Ho's, nor humorously belligerent like Chen's. Yes, he'd have trouble with Lin. He made a mental note to watch him.

In a flash of intuition, he became certain, too, that Ho held the key to this territory, and could tell him much that would help him. If only he could make a friend of Ho! He resolved to take a long trip with the merchant, though Jenkins had said that Ho would not travel. So far Stephen had sought to avoid any clash of wills, but now he no longer feared to ask Ho, feeling certain that his suggestion would be accepted.

Planning the trip, Stephen determined to cut away his last prop; he'd leave Kin at home. He would no longer be nursed by his servant. In this illumination of the Chinese world, he knew Kin had always done this. Henceforth he should be plain house servant. Another thing— he would not take a book or magazine with him to clutter his mind with Western ideas. He must let his own world go, if he was to get the texture of the Chinese mind. Only so could he make a friend of Ho, and he must have Ho for his friend.

Two weeks later, Stephen and Ho sat on the deck of the Company launch. The trip had been peculiarly devoid of revelations. Barriers of reticence and caution are thick, holding mature men of the same nationality apart, but with these two of different race, the barriers were buttressed by their alien cultures.

Sitting in silence, as immobile as the tall Chinese at his side, Stephen was trying to free his brain of activity. To do nothing was the hardest thing he had had to learn—to let go his usual tension of mind and become passive. Tonight the desire to do something gnawed at him as hunger gnaws at the stomach. It was with the utmost difficulty that he held his mind closed to the things of his own world.

The sailors on the launch moved about, setting all to rights for the night; then one by one, attired in clean blue garments, they dropped into sampans, collected like a brood of chickens around the boat's stern, and went off to feast in the town. Now Adviser Ho spoke, opening the conversation with the usual bland formalities. Stephen felt defeated, bored, as he responded to these often repeated phrases so meaningless to him. Then Ho bent toward him, as if fearful that even the quiet waters around them might have ears, speaking very softly. Stephen's boredom vanished. His moment had come. Al-

191

though he only half comprehended the meaning of Ho's remark, one thing he did know—a gossamer thread was being extended to him, out of the closely wound ball of Chinese business methods, a cocoon-like growth of centuries. Stephen had a fantastic illusion that his fingers were reaching for that gossamer thread, but that they were too short to grasp it. To do so, they should be long like Ho's, spread out on his silk-clad knees.

Then he had it, grasped between his short fingers. Guilds, the concealed force in Chinese life, as in Chinese business! It was the thread that would unravel for him the cocoon. A guild of oil men, the ancient, secret, binding organization of the Chinese, now controlling this modern business of oil, though he had not suspected it, as it had for centuries controlled the business of silk, rice, tea. Even artizans had guilds.

The minutes passed. Let him be silent. Even though his silence might seem like incomprehension to Ho, it was better than to risk wrong speech. How much understanding was he supposed to declare? The cocoon unwinding. Ho, a retired merchant, but not therefore out of the stride of business, as he would be in America. Ho, the center of the guild, the most important oil man in the province. Perhaps of the oil men all over the country. . . . Hold on, don't unwind the cocoon too fast. The threads might get tangled. Guilds were not simple. Stop right there—Ho, the most important oil man in the province. And Jenkins had made him stand in his presence! Had not stood himself in greeting! And the Company had even been on the point of dismissing him!

Still Stephen dared not speak for fear of shattering the confidence between them. When at last he did, it was with the frankness with which he would speak to a fellow-countryman, knowing he could do this, because Ho was his friend. There was a chamber of friendship in

192

China where men removed their masks. He had entered it. Very simply he said:

"Teacher, will you help me?"

Adviser Ho answered him quietly. "This is a personal matter between us. The *tong ja* I will help, not the foreign Keepers of Light business."

"What you do for me, you do for the Company. The Company and I are one here. I am their servant." Stephen spoke the word proudly. "Because of the rudeness of one man——" He hesitated. "Surely the teacher understands that the Company would not have permitted this discourtesy, had they known—and Jenkins is leaving their employ."

But the dark look on the Oriental face beside him was not dispelled.

"The Keepers of Light walk not the true path. Watch my fellow-countrymen in your outer office. When their wages have been increased so many times—like that Jenkins—some reason will be found to let them go."

"But Jenkins failed!" cried Stephen. "He should go."

"The Keepers of Light owe him rice. We are all one family now."

"But look what the idea leads you to! That is why your government fails. You put your personal relationship before your duty." Stephen spoke impetuously now, risking that gift of friendship so seldom offered a foreigner.

"You look at business; we look at relationship."

"But one's duty! Surely it comes first," insisted Stephen.

"*Ai yah,* the Prior-born's duty!" Ho spread his knees far apart, so that the skirt of his gown fell between. He placed his long narrow feet, encased in their satin slippers, more firmly on the deck, then he spoke:

"Our two customs we put behind us now, so that we may see each other. Good? Not good? So that our hearts may speak the same words."

"Yes," said Stephen, "it is good."

A clue here, a clue there, of this and that agent, Ho now gave him, speaking softly so that the ears of the night should not hear. Some comprehension of the intricacy of life for every man in this ancient country came to Stephen. Each man entangled in clans, in guilds, grown more intricate through centuries, each man inheriting the intricacies of his father's and his father's father's life. And yet Ho trusted him enough to speak a little openly! He felt humbled and very proud all in the same moment.

Then of a sudden, intimacy was gone. Ho rose, dignified, aloof, formal, speaking again with conventional ceremony. For a moment, Stephen was dismayed. Had he offended? Then he perceived that this was courtesy— Ho was giving him back his personality intact, the mask of formality again adjusted as it had been before entering the secret room of friendship. One did not end an evening on a note of intimacy. The formalities which had seemed so banal at the opening of the conversation did not bore Stephen now. He saw their purpose—freeing them both from the embarrassments of intimacy. After a little, Adviser Ho went to his cabin.

If the new manager had thought that everything would be simple for him after that night, he soon found he was mistaken. That intimate moment with Ho was not repeated after their return.

But Adviser Ho came every morning now to the hong. After the clerks were in their places in the back office, with due ceremony he would come in his sedan chair, taking his place of honor at Stephen's left hand. In perfunctory fashion, he advised on routine matters of business. But Stephen understood that this was all Ho dared to do, involved as he was in the intricacies of Oriental life. It was his own hard luck, he told himself, if he could not work out a strong organization from the clues already given him.

No longer was Stephen outside as he had been in Manchuria, fumbling in the dark. Day by day he found himself exploring minds developed in a different school of thought than that in which he had been trained. Now he saw that "face" at which foreigners laughed was not a light thing, not something theatrical as he had imagined; essential in such intricate surroundings. Stephen began to speculate. Would not the complete loss of face, the surrender of dignity, be for the Chinese the great sacrifice, more to a man than the sacrifice of life?

It was mysterious and silent, this coming together of alien minds. He led now a secret inner life apart even from Hester. In confiding in her, translating his knowledge into Western thought, he might let slip the gossamer thread of understanding, or a listening ear might lose Ho to him for ever. Even their bedroom he now knew was a part of the huge whispering gallery of China. Hiding his new understanding behind a quiet reserve, he forced his mind down strange alleys of thought.

Stephen glanced up from the empty desk he was contemplating. So Ting had come, just as he had expected. It was he who had set the snares that had beguiled Agent Ting into coming. This man would not work. Well, Stephen was going to make him. Knowing now the rules of wearing the mask, he was going to change them a little like an artist who knows the laws of his art well enough to break them. He meant to make a thrust behind this man's mask.

Ting refused to be seated. He was a short thick-set Chinese, with a large paunch which gave him the effect of strutting. He was cross-eyed, and now in his excitement the gaze of his left eye seemed to wander off at its own will in a rakish, devil-may-care way.

"And once I thought that all the Chinese look alike!" was the passing thought in Stephen's mind, as he listened to Ting's words exploding like bombshells.

"For years I have set at naught the interests of my miserable self, making a mere pittance, striving night and day, selling thousands of the tins of the foreign oil, and now Prior-born accuses me of . . ." The agent stuttered, grew almost apoplectic. Did not this fool know that there was not such another agent in all the south of the province? No such fine credit as his? Ting's attitudinizing turned suddenly into a burst of real anger.

"I resign." He leaned near Stephen, shouting the words almost in his face.

"I say you cannot resign."

Ting's left eye shot up to an even higher angle, but the fireworks of his speech died away in sputtering. The barbarian telling him, the leading merchant of the south, that he could not resign. Final indignity!

"No," thundered Stephen, bringing his fist down on the table. He was venturing far. According to Chinese custom, by that bang on the table he had informed the agent that he was his master.

"Mr. Ting prattles about losing face. Face! What is the little outer mask stripped off, compared with the face Mr. Ting will lose if he resigns? A merchant of China who does not know how to sell. See, they will know, for I shall tell them." Stephen pushed a paper full of Chinese figures toward the agent.

Ting brought his left eye down to survey the paper. How had the foreign one learned all this? No other barbarian had known so much, where he sold, and where he did not.

"Resign, and to the Thousand Li Wall I will tell that the honorable Ting could not get business."

Did this insignificant barbarian know of the Oil

Guild? Ting regarded the white man with a degree of respect.

"Talk about resigning! It is I who should dismiss you," Stephen whispered across the desk. "But how could I think of doing so, when it would mean that you would leave this room without even the thinnest tissue mask over your naked heart? Go out now, Ting, chief merchant of the south of the province, and get me the business. And when in every one of these shops Mr. Ting is selling the foreign light, then he may come to me and resign with safety."

Ting folded his hands within his long sleeves, bowed gravely, murmured, *"Tai-pan, tai-pan,* manager, manager."

There was something of servility in his tone. He would go out, and he would exert himself like a barbarian. This foreign one knew how to ruin him, so that he could not live in this province. Never before had he felt respect for a barbarian, but he hated Stephen, too, for forcing him to energy, an exercise as terrifying to men of an old race as a child's activity to his elders.

The door closed upon him. Stephen dropped his grand manner. He had gone pretty far with cock-eyed Ting. He had thought for a moment his thrust had gone too deep, and that it would be necessary for Ting to resign. But he had had to take the risk in order to rouse the agent to energy; the head office was already demanding his dismissal and Stephen knew that if he were dismissed, Ho would regard it as a violation of the personal relationship. He could write the Company now that Ting would work. He personally would guarantee it.

That afternoon as he wrote the letter, a sweet sense of power possessed him.

There was a knock, the door swung open, and the engineer from the Company launch stood with a broken part of the engine in his hands.

197

"Tai-pan, it refuses to work."

Stephen in an instant had the parts in his hands, studying them. His knowledge of machinery told him what was wrong. There was nothing to do. This part would have to be discarded. There'd have to be a new one. He turned to give his order—a copy could be made at the ironmonger's in the city. Then he remembered. He could not make this small expenditure without the consent of the main office.

"Go now, manager of the machinery. I will attend to this," said Stephen.

When the door closed, he sat drumming on the desk with his fingers, hating to write the main office for permission to spend this small sum of money. A moment before he had felt the fine enthusiasm of the administrator. Now his house of cards had collapsed. He was only a clerk!

Again there was a knock. Fenton, of all people, that annoying boy who seemed to spend his time planning how he could get out of work.

"Would you mind," began Fenton, hesitating, for he saw that Stephen was in a black mood. "That trip I was to start on this afternoon—if I waited until after Sunday? Today there's a port picnic, and I'd like to be here Sunday, too."

"It can't be done," snapped Stephen, turning to get some papers out of the files.

Fenton looked angrily at Stephen's unresponsive back. Then, not daring to ask again, he went out.

"I might have given him his Sunday," Stephen thought with a secret sense of shame. "But he's always loafing on the job." Somehow with that command he had been released from his own humiliation. He had power over men. Fenton had to obey him. He did not know that some bit of common humanity went from him when he gave Fenton his orders. He only knew that he was beginning to make a good manager.

IV

.THE spring rice was harvested. Again the fields were plowed and flooded. Not the tiniest space of land at the head of the mountain valleys ignored—a field no larger than a man's head-cloth would bring forth its bowl of rice. Only the graves of the ancestors were not plowed, standing up like haycocks, but they would yield their rough grass for fuel. Now the fields were again ready and the rice stood thick in the seed beds. With the first streak of light men and boys walked in the black ooze of the paddies transplanting the rice. And so summer broke, forced into early abundance by the needs of the millions packed in the valley.

The highways of the valley—the river, the streams, the canals, there were no roads—were fair things to see. Through the long day flotillas of brown-sailed junks sailed upon them. So level was the valley floor that the low standing rice hid the shimmer of water, making it seem that the junks sailed through the green sea of rice. Now when the water was deep in river and canal was the moment of communication in the green valley, even as the winter had been in the north; now was the moment to supply the farthest village. Stephen was told to offer long credits, and the junks went weighted with the foreign oil. Thus was China drawn into world trade. Her progress hurried, the delicate balance of the green valley disturbed; native peanut oil standing unsold, replaced by the foreign product.

The heat, even now, lay like a blanket over the earth,

sapping the strength of white people. The white women were going away. But Hester was not going. It was unthinkable to her to leave Stephen.

The women, her neighbors, drifted in saying good-by, urging her again and again to go with them. "But the heat, Mrs. Chase. You can't guess how dreadful it is," they argued.

"All of you have children," answered Hester. "I have no reason to go."

With a sense of relief, she heard the last one go down the steps of the gallery.

Only a narrow alleyway separated the hong from the ancestral home of Ho, but the women of the two families did not mingle. Ho's mother hated the outside barbarians —bringers of new customs. She spat when she spoke of them, refusing to meet Hester, although her son desired it. But there was nothing harmful in the barbarian's money, so she did not oppose the intercourse between Ho and Stephen.

When Hester first realized that the two men were becoming friends, she thought she too might find friends in Ho's household among the women. Looking across the roofs to the sweet olive tree, spreading its pattern of leaves on the gray roof-tiles, she wondered if some time she might know that powerful woman, whose court was shaded by the great tree. One evening her quick ear caught, above the noises of the alley, a fragment of melody played on a strange instrument. It revived in her an old desire to find music in this country. She asked Stephen if he could get the song from Ho.

"It is nothing," said Ho, "one of the servants playing."

Then Hester asked Kin if he could get the song, but he did not seem to comprehend what she wanted. He did not tell her that when Ho had brought word of Hester's desire, the old *tai-tai* was very angry that the

200

white woman should thus intrude herself. For if Hester were to have the song, she must come to the great house, or the daughter-in-law who had played must go to the barbarian's house since the Chinese do not write their music, the listener remembering, rendering it again according to his own interpretation.

"This is what it has come to!" said the mother of Ho. "Admitting these barbarians to our city. Their curious ears would listen even at the inner courts. When I was a girl the officials would not allow them in the city."

As she talked, the *tai-tai* became more and more angry until the house was filled with her wrath. Slaves, servants and daughters-in-law alike fell under her anger, and none could please her while the anger lasted. Even Ho's head wife did not escape her displeasure. As for the young daughter-in-law—just a month in her house—who had played the song, the old *tai-tai* lashed her with her tongue.

"Exposing yourself to attention like a common woman! Wanton! I'll teach you!" And the *tai-tai* clapped her hands sharply for her own serving woman to come.

Although the *amah,* standing outside listening to all that was said, waited only long enough to have it seem that she came from the servants' quarters, the mistress rapped her sharply over the hand with her fan.

"Sluggard!" she shouted. "Worthless and lazy one! Call me the servants!"

When they came, she went with them to the court of the young daughter-in-law, herself seeing to the moving of the daughter-in-law's possessions to a court near her own. All day the wretched girl answered the call of her mother-in-law, bringing steaming towels for her face, bringing her pipe, bringing sweetmeats, trembling with fear as the *tai-tai's* anger mounted, while she whipped the great household with the lash of her tongue.

When evening settled down over the city and the birds

twittered their night call in the sweet olive tree, the old woman's anger left her and she dozed in her straight chair, her black brows drawn together, her full face, despite its coating of white rice powder and rouge, a vulgar common face, very different from the delicate countenance of her daughter-in-law.

The young girl, near by in her own quarters, slept too, but she was alert even in her sleep, fearful lest her mother-in-law call her and she not hear. The servants and the slave girls sat about in watchful ease, like people living in a country of sudden storms, snatching rest when they can. An old man went out of the gate at the back, in his hand a lacquered basket. He was walking quickly for so aged a man.

"Open, open," he called, knocking on the door of a hut.

The woman who pulled back the door was as old as himself and as poorly clad. But her face bore the mark of breeding, intensified by the fine etching of suffering. She spoke quietly but with a note of authority in her voice.

"Ts Dong, you are late to-day."

"Mei yu fatsu, tai-tai, it could not be helped. The old one's eyes have been everywhere to-day. Only now that she sleeps could I leave. Days like this did not come when the honorable one was our mistress."

Once, indeed, this woman had been mistress in the great house, honored first wife of Ho's father. But she had borne him no son. So when his concubine, mother of Ho, had desired not only the place of honor in the house, but the putting away of the head wife, he had yielded. For many years now the first lady had lived in this hovel, attended only by the old servant appointed by Ho's father to serve her.

"It was all on account of these Keepers of Light," Ts Dong explained. "The old one was angry over their impertinence. And even the great Ho, gentle as he is, is annoyed that this one he calls friend should seek to penetrate into the secret entirety of a man's house."

Hester would have remained in ignorance of all this had she not, a few days later, heard children in Ho's garden singing at their play, and summoned Kin to listen so he would know what she wanted this time.

But Kin never brought her the song. At first he said, "Wait a little," and when she again asked him, he feigned ignorance of her meaning. Then Hester, whom long ago Kin had taught the futility of beating her will against his passive resistance, knew quite as certainly as if he had told her, that she was excluded from the house across the way.

Still she hoped she might know Ho, of whom Stephen talked so much. It was at the beginning of the summer that her husband sought to include her in the friendship. He had waited to do this until he knew Ho very well, for he did not wish to repeat that mistake he had made in Manchuria.

On the day appointed for his call, gravely respecting the custom of his friend, Ho came through the door of the living-room, bending his great shoulders, bowing gravely to Hester, not dishonoring this good woman by raising his eyes to look upon her.

He took the tea Kin gave him, and nibbled at one of the foreign cakes. And when Stephen asked him where Hester could secure old bits of porcelain, he said that he himself would send the dealer with whom he dealt. Then from his long sleeve he took a bowl. Hester exclaimed over its color and shape which delighted her eye. When Ho held it again in his hand within his sleeve he moved his long delicate fingers over it, telling Stephen its shape was beautiful to feel.

Before he left, Ho stood for a time before a painting Hester's father had left her—a single stem of bamboo—

and the next day he sent his friend's wife one to companion it.

Stephen felt the visit had been a great success. His friend and his wife had many tastes in common! But this time Hester understood. She knew that, notwithstanding Ho's politeness, she did not exist for him in the things of the spirit. Depression crept upon her. This dwelling in alien minds made of her a gray ghost, brought an emptying away of her personality.

For some time now when Stephen's agents came to consult him, he had turned to Ho, asking him to make the Company's wishes plain to them. Then one day Ho said, "Send the agents to me first. The *tai-pan* can tell me whether he will grant their petitions. If not they will not lose face with the *tai-pan*. The *tai-pan* is a hard man, but he is a just one."

Often after that, when Ho spoke for Stephen, he softened his words without changing the meaning. And sometimes he added more than Stephen had spoken. He told the agents that the manager's heart was gentle; only his lips spoke sternly. Because of the organization, he was stern. It was his *dauli*. His relation to the Company was to him what the relationships of father to son, friend to friend, were to Chinese. He spoke thus because he did not wish Stephen to harm himself.

In other ways, also, it helped Stephen, this sending the agents to Ho. It saved him time, for each one of them, trying to wear him down in order to get more privileges from the Company, often contended with him for an entire day. And, as the weeks went by, he knew that he needed his time to find out and curb the "squeeze," if this illegitimate gain of every agent, clerk, shipping man, junkman, coolie in the employ of the Company was not to become so large that it would ruin the business. Especially were inroads increasing at the

204

oil tanks. Stephen and the white man who guarded them night and day waged a continuous fight against the slow dribbling away of the oil. Long ago, guards had been brought from another province, so that there would be hatred between them and the workers, and each would check the squeeze of the other. But now it seemed they were in league, for more than a little oil was going out secretly.

Increasingly, as Stephen felt out the Chinese mind, he discovered that the idea of squeeze permeated it. And he realized that the Chinese did not consider it dishonest. They had no sense of guilt about it.

He wished he could get some help from Ho on the matter. But even when they were alone, Ho gave him no clue. At last Stephen spoke openly. They were together in the closed-in tea-house in the center of Ho's garden, where they had formed the habit of sitting at the end of the day—the square table between them, teacups and cigarettes upon it. Here, better than in the office, they could talk. This tea-house with its fretted windows, the oiled paper panes changed by Ho for foreign glass, gave them a view of the whole garden—no unseen listening ears here to make them wary of speech. Stephen spoke of his suspicions, telling of his worry. He watched Ho narrowly. If his friend did not tell him directly, perhaps some faint expression of knowledge passing across Ho's face would indicate that his suspicions were correct. But Ho sat in contemplation, the lids of his eyes lowered, as the Buddha's eyes are lowered; his mouth, as usual, serene; his beautiful delicate hands, oddly feminine on this huge man, crossed inside his purple silk sleeves, as always when he was at rest. For a moment Stephen had the illusion that he had not spoken to Ho, only thought the words. Then he was filled with bitter disappointment. He had been rebuffed—and by his friend! What was the meaning then of this thing called "squeeze" so

lightly spoken of by foreigners? Something sinister behind it.

He pondered his friend's withdrawal from confidence,
more perhaps than he would have done, had he continued
to see Ho each day as usual; but the day after their conference, a message came, saying that Ho could not come
to the office as the old *tai-tai*, his mother, was ill. At first
Stephen worried lest he had destroyed the friendship.
Squeeze, he knew, was as a rule taboo as a subject of
conversation—had Ho made pretense of his mother's
sickness in order to declare indirectly the ending of their
relationship? The sickness of the honored mother was
the excuse most often given, in lieu of the correct reason,
when any one in the office wished to absent himself.

Then a second message came telling Stephen that the
old *tai-tai*, head of the clan, had died. Stephen knew that
this was so. Already, the wails of the two hundred-odd
members of the clan rose from the great house across the
way. Men passed in and out of the gates, dressed in white
robes of mourning, white shoes with red at the heels.
The red strips of paper at each side of the gate were taken
down, white ones put in their place.

Then a third time Stephen received a message from
Ho. One of the servants came bearing two flat packages of
white cloth which he presented to Stephen, mourning
for Hester and himself, invitation to enter the house of
Ho and wish the *tai-tai* safe passage to the other world.
But Stephen could almost hear the old lady's cane tapping
in angry dissent. No foreigner should enter her presence.
He knew, too, that Ho had invited them only out of
friendly courtesy and did not expect them to come. So he
sent regrets and a silk scroll to be hung in the ancestral
hall; bright blue with white characters, long enough to
reach from floor to ceiling. But he kept the bundles of
white cloth, tangible evidence of the great Ho's friendship.

During the days that followed, the days of the beating of the drum in the outer court at the arrival of each guest, and the days of the chanting of the priests opening up the way to the Western Heaven for the *tai-tai*, and for many days after, Stephen held this courtesy in his heart to assure himself that Ho still was his friend. Yet he did not wholly sense how significant had been Ho's act. This was a time of important ceremony in his friend's household, the most important until his own death, and there was much to be attended to. Also Ho was a superstitious man and many fears attended him, lest by neglect he omit some precaution against evil spirits and bring disaster on the family. There was, too, the proper choosing of the time of the old one's funeral. It disturbed Ho that the necromancer had set the lucky day but one moon away. He felt in his heart it was too soon to be properly ceremonious. Yet in the midst of these grave family matters, he had thought of Stephen.

Gradually the blanket of heat lying over the valley sapped the strength of Hester. She lay all day in a long chair between window and door to catch the faintest stirring of air. Her languor seemed to loosen her spirit so that it dwelt lightly in her body, borne aloft on the laboring heart of the land, on the chants of labor. *"Hai yo-oh! High low-oh!"* . . . the syncopated chant, made by the jarred breath of the human pile drivers; *"E-au! E-au!"* . . . the breath forced from a man's chest, the chant of the heavy-laden.

There were no duties to worry Hester. Kin had been solicitous of the *tai-tai's* ebbing strength. He would look after the hong. Only let missie give him the keys, so he need not disturb her when she slept late in the morning. And Hester had given them into his care, taking delight in the homage of service. To be served was to have existence heightened. No longer did she look at Kin with hostile eyes. All he had ever wished was to serve her, and she had been unwilling.

Kin, sensing her acquiescence, knew that his time had come. *"Ai yah,"* now he could rule her.

Stephen came often and sat by her chair, solicitous too. "Are you all right, sweet?" His love for Hester had become the rock on which he erected the structure of his activities. Sometimes he would come up from the office after hours, stand a moment looking down upon her, gaining vitality from her presence, then go back to do some bit of difficult work he had saved until the place was empty and quiet. And, sometimes, looking at her in her idleness, he would experience a sudden pleasure in his own intensely lived days—those arduous days of his which made it possible to keep Hester secure.

One day she heard him hurrying up the stairs. "Hester," he cried, "read this."

"What is it?" she asked.

"I'm not even saying it out loud," he answered.

"How nice!" exclaimed Hester. "It's such a big increase this year."

"Sh!" Stephen, put his hand lightly over her mouth. "This house is full of ears."

"Now I can have the number two boy that Kin says we should have, because master is the great *tai-pan!*" exclaimed Hester, hardly noticing. "Yes, and a second coolie———"

Stephen put the letter into his pocket. "It means they like what I've done up here," he said.

"Strange," thought Hester, as he went away. "It wasn't the increase he cared about, it was the Company's approval." But for the first time in her life she contemplated the value of money for the power it gave her.

The next morning, passing for a moment through the butler's pantry, she was attracted by a letter lying on the morning tea-tray. Opening it, she saw it was the letter telling of Stephen's increase. How had it come here? Had Stephen carelessly dropped it that morning and Kin picked it up? Odd that it should have been this particular letter that had fallen into Kin's hands. Odd and a little disturbing. When she gave the letter to Stephen, for a moment he was angry.

"Damn Kin!" he said. "He must have got it out of my pocket when he arranged my clothes this morning."

Then his anger was gone. *"Mei yu fatsu,"* he said, "it can't be helped. He'd have found out somehow. I've noticed that one's expenses go up with one's position. It's good we've got a pension ahead of us."

Kin, coming into the pantry, saw that the letter was not there. Had the white vixen, then, returned to her ways of a common woman? He had been at such pains to teach her that she lost face in exerting herself. *"Mei yu fatsu!"* Fortunate that he had already taken the letter to the reader of the barbarian's language who sat in the outer office. The extra money to come to the household was better than he had hoped. He had done wisely when he stayed with this master. To-night when he went to the tea-house he would arrange for that woman he had long desired. The gambling among the servants of white men should be moved to his quarters, his now should be the place of importance.

When finally that night he lay down in his bed, he had gambled away a great sum. *Ai yah,* fortune had not attended him. The entirety of his master's increase must fall into his hands, if he were to pay his debts. The number two house-boy must be hired, and the extra coolie, so he could receive part of their wages. From everything that came into the house, he must take an extra commission—and missie must buy more. How could he teach her to want more? In this he had not yet succeeded. When he tried to entice her with the treasures of the

209

pedlars—the embroideries, the little trinkets, the laces, the bronzes—she bought sparingly as a man would buy.

The "little heat" was passed; the "great heat" drew on toward its fulness. Day after day no rain fell, and the second rice began to turn yellow before its time. The water that had been garnered in reservoirs was fed to the fields, and along the streams and the river all night the feet of men walked the endless treads of the chain pumps. Then, except along the river, the foot pumps were still, for there was no more water in reservoir or stream. In the city, there came a time when the water taken from the wells was thin mud. Each day the line of water-carriers at the river grew longer. In a lengthening queue, they moved over the river bank, a thin yellow band in the distance.

The farmers, idle now, moved along the alley-like streets of the city, along the bund, crowding the sampans, going to the temples, going to the sacred mountain across the river. They would petition their gods for rain. What did the gods want? Reverence? Three steps and we kneel. Sacrifice? Hooks hung in our flesh that the gods may see and give us a little rain, in order that our sons may live. No meat or fowls or eggs sold in the city; no life of any kind taken, except for the sacrifice of bull and ram made by the governor.

Stephen, walking daily through the city, watched the money market grow tight, the price of rice go up. In many small shops men sat idle. It startled him to see how small was the margin on which the people of the valley bought; how quickly it was wiped out. In his offices, although they had wages and would not starve, clerk, junkman and coolie squeezed as they had never squeezed before. They seemed to partake of the common fear.

Stephen forgot the delight of his intellectual adventure

210

in exploring the Chinese mind, forgot his bafflement in its blind alley. During these days he was unconsciously one with those around him, some instinct within him vibrating to the fundamental calamity. When he found the office coolie palming stamps from letters, he did not dismiss him as he would have done a month ago. And although he watched now more closely than ever to keep down the squeeze, it was in a new mood. Not with the censoriousness of an outsider, but with the sympathy he would have felt, looking upon a like manifestation among his own people.

Stephen tried to keep from Hester that there was danger of famine. High at the top of the hong, sheltered, secluded, she failed to understand the full significance of the drought. She saw only a gay pageant moving across the bund: peasants with yellow knapsacks bound for the temples; the gods, decked in bright red robes, riding in chairs on the shoulders of men who carried them out to view the metallic sky, the bright sterile clouds. Finding delight in sound and movement, she grew excited over the spectacle.

Her imagination seemed to come alive. She craved activity, she knew not what, and when Kin came, saying a white pedlar stood outside with a bundle "great big," she welcomed the diversion. It was a Russian, tall and gaunt, who entered at Kin's bidding. Kneeling by his pack, he took from it rugs glowing in color, soft as silk. Hester, coveting the most beautiful of the rugs, began bargaining, seeing in the man's eagerness the desire to sell at any price.

She had just completed her bargain, when Stephen came at her summons to pay the man. He looked at Hester, vivid with the excitement of possession, bright spots in her cheeks. He heard the sounds coming up from the bund. Bang! Bang! Men beating upon brass gongs, a frenzy of gongs, propitiation of the gods, the heavens,

211

he knew not which. But he knew that it was desperate entreaty to end the drought. Famine at the doors—and Hester buying a costly rug!

"Hester, we don't need it. The hong's full of Company rugs."

"But they're so ugly, Stephen. Look at this one on the floor. It's got two darns in it. The new one would look lovely in this room." She laid her hand on the soft surface of the rug.

"We can't, Hester."

"Why not?" she demanded, feeling resentment over his unwillingness, remembering his substantial increase.

"Because there's famine."

The pent-up strain under which Stephen had been laboring broke its bounds. "When there's famine, the people can't buy. This is my first managership. I haven't made good yet. My whole future is built on sales. I don't know yet how bad the famine will be, how far it's going to spread, maybe over the whole province. Suppose the sales drop instead of increasing? The Company sees no extenuating circumstances—either I win or I lose. Suppose I lose———"

Hester sat back on her heels. "No, not if that's the case. But I didn't know, Stephen."

He was angry with himself. He had not wanted to shatter Hester's sense of security. It was for that he was working. "Better buy the rug, I guess we can swing it," he added hastily. "We haven't famine yet. I'm probably borrowing trouble."

Hester looked at Stephen as he counted out the money, but her pleasure in her purchase was gone. Famine looked out at her. She remembered the trek of the peasants in Manchuria, their faces. That was what had stalked behind their eyes—hunger! Famine! Her spirit drew back. Stephen went to his office. Bang! Bang! The noise grew louder, a frenzy of noise.

There came a day when the sun, shining as brilliantly as before from the glittering sky, wrought some new tension in the city. Along the streets, in every house, every one's eyes were turned skyward. The servant passing through the hong stopped at the windows to look upward. If there is no rain to-day, for forty days there will be no rain, they told Stephen. Toward noon, a few clouds drifted across the sky; clouds empty of rain they seemed to Stephen, standing at the window. Then, as if dropped from the blue, raindrops fell. But they had no vigor, none behind them to push them on. The servants moved through the hong closing the windows. "The rain, the rain, it will come." It did not matter that the rain had stopped. The soothsayer had said it would come like this, at first a little.

Early the next morning Hester was wakened by the silence. No murmuring voices, no cries of children came up to her from the poor who of late had been sleeping on the bund, no clang of cymbals as the gods rode forth. Only the gentle and monotonous fall of rain. Her spirit took back its buoyancy. She turned on her pillow and slept. The shadow of famine was gone from the green valley. But for Stephen there was less resilience of hope. A partial famine, insecurity pushed only a little into the background.

Well before sundown one afternoon, the black gates of Ho's ancestral house were opened wide. The men of the family, all in white sackcloth, Ho looming above them, came forth bearing the things of the spirit world, all of paper. Paper servants—*amahs* and gardeners and men servants; a handsome chair with six bearers; rickshas, perhaps not too frail for the shadow world; a house with its many courts, replica of the ancestral home the old woman's spirit had so recently quit. A full-sized stage, held above the heads of men by means of bamboo poles,

213

was borne forward, a hundred paper actors were carried jauntily on the shoulders of coolies.

Amah called Hester. The hong windows were full of servants and office staff. *"Ai yah,"* they exclaimed, as the spirit things were laid in a great pile. "Grand beyond measure!"

"Ai yah! Tai-tai will have a good time. It costs the Ho clan thousands upon thousands of coppers!"

A half-hour and the things of the spirit world were a heap of ashes.

The next morning around the ancestral dwelling there was a bustle of an important journey about to be undertaken. So had the *tai-tai*, the one-time concubine of Ho's father, long the first lady in the household, looked upon it—the one important journey, the supreme adventure. Many years before she had arranged every detail.

And now at last she, who had not often been beyond the confines of her own domain, started on her long anticipated journey. The gates were flung wide. Out came the musicians, out came the banners carried aloft by men in green robes, out came the mourners in white— the great Ho leading his brothers, his sons, his cousins behind, the last outer ramifications of the family following. What a family it was! Only now did Stephen realize how many of the Ho clan were in the employ of the Company. His office force had been depleted in the last few days. Even the gateman had asked leave to go home, saying his mother was very sick. There he was now, humble member of the clan, almost the last in the line of white-clad mourners turning left on the bund.

Now came the great lacquered coffin, escorted by a monstrous paper dragon. The head, supported by men, rose in front of the coffin, which appeared to rest on the undulating body. The tail, supported by many children, flapped behind. An angry monster, guarding the precious freight that rode upon its back.

Last came the women of the clan, those of importance hid behind the drawn curtains of their chairs. Now and then there was a glimpse of a white slipper, a white sleeve, a delicate yellow hand. *Amahs* with children in white, white cloth around their heads, rode in rickshas at the end of the procession.

Even in a city of magnificent funerals, this one caused excitement. "It's worth all of ten thousand dollars," murmured the crowd.

The great family crowded the bund in front of the office. In noise and confusion they filled a flotilla of sampans. Then the dirge rose into its last high wail, as the coffin of the *tai-tai* came to rest on the deck of the Company launch which Stephen had lent for the occasion. Lost in the dirge were the signals to the engine-room. As the engineer's head rose above the hatchway to get his orders, Stephen caught a glimpse of him, his head swathed in the turban of mourning. He, too, a member of the clan! The launch moved out into deep water, little boats, sails set, trailing behind as if pulled by the band of moving water in the wake of the launch.

The hong seemed very still. Across the way there was no perceptible movement in the courts of the Ho compound, only the leaves of the olive tree moved in a little wind. Now and then a leaf dropped, drifting down into the empty court below.

Stephen closed the door of his office. He wanted to think. His friend Ho—was he a friend? Or was he simply trying to see what he could get? Stray incidents, at the time insignificant, came back to him: Ho suggesting a new gateman at the hong—the other was not trustworthy; Ho, when the new launch was to be sent up from Shanghai, asking Stephen to write the Company of a local man who knew the treacheries of the river—a local man who had not proved to know so much about the river after all, thought Stephen, with a wry smile.

Doubts of his friend assailed him. In how many other ways did Ho use his friendship for gain? Ho, too, not to be trusted? The old reaction—all of them crafty. He arraigned Ho before the tribunal of his own standards and found him wanting. Disgust filled him; the friendship, as far as he was concerned, was finished. But not so easily could he destroy it. Tenaciously, this friendship was rooted in Stephen, for he loved Ho.

Closing time came. The coolie looked in to see if the master had left. If he could attend to the master's office, he could go to that second job he never told about, which he held with those other white people across the city. He squatted on his heels outside the door, patiently waiting.

Stephen sat on, tipped back in his revolving chair, his hands behind his head, trying to save his friendship, trying to understand. Since the days of threatened famine with their terror of starvation, a new pattern lay over his mind. Things he had seen since he had come to China, isolated in his mind heretofore, now fitted into that pattern like the parts of a puzzle. The peasants on the ample plains of Manchuria making a last gleaning of the fields, not bold and daring pioneers, those peasants, but men with the memory of want and poverty. And now, even here in this fertile valley, poverty—everywhere its manifestations. Paper-thin bottoms of kettles, a few twigs beneath; no heat in the houses during the damp coldness of winter, only charcoal hand or foot stoves; people coming from market, a two-inch piece of pork, or a chicken's wing, the day's supply of meat; vegetables bought sparingly, water used sparingly. Now he knew what lay behind squeeze—centuries of want. But Ho—there was no excuse for him; he was rich, as riches go in the East.

Then across Stephen's mind the scenes of the day marshaled themselves. The long line of men in their sackcloth, the rickshas and chairs of the women. He sensed the solidarity of Ho's life with the life of his clan; not a separate life, as Stephen's. Ho, the head of the clan; Ho, with two hundred pairs of hands clinging to his garments; Ho, every day vicariously partaking of want. And suddenly Stephen did not doubt Ho's sincerity of friendship, even though he knew now that he must watch Ho as he did the others.

Hester was calling him. He rose and went thoughtfully to the top floor of the hong.

That evening Stephen made his second great contribution to the corporation. In his youth, as he had sat on a brick *k'ang* watching the flickering light of a peanut oil lamp cast on a dirt floor, had come the inspiration of the lamp. Then he had seen a vision of China recreated on the grand scale of America, also power and recognition for himself. Now, in his maturity, he sat in his comfortable suite in the hong, slouched down in his easy chair, his eyes upon the rug Hester had bought, his mind turned inward, seeing success for the Company in fitting the business into Chinese poverty. A picture stood in his mind of a corner of Ho's wall and the seller of peanuts who sat there day in day out, in cold and heat, rain or sun. Before him, resting on an old tub, a wooden tray; and neatly arranged upon the tray, piles of shelled peanuts, three, four in a pile. He must think as the man who sold four peanuts thought, as millions like him thought, if he would put a lamp in every house throughout the province.

A three-cent lamp—many a man's wages for a whole day. If he increased the business, he and his men must be patient enough to make a shop-to-shop inspection of the province. The tiniest shop which sold native oil must not be overlooked. He would make a record of the infinitesimal sales of the province. After that, the agents should be pressed to make these "four peanut sales," as

217

Stephen called them now. Insignificant in themselves, gigantic when you multiplied them by the millions upon millions who bought in such minute quantities.

This time Stephen dreamed no dreams of personal greatness. He would try the scheme out. If it worked he would pass the plan on to Shanghai to use as they saw fit. That they would adopt the idea without comment if they liked it, now seemed natural to Stephen.

V

WHEN the "great heat" was over the spent and exhausted city by some mysterious process of its own took unto itself renewed life. The hong regained activity. Boynton and Fenton had returned from their vacations. All the clerks who had absented themselves on one pretext or another were back in their places—the coolie was busy carrying them tea and steaming cloths to wipe their faces. The substitute gateman had departed, the former one was again at his post.

Once more Ho sat each morning at Stephen's side, a grave and astute adviser. Now Stephen determined to try out his new scheme for increasing the business. He wired Shanghai for permission to travel, and leaving Boynton in charge of the office, started forth with Ho to visit the territory of the cock-eyed Ting. As the chair coolies trotted forward, carrying them in on the valley floor away from the river, he noticed with concern the effect of the drought. The flagged path wound along the raised rim of the paddies, and he could look into the fields— not a thick carpet of yellow rice heads; the rice stood so sparsely that he could see the black earth beneath. Men and boys were going carefully over the paddies cutting the scant rice heads. The beat of thin sheaves on the edge of the threshing boxes reached Stephen's ears. A year before he would have thought such fields not worth harvesting, and he would have asked Ho why they bothered with this meager crop, as they had the spring rice for their winter's supply. But now he knew that, even in this rich valley, it was a hand-to-mouth existence.

In the distance appeared two broken gray and white lines edging the path on both sides; gradually the lines revealed themselves as white plastered walls and gray-tiled roofs. "How little the towns take from the fields," thought Stephen. Then at last they were hard upon the village, entering the narrow street between the shops. A rap on the chair-poles. With sighs and grunts, the chair coolies lowered the chairs, and Stephen and Ho stepped over the poles into the street, entering together the first shop that sold oil.

Inside the shop, they sat side by side on a bench, facing the high counter and the shopkeeper behind it. In a dark recess beyond the counter, they were aware of half-revealed figures—a woman seated on a low chair made of bamboo, a child standing beside her pulling at her breast, a baby asleep on her lap. The woman's black hair merged into the shadow of a bed, its interior like a dark lair beyond the looped-back curtains of coarse cloth. Shop and house was this room.

Once Stephen would have felt the oil business superior to such petty trade. But now, realizing the enormous numbers of such shops, he noted with interest the supplies—two pieces of cloth neatly folded lying on a shelf behind the counter, a few red candles, a jar probably full of coarse sugar, and a discarded oil tin of his own Company, half full of peanut oil, heavy and brown as lubricating oil. How could it be replaced with a quarter-tin of the Company's oil? How could the man be made to change?

The open shop front filled quickly with faces—the

curious of the town. Into the air, heavy with the odors of unwashed bodies and the dank smell of the earth floor, the guttural speech of Ho fell, uttering the polite phrases of his race, speaking of that matter of supreme importance—sons.

"I, the miserable one, have only two," answered the shopkeeper.

Speaking later of business, he said, "For generations have we sold oil in this shop—I, and my father before me, and even before that. At the time of the winter moons, twelve catties; at the time of the summer moons, six. It is good oil. Is it not so, to sell so much each moon since I was a child, since my father was a child, and his father?"

It took long to break down the shopkeeper's reticence and to learn that he had a capital of ten dollars on which to run his business. Sugar and oil, dye and a little cloth, he sold. When they had entered the shop the sun shone straight down, making a sharp line of brilliance along the center of the street; when they left it had moved westward so that half the street lay in shadow.

There was one more shop in town which sold oil; but when they came to it, a bargain was going on and they must wait. Joining the onlookers, they peered within.

"He is selling the earth of his floor," explained Ho. "The *tong ja* can see it is wet, and that the shoes stick to it as one walks. Now it has value for the fields, or to the maker of gunpowder; a little saltpeter can be drawn from it, so the owner is selling it."

"A man makes his living in this way, buying the dirt of such floors!" exclaimed Stephen, realizing how meager must be the money gained from the extracting of saltpeter from the slimy surface. Literally nothing was wasted in this country!

"*Ai yah!* It is too much," contended the buyer, a spare man, wearing a gown of thin silk marked with a solid line down the back. "His queue must have rested there in times long past," thought Stephen. There was a gray line, too, where the long sleeves were turned back from his thin hands.

"You are charging for three inches of earth and there are but two of value," the man went on indignantly.

"Three, I say." The shopkeeper brought forth a pointed stick. "See, I will loosen it here under your feet, that all may say I speak truly."

"Over in this corner I will dig a little," answered the buyer. "Perhaps water from the watering pails has fallen where you dig. *Ai*, less than two inches is wet in this corner! But I am a just man and I will pay you for two."

"Three, I say."

"*Ai yah*, it is too much. You will take away my profit. There is leaching to do, and the ashes of plants that I must buy."

"Three."

"And only a little saltpeter when all is finished. Many floors, before I have enough to sell at the gunpowder market. *Ai yah*, two and a quarter."

"Two and three-quarters."

"*Ai!* The paying of my tax! I forgot the paying of the tax. Ninety cents a month. Two and a half, I will pay, but I make nothing."

The bargaining went on, dragging itself through the afternoon, buyer and seller struggling for the minute profit. At last they agreed on two inches and two-thirds.

When night came, what with the slow Eastern politeness and the slow winning of the confidence of shopkeepers, Stephen and Ho were only a little on their way. Stephen had for his day's harvest of work only the record of the tiny kernels of business of four country villages, and the knowledge that the saltpeter gleaned from old floors made a man a living. Weary with the long drawn-out talk over little happenings, he passed through the tea-shop that made the front room of the inn where

221

they were staying the night, hoping to find an inner room where he could be alone. In one of a number of cubby-holes, evidently used here in the South for sleeping-places, he found his boy spreading his mattress on a bed frame of woven cords, evil-smelling and filthy.

"Take it out quickly," he commanded.

He was looking around for a place to sleep, when Ho joined him.

"*Tong ja* can sleep in the court if he wishes. I have arranged it."

Stephen hesitated.

"But the innkeeper's shrine is there. He will not object?"

"I have arranged it," said Ho.

After each had eaten his evening meal—Ho in the front shop, and Stephen sitting on his cot, a table before him on which his boy had placed a plate of ham and eggs and a great pot of coffee—the two men sat together, smoking, in the dim courtyard. Ho, in his dark cotton traveling gown, was but a blotch of black beside Stephen, except for two light streaks where his snowy under-garment made little cuffs beyond his sleeves. The bands of white were parallel, showing that Ho's hands rested on his spread knees.

A crowd of villagers which had gathered at the edge of the court, gradually moved nearer until their faces were close to Stephen's. One man, more bold than the rest, was fingering the cloth of his trousers. At Ho's words they moved back, but soon they were edging forward again, until once more they were peering into the white man's face.

Stephen toyed with the idea of offering the innkeeper the sum of his evening's business in the tea-shop, if he would put up the wooden shutters across the open front, shutting out these curious onlookers. He computed the probable returns for the evening. Three ten-cent pieces, small money, would be the top price he would offer. Then he gave it up. It would take half the evening to make the bargain but, even more, such a bargain might lose him too much prestige with Ho. He remembered a recent talk in which he had asked his friend how best to govern the servants of the south.

"Tong ja," Ho had said, "this is the error in your countrymen's conduct. You send to buy a trifling thing on the street. The coolie returns and counts out the change, lays it before you—two silver pieces, a copper and ten *cash*. Let not the *tong ja,* as so many of his countrymen, leave the *cash* for the coolie. The coolie is not grateful. In his heart, the coolie thinks such a man a fool who does not know the value of money."

No, better endure the crowd drawing in once more. He felt that Ho would think him a fool, too, if he should waste money, paying the innkeeper for the evening's business.

But at last the innkeeper drove out the loiterers, slid the wooden shutters into place along the front of his shop.

Day after day, Ho and Stephen moved slowly over Ting's territory, visiting every village. The humblest was not neglected. At last they drew near to the city where Ting lived. In more and more shops, they saw the oblong cans of oil bearing the chop of the Keepers of Light —two flaming red characters across the top of the large label—and beneath a picture of the little lamp, its burning wick turned high, radiating yellow flanges of light. Ting has indeed been at work. But he shall work even harder, now, said Stephen to himself.

As their chairs were carried along the Great Street of the city, they saw the gilt sign of the Company hanging in air above the shop of Ting. Their chairs were brought to rest. Stephen looked up. Ting's shop was by far the grandest building on the street, two stories high, and its front decorated with ornate carvings.

Ting, the skirt of his gown shortened in front by his paunch, larger even than in the spring, stood at the door of his inner room, holding up the bamboo curtain for Stephen and Ho, urging them to precede him into the room. Seeing him thus against his own background, Stephen recognized that Ting was indeed an important man in the province.

Two contending emotions filled Stephen: astonishment over his own daring in treating Ting as he had—perhaps if he had realized the man's position he would not have risked experimenting with him in the matter of face; pride, that he had saved such a man for the Company. There was no talk of resigning now, even when the new scheme was discussed. "Mr. Ting will have to have more men to do this."

"*Hao la, hao la,* all right, all right," replied Ting.

He was in excellent humor. His business must have increased even more than his reports showed. "Holding back a few sales; speculating in wood oil, I'll bet," was Stephen's secret thought.

"The *tai-pan* will feast to-night?"

It was while they were feasting in the city's chief restaurant that Stephen felt moved to twit Ting a little.

"Is it to-night that the honorable one would resign?"

"Very good, very good, *tai-pan*. I recommend for the Keepers of Light a great merchant." Ting inclined his head toward a mean little specimen of a man at the next table.

"Very good," answered Stephen solemnly.

Ting's left eye shot up, and he settled himself to his feasting. Through the meal they continued to chaff each other, even Ho occasionally joining in.

* * * * *

On a day late in September, Stephen and Ho reached their home city. They were almost at Ho's gate when the chair coolie swerved suddenly to avoid a kneeling figure. A beggar, Stephen thought, then he saw that it was a young girl who knelt on the stone flagging. She was evidently well born from the cut and material of her short jacket and trousers and the smallness of her feet. She might have been twelve years old, he imagined. With his quick eye for detail, he noticed that this girl did not wear her hair in a long braid, the style followed by Chinese women before marriage. Her hair was short and, odder still, curly. He caught a glimpse of her face, the black loose masses of her hair accentuating its paleness. The girl had risen now and a coolie woman, evidently her *amah*, pulled forward a mat on which her mistress had been kneeling. The young girl took three steps upon her bound feet, then knelt again. "What penance is she doing?" Stephen wondered.

As his chair swung round the corner toward the front of the hong, he looked back, for another thing had struck him about the girl. She was beautiful. He had never before seen beauty in the Chinese. He wanted another glimpse of her, but she had vanished. And in another moment he had forgotten her in his delight over his home-coming.

The next morning Stephen called Boynton and Fenton into his office and laid his new plan before them, giving each a territory to cover.

"You can start to-morrow," he said, closing the conversation.

Back in their office, the two young men faced each other. Even the loyal Boynton was for the moment nonplussed. Fenton, feeling no reserves, stormed about the office expressing his criticism.

"Well, that finishes him for me. You can say what you like. Just imagine a man at home wasting his time over little sales like that, instead of seeing the big opportunities. Men connected with a Company like this, spending their time over the picayunish buying of the poor! Why, it's like the Chinese splitting sunflower seeds with their teeth and pulling out the kernels with their tongues, instead of eating real food!"

Suddenly, the amount of work the project involved occurred to Boynton.

"Imagine the patience it's going to take, the patience of a Chinaman. We'll be gone for weeks!"

"Well, you'll see how fast I get it done," Fenton answered. "I don't intend staying out longer than . . . Let's see, there's a big party on, three weeks from to-day. Must try to make that. Guess I'll get going this afternoon. I'll surprise Chase for once, and start sooner than he told me to." He grinned, rang the bell for the coolie, sending him for his houseboy.

"Get my traveling kit ready, savee?"

Hester, in her living-room, arranged and rearranged short sprays of the glossy-leafed *kwe hwa,* sent her as a present from Ho. Coming in through her windows, she heard the high squeak of wheelbarrows, the thin rasping of insects in tiny wooden cages—the cicada vender down in the alley—and the easily detected cadence of white women's voices, her neighbors, gathered in a knot down below on the bund. Like an echo from some other scene, their voices reached her.

Stepping through the long open window that gave on the gallery, she went to the top of the stairs, looking down into the uplifted faces of three women, and the small oval of a little girl's face.

"Hello!" the women called up to her in chorus. "We're coming up!"

They mounted the stairs, talking and laughing, the little girl in their midst.

"We want to hear all about what you've been doing," said Mrs. Breckenridge, the tall thin wife of the manager of the British Oil Company, as they entered the room. "Robin wrote that that husband of yours doesn't play fair, works all the time. He daren't take a vacation because of him."

Hester poured tea for her neighbors as they sat in a circle round the tea-table. The *kwe hwa* gave out its rich and heavy perfume, mingling with the scent of the tea. The crisp blue native linen dress of the consul's wife made a spot of clear color set between the dun-colored pongee of the other two. The little girl leaned against her mother, looking with bored eyes from face to face, clutching at the conversation of her elders for something a child might enjoy.

"Don't lean on me, Geraldine," said the mother, pushing the little girl away. "It's too hot." She added, "I don't know what I'm going to do with her all winter. She hasn't a soul to play with, now the Dentons have gone away. Joey was twelve, but he was nice to Geraldine. She's fretful already, the way a child alone gets in these places."

All four of them looked at the little girl, who stood, staring dully into space.

"I don't see how you stayed here all summer, Mrs. Chase. What'd you *do?*"

"It's been nice," began Hester.

"Nice? How nice in this heat? Just tell me that," one of the women demanded.

Hester started to speak, making an effort to explain. Then she stopped, laughing lightly.

"I believe I can't tell you. I'm beginning to think it was just because I'm lazy. I didn't do an earthly thing."

"I thought as much from what Ted wrote me," said the commissioner's wife.

"Well, girls, let's get down to business," said Mrs. Stanton, the consul's wife. "We came to see if you'd make a

227

fourth at bridge three mornings a week this winter, Mrs. Chase."

Hester hesitated.

"Please do say you will. You see we can't play if you don't. You owe it to the community."

When it was arranged to their satisfaction, the three women rose to go. Then the consul's wife remembered something she had meant to mention to Hester.

"You know we heard this summer, while we were in the mountains, that you play beautifully . . . the piano, I think. It's naughty of you not to have told us. We need everybody's bit to keep up the spirit of the port."

"Oh, but I don't," expostulated Hester.

"Really, my dear? It's strange. The woman that told us said she used to live in the same town with you in Manchuria."

Deftly, Hester changed the subject. She did not want to tell them that she played the violin.

When the callers had gone, she turned to watch the outside coolie lower the screens of strung reeds at the edge of the gallery, then passed into the darkened center of the room beyond. She gave pleased attention to the house coolie with slow movements pushing a cloth over the high polish of the native varnished floor, erasing the pointed footprints of the neighbors, leaving the space between Hester and himself gleaming like a dark red mirror. Seeing her, the coolie waited to let her pass. His eyes, black and moist as a dog's, full of the faithful devotion of a dog, raised to Hester's, became a new pleasure. He moved behind her now, patiently polishing the piece of floor over which his mistress had just passed. He had restored the gleaming perfection of the mirror, when Hester came in again from the hall with Stephen.

"What is it, Stephen?"

When she had met him in the hall, as he reached the

next to the top step of the stairs and she had leaned forward to kiss him, her mind had taken hold of some difficulty within him which had not been there in the morning. But she had not spoken then, with the black pitlike descent of the stairs falling away below them, creaking, sighing, with the mysterious life of the hong.

"Come in here," he answered her, passing on into the greater privacy of their bedroom. "I can't get their cooperation, not even Boynton's this time. If they don't do it with understanding, it won't be any good."

"What is it you want them to do, Stephen?"

"I couldn't explain it to you, I mean I couldn't now. It goes back . . ."

"Perhaps if we had them to tiffin, you could make them understand. I'll send a chit right now." She rang for Kin, scribbling on a leaf of Stephen's memorandum pad, surrendering the joy of this meal alone with her husband to the larger demand of the Company.

It seemed not two minutes before they appeared, Boynton leading, waving a white napkin.

"See, Mrs. Chase, for you to speak is for us to obey. We were just starting our own tiffin when your message came. I arose, obeyed." And he bowed his blond head before her.

At first Boynton, in his exaggerated politeness, was as disconcerting to Hester as Fenton in his silent moodiness; and then a pleasant little thrill shot through her. She was the mistress of the hong. There was deference behind the mockery of Boynton's speech.

As they took their places at the table there was a constrained moment. Then Hester began searching out the dissonances of the group; the contempt that was Fenton, the bantering rebellion—"Oh, I say, have a heart"—that was Boynton, the fierce drive that was Stephen, the manager. She drew forth the youthful self-assurance of Fenton; and lest to Stephen he seem insolent in his cock-

229

sureness, she turned the theme away from business, to allow him to talk of his fiancée in America.

"She's awfully popular, that girl of mine," he said. "You know, Mrs. Chase, sometimes I'm afraid some other man'll get her before I get back. Of course I want her to be popular, but it's a whole year yet. Wish I were Boynton: he has only three months more. He's got the hours worked out."

"Oh, shut up," said Boynton.

"Why, I didn't know you were engaged," exclaimed Hester.

"I am, on and off. It's on just now."

"Have you written about your leave?" asked Stephen.

"Well, no," said Boynton. "I thought the Company would let me know when I could be spared. I don't want to seem too eager. They might think I'm not enough interested in my work."

"Would you care to have me write?" asked Stephen after a moment's hesitation. "I'd like to keep you here, but I think . . . well, this is something due yourself."

"I'd be awfully grateful if you would," said Boynton. "It would come better from you."

Now the conversation swung comfortably back to their work and to the discussed problem. Boynton, sitting at Hester's right hand, half turned in his chair, forgetting her in his interest in what Stephen was saying.

"You see," Stephen began, "this plan is aimed at making another class of Chinese want light. At the top, the electric light is coming in. That presses the big lamp a little farther down in the economic scale, but not much. The class that can afford it is small. A night's burning of a big lamp would take a week's wages of nine-tenths of the people in the valley. What's got to be done is to get small tradesmen out in the country districts thinking about light, wanting light. Now, for instance, in Man-

230

churia. Most of the people there had passed through the big cities of the coast on their trek into Manchuria, and they'd seen cities really lighted. They had a conception of light, and they made chimneyless lamps out of old bottles, even before they had seen our lamp. To get the business I want, you've got to imagine the state of mind of men who count their day's business in *cash—cash*, a two-thousandth of a dollar."

Fenton, who had been maneuvering two salt-cellars along a road he had made of a spoon and a knife, looked up, for one moment, giving his will for understanding over to Stephen. Kin gently removed from under his hands the spoon and the fork, setting them in their rightful places.

Stephen was leaning forward, forgetting his habitual restraint. "You've got to understand poverty to succeed," he concluded.

"I don't want to feel poor," said Fenton. "Unfit me for big enterprises."

"If you mean America," Stephen answered, "men rarely go back; and if you mean big enterprise in China, there is no such thing, only a multitude of little sales."

"Well, I guess it's a sound idea," Boynton conceded. "We've been shooting too high."

Long before, Hester had let go their talk, her mind idling outside the orbit of their conversation, aware only of the soft stroke of the silk of her sleeve as she moved her arm, and the faint breeze set going by the punka, fanning to coolness her skin, moist, as the heat of the September day mounted in intensity with the hours. And a new sound, heard for the last hour but hardly noticed, which, by the weight of its repetition, at last bore down upon her. *"Hai yo-oh, hai yo-oh,* High-low-o, high-low-o!" A great weight thudding down, accenting the chant made by the jarred breath of the laborers.

"Ho's begun his foreign house," said Stephen, breaking into the theme of his own conversation. "The pile-drivers are at work."

Kin came and spoke softly to Hester, telling her a new curio man had come.

She made a little shift of her chair, essaying her departure. Stephen looked at his watch and rose quickly.

"I had no idea it was opening time."

For a moment they all paused at the window, looking down at the preparations for Ho's three-story brick house. A corner of the garden wall had been torn away, a scaffolding of bamboo poles had been erected. Four men stood upon a platform, ropes in their hands.

"Hai yo-oh, hai yo-oh." The human pile-drivers hauled up the enormous wooden hammer, dropped it.

"Look at them, millions just like them in this country, little more than animals," said Fenton. "Do you expect us to make them want light?"

"Yes," said Stephen, "that's our market."

As the men went away to their work, Hester knelt by the pack of the pedlar, idly watching him take out his wares. From the events of the morning, the question of her music was thrust forward into her attention. All through the luncheon she had been putting it from her. Why did she not play? Why could she not play her violin? Even now when she felt to the point of pain the need for music, she was unable to feed her own hunger. Something hypnotic in the bright hot minutes of the afternoon, empty of endeavor, filled with the little entertainment before her, held her spirit: blue glass beads on yellow cords, bone beads patiently carved with flowers falling on the blue ones, coral flung in a red pile on the top, the bright blue of the kingfishers' feathers enameled into earrings crowning the mounting heap. Then the beads and the tangled tassels, the bits of brass, the small incense burners bought by the white people for ash receivers became an offense to her, disfiguring the polished beauty of her floor.

"Tell him to take it all away, Kin," she commanded, pushing from her lap a little pile of objects she had half thought she would buy.

"*Tai-tai,*" the old man spoke softly, picking up a cloth-covered gray box, pulling the inch-long bone spear of its fastening thrust through a loop of red braid, "look see."

In a shaped space fitting it accurately there lay a perfect piece of porcelain. An artist had made that, Hester knew. An artist of centuries ago, for the making of such porcelains is a lost art. She coveted the vase.

Quickly she turned her attention to a vulgar brass image of the Laughing Buddha, cunningly expressed interest in it and none in the treasure she coveted, thinking to lessen its price by her indifference. Kin, watching the old man sitting back on his haunches bargaining with Hester over the Laughing Buddha, detected a slight movement of her hands toward the valuable porcelain. He moved his foot a trifle, indicating to the pedlar that it was there that *tai-tai's* interest lay.

No, said Hester, she did not want the image. Not good, there were flaws in it. But what of this other thing, this bit of porcelain? If it were not too dear she might take it.

When the curio man stated his price she rose and walked away.

"You no wanchee anything?" he called after her. With a patient sigh, slowly and carefully packing away his trinkets, he raised his pack on his shoulders and went out.

But when Hester returned, the bowl stood upon the table where she had planned to place it. When she summoned Kin, asking the reason, he said the man had insisted on leaving it a day for her to look at. He would come again.

Suddenly the afternoon was vivid with interest for Hester, a new idea forming in her mind. Everthing in

233

this room beautiful, the other rooms too. Things which only the privileged manager's wife could own. She reached out covetous hands for the vase. She must have it at any cost. Things beautiful, things to deck the spirit that had refused the travail of creating beauty of sound. In the days that followed, with excited energy she offered her spirit one lovely thing after another.

VI

DAY by day Ho's foreign house grew taller, the scaffolding of bamboo poles, tied together with hempen strands, standing so high that the red flags on their tips, placed there to keep away the devils, floated level with Hester's windows. The red brick walls were a floor high, and down in the alley the apprentices, through the slow hours of the day, trod water into the cement. Thin stockings of gray formed on their legs; their chant took the place of the heavy chant of the pile-drivers, boys' voices, sleepy, soft, and sometimes shrill:

> A ha, a ha,
> Six years we work
> For our master.
> A ha, a ha,
> His old trousers to wear in the summer,
> A padded coat in winter!

One day after Stephen and Ho had ended the morning's business, Ho spoke, *"Tong ja,* there is a little matter that pertains to my family."

Stephen was startled into attention. Ho speaking of his family to him, who had never been beyond the garden of the great house!

"The wife of my third son . . ."

234

Ho considering his daughter-in-law! There was a change coming over him since the death of his old mother. First the foreign house, and now speaking to Stephen of the women of his household. Occasionally Ho had spoken of this or that son. His oldest son, Stephen knew, was a disappointment; and that the third son was his favorite. Once Ho had brought this third son to the office. He had seemed an odd mixture of gentleman and coolie; a thin face, aristocratic in shape, the mouth heavy and the nose as flat as a Negro's, the nose of a coolie. But the eyes were what impressed Stephen—honest, faithful eyes, strangely revealing in their expression for a Chinese. Ho's third son was tall, too, like his father. Stephen wondered what the wife of this boy of seventeen would be like.

"My son talks of the school in the city where girls learn. Day and night, he does not cease to speak of it for his wife. It seems it is becoming the custom. Perhaps good, perhaps not good. He wishes her to learn your speech."

Stephen was silent for a moment. Possibly here was a chance to return Ho's kindness to him; here too, Hester's opportunity to know the women of his friend's family. Perhaps this was what Ho desired now. Friendship between the two families.

"Teacher," Stephen said at last, "I do not know your custom, and whether it would be pleasing to you, but my wife could teach the woman our speech. She reads and writes."

There was a long silence and no answer. Ho rose and, after formal salutation, went away. But after another day the matter was arranged between them. Stephen was happy that he could do this thing for Ho; and happy, too, that Hester was to have her desire.

For three afternoons of sunshine Hester held herself ready to receive Ho's daughter-in-law. Each day Kin brought her word that her pupil was coming, then that

235

there were affairs at home and it could not be arranged.

On the third day, weary of waiting, Hester went in where her *amah* sat by the window in the guest-room sewing, and talked to her about the matter. *Amah* did not lift her eyes from her work, but Hester felt there was knowledge in them, for about *amah's* mouth played the faintest of knowing smiles. Hester was baffled and annoyed, feeling that she had some right to knowledge of the delay, a knowledge which every one else seemed to possess.

That night, while they were seated at dinner, she asked her husband if he would not speak to Ho, but Stephen said Ho had unexpectedly gone away that very day on some business of his own. "Besides it would be discourteous to force an explanation," he added.

"It seems to me," said Hester, "that it's discourteous to me, to keep me waiting."

"Not in the eyes of the Chinese," answered Stephen. "Probably it's their lack of sense of time that's causing the delay. Time to them is not split apart into small units, as it is to us."

Hester was almost persuaded, when, looking up, she caught the ghost of a smile playing around Kin's mouth, like that she had seen around *amah's*. Kin was serving at the time, and his eyes were lowered as *amah's* had been.

She felt uneasiness rising within her, remembering that night in Manchuria when they had waited in vain for the agent to escort them to the feast. Was she again the recipient of Oriental insult? She began to feel herself losing the footing she had gained in this Oriental world —again that dwindling of personality so painful to her.

But the house of Ho had no idea of insulting the wife of Ho's friend. Neither was there indifference to the hour set for the lesson. The matter had taken on too great importance for that. Not since the death and burial of the old mother had emotion swept with such vehemence

236

through the courts of the Ho household, although for some time a storm had been brewing.

Since the death of the old *tai-tai,* new contents and discontents stirred the courts. The eldest son of Ho had been the darling of his grandmother. At thirty, he was effeminate, loitering in the courts of the women, a man given to many women, squandering the clan's money in gambling at *mah jong.* Only the commands of the old *tai-tai* had kept Ho on several occasions from beating him with bamboos. But now, no longer could this waster make free with the family money. His father governed him strictly, and when Ho had gone on the long trip of investigation with Stephen, he had placed the money affairs in the hands of his third son.

The night Ho had returned from the trip, his house apparently was filled with the quietness and peace of Oriental seclusion, very satisfying after the weeks of travel, travel which, as to most Chinese, had been anathema to him. The lanterns had been lighted in the courts, and, as Ho's chair coolies carried his chair through the gate, there was the scurrying of servants' feet, and the cry echoing through the courts, "The master comes! The master comes!"

In the ancestral hall, there was quiet reverence. The food had been placed for the old matriarch's use. It added a homelike air. Outside the apartments of Ho's head wife, the table for the children was spread. There was the soft hubbub of their voices, the subdued laughter of their *amahs.*

The servants came to him, bringing steaming cloths for his face, hot food and his water-pipe. And then, with a loud sigh of satisfaction, Ho had stretched himself out on the clean and tautly laced brown string mattress of his bed, resting his head on the hard pillow, as he commanded the servant to loosen the bed curtains from the brass hooks which held them back. He would sleep a little before the evening salutations of his family.

But the peace which lay over the courts was brittle with the tension of jealousy. The first son's wife sat in the doorway of her court where she could see all who went forward toward the room of her father-in-law, and all who went to her mother-in-law's private apartment. There was restraint in her dress and in her posture, but in her face the hunted look of one strained to the breaking point.

In the court nearest to the head lady's, the widow of Ho's second son awaited the return of her sons from their evening meal. A little boy skipped gaily through the doorway into the court.

"Where is thy elder brother?" asked his mother.

"The old one desired him," he said, tying the skirts of his coat into his silk girdle and getting out his diabolo. His mother was pleased. Her son detained by the *tai-tai*. He was gaining in favor daily. She, a widow, must depend upon these sons to give her position in the family. All she did that was asked of her, all and more—her girl-child performing this extra sacrifice at the temple.

The third son's wife, Still-Water—she who had brought down wrath upon herself that day she played where the white barbarians could hear her—she, too, was thinking of her father-in-law's return. As a sweet taste in her mouth, she savored her newly exalted place in the household—her husband, the one handling the money in the master's absence.

The next afternoon, the third son of Ho came from the apartment of his father well pleased. In return for his satisfactory handling of the money, his father had granted the thing he had desired. He went directly to his wife, Still-Water, telling her she was to go to the Keepers of Light for the new learning. Still-Water pouted a little. She had never studied in her life, and did not want to study now. Why should this be asked of her?

Her *amah*, leaning between the pair to pour a little tea and set down the dish of sweetmeats, exclaimed:

"*Ai*, my lady privileged among all the ladies of the household. Her face is very great!"

Then she went away, spreading the news through the courts. As she had hoped, word of it was carried to the wife of the first son, who lay down immediately, drawing the curtains of her bed together. Tears fell from her eyes, and over and over she said to herself, "Favor again for that silly Still-Water. *Ai*, I eat bitterness! I eat bitterness!"

Toward evening, she was sick with the bitterness she had eaten and her flesh put forth fire. But she rose to obey a command of the mother of her husband, her ruler. She dared not send word that she was sick. She was hated by her husband's mother because she had never borne a son. Daily she lived in fear that one of her husband's concubines might be given her place. Feeling too weak to walk alone, leaning on her *amah* as she went toward the head lady's apartments, the wife of the first son met the *amah* of Still-Water coming chattering forth from the court of the widow of the second son. Then the first son's wife felt black rage rising within her and she slapped Still-Water's *amah*, shouting at her to stop her foolish talk about her great face.

Amah, blubbering noisily, hurried away to her mistress and set up a loud wailing, telling Still-Water what the wife of the first son had done to her. "Insulting you through me!" wailed *amah*.

Then Still-Water went to see the first son's wife, and they berated each other. Anger ebbed and flowed through the courts. *Ai yah*, it was a fine drama. The servants of the household took sides, some with the first son's wife, some with the third son's wife. Even into the garden where Ho sat talking to Stephen, word of the quarrel was carried. The servant who brought tea told the master,

239

speaking in such wise that the white man did not grasp the meaning.

Stephen, looking at his friend, immobile of countenance, wondered if the way of life of the East did not offer more serenity than that of the West—this quiet garden, the sheltered courts beyond.

Ho, who had not been at all certain that education among the women was a good thing, decided now that it was not, and sent formal summons that evening to his third son to come to his apartment, telling him it was better that the women change their ways. The next morning word was brought that his third son's wife was very ill, having put forth great fire. It was wise not to oppose her, for there was hope that she was soon to have a son. Then Ho decided he would go away for a little meditation, and leave the affair to settle itself.

Had the matriarch, Ho's mother, been alive, she would have governed them by doing as her favorite wished, but the wife of Ho could never decide between her three sons. Another day the battle raged, even the little boys of the household slipping away from their teacher to peep into the court of the first son's wife, where Still-Water rocked herself back and forth, insisting she was going to the foreign house, and the first son's wife, calling her names, said she should not.

Now the ten-year-old daughter of the dead second son, who had long wished to study with the boys of the household and had been refused, came and stood up bravely between the two angry women, making herself a go-between.

"If I, this little insignificant one, lowest in the families of the sons of Ho, should be sent with the third son's wife, the honor of learning would be shared with the second son's widow, my mother. Then neither the wife of the youngest or the oldest son triumphs to the full."

"It is a good compromise," said some one.

240

"It is a good compromise," said every one.

Then all at once the rage between the two women had spent itself.

"It is now the hour to go," said the little girl, pressing her advantage; and, after smoothing the hair of Still-Water and putting rice powder on her face, she led her forth.

"They come, they come," announced Kin.

Hester saw entering the room not one but two young girls, holding hands as if to give courage, each to the other. Their tiny feet struck the floor with the clump, clump of padded sticks raised and lowered, raised and lowered. They sat side by side on two straight chairs Kin placed for them, their *amah* attending them, standing behind.

"At last!" Hester said to herself. "After four years in this country am I to know its women?"

The older girl's face did not interest her. It was heavy and expressionless. She did not know that it was dulled by the fierce part the girl had played in the recent happenings of Ho's household. The younger girl was fascinating. The child sat squarely on her chair, a humorous likeness in her attitude to that of Ho himself. Behind her composure, Hester was aware of magnetic power and a strong will. This girl must play a big part in the Ho household, maybe the favorite child.

"What is your name?" Hester asked.

"Shiao Pao, Little Precious."

Ah, she was right; the little girl was a favorite.

Now Hester began the lesson, leading the girls about the room, to chair and table and window, telling them the foreign words.

The news spread through the hong that women from the household of Ho were in the house. The word reached Stephen. Two? He had arranged for only one, the wife of the third son. Who was the other? Filled with curiosity to know what the women of Ho's household were like, he went up the stairs, passed by the open door, hoping to catch a glimpse of them. Standing in the dark hall, he could see and not be seen. They were facing him. Why, one was the girl he had seen kneeling in the street, the little girl with the black hair waving about her face, like a child of his own race. That strangely appealing figure had been on pilgrimage from the Ho household! How little after all he understood Ho's life!

VII

KEYED higher and higher were the days for Stephen; the business was beginning to grow. But coupled with the excitement of success, was the fear of threatened failure. This fear was not long absent from his mind. Through letters, telegrams and the "grapevine telegraph" made up of the Chinese of the Company, it traveled to him: a young man, marrying before his two years were up, dropped from the Company; a man on leave, talking too much to newspaper men, had not returned to his post; a manager who had exceeded his authority, another who had lost money for the Company, returned to the ranks. Each day Stephen surrendered a little more to the demands of the Company, striving to make good in his first managership. Now that dreaded thing "squeeze," not only had not been checked, but was taking on formidable proportions at the tanks. If he could not check it, it might cost him his position. Each morning he went to the telephone, calling McBain, the Scotchman in charge, and each day the answer was the same. The oil was disappearing and right before his eyes! Yet how? Day after day, as soon as the office was closed, Stephen made the two-mile journey to the tanks.

There were four huge gray tanks here, and two long slanting-roofed godowns, where machines took the great sheets of tin plate, fashioning them into the oblong cans. These were placed on a revolving platform, the oil flowed into them, the seal of the Keepers of Light was soldered into the opening. The men in the filling-room sat naked to the waist. What place of concealment had they? The long lines of carrying coolies, oil tins hung from the ends of their poles, jog-trotted their loads to junks waiting at the pontoon. No receptacle other than the sealed tins passed the guards without being challenged. Even the cook's basket was examined each morning when he went to market for the McBains. And yet the oil was disappearing.

Things like this were blots on a man's record, the Scotchman's record, Stephen's record.

The long autumn tarried in the fields and in the town, a slow march of days of sunshine and haze, of *kwe hwa* passing, chrysanthemum buds swelling; the fields after the two harvests of rice, plowed into furrows, planted with the winter crops of clover and vegetables, renewing the habitual green of the valley, flowing like a green sea around the fortress of oil from which, despite its strong walls, its guards, the oil continued to trickle away.

The quiet of late afternoon lay over the countryside. Stephen and McBain, long in consultation, came from the Scotchman's office, waiting for Hester and Mrs. McBain who moved slowly down the path from the house. Stephen watched them passing between the tanks. How tiny they looked walking between the great towers! Mrs. McBain's voice drifted to him.

"Please stay for dinner. You owe it to us, Mrs. Chase. It's as lonely as a lighthouse down here. And now with this trouble hanging over us . . ."

Hester hesitated. She didn't like the place; she didn't want to see night come down over this isolated spot, giving her a picture of the McBains shut away by the darkness and the walls. But the pleading in the other woman's voice was too marked; she could not say no. The four walked to the gate, Stephen giving the order for his launch to come back later. They stood watching the last of the workmen, the coolies, moving toward the gate, going home for the night. In a moment now, they would all be gone. There was no sound except frogs croaking in a pond outside the wall, and the *walla-walla* of talk—the last group of coolies passing out, their round bamboo carrying poles slung across their shoulders, no tins suspended from the ends now.

Suddenly Mrs. McBain gripped Stephen's arm, whispering excitedly, "Mr. Chase, Mr. Chase, look at them! Something's wrong. Stop them! Stop them!" she cried to the guard.

Stephen thought she had lost her wits, then in a flash he saw what she had seen. Why had he not noticed it himself? Each man walked under his carrying pole as if it had weight; and yet bamboo was hollow and had little weight.

"Guards, close the gates!" commanded Stephen. And to the coolies, "Give me your poles."

Out of the cluster of coolies, one advanced and laid his pole in Stephen's outstretched hands. Examining it, he found at the end a cunningly contrived opening and, when he drew out the plug, oil trickled out, falling in a little pool on the gravel path. In that very moment of delight over finding the squeeze, he pondered over the greatness of the loss from so small a leak. The reason came to him, why he had not found out before—he had been looking for something larger. Would he ever learn from these people how much the small things counted?

"I'll be damned!" cried McBain. "But how'd they get it in, without our seeing them?"

"That will probably remain a mystery," said Stephen.

When the gate was opened the coolies slunk away quickly, going home disgraced now in the eyes of the village. To be detected in squeeze! And the extra revenue gone from the village!

Within the walls of the fortress of light, the four gathered around the dinner table in celebration, a bottle of special wine opened by McBain. The fear gone now, the blot on the men's records erased.

"The first toast must be to Mrs. McBain!" said Stephen. "We shouldn't know now, if it weren't for her."

Spots of color glowed on Mrs. McBain's thin cheeks. She couldn't get away from her part in the affair. "You see," she kept saying, "it just came to me all of a sudden what it was."

The next morning, Stephen came running up the stairs to Hester, a letter in his hand, crying, "News! Boynton's got his home leave and the Burnhams are being sent here."

"Oh, how nice!" cried Hester. She'd never forgotten Elsie Burnham and the way she had slipped her hands into hers. And Elsie had written her after the baby came, telling her it *had* been all right, just as Hester said it would be. Elsie and the baby coming here.

"But, Stephen, I thought Burnham was a manager."

"Well, he's had a little bad luck, so they're sending him here for a while," he answered.

They looked at each other, the same thought in both their minds—suppose Mrs. McBain hadn't found out about the oil in the carrying poles!

The day of Boynton's departure, the day of the Burnhams' arrival, Stephen was checked as he passed the door of Boynton's old apartment by the sound of Hester singing. A trill of high notes fell from her lips without effort, bubbling up like a bright spring from some source within her. It was the first time he had heard Hester singing in the hong. Vaguely, through the tense and absorbing interest of his own struggle, he wondered about it as he pushed open the door to see what she was about. She was looping back the heavy Soochow curtains from the long windows. These curtains, part of the equipment of every Company house, heavy and coarse as an ingrain carpet, defied her deft fingers.

As he watched, this woman, so intimately dear to him, seemed unknown. Why had she not sung before, why did she sing now? And then, disturbing in its vivid reality, came the memory of Hester long ago in Manchuria disclosing to him the secrecy of her heart. What was now the secrecy of her heart? Had she been so lonely that she did not sing? Did Elsie Burnham's coming mean so much to her?

When, for the third time, the cumbersome material fell away from her hands, he went over to her.

"Can I help?" he asked. "But why tire yourself like this? Why not let Kin do it?"

"I don't know, really," she said. "I had some sort of idea of making the place more homelike for Elsie Burnham by doing this myself." She spoke a little ruefully, looking at the unruly curtain. "Absurd, really, as if it would make any difference whether I did it or Kin."

She was facing him, standing against the brown curtain, the darker brown pattern of bamboos stretching away into the dim high top of the room. Stephen looked deep into her eyes.

"Hester," he asked, "are you happy?"

"Why, yes, Stephen."

They stood, not touching each other, approaching some new understanding. Her eyes, held to his by the intensity of his gaze, saw into the innermost place of his heart, saw that she was its occupant, giving every delicate offering in this place so secret, so guarded that the

246

door, perhaps only in this moment, would ever swing in for her recognition of her presence within. If she could only remember when the door swung to.

Into the charmed moment broke the whistle of a steamer.

With one motion of his hands, Stephen swept back the curtains. The wooden rings slid along the curtain poles with a wooden clack. The spell was broken, his thoughts back again in the groove of work. "It's the steamer," he said. "We'll have to hurry if we meet the Burnhams."

Looking through the window that gave on the alley, he caught a glimpse of Ho walking carefully across the white flooring boards of the second floor of his new house, and he heard the apprentices at their work, the sleepy chant of boys' voices:

"The cotton padding in my coat is thin . . ."

*   *   *   *   *

The breakfast was done, Stephen had gone away to his office. Against the long windows fell the fine sheets of rain—indication that autumn was ended. Above the noise of the coolie raking out the huge stove in the hall, Kin patting the pillows on the bed, *amah* coming up from her morning meal sighing audibly, settling to her work, Hester heard a door shut on the floor below, the clatter of Elsie's mules clop, clopping on the stairs, and Elsie, as she came, singing a popular song. Then she was there, entering the room with a hop and a skip like some pretty gamin. Her baby was tucked into the hollow of one arm and under the other a box of chocolates.

Amah trailed behind, complaining, "Missie, pay me small baby. Yo no savee. True must sleep." And Elsie, laughing. "Oh, go away, fat *amah*. He's my baby. I'm going to enjoy him my own way. Go and eat your chow, *amah*."

247

She curled herself into a big chair, settling the baby beside her.

"Isn't he marvelous, Hester? He knows better than to cry, or I'd give him to fat *amah*."

"*Ai yah*," *amah* wailed, "I come back chop chop. Then you pay me small baby."

"Elsie looks like a pretty child with her doll," thought Hester, when *amah* had gone, stooping to pull the corner of a pink blanket into a little peak over the downy head of the baby, hardly knowing whether the exquisite sense of protection she felt was for him, or for her friend who looked up now with a gay smile. Perfectly happy, was Hester's verdict, not knowing that this was a valiant gaiety of Elsie's, shutting out the humiliating thought that they would not be here if her husband had not failed.

"Now, let's talk," said Elsie. "I'm simply dying for a chance to talk. You see, up-river was nice enough in some ways, prettier than here, hills all around us. But sometimes for days I didn't see any one except the servants. Every one in the foreign community lived on a different hill, or across the river in the city. But it was all right about the baby, just as you said it would be. How'd you know, Hester? You don't mind if I call you Hester, do you, even if your husband is boss around here?" Then she was smitten by her own words and fell silent.

"It would be dreadful to have you call me anything else. I loved you the first day I saw you." Hester fell silent too, made uneasy by this revelation of herself which took her out of that world where she dwelt separate from all save Stephen. Then the warmth of friendship ran into her heart and she swept on into confession.

"I worried, after I told you you'd be all right up there. I don't know why I told you that, because you see—I wasn't—sure. My baby died up in Manchuria. At home he wouldn't have."

248

Only the sound of the rain driving in sheets against the long windows. Elsie, with a little rush, was kneeling beside Hester, her baby on one arm, the other thrown round her friend. "My dear, I didn't know."

"Don't tell any one," said Hester hastily. "So you see, I have no honor in the eyes of the Chinese."

"But surely you don't care about that!" exclaimed Elsie. "What does it matter what they think?"

"It used not to matter but I suppose it must now—the way I've spoken to you," said Hester.

The *amah* came now, bearing down upon Elsie like a ship in full sail, the skirt of her short white gown blowing out behind.

"I takee little Dee-dee (small brother). He *amah* savee. Pay he bath, pay he chow, pay he sleep."

When Elsie was once more in her own part of the hong, she threw herself on her bed, crying her heart out. At last she sat up, dabbing at her eyes, putting her hands to her ears to shut out the incessant cries of laborers coming up from the bund and the streets of the city. Why had she been so disturbed over the fact that Hester, the manager's wife, almost a stranger to her, had lost her baby out here—lost it because she was beyond the reach of the help she would have had at home? It seemed so dreadful for them to be stranded here. Some vague understanding came to her of why she had cried. Hester, herself, her husband, Mr. Chase—even he in his success—the sports of fortune. She had come bent on adventure, now she knew where the adventure led. Sacrifices like Hester's, humiliations like her own husband's over his demotion, a part of getting their living. Well, whatever it cost her it was worth it if that young man she heard crying in his tub was properly cared for.

She got up and opened the door into the bathroom. The moist hot air rushed out at her. In the corner was the round green pottery tub in which she had sat that morning, like a Buddha, for her bath. Above it, suspended from the ceiling, hung an oil tin, a sprinkler spout soldered into the bottom—their shower bath. An oil stove burning brightly had eaten up the oxygen in the air, making Elsie gasp. A small tin basin stood on a stool beside *amah*. On a towel spread across *amah's* thighs, well cushioned by her padded winter trousers, lay Dee-dee, naked for his bath. "Plenty fat, Dee-dee."

"I'll bathe him," said Elsie. "And put out the stove. How many times have I told you to use plenty of water, *amah*, to bathe him? Now go and get another pitcherful."

Protesting, *amah* surrendered the baby, and went away grumbling. "Sin of waste, water wasted. So much to drink in the next world in punishment."

"Bye, Baby Bunting, Daddy's gone a-hunting," sang Elsie. "To get a pretty rabbit-skin, to wrap his darling baby in!"

Into the Narrow House discord came. From the day of his arrival, Burnham flushed hotly whenever Stephen gave him an order, a flush of humiliation and resentment. Chase ought to recognize the fact that he had been a manager himself. Probably only temporary, this being put back into the ranks. If he could have it out with Chase, if Chase would tell him . . . well, why he was here. He could explain about those defaults. He was not to blame. It might have happened to any one. Just bad luck; surely he could make Chase see that. He went over in his mind how he would present the matter to Chase, if Chase would give him the opportunity.

The Company had not told Burnham what they had told Stephen, that they considered him too easy-going; the Chinese could hookwink him. They had sent him to Chase to whip into shape, passing the burden of discipline and possible ill-will from the Company to the individual. When Stephen had received the letter telling him to work Burnham hard, he had held it in his hand for a long time. Not a pleasant task. Should he make any mention to Burnham of the letter? The Company surely had informed him why he was here. Perhaps they should thrash the matter out between them. But no! Unnecessary to cause Burnham to lose face. That would make the situation intolerable for him. It was sufficient that the man knew why he was here, Stephen concluded, putting the letter in his private file. But as the days went by and there was no understanding between them, Stephen decided to give Burnham a bit of independent work. Lin, the agent he had never trusted, was in arrears. He'd send Burnham to collect the outstanding money—a task where he could be on his own. Putting confidence in him might lead to a better understanding.

A week later Stephen glanced from his office window, hearing the last forced-out groaning note of the chair coolies, as they lowered from their shoulders the weight of a man. Burnham returning!

Stephen's lips set in a stern line. "You're to stay until you get the money," he had said. No remittance had come in from Lin.

As Burnham went past the office to the stairs that led to his apartment, Stephen hailed him.

"Just a moment, Burnham."

The other man turned, his hand on the stair post, looking up toward Elsie and Dee-dee. "After I've seen the family and cleaned up I'll be down."

"I want to see you now."

A moment, Joe Burnham hesitated. Elsie, Dee-dee in her arms, fell back into the shadows above, and her husband strode into Stephen's office.

"Have you the money?" Stephen asked. "I've had no remittance."

"I've used my best judgment," answered Burnham. "I think everything's all right."

"I did not ask you what you thought," said Stephen, "I asked you if you had the money."

Burnham's eyes fell. "He said he'd remit."

"And you believed him?" Stephen's words had the cold cut of scorn. He remembered Lin's shifty look—it had been his own first reading of character in a Chinese. Couldn't Burnham see that Lin wasn't to be trusted? Burnham, who had been born in this country?

"Why shouldn't I trust his word?" Burnham's humiliation and resentment of weeks flared into defiance of Stephen. "I believe in trusting them if you don't."

"It isn't a question of trusting the Chinese. You want to look at them as individuals. Lin couldn't be trusted, whatever race he belonged to. Besides it was up to you to follow my orders; it's I who will have to take the blame, if he defaults."

Stephen's words sounded harsh and arbitrary to Burnham, justifying him in his feeling of superiority. There came to his mind the delicate attention of the agent, the inference that the man preferred to deal with him rather than with Stephen. He turned and left the office.

For forty days the sun did not shine, the gray city lay under the gray pall of the semi-tropic sky, and a misty rain wrapped the city about like a death shroud. In the sunless unheated houses, the women sat shivering in their cotton-padded garments, the more fortunate resting their hands upon covered charcoal braziers held in their laps. The men worked incessantly at their trades, cumbered by their heavy clothes. Members of the beggars' guild, drawing their rags of rough sacking around them, moved each day like an army of vultures through the narrow streets, whining on the door-steps of rich and poor alike. And no man dared turn a beggar away empty-handed, lest the guild of beggars turn upon him and rob him. Every mission in the city, every house on the bund, was surrounded by a sea of muddy streets. The river was shrunken, a muddy line in the distance, destitute of steamers.

Burnham had charge of the office, for Stephen himself had gone to see Agent Lin, seeking to collect the money owed to the Company. But the number two found no pleasure in his position. Stephen's absence was a constant reminder of his own failure, and a round of petty annoyances had cropped up in the office. He laid these annoyances to the rain, the gray monotonous fall of the rain. But it was not accident that the translations were wrong, that there were mistakes in the reports. The "go slow strike" had been declared, because the Chinese clerks had contempt for Burnham in his failure.

Dee-dee was now the only bond between the second and third floor, for the Company stood between the two women. Each morning Hester waited in vain for Elsie's appearance. And when she passed the Burnhams' bedroom and living-room doors, going down the stairs, Elsie, hearing her light step, would busy herself out of sight. Caught in the back-wash of her husband's failure, she felt Hester's success, through Stephen, as a constant irritant, setting them apart.

Hester was proud that Stephen was making good. Little by little the code of a manager was being made known to her—service, that asked nothing for extra hours, or long periods of strain; expected no part in the huge profits, accepting whatever the Company cared to give as an increase in salary; walking in step with the organization at all times, subordinating himself to the will of the organization. By this road only could come that security Stephen talked about, the need of it growing greater with her mounting desire for luxury.

She did not understand Elsie in her aloofness—she had loved Elsie, and this coolness growing up between them troubled her. She began to wish that she and Stephen could have a house to themselves, away from such irritations. Many of the firms were building houses for their managers on an island out in the river. Stephen might ask the Company to do this for them—the hŏng was so crowded.

VIII

STEPHEN had taken. Ho with him, when he went after the money. Twenty thousand dollars owing! The sum stood in his mind in bright red figures. Red ink! A loss, a blot on his record. As he sat on the launch, on his way to Agent Lin's shop, he was tempted to write the main office that it was not his fault . . . Burnham's. But there was Dee-dee. No, he couldn't do it. Might mean Burnham's discharge. Ho, sitting immobile by his side, had he known Stephen's thoughts, would have felt satisfaction. A follower of the good custom. One of the relationships kept —duty of friend.

The agent's shop, perched high on the river bank, was closed. Upon the door were large strips of paper pasted criss-cross, stamped with the magistrate's seal. A groan escaped Stephen.

"Let us go to the magistrate," said Ho.

After they had passed through court after court of the official's dwelling, the magistrate's servant came to meet them, holding Stephen's card high in his hand, crying, "*Chin!*"—an invitation to enter the presence of the great man. The magistrate then was willing to help them. During the long interview that ensued, Stephen held himself in control, lest the intimacy of anxiety intrude upon the aloof moment of greeting.

As the two men rose to go, the magistrate said he would send an assistant to break the official seals he had placed on the shop—done to preserve its contents for the

Keepers of Light. But when the seals were broken, the door opened on a scene of desolation. Every article had been removed. Only the bare shelves remained.

Ho sent away the rabble that had collected, and together he and Stephen slid the great shutters into place. In the dark and bare interior, in every silent room around the court, they hunted for the account books, sticking their fingers into the cracks. Finally, under a bed in a back room, they came upon a small chest; and, when it was opened, there lay the small limp paper books used for accounts. Stephen turned to the last page, and beginning at the right-hand corner he followed the characters down the long row. Yes, here were names of various small shops in the city, and the amounts due.

"These would mean a few hundred to us," he said. Then something made him look at the accounts more carefully, and he saw that the entries were false. The books had been painstakingly prepared but he noticed that each item was in the same shade of ink. The Chinese ink, rubbed from a block, and made fresh for each using, could not possibly have given this uniform effect, if the entries had been made on different days. These must be the books prepared for Burnham and left with the thought that they would fool any other stupid foreigner, causing him to consume days in the city trying to collect the accounts.

"There is but one thing to do," said Stephen. "Make use of the deeds we hold as security. Sell the land."

"It will bring little," said Ho.

The white man knew this was true, for land sold by the magistrate would pass through the hands of many officials, and each would take his squeeze.

"There's a better way," Ho went on. "According to the good custom of my country, the family of Lin, if they are worthy, hold themselves responsible."

It was late afternoon when Ho learned where the family

of Lin lived. Thirty *li* away in the country. Only ten miles, but the chair coolies could not make it before dark. Stephen felt he could not wait until morning, so they started.

The thirty *li* named in the town lengthened to forty, to fifty. Darkness had long since fallen when they reached the great farmhouse and Ho knocked on the outer gate. Inside there was barking of dogs and a murmur of consultation. Then, at Ho's second knocking, a voice called through the heavy timbers of the gate, "What man is without?"

But even when Ho gave his name, there was no slipping back of the bolts. Stephen realized that the family were fearful, thinking they might be bandits. He cursed himself for giving way to his Western impatience, coming so late, instead of waiting, as Ho had suggested, until morning. But at last the gate was opened a crack; and when the man within saw it was indeed the great Ho, known throughout the province, the halves of the gate were pushed back on their wooden hinges.

A very old man, leaning on a stick, beckoned them to come inside. Walking ahead of them—his shoes, made of new rushes, creaking as he went—he led them across a court and into a dimly lighted room, where two old men with thin white beards sat in armchairs, one on each side of a table.

Stephen could only conjecture what consternation they must be feeling at this intrusion into their house of a pale-eyed barbarian, perhaps the first they had ever seen. But the old men gave no sign, advancing with Chinese calmness, giving the visitors greeting.

The long negotiations that went forward through the night seemed a kind of dream. At first only the two old men took part in the conference, then other men, younger, but all in blue homespun, stepped out of the shadows of what must have been an inner court, and entered into the discussion. The ancient who opened the gate joined in the talk, whether as member of the clan, or simply as a privileged servant, Stephen did not know. But he knew that the imperious old woman who finally hobbled in, seating herself in one of the big chairs at the center of the group, was the most powerful person in the room. For a time she sat without speaking, leaning forward, her gnarled yellow hands resting on the back of the wooden bird that made the top of her cane. Then all at once, when Ho was telling them that the account books were counterfeited, she raised her head, and, in a voice vigorous and shrill, harangued the men of the household. What she said Stephen could understand only in part, but he knew that she considered the forging of the account books Lin's most serious offense; an offense punishable by death, he knew, under the régime of the Emperor, the régime the old woman understood best. It was drawn when all seemed to understand just how much had been gambled away by the scapegrace of the family, who had fled, leaving them to pay.

One of the old men spoke gravely now. "If the Keepers of Light will give us three days of time, we will bring to them the full sum of our indebtedness."

When a few details had been arranged, Ho rose to go, saying, "Until then we hold the deeds."

"Until then the great Ho may hold our deeds," they echoed.

Stephen was passing through the great gate, following Ho, when he turned with the sudden motion of the Westerner, realizing he had left behind him his stout stick, which he always carried when he was in the country.

And there in the room which they had just left, in a streak of gray light where a shutter had been taken away from the opposite wall in the midst of the assembled clan, stood the scapegrace himself, Lin, the agent of the Company! So he had been here in the house during the in-

257

terview, hiding behind his family, shifting his responsibility to them! In a flash Stephen took in the whole scene. The agent was bare to the waist, and his hands were pinioned before him. The other men had fallen back, except the tall old man, spokesman throughout the night. Over the half-naked figure of Lin he towered, golden yellow with rage, his arm raised, in his hand the long bamboo used for terrible punishment. Power of death, fathers had over their sons. Stephen felt himself shaken with the sight.

The gate-keeper pushed forward the two halves of the gate, forcing him outside. As he walked through the silent countryside, following the chair swinging like a plaything between the stalwart coolies, the morning breeze coming up from the fields revived him and he felt his brain clearing. Nevertheless, the anger of the outraged father of the agent could not be brushed from his mind.

Five days passed and no word was received from the Lins. Ho counseled patience, mentioning that this was a bad year. Even well-to-do farmers like the Lins felt the pinch. Because of the drought, the second rice had been thin in this area. Ready money was difficult to obtain. On the sixth day Stephen, sitting idly on the deck of the launch, saw a sampan moving toward them, and in it the elderly man, spokesman that night of negotiation.

He called Ho, and soon Ho's great shoulders rose above the hatchway. The two stood together, waiting.

After the salutations had been completed, the man told Ho he had brought the major part of the indebtedness. "But a small sum we find difficult to raise, and would substitute a deed to a piece of fine farmland."

"Fine farmland!" said Ho, looking at the deed. "Drought has been there for three years."

The bargaining that had not taken place that evening in the farmhouse, now took place on the launch, dragging itself out through a succession of days. Stephen was tirelessly patient, realizing that this bargaining over the final bit of the indebtedness gave a little face to the Lin clan. At last a piece of property was agreed on.

When the bargaining was concluded, Ho and the old man went off to the town to arrange details with the magistrate. Stephen, pacing the deck of the launch, awaited their return. Presently, along the ridge of dike, he noticed a line of country folk slowly advancing. He wondered if, a little before the usual time, these people were making their spring pilgrimage to the temple. Then he noticed they carried no knapsacks bulging with offerings, and as they drew nearer, he saw that their full figures typified excess, as he had never seen it in this country of close margins. Exaggerated to the grotesque was the greatly desired full form of plenty, bellies bigger than the laughing Buddha, god of plenty. Erratic in their walk, they staggered forward, excess of revelry manifested in every movement and posture. Such a Bacchanalian march of men, women and children was startling in this country of sober toil. And then, as they drew still nearer, Stephen saw the specter of famine in their faces—their eyes sunken, their cheeks fallen in.

"Who are they?" he asked the captain of the launch.

"Eaters of bark and grass," the boatman replied. "It was rumored in the city yesterday that farmers from ten villages away were coming."

All afternoon, advancing along the dike paths, these victims of famine came. Not one stepped into the fields, snatching at the vegetables, such was their acceptance of fate. But they stopped at the launch, using the ancient cry of the beggars, "Do good, do good!"

Their faces pressed in upon Stephen, until each tragic

259

mark of suffering was written vividly on his mind. From further knowledge of this land of starvation, he drew back. He felt a foreboding of disaster.

It was late on a rainy afternoon that the launch bearing Stephen and Ho came in sight of the narrow white building—the hong. After weeks of patience, suddenly impatience mastered Stephen. He put on his slicker and stood at the rail before the gangplank was down, finding it difficult to fit his step to Ho's, as they walked together across the muddy bund. Now at last he was at his own gate. Past the offices he hurried, glad they had closed for the day. Up the stairs, gaining the second floor, hoping no doors would open, none of his staff come out to greet him. Sometimes of late he had wished he could have more privacy—escape for a moment from his business.

No one appeared and he took the last flight two steps at a time, giving his own particular call for Hester. But there was no response. She was out somewhere evidently, not knowing he was coming. The rooms of his home were full of the fragrance of her personality. That quiet place of her making gave him the sense of sanctuary he craved. He closed the door of the living-room behind him, moving about the spaces of the room, delighting in its beauty, delighting even in its luxury, the world of poverty shut out. Sometimes he had demurred in his heart at the money Hester spent for these beautiful things, feeling secure only when he was saving. But this dark afternoon of his return, it was the room's very luxury that gave him his sense of security.

The door-knob turned, and he held himself tense, fearing it would be Kin, or the coolie, interrupting his moment of privacy. Then he heard a cry of joy and he turned quickly, holding out his arms to Hester. In the long embrace, there slid from his mind the pinched features of the starving peasants.

The next day Hester felt the hong to be pervaded with an indefinable unrest, clouding her happiness in the return of Stephen. Late in the afternoon, when she had shut herself away in her own bedroom to escape the uneasiness, *amah* came, closing the door behind her.

"For a long time the *tai-tai* has not made the inspection of the quarters of her unworthy servants to see that all is well."

Why should discreet little *amah* break the solidarity that existed among the servants? she wondered. A little later, she walked down the long flights of stairs of the back gallery to the servants' quarters.

Kin had just left, bent on giving his birds an airing. It was a three-coat cold day, and he owned but two coats. He had pawned his third the day before, when he had bought himself another woman. She had come with her family from the upper part of the province where famine existed this winter, and he had got her cheap, but, *ai yah*, he had no luck in women. She was a poor starved thing. He had her hidden in the coal house. He wished now he had the coat instead of the woman.

A three-coat day; he certainly could not go forth in two. Did he not represent the hong of the Keepers of Light? Better he place a coat belonging to his master over his own. Thus attired, carrying his bird cages, one in each hand, stepping gingerly on the stones close to the cubicles of shops, avoiding the slimy mud, he had gone forth.

Kin's birds sang well, as he squatted with other bird fanciers in an open space. The fruit vender, who stood at the corner blowing on his fingers to keep them warm, looked upon him with admiration as he stopped to chat

261

a moment on his return. Kin was filled with well-being, as he entered the hong and leisurely prepared to answer the summons of his mistress, divesting himself of the coat that was Stephen's, and donning the long white gown of his office. All was well. He had told his mistress before he left the thing she was pleased always to hear, that he wished to take time to go to the bathhouse. Not until he entered her presence, was he uneasy. Then he saw immediately that matters were not as he might wish.

"One moment," he said, and went out, bringing in from the butler's pantry a gnarled peach-tree a foot high in full bloom. He had meant to sell it to Hester, but he now presented it to her.

Stephen, arriving from the office, came upon the incredible spectacle of Kin offering the lovely thing to Hester, and Hester disdainful in her refusal.

"Kin, the woman you have hidden in the coal house cannot remain the night. Go now and take her away. I am angry."

Stephen remembered a little uneasily the old conflicts between Hester and Kin.

"The missie does not comprehend. My family have burdened me with a wife I did not seek. Surely for a night the *tai-tai* will give her shelter here," whined Kin.

"Stephen," pleaded Hester, "will you see that he does what I say?"

Stephen walked quickly down the stairs, angry that Kin was annoying Hester. He'd see that Kin's woman left. But when he opened the coal-house door and saw the woman, her black hair disheveled, her features gaunt, her yellow hand, its flesh unwholesome, hanging down over the side of the boards on which she lay, he shut the door and, without a word, went back to Hester.

"Hester, we can't send her away," he said. "She's half starved. Even to discipline Kin, we can't do it."

His words fell without their true meaning on Hester's

ears, thinking he used "half starved," as the words would be used amid the plenty of America. "Nonsense! If we allow her to stay, every other man will bring a woman here."

"Hester, you don't understand. If Kin turns her out, she will really starve," pleaded Stephen.

"You tell me not to let Kin squeeze so much and then you tell me to keep this woman. You know Kin would keep her at our expense. Stephen, you're protecting Kin, undermining me with him. And he's fooling you just as he always has! Why, the woman's a disgusting creature! I won't have her here."

Stephen was aghast that it could be Hester doing this. Then he knew that she did not understand. "They look like that when . . ." He stopped. He did not want her to understand. That image of starvation in Hester's mind. No! Better that she think him harsh and unyielding.

Hester caught a hint of some trouble within him. She waited for him to go on, but he sat withdrawn into himself. The set line of his lips told her that he would not speak.

As she looked at this man, so intimately known to her —the texture of his skin as familiar to her as her own, the cadence of his voice giving her the sense of stability —the incompleteness of such intimacy brought sharp suffering of the spirit shut out. Her throat tightened and her eyes were hot with tears. She rose and went into the bedroom.

After a little Stephen followed her. He drew her to him, looking deep into her still wet eyes. He kissed her eyes, her lips, the curve of her throat, the palms of her hands.

"Is it all right now?" he asked gently. "You must let me decide this time, sweet." He felt the wistful desire for her understanding, but he would not tell her what

263

troubled him. Keep her secure from any knowledge of want, never let want come near her. Deeper within him than ever before, he felt a bondage to his job.

That night, very late, after Hester and Stephen had returned from a party, there was a light knocking at their door and they heard Kin speaking softly, "Master, open."

"Master," he whispered when Stephen was in the hall, "there is gambling in the servants' quarters. As the *tai-pan* knows, it is against the law."

Stephen went softly through the house, avoiding the back galley, wishing to surprise the gamblers. For a long time he had suspected that there was organized gambling going on in the hong, but he had seen no way to control it. But now here was this sudden help from Kin.

He stood listening at the closed doors of the servants' rooms. Yes, there was the sound of *mah jong* tiles! The cook probably; for a long time he had suspected him. He threw the door wide, disclosing Hester's *amah* and three cronies in a harmless game! Now that he was here, he must speak, although it meant that *amah* would lose face and leave—obviously Kin's intention in bringing him here. Some drama between Kin and his women was being enacted, with Hester and himself playing leading parts, but as whose enemy, whose friend, he did not know.

As Stephen expected, *amah* made a great scene the next day over the master's visit; then she went away and Kin got another *amah* for Hester. The solidarity of the servants' quarters was restored. Hester again rested on their outward serenity, and Stephen did not demur at the slight increase in the expenses. He knew that the cost of Kin's extra woman must come from his pocket.

IX

THE leaves of the mustard fell. The stems and the ripened seed-pods turned to ash-gray. The pods were harvested, the oil crushed from them; the residue and the stalks were returned to the fields lest the soil be exhausted, now in the fortieth century of its use. The rice land was flooded. The valley became a glistening, shimmering floor, awaiting the spring planting.

The hong had grown more crowded. Every one was a little cramped, now that Stephen's tireless energy was increasing the business. More men were needed. Stephen and Hester no longer had the top floor to themselves. It had been divided by the simple means of a partition across the hall. Two bachelors lived at the back. It made Hester more desirous than ever for the separate house. On the floor beneath lived the Burnhams, Fenton and a young man named Lunt, just out from home. The floor below that was a veritable beehive—six white men, Chinese clerks, shipping men, agents and captains of oil junks, constantly coming and going; and on the ground floor, twenty men-servants and two *amahs*. Up and down the outer stairway at the back, from gallery to gallery, they tramped, talking, quarreling, gossiping. At night there were more, for Kin had them sleep two in a bed, renting out the vacant space.

All day through the hong the hum of life went on, a voice now and then dominating the usual murmur—Stephen's voice, light in timbre; Hester's *amah* scolding some one. Dee-dee, little brother to all the hong, nine months old now, commanded the servants of four households. Even Kin stopped to ride him piggy-back down the long corridor, on his way to answer the missie's ring.

At night the voice of the hong was less constant, although it never altogether ceased; laughter and conviviality in one of the apartments; Dee-dee crying out for a drink; soft click of *mah jong* tiles as Kin gathered the servants together from the white households; Dee-dee's *amah* praying to the white man's god for a son—a little boy like Dee-dee with blue eyes and yellow curls, for Elsie's *amah* did not think the pale child grotesque, as most of her countrymen did, but beautiful to see. Nor did she envision the anger of her one-eyed husband, if she were to bear a child like Dee-dee. She continued to pray in peace.

Now came a wave of excitement spreading through the hong. The general manager, Mr. Truesdale, "the Gentleman," was due on the next steamer. Every one in the hong had his own particular interest in the event, the younger men hoping the manager would think them outstanding and promote them; Joe Burnham hoping that Stephen would be transferred and himself made manager —undoubtedly that was why he had been sent here in the fall; Elsie hoping they might be transferred to a larger city for Dee-dee's sake; Hester hoping Mr. Truesdale might grant the new dwelling; Stephen filled with concern that his office should be in perfect order, and that the manager should be satisfied with what he had done in the territory.

Hester prepared the hong for his coming—each piece of Company furniture accounted for; the building, ramshackle as it was, made to give forth a well-cared-for air. Kin supported her valiantly in her efforts. What a catastrophe, if he should lose face before the great one coming from Shanghai!

The general manager was impressed. On the first day of his stay, he said to Stephen, "I congratulate you, Chase, on your wife. She is a help in the Company." A little later Stephen, managing to get away from the conference for a few moments, rushed up-stairs to tell Hester what Truesdale had said of her.

That night, at the dinner given for the Company

people to meet the general manager, Hester was in a warm glow of happiness under the memory of his praise. Elsie should be thankful she was starting under such a man, she thought, remembering her own beginnings with a general manager who did not say gracious things to wives.

Imagine talking to the old manager, the way Elsie Burnham was now talking to this one, telling him all about Dee-dee! But then who would not be interested in Dee-dee? Hester smiled to herself, thinking of how masterful the little boy had looked, riding triumphantly on the back of his *amah* that morning, beating her with his fists until she quickened her pace to a jog trot, her bound feet pounding the floor like tiny hoofs.

Elsie was wondering if she dared hint to Mr. Truesdale her fears about living in the hong, situated at it was in the midst of the Chinese city. Not a safe place for a baby. Now, if she could live in Shanghai. . . . Only this morning *amah* had said, upholding Kin in his zeal for women, "Number two great lady, you no savee. My side must catchee plenty wife, plenty son. Suppose many die, have got p'laps one left. Your side all belong live. But my thinkee you more better catchee one more all same Dee-dee."

Elsie had laughed at *amah's* quaint philosophy, but a faint dread remained. She gave her attention to the general manager who was saying graciously, "I met a handsome little boy in the hall to-day."

"Oh, that must have been Dee-dee!"

Impetuously she spoke and all at the table laughed.

"If there were a dozen children in the house, you'd be sure it was Dee-dee," her husband teased her.

"But it *was* Dee-dee!" There was no room in Elsie Burnham's mind for humor in regard to her son, and she was a little affronted at the laughter. Mr. Truesdale came to her rescue.

267

"Stand by your guns, Mrs. Burnham. I have two sons and I know how you feel."

They disregarded the rest of the table and fell to talking of their boys.

"Mine are at college," said the manager.

"Mine is going to be. What do you think is the best college for a boy?" Elsie was dreadfully serious.

"Well, I don't know that you need to decide now," he answered, looking at her kindly.

"He's so friendly, so kind, and *so* human," thought Elsie. And then, without her volition, the words spoke themselves.

"Oh, Mr. Truesdale, this isn't any place for a child. If only we could live in Shanghai!"

She was not prepared for the instant change that came over him. No longer did the kind father look out of his eyes. Now he was the general manager of the Company.

"You know we can't any of us be choosers in the Company, Mrs. Burnham. Of course, if I had my way, we'd all live in Shanghai." Then he turned back to Hester.

Elsie attended closely to the eating of her salad, seeing through a blur the three stalks of asparagus thrust through a ring of pimento, Kin's special company salad. Her husband would never forgive her for this. It was his proud boast that he had never asked the Company for anything. Too late she had perceived that the general manager's first allegiance was to the Company.

Angrily she dug into the asparagus, thinking how naked it looked, lying there without any lettuce. Some Company people had gardens and could have lettuce. She felt ill-treated. The general manager ought to know she was a good sport, after the way she had stuck it out off there in Szechuan, and the baby coming and all. She wasn't asking anything for herself but for the baby. And wouldn't he feel the same way if it were his baby? Elsie felt desperate. Some people in the Company got things. How'd they do it?

She realized Mrs. McBain was speaking to her from across the table.

"Mrs. Chase has promised to send the kitchen scraps, when the Company launch comes down each morning. Will you send yours? I'm feeding the poor Chinese doggies. I make them a warm mash. You should just see them. They come in droves, and they're so thin. Somehow, lately, I haven't been able to think of anything else but those poor doggies."

"But wonks, Mrs. McBain! There are millions of them in a Chinese city," protested Elsie.

Stephen was annoyed. What would the general manager think of them? His staff wasn't showing up so very well. Sentimental talk of wonks as doggies, and Elsie Burnham going on about the baby. What possessed her? She who spent her time at gay parties, leaving Dee-dee to the *amah!*

Hester saw Stephen's look of distress. She hastened to rescue the conversation by asking the general manager if he wouldn't tell them about his recent trip to America. "None of us has been there for a very long time."

"You don't think you are losing your nationality?" Mr. Tuesdale asked mockingly. "You know that was Mrs. Fulton's reason for getting her husband to resign."

They all laughed.

"But seriously, now," said the general manager, "she didn't know when she was well off. It's hard getting started at home. By the way, Chase, you knew Cheatham, didn't you? Ran into him one day in a candy store in New York."

"What's he doing?" asked Stephen.

"We knew him well in Manchuria. Why, he took over from Stephen when we left," broke in Hester.

"Doesn't seem to be doing so well. Didn't look too

prosperous. Tried to avoid me when he saw me come in," said Mr. Truesdale.

Hester felt thankful for her financial safety. Risk was ugly. She was sorry for Cheatham in his shabby struggle. Once she had thought there was something glorious in such a struggle. But she knew better now.

Stephen was thoughtful, too. The security of the Company was becoming a necessity to him. Between him and poverty stood the Company. The Company took care of its men.

There was a lift to all the heads at the table and a drawing together. Something uniting these people, a few moments before so jaggedly individual, each with his own happiness, or discontent. The manager had drawn them together, bound them into the Company by injecting into them the fear of the unknown, the uncharted, for such America had become to them.

"But going back to your request, Mrs. Chase, to tell you something about America. You know the thing that impressed me most—perhaps because I'm an oil man— was the sight of some newly developed oil wells. I'd never seen any before. I suppose none of you have. Well, you've never seen such a sight. Derricks, not one, but hundreds. And excitement as great as if gold had been discovered. It *is* gold—liquid gold. And people, poor, suddenly rich, and then poor again. The little men not having much chance against the bigger concerns, and each one hurrying to get down his well, before the oil was drawn off by the man next to him. Our Company had bought up a lot of small men, and you know our record for efficiency. We were doing better than record time in getting down our wells. Couldn't wait, or we'd lose the oil. But we're overproduced. It's a challenge to us to sell more oil. They want us to make a record this year, men." Challenge and stimulus of fear stimulating the men to the greatest service.

"Ah, I've talked too much of business, Mrs. Chase. I must apologize," continued Truesdale, turning once more to his hostess.

"Oh, no!" cried Hester, feeling how close together they all were now. She was grateful to him.

It was only at the end of the general manager's visit that Stephen brought himself to present the project of better living conditions. He knew it was not good for a Company man to ask for things, but for Hester's sake he must speak.

"We're overcrowded, Mr. Truesdale. Many of the business companies are buying land on the island out in the river away from the city."

"Well, Chase, I hardly feel I could put anything like that up to New York now. You must remember that I have just started in as general manager. I can't advocate big expenditures. Business has grown since you came up here, but it hardly warrants the expense of an extra house. Matter of fact, I thought you seemed pretty comfortable."

He was thinking of their living-room and its beauty. Two or three Chinese pictures hung on soft gray walls. Here and there the sun making pools of light on the polished surface of an old Chinese table; bronze vases in studied pairs, black with age; porcelains, exquisite in form and color; the rugs and hangings gorgeous and rich. He shut his eyes to the Chinese city pressing so close, and to the complicated life of the Company people within this House of Business. The Company had told him to keep down the overhead. His position depended upon it. He too must make good, he too knew the flick of fear.

"What would you consider a business that would warrant it?" asked Stephen.

The general manager named a figure that made him draw in his breath.

After Truesdale had gone, Stephen began planning. If Hester was to have this separate dwelling, he'd have to touch that figure within the year. He gathered himself together for the effort. Now, early in the morning, he went to his office in order that before the steady hum of big business began, and he was surrounded with the substantial success he was bringing to the oil business, he might imagine more and more fully how a man living ever on the edge of starvation could be taught to want light. Often in the days that followed, thinking so much of poverty, he imagined his own life forced down into its dark and hampered mold. He never got ahead in his savings. He had thought he could put by the amount of his increase, but the expenses of the house had gone up enormously. How did Kin manage it and never get caught? He had no time to watch him, it was all he could do to follow the squeeze going on among the men in the business. He might dismiss Kin, but he might be worse off in another house-boy's hands. Kin doesn't take more than my increase, he thought, but I suppose he takes that.

And Hester—Hester believes we should spend the increase. Saving is ugly to Hester. Then there's mother—exchange bad for me. Silver changes into so little gold. He began to wonder if perhaps the secret of saving, as in profit by squeeze, did not lie in the little things. Kin took away his increase by a few coppers here and a few coppers there—a slow but persistent seepage. If he were as persistent in the small savings, perhaps he could get ahead. Begin on himself. He didn't seem to have many wants but still—club chits, smokes, clothes—didn't bother much about clothes, but might save a little there. He must! He must make Hester safe against poverty.

X

WITH the stirrings of spring came the stirrings of soldiers awakening from their winter torpidity, and in the districts where there had been famine, bandit groups sprang up. There was a corner of Stephen's territory where none dared venture now, a stronghold of bandits. Still the peasants held the valley to its green productivity. The rice and the silk-worms flourished. All was well.

Then summer came. In this ancient civilization the summers were terrible. From the city the odors, mingling in the narrow streets and never quite blown away, rose, filling the hong like a noisome perfume, and the still heat lay in the rooms like a hot fire. The house seemed very empty. Two of the younger men were away on their vacations. Elsie and Dee-dee had long since gone to the hills, and Burnham had joined them recently when news had come that Dee-dee was not well.

Hester and Stephen were making ready to go, too, leaving Fenton and the new boy, Lunt, to carry on, when the evil spirit of cholera entered the city. Melons were in abundance, and they lay on the fruit vender's trays cut into small pieces, so that even the poorest might be tempted to buy. Half asleep, the fruit vender forgot sometimes to wave his horse-tail brush over his wares to keep off the hordes of flies. But no one minded very much. Rich and poor bought his wares. It was not good to be hungry. And then, mysteriously, the black scourge of cholera entered the city.

Stephen would not go now, leaving the younger, inexperienced men in the midst of danger. This was his post. And Hester understood his anxiety, as she had never understood his anxiety over famine. There was something tangible in this threat of death which roused her. The inactivity of the past year fell from her, a discarded garment.

She ministered to all around her, quieting the fears of both yellow man and white. Through kitchen and servants' quarters, she moved like a white spirit, for the moist heat had taken her last vestige of color. Like children, the servants came to her, shaken with the fear that the black death would snatch away their lives, and she calmed them.

"If you do as I say, I can keep you safe. The evil spirit enters into the melons, into all cold things. Eat only the hot food, and the evil spirit cannot touch you. And bathe your hands in this special water when you come from the street."

Tirelessly she worked, even entering the offices and superintending the baking of some papers handled by a victim of the dread disease.

Three times a day Stephen, Fenton and Lunt gathered around her, eating only what she gave them. The red flare of the charcoal in the brazier upon which Kin cooked all their food, there in her presence, threw its heat up in shimmering waves, fanning her cheeks with its hot breath, but she never relinquished her oversight.

Round the slender figure of Hester these men pivoted. Lunt, straight out from home, was frankly her slave. And Fenton, like a little boy who, once the veneer of braggadocio is gone, clings without shame to his elders, frankly took his courage from Hester.

"So long as you're not afraid, I'm not," he told her. "But, say, couldn't I call you Hester? You'd seem a little nearer to me then."

The men from the other hongs dropped in casually at mealtime, hoping Hester would ask them to stay. And she always did. The mission doctor, pressed as he was, came often, making as his excuse the need to look after them; he took strength from the presence of this woman so full of courage, but he scolded her for risking herself thus. She ought to leave the city.

Stephen himself said little, but in Hester's presence he kept his eyes always upon her, as if thus he gained strength to forget the horror of this death, repeated so often around him, so needless if the people were not so ignorant. And the threat of war that hung over the city, that troubled him too. Disease, war, more poverty. A haven from it all was Hester. He felt healed by a lovely compassion in her.

The city pressed closer with its hundreds of dying men. Coffins could not be made fast enough. Shrouded in bright red, the people bore the biers down to the junks on the river, some taking their dead to ancestral burying-grounds under ancient cypress trees, others carrying them over the narrow green dikes between the now golden rice-fields, up into the hills to other ancestral burying-places. Across the bund, night and day, the red-decked coffins and the white-clad mourners moved. From every window of the hong, the pageant of color could be seen, and all the rooms were filled with the wailing, shrieking dirges. But as day after day the scourge passed them by, Hester grew in her belief in the white man's immunity, the immunity science had brought him. This Western house, surrounded with the song of death, a house of security—made so by her presence, keeping watch. And as the realization that all the household needed her, greatly depending upon her, grew, there was in her demeanor an indefinable air of authority and power, upon which the people—both yellow and white—rested.

The drama of death moved on to its climax. The night came when the paper steamer which had stood in the temple for many days, heavily provisioned with rice and fruit to eat, wine to drink, clothes to wear, opium to smoke, in the hope of luring the evil spirit of the black death to enter it, had at last its guest. From the lowest to the highest in the city, the people had given freely for the spirit's comfort. Ho had given two hundred dollars, and the fruit vender at his gate had given six *cash*. So great had been the sum, that the city had been able to provide the spirit with this fine steamer, exact replica of the one the white barbarians used.

The night was oppressive, the blanket of moist heat made breathing labored and unnatural. The four in the hong were sitting on the upper gallery when, from the city which lay behind them with its hundreds of dying men, there arose a wailing that curdled their blood. Then came a roar of men's voices, and sweeping down the bund, long phalanxes of dark figures carrying paper lanterns, carrying flaming torches, chanting the wild beseeching cry of the boatmen, used when they call upon the wind to come. On, on the chanting thousands moved, sweeping forward, more following, carrying on their shoulders the huge paper steamer lighted from stern to stern with electric lights.

As they passed, Hester, turning, saw Kin switching off the current in the room behind them.

"Kin," she called, "what are you doing?"

Covered by the darkness Kin slipped out to the veranda, speaking with a soft Eastern chuckle in his voice.

"Fool the evil thing. It cannot find its way back." And looking, Hester saw that the city was shrouded in blackness.

That night Stephen could not sleep. When he came and lay down beside Hester, she pushed herself high on her pillow, throwing her arm out, encircling him. A tall and hovering presence she seemed to Stephen, as she drew his head down until it rested in the hollow of her breast. Slipping off to sleep, he gave a sigh. Dimly he felt the cycle of a man's need of woman completing itself. He drew his knees up, his hands to his chest, as if he had come back to the same darkness of his mother's womb.

*   *   *   *   *

276

Gradually the cholera grew less and less; the spent and exhausted city took unto itself renewed life.

Autumn came. The second threshing began. There was the soft hollow thud of rice bundles beaten against wooden bins, set up in the stubbled paddies. Shocks of rice straw dotted the valley floor. Red persimmons lay on the trays of the fruit venders. Behind the high walls of Ho's foreign house, the *kwe hwa* tree was sending forth the sweet smell of its thousands of clusters of tiny yellow flowers, hidden under the thick green leaves.

The hong again had its full quota of workers; the men back from their vacations, Fenton bringing with him a bride, a Russian girl he had met during his two weeks' vacation; the Burnhams back with Dee-dee, rosy and fat and attempting his first speech, a jargon of English and Chinese. His first word, Chinese, spoken to *amah,* who had come running to Elsie boasting proudly, "He say '*ao sao,*' hurry! All same proper white man."

It was Saturday afternoon, an autumn day of pure beauty. The hong was all but empty. Every one had gone to the club, either to watch, or to take part in, a tennis match. The house-boys were there, also, for this was the day for the hong to serve tea at the club. Two coolies left in charge were drowsing by the back gate.

Dee-dee, little brother of all the hong, had just waked from his nap and was demanding imperiously of his *amah* that she ride him piggy-back up the long stairs to find his Aunt Hester. When he found her domain empty, he demanded that *amah* take him down the flights of the back gallery. He brought her to a halt at the back entrance. *Amah* looked wistfully out. Just two short streets to the little hut she called home. The members of her family had not seen little brother since he came home. It was a fine afternoon. The temple was on the way, another prayer for a son. A sudden idea—leave among the clay images given by other women desiring sons that

277

little image in Dee-dee's hands. "Doll" he called it—an image with light hair, blue eyes. Her time was very near now; she had bound herself so tightly that missie did not know, for missie would send her away if she found out, and *amah* needed every penny to help her one-eyed husband to pay for the funerals of his clan, many this summer. Thirty per cent. must be paid on each dollar they had borrowed from Kin.

"*Ao sao tih,* hurry—gee-ap."

Amah on her bound feet broke into a jog trot going down the street. A spray of *kwe hwa* for the coils of her black hair, haggled for and at last bought, from the bottleful sitting among the bright persimmons on the fruit vender's tray. The candy-maker coming along the way, beating his gong, crying, "Sugar blown by my breath into horses, into men!" Dee-dee reaching out his hand.

"Little brother of all the hong, thou shalt have one! Only give me the little image in thy hand."

That night, summer's hot ghost stole back into the city. In the breathless heat, every one in the hong had left his doors and windows wide open. Stephen had just managed to get to sleep, when he heard a child's sharp terrified scream. Dee-dee having a bad dream, he said to himself, closing the door quickly so that the sound would not wake Hester. But he was only just dropping off to sleep again, when there was a knock on his door.

"Say, Chase, I hate to disturb you, but the boy's awfully sick." It was Burnham's voice. "Elsie's frantic, and I don't know what to do." Almost like a child himself, he appealed to Stephen.

It was a long time since it had been necessary for Stephen to care for the sick. At first, as he leaned over the crib he thought it was colic, then his heart stood still. That little writing figure growing momentarily thinner before their eyes. He had seen that too often in the streets of the city this summer not to know. Cholera!

"Burnham, we've got to have a doctor immediately."

"Answer, answer," Burnham called frantically into the telephone, trying this doctor, that. Were all of them out this night? At last one, but across the city—coming as fast as chair bearers could bring him. The hong was roused now, the cooks heating water, the coolies toiling up the stairs with full pails, the boys under foot trying to help, Hester begging to come in, but denied admittance by Stephen. "No use risking yourself for nothing, Hester." But careless himself. It was Stephen who handled the moaning child—Dee-dee seemed to cry less under his dexterous touch. It was Stephen who did the things a servant would do. *Amah* was no help, kneeling by the crib, chattering, "Dee-dee, *amah* callie you."

Burnham looking on, too, not resenting Stephen's command this time. How deft and gentle he is, thought the father gratefully, as he watched Stephen lift the sick baby from his crib, slipping a fresh sheet under him. Elsie, white and determined, moved about helping Stephen.

"Where's *amah*?" she asked once. "Call her."

But *amah* had gone, stopping in the kitchen only long enough to get one of the little red lamps burning there. Then out of the back gate into the dark city she went, looking for the fair spirit of Dee-dee. She held the lamp high, peering into every corner. In the still night, its flame, inclosed in the beautiful glass holder, burned brightly. Better far than a candle.

"*Lai, lai,* come, come, little spirit, back to your pretty self. Don't you see this fine light? Follow it. *Ai yah*, I hear the little white spirit." "Gee-ap, *ao sao!*" Surely she heard it.

But, no, she could not find it. Perhaps the little white spirit was teasing, just as its master did. Perhaps it had whisked behind her and was on its way home. Holding the lamp lower now, peering into every cranny, fearful lest she pass Dee-dee, she made her way back to the hong. But the spirit of Dee-dee had not returned. How had she failed to find him with so bright a light, she wondered in her bewilderment, as she came into the room, seeing the body of Dee-dee lying shrunken and still.

The doctor had been too late. "If only we had modern transportation in this city," thought Stephen, as he sat with Burnham, keeping watch over Dee-dee, as he had kept watch long ago over his own dead son. And Burnham, at last penetrating the mask of Stephen the manager, saw Stephen's real self, his quiet dignity, his gentleness, his self-control and his capacity for friendship. In the dark hours of the night, free now from the anger and humiliation that had consumed him for so many months, Burnham came to know Stephen as friend. Back and forth like a shuttle his mind flew from these thoughts to the unbearable loss of his son.

Hester had taken Elsie away to her own apartment, making her lie down. And when Elsie moaned in sleep, Hester lay down beside her and drew her into the shelter of her arms. Strange sensation. After so many years of nights knowing only the touch of a man's strong body, Hester was startled with the fragile delicacy of Elsie, who lay against her in a thin sickle of life. Suddenly she was robbed of the illusion of strength she had had through the summer. She and Elsie were too frail to be anything but the sports of fate, fate which had taken their children. She sobbed and Elsie woke. They held each other close, crying together.

Down the worn stairs of the hong they carried the coffin, not half a man's load. For a moment they halted in the hall. Above them on the wall hung the picture of the great skyscraper of the oil company. Then they moved on to the white man's cemetery, a tiny unsheltered spot among the rice-fields.

When the news of Dee-dee's death reached the general manager, the father in him transcended the corporation servant. Emotion broke through. Nothing too good. That place in Shanghai that Mrs. Burnham had wanted.

"What do I want of it now?" said Elsie. "I never intend to have any more children. China's no place for children."

The Company felt her ungrateful. Here she was offered the finest place to live the Company had to offer, and yet she was dissatisfied. How many Company people envied her!

On the steamer going to Shanghai, Burnham tried to forget his gratitude to Stephen. It gave him a feeling of uneasiness, because of what he had told Creighton—the man sent to fill his place. Hang it all, how could he know that Creighton would take the joke he had told on Chase so seriously, dwelling on the fact that a man with a salary such as Chase must have, should hoard coppers, even *cash!* "Most of us, of course, when the servants do an errand for us, just let them have the change, but not Chase," Burnham had said.

"Oh, tight is he, with his money?"

"Oh, well," thought Burnham, "it doesn't make any difference." What difference could it make with a man who stands in, as Chase does, with the Company? Some men get all the luck. As to Chase being his friend—after all, who wouldn't show a little kindness when a baby was suffering?

XI

THE transfer of Burnham had not slowed down the Company's business for even a day. The matter was arranged

281

by telegram. The steamer that took the Burnhams away had brought the exchange man, Creighton. That night there was the sound of tacking and pounding in the rooms below Hester. Creighton was busy getting his part of the hong ready for his family. They would come in a week or two when the last of the heat was over.

"Wait until you see my kids," he had told Hester at tea-time. "Three of them. Twin boys and a girl. I've taught those two boys to fight. Husky kids all three of 'em. I'd risk 'em in any city in China. We've got a flock of goats, too. We're a self-contained unit. Pity about the Burnhams, but I guess they didn't know how to manage."

Creighton asked all the Company people to go with him to meet his family. Hester disliked to be caught in the wild rush of coolies for baggage, and made the excuse that some one should be at the hong to welcome Mrs. Creighton.

It was five o'clock when the steamer was sighted. Hester went out on the gallery, sitting there high above the rush and violence, to watch the landing. Finally through the milling crowd, she saw the Company people coming. Fenton and Lunt each had one of the twins grasped tightly round the wrist. The children were bare-footed, carrying their shoes. Hester gave a little gasp. No one went barefoot here. It was not safe. Stephen was with Mrs. Creighton, taking long strides to keep up with her for she advanced in quick spurts like a thin distracted hen, her eyes on the children ahead. Creighton followed, a small girl in his arms. The child bobbed up and down like a cork afloat, as he ran about here, there and every-here, shouting, commanding a long line of coolies, from whose shoulder-poles dangled bags, bundles, even little trunks. The coolies were laughing and chattering over this sudden windfall in the shape of a rich foreigner. So many bundles, he must have money, they would raise the price a copper. Then Hester beheld, stepping bravely

282

along the bund, a goat-herder marshaling a flock of goats.

In a moment the Creighton family had invaded the hong. Hester, looking down, saw the men running up the stairs pulled along as if by wilful puppies on leashes, Mrs. Creighton hurrying after them, and Stephen, who had taken the little girl from her father, carefully carrying her, as if she had been marked, "Fragile, Handle with Care." Then came the coolies with grunts and sighs, laboring up the stairs with their heavy loads, running swiftly down, crowding at the entrance where Creighton awaited them to pay them off. Their *walla walla* echoed along the galleries, filling even the dining-room, where the servants moved back and forth now, serving the Company family. The twins were eating ravenously.

"Don't you think we'd better put their shoes on?" said Hester to Mrs. Creighton. "The doctor says it isn't safe here to go barefoot."

"They wouldn't," said Mrs. Creighton. "They're Montessori children," she added proudly, "so of course I couldn't make them."

Stephen sat at the head of the table, the little girl still in his arms. She had fallen asleep, her head against his breast. Mrs. Creighton moved to take her from him.

"Leave her alone," said Stephen. "I like to have her."

The *walla walla* of the coolies rose now in a new note of anger. "Kin, go down and see what's the matter," said Stephen, speaking softly so as not to disturb the sleeping child in his arms.

Kin returned, raising his voice above the babble of the coolies.

"Carrying men, they demanded a copper too much. They say the white man is rich. See all he owns. When they would not take what he offered them, the number two master threw the money upon the ground and shouted, 'Because you would cheat me, charging me a

283

copper too much, I pay you a copper too little.' Then the bearers were angry and ran after the number two master and held him. But when I spoke, they obeyed and went away."

Creighton entered, rubbing his arm. "These brutes are husky but they can't scare me. I beat them at their own game," he said, with satisfaction, sitting down to his meal, eating and drinking with gusto. "Gave 'em less, to punish them."

"I've got to have an *amah* right off," Mrs. Creighton was saying. "My old one wouldn't come up here."

"Kin," said Hester, "call the Burnhams' *amah*."

"Not here," was his answer.

"Surely, Kin, I saw her."

"But she has gone. There were affairs of her family. I think she go far," answered Kin.

"But, Kin, I thought she wanted to be *amah* for the new missie?"

As Kin remained in stony silence, Hester knew it was useless to press the matter.

The next morning Adviser Ho came to the office on a serious matter. He was acting as go-between for the carrying coolies. The new master had deprived them of money.

"How much?" asked Stephen.

"Two coppers for each coolie, one for each end of the load. It comes to one silver piece."

"I will speak to him of the custom." Stephen took from his pocket a thin silver coin, handing it to Ho.

"It is insufficient," said Ho. "A silver piece, big money is required."

Stephen gravely added two coppers.

A little later when Ho had gone, he explained to Creighton what the custom was; it was important to keep it.

"I paid it," said Stephen.

"Oh, well, if you paid it, here it is!" Creighton tossed

a coin on the desk. "By jinks!" he said to himself. "So Chase is close with his money! I thought Burnham was probably jaundiced." He did not understand that Stephen had meant to show him that the custom must be kept. Essential that a man should start right.

Creighton was a worker, but there were two flaws in Stephen's satisfaction in the man. Creighton did not get on well with the Chinese, and Creighton's sons proved to be *enfants terribles,* increasing the complications in the intricate life of the hong. But the new man only laughed when he heard of his sons' escapades. "What can you expect of two lively boys shut up like this? Why, for them this hong is like doing the Olympic games on a pocket-handkerchief." The hazards were great for any one going through the common passageways of the old building. One never knew when a missile might hurtle down from the landing above; one never knew when, issuing from one's own apartment, Indians or bandits might fall upon one. Olga, Fenton's wife, who lived across the hall from the Creightons, resisted the twins' onslaughts volubly, chattering to her adversaries in a conglomerate of English and Russian.

Stephen was fearful of the effect the racket would have on Hester, for she was not well. But she did not seem to mind. The children rested her, she said. Secretly, she rejoiced in each burst of sound coming up from the floor below, imagining herself the hurried distracted mother. But she gave orders to Kin not to let the boys beyond the gate she had erected at the top of the stairs, fearful lest they destroy the luxurious beauty of her rooms. Sometimes the little girl, escaping from her rôle as captive to fierce Indians, would creep up the stairs to nestle in Hester's arms. Often she fell asleep and Hester would sleep too, freed from her sense of weakness with the child against her.

Strangely enough, notwithstanding the commotion,

there was a harmony in the hong not there when the Burnhams had made part of the household. Creighton gave wholehearted cooperation; he found himself liking Stephen in spite of the episode of the silver piece. "I'll make my own estimate of a man after this," he said to himself. In time he came to admire especially Stephen's ability to get on with the Chinese. He'd give his hat to have that tall old fellow, Ho, friendly with him. Why, the way Ho said *"tong ja"* to Chase ought to make a man proud.

But Creighton could make no headway with the men of this province. He had understood that they were proud fiery men, but he had not anticipated that they would be so hard to get on with. In reality, the Chinese were making it as difficult for him as they could, for they had raised against him that ancient weapon of their race, passive resistance, more to be feared than any declared opposition. Outspoken resistance one could meet. But these thrusts in the dark! A man lunged toward his adversary and found—nothing.

Only the poorest of servants could be secured by the new family. The *amah* was an unkempt coolie woman whom Mrs. Creighton hated to have touch the children. After the clumsy creature had spilled a kettle of scalding water almost over Little Sister, the frightened mother scarcely stirred from the house. The house-boy served the meals a half-hour to an hour late. Often as the family were about to sit down to dinner, he would announce that the cook had secured no meat that day; or he would come in the morning to say the cook had risen late and there was no bath water. Creighton threatened and sometimes used his fists, but no fear of punishment lessened the mishaps. The office staff lost memoranda that were to go to Creighton's desk, the records they gave him often proved to be incorrect, and time after time Creighton had hours of work to do over. Although Stephen knew there was opposition to Creighton, he did not realize how ruthless it was, for in his presence both servants and office staff rendered to the number two suave counterfeit of service.

Creighton was reaching the limit of his endurance, harassed to the point where he felt he must get out of the province—the object the Chinese had set out to accomplish. He was on the point of risking a request for a transfer. Not a good thing to do, he knew, in the Company. Assertion of personal desire or need was not forgotten.

It was a warm afternoon, the sky hazy. Such were the autumn days in Creighton's boyhood home in the South. It was difficult for him to be discouraged for long. As he strolled along the water-front after office hours, memories awoke taking him back into the happy-go-lucky spirit of his boyhood. Certain sleight-of-hand tricks he had once enjoyed performing popped into his head, as he passed an old man peddling a tray of early tangerines.

"Venerable One," he said, "those are fine tangerines. How much for one?"

"Two coppers, I say."

Creighton, without bargaining, paid the two coppers.

"*Ai*," said the crowd, "when this barbarian came among us, he broke the custom, cheating the carriers of two coppers apiece. Now he breaks it, paying a fool's price for a tangerine."

In the midst of the crowd gathered around him, Creighton ostentatiously peeled the tangerine. And lo! when he split it, there was a thin silver piece in its center.

"*Ai yah*," exclaimed the crowd.

"It is a good bargain I have made," said Creighton, pocketing the dime. Then he spoke again to the vendor. "Sell me, old man, another tangerine. Here are the two coppers."

"That was a small and inferior fruit," said the vender.

"The rest are big—greatly big. Ten cents is the price."

Creighton, again without argument, paid the man what he asked. The crowd pressed him close, peering into his face, jostling his elbows.

"Stand back," he cried in lordly fashion, "that I may eat this expensive fruit with satisfaction."

Slowly he peeled it, and when he tore the sections apart, there lay a silver dollar.

"Sell me another!" he cried with assumed anger. "I wish to eat, and I cannot eat money."

But the old man shook his head. No, no more were for sale to-day.

Creighton turned on his heel, walked along the dock in nonchalant fashion, then came back, parted the crowd, dense now around the fruit vender who was cutting open one tangerine after another.

"Old man," said Creighton, "why seek money in the fruit when it is in thine ear?" And, leaning over, he took from the man's ear a dollar and laid it on the tray before him.

A heavy guffaw of laughter broke from the crowd. "He is a magician," they cried, "like our own magicians! And he has paid a lordly big dollar to the old man for his fun."

Carriers, poles on their shoulders, ricksha-men who had left their rickshas, street idlers, small boys, went away murmuring, "*Ai*, he laughs as we laugh! He is a man like ourselves."

When Creighton reached the hong, he found that his wife had gone out, the children with her. "I'll not ring for tea," he thought. Usually at such times there was no afternoon tea for him or, if he did get it, the toast was burned and the cake stale. Stretching himself out in a big chair, his legs thrown over its arm, he began thinking of his performance on the bund. "Well, I suppose I've gone and done the wrong thing again," was his conclusion. Then the door opened to admit the boy. Deferentially, he placed a tray on a table beside Creighton.

"Master, I think, perhaps want tea," he said.

When the boy had gone, Creighton whistled softly. "What's happened to him?" Suddenly he slapped his thigh, exclaiming, "I'll be damned! I've broken down their opposition. Who'd ever have thought that a bit of tomfoolery would turn the trick?" He'd found his way to win them and, by jiminy, he'd stay on the good side of them. Hurrah! he wouldn't have to ask to be transferred! He settled to his tea with zest.

Two minutes after Stephen reached his apartment, Kin was launched on a dramatic account of the happenings on the bund. All his decorum seemed broken by his inner laughter. Not since a day long ago in Manchuria, when a man in an inn had leaned against a door he thought closed and had fallen sprawling at Kin's feet, had Stephen seen Kin moved to such merriment. The grave Kin, immaculate in his white gown, suddenly was not Kin but a little old man searching oranges for money; and, then, casting aside his last scrap of caution before white men, Kin became Creighton, walking with the rolling stride that was Creighton, cunningly giving to his manner a faint flavor of braggadocio and swagger that, too, was Creighton, taking the dollar from the man's ear.

"I think second master very clever," he ended.

"I needn't worry any more about Creighton getting along with the Chinese," thought Stephen. "They'll take him at his worth now and he's smart enough to build on the advantage he has gained."

He was right. Little by little, Creighton won himself the liking of this, or that, Chinese on the staff. In time he became to Stephen a kind of second self—a large ample self.

XII

THROUGH the long slow autumn, the city and country set themselves to the replenishing of life lost in the valley during the cholera. The business of marriage and birth was carried on with renewed zeal. Wives and concubines were taken in order that there might be sons in the families depleted by death during the summer. Sometimes a man took upon himself the bearing of sons, not only for himself but for a father's brother who, dying in the epidemic, had left no heirs. Wives were taken for the dead, raising up families for them.

At the time of marriage, no symbol of fecundity was neglected. The right food was sent by relatives and friends, the right food prepared by the family—rice that symbolized plenty, cakes that symbolized productivity; and about the marriage bed embroideries inducing fertility were hung. Everywhere in the decorations, the *pa kwa,* the circle enclosing the symbols of male and female locked together, was used. Birth was the ecstatic concern of the teeming millions.

Money borrowed for weddings, following hard upon money borrowed for funerals, was at an ever-increasing rate of interest. Early and late the people of the valley labored to meet the demands of the dead and the living. Even so, there were times when it was necessary in the homes of small traders and coolies, in order to stop the incessant cry of the small ones for food, to give them their rice half cooked. The half-cooked grain swelled slowly in the stomach, and for a long time, the children did not wish to eat again.

Despite the close struggle for existence, the business of the Keepers of Light prospered. The shop-to-shop inspection made the autumn before, repeated in the spring and now again in the autumn, was bringing up the volume of sales as Stephen had foreseen. But even Stephen had underestimated how great his gains would be. Fascinated, he watched the mounting totals of the daily sales-reports from his agents. Business built on the little *cash* with a hole in the center, twenty-five hundred *cash* now to the dollar, swelling the profits by thousands of dollars! This year the province would yield the Company three million dollars. Stephen began to get some conception of the millions upon millions of people who made up that sub-stratum of society in which he was creating the desire for light.

And now war, that each year since the coming of de-mocracy had taken its percentage of the people's earnings, touched Stephen's business. One morning as he went to his office, he found his Chinese staff talking in high ex-cited voices, *"Ai yah, ai yah,* we must draw in our hearts, draw in our hearts. It may happen here."

"What is the matter?" he demanded.

"The soldiers of the old governor have looted the city to the south! A new lord has entered and taxed the mer-chants one hundred thousand dollars."

"Impossible," said Stephen. He had a mental picture of that city with its rows and rows of petty shops, its few merchants of moderate means. "Impossible; there is not that much money in the town," he cried.

"It is paid," was the laconic response of the shipping clerk.

Stephen stood aghast. The town would be ruined. Cock-eyed Ting, what had happened to him? Could he pay for the oil stocks he had undoubtedly lost in the looting? What part of the tax of a hundred thousand dollars had Ting had to pay? He himself must go imme-diately and see.

Stephen was thankful in his heart that he had a friend like Ho. Ho would know almost to a copper what would have been Ting's part in the tax. Then he realized it

291

would not be fair to ask Ho to take this trip. He would be a rich prize for any war-lord—the great Ho. No, he could not ask his friend to go with him. But before he left he was closeted with Ho for a half-hour.

As the coolies carried Stephen's kit down-stairs, the number one interpreter of the office came to the master.

"*Tong ja,* you never take an interpreter with you, but may I go with you this time? I want to go home."

"Why do you ask? This is no time when we are hard pressed." Stephen spoke sternly.

"*Tong ja,* for two centuries my family have lived in the little village at the top of the pass on the great road."

Stephen's attention was arrested. How often he had gone through that village, and Tsen had never told him of this!

"Many times we have paid forced taxes. Always before, it could be arranged. But three times armies have passed through this year. Two times ago my mother and father fled to the hills. My father ate too much bitterness and died. Now the troops have passed there again. I do not know where my mother is."

"Are there others?' asked Stephen.

The interpreter spoke with reserve, "My wife and my son."

"Yes, you may take leave," said Stephen.

Still the man hesitated. "May I, *tong ja,*" he begged, "go with you? Alone I am not safe. They will not touch the foreigner."

So Stephen and the interpreter set out together, each on his own errand.

At nightfall, Stephen entered the stricken city. Occasional furtive figures skulked along side-streets, seeking the food shops. But for the rest, the city was like a dead man's abode. The little shops, once bustling with life, had their night shutters in place, even so early in the evening. The great shop of Ting, general merchant, showed no ray of light between the shutters, and no sound came from within. Always before when the shutters were closed—even at China New Year when they were closed in the daytime—if one listened, one would hear a murmur of life, life urgent, too insistent in its demand to be hushed for a moment. Now there was silence.

Had he better knock? Stephen raised his hand. Then he heard a whisper, *"Tong ja,* take care." He turned to see a man at his elbow, motioning him to follow. They passed down a back street and his guide knocked cautiously at a small door in a wall, the rear entrance to the shop of Ting.

"A friend comes," the man whispered, his lips close to the crack of the door. Some one must have been near for the door was opened quickly and as quickly closed behind them. Out of the shadows of the shuttered shop a figure materialized carrying a lighted lantern, its wick turned low.

"Come, come," whispered the figure, and they passed into the front shop. Stephen caught glimpses of the empty shelves above the counters. They went silently through court after court, into the innermost recesses of the dwelling. Once a man's foot, clad in white stocking and cloth shoe, was caught in the lantern's glow, once a woman's pointed blue cotton shoe and white anklet stocking above, loose at the top, flaring out beneath her trousers; and several times black startled eyes peered out of the dark like deer's eyes, held suddenly by the flash of light.

At last they sat down by a high Chinese table; the lantern was put out. Stephen heard whisperings and the rustle of bodies moving, then close at his side the familiar voice of Ting, but muffled and frightened.

"Yes. Everything lost, and my tax was heavy. But I will be generous to the Keepers of Light. I will pay them a tenth of what the soldiers have taken from me."

293

"A tenth?" answered Stephen. "It is not enough. It is but a tenth of the loss that the Keepers of Light should bear."

The bargaining began, and Stephen was secretly delighted that with each point gained, Ting's voice lost a little of its fright. Ah, the bargain. Well, he guessed Ting had spirit enough to weather this catastrophe.

As he made the journey back, he could think of nothing but the paralyzed city. The heavy tax, the loss of silks and cotton and oil during the looting. The city had been dealt a mortal blow. It would take years for it to recover. Forced contribution. Where would it end?

At last he came round the mountain and struck into the flagged path that led across the valley floor. The moist autumn air was like a narcotic, and he was reassured by the scene of peace and plenty spread out before him. Like the Garden of the Lord indeed, the valley appeared to him. The peasants had finished threshing the second rice. The black, heavily fertilized soil was being ridged for its winter crop of vegetables. And a little way from the road, set in the midst of the fields, was a farmer's hut, smothered in bamboos. By the house-door, a woman was chopping some twisted tangled roots into fire-wood. Along one of the dike paths a boy, singing in a high falsetto voice, drove forward a flock of geese. From overhead came the honk of wild geese as, in wedge-shaped formation, they flew north toward the Great River.

There was no other sound, except the rhythmic creak of Stephen's chair, as its wicker arms rubbed against the limber poles, and an occasional grunt from the chair bearers as they shifted the weight on their shoulders, or lifted the chair an inch or two to ease the rub on their bare flesh.

Suddenly Stephen heard a scream and, turning in his chair, he saw a gray-clad soldier wresting the short-handled ax from the hand of the peasant woman. Then the soldier picked up the fire-wood, and ran off along the path, the ax in his hand, the wood under his arm. The woman stood for a moment by the chopping block, then without protest, turned and walked into the hut. The valley returned to its peace.

But the scene had destroyed Stephen's peace of mind. He felt irritated with the resigned patience of the peasant. Suddenly he realized that Ting had been resigned, too, over the looting. He had used the time-worn expression, *"Mei yu fatsu,* there is nothing to do about it." It was incredible that Ting, clever, astute, spirited when it came to a bargain, could be so passive about the disasters these floating armies had brought upon him. Was it fear? Perhaps. Fear of the official was ingrained in the race. But these merchants had strength, if they would only use it. He thought of Ho, and what he had told him of the ancient guilds. Ho, perhaps head of one of the most powerful of guilds. There stood the organization ready-made to combat the military, not as feeble individuals but as guilds, many guilds—the guilds of the money-changers and the gold workers, the guilds of the rice merchants, the guilds of the oil men, spreading a network over China. Let them assert their power, they were the moneyed element of China. The military could do nothing without their money. Withhold it, and these generals, weak without "silver bullets," were done.

The next day as Stephen sat with Ho in the tea-house, he spoke of the matter.

"Why don't the merchants do something?" he asked.

Aloof, unresponsive, Ho sat as he had on that occasion when Stephen had approached him on the matter of squeeze. In the silence that lay between them, Stephen felt Ho's passive acceptance of calamity as some bedrock strength—a mysterious strength that his Western mind

295

could not grasp. And he felt he had been presumptuous in the house of his friend, pressing his Western aggressiveness.

Through the winter the valley lay serene, no violent manifestation disturbing its productivity. There was no fighting. The soldiers were faithful to the ancient saying, "No man fights until the fleas stir in his coat in the spring."

During this period of quiet, a mysterious process of recuperation went on among the victims of bandits and soldiers. Early in the spring, Stephen visited the city where Ting lived and there was no sign of the looting of a few months ago. All the shops were open, business going on as before. Cock-eyed Ting paid the Company the last of his indebtedness on the oil lost in the looting. Stephen began to see that some endurance lay hidden in the acquiescence of the Chinese, forcing its way triumphantly through disaster.

Then summer came, bringing the annual catastrophe this year, flood. The city and the valley had said there would be flood—once in five years, was the saying. Stephen had paid little attention to the talk; he had not yet lived enough with disaster to accept it before it came. May wore away into June. The rain fell day after day, not in fine mist, but in devastating sheets. Reports began to come in from up-river that all the streams were in flood. The hillsides, for centuries denuded not only of trees but of shrubs, for the people used even the brush for fuel, did not suck in the rain, but let it run down into the streams. Hour by hour the river rose and now Stephen felt the power of nature, and he, too, knew there would be flood.

In front of the hong the water lay, a thin yellow scum. Inch by inch, it rose until it stood in the servants' quarters. The office force arrived in sampans and Ho sent word that he was delayed with affairs of the flood. The water lay over his garden and in the courts of the old house. All the great family was taking shelter on the second story of the new house.

Hour by hour the water made its way over the city. The people worked with dumb resignation, placing in the rafters of their huts their rude chairs, tables, wooden mallets and hand forges. Then they crouched—patient and acquiescent—among their belongings.

Offerings of rams and bulls thrown into the foaming yellow waters had not stayed the cholera, nor did they stay the advance of the flood. The river continued to rise, breaking through the dikes not repaired by the avaricious war-lords, erasing the green from the valley with its brown smudge. Here and there green lines, fragments of the dikes, stood above the waste of waters.

Then there descended over Stephen the shadow of the tanks. Was the embankment around the place high enough? Each visit he made, the water stood higher. McBain looked excited, alert and heavy-eyed. What with the summer's quick succession of tankers coming in at all hours of the day and night, and the threat of flood, he had little time for sleep.

It was after nightfall; Stephen had just returned to the hong, riding in the launch up to the first gallery. He was weary but hopeful, for the water seemed to have reached its height. He was eating his dinner when the telephone rang.

"The water's rising; it's within an inch of the top of the embankment," came McBain's excited voice. "I'm getting the oil pumps into readiness for pumping out the water; it is seeping up through the ground inside the wall."

"I'll get there as fast as I can," Stephen answered.

He gave his orders quickly to Kin to get his slicker, his boots.

"Creighton, look after things here," he said, "if I'm not back by morning."

Hester watched him hurry away, a dim figure making the dark descent of the stairs. The electric power plant was flooded and the great horn lanterns full of electric bulbs hanging in the hall were unillumined. Above the downpour of the rain she could hear the ominous stealthy licking of the water around the newel-posts at the stair foot. She caught a last glimpse of Stephen. The light from the lamps placed on the stair-posts fell on the black water flowing past the office doors and upon Stephen with sure tread walking a plank raised above the water.

When Stephen reached the citadel of oil the water stood almost at the top of the embankment. The storage grounds inside were like a great cup prepared to receive the waters.

McBain gave a sigh of relief. "We may have to let the water in to save a sudden rush. I'm glad you're here to decide."

Now was the inevitable emergency stealing upon a man in the moment of his success. No time now to consult Shanghai.

Stephen waited. The water rose another half-inch. "Open the gates. Let the water in." He gave his order calmly, satisfied he had chosen the last moment when daring would not be foolhardiness.

An hour he stood alone on a bit of embankment watching the destruction he had commanded. The water mounting on the godown walls covering the tins of oil, the boxes of tin plate. Already his mind was busy with the problem of the rusting tin once the waters subsided.

The cup of the compound was full, the flood waters leveled over the cup. There the water held. A half-hour, an hour. Then in the light of his torch Stephen saw the line of water on the godown creep slowly upward. No need to justify his act to the Company. His decision had justified itself. Had he not acted the godowns would have been swept away.

The emergency was over and the need for decision. Immediately Stephen sank himself in the organization, wiring Shanghai asking what they wanted done with the tin plate.

The flood's peak was gone. Stephen was helping McBain in the unloading of a tanker; a telegram was handed him:

"Put tin plate in your empty tank. Flood it with oil. Have coolies wipe it."

Stephen sent for McBain who was down at the pontoon.

"How many sheets of plate have you?" asked Stephen.

"Two hundred and fifty thousand."

"Umph," said Stephen, "two surfaces to a sheet, that means a half-million surfaces."

"Coolies are hard to get," said McBain. "All helping their families in the fields after the flood."

"How many could you get, McBain?"

"Well, perhaps twenty."

Take them weeks. In the meantime the most of the plates would be rusted.

Suddenly Stephen thought of the great tanker going back empty. Load it with the tin plate, send it down to a larger port . . . where there were plenty of coolies . . . the wiping quickly done, the tin plate saved.

He gave his orders. Soon the place was ringing to the chant of the coolies carrying out the boxes containing the tin plate.

The tanker had gone. The compound was quiet. Suddenly Stephen realized what he had done—actually disobeyed the order of the Company.

"Well, I saved the tin plate, anyway," he said to himself. . . . "But the question is, Do I get hell?"

In fact nothing was said by the main office in Shanghai, neither praise nor condemnation.

From this catastrophe of the flood, as from other catastrophes, the people recovered.

"*Ai,*" they said. "*Mei yu fatsu,* there is no help. Once in five years flood takes our early rice."

They spent no strength in lament but, when the waters receded, brought from untouched seed-beds more rice, replanting their fields. Stephen began to have an almost superstitious belief in the recuperative powers of the Chinese people.

Two years, of the three allotted to Stephen to build up the business of the province, were completed. Through his office, the chant of carrying coolies echoed and re-echoed—an endless flow of jarred rhythm, shaken from bodies weighted with heavy loads. Like a syncopated moan, the chant rose from the long line of coolies carrying great sacks of rice upon their shoulders down to the loading steamer. The military, needing more revenue, was shipping away the stores of rice, threatening the Green Valley with a new kind of famine.

This summer afternoon Stephen was completing the graph of his last year's business on a piece of cross-section paper. The black line rose and fell, dipping down in the summer months, rising in the winter months—the general trend of other years—but each dip and rise was several squares higher than the corresponding curve of the year before. However, the total of the year's sales fell short of the high mark Truesdale had set for the province.

Stephen saw he would have to give up the idea of reaching that total in time to give Hester the benefit of a new house. "I would have liked to get it for her," he thought wistfully. Too late now. The house could not be started for another year. Flood and confiscation of rice had settled that. But surely one more year would bring the desired volume of business. It must.

That was the mark the Company had set for him, the criterion of his success as manager. With hard work he believed it could be done, for, despite extra taxes and the rising price of rice, the business had steadily, if slowly, mounted. In this last year of his managership, he must put behind the business the whole of his mind, his knowledge of poverty, and his faith in the recuperative powers of the people, sparing neither himself, his men, his agents, if the four million dollars that the Corporation desired from the province were to be secured.

In the hong, overshadowing the occupants, dwelt that corporate person, the Company, its tenacious, unyielding will that desired four million dollars from the province, shaping the life of the household. Silently, the master will of organization strove with the little wills, subordinating them to its own use. In spite of it, each individual in the hong still fought his way towards his own happiness. Olga, Fenton's wife, sought hers with a vehemence terrible to the Americans, better understood by the Chinese members of the household, who themselves loved their emotions. When Fenton was delayed at the office, there was a little scene. When he was sent on a trip, a big one. Then the sobbing of Olga filtered through the thin partitions, filling the house. Sometimes she threw herself among the rose-colored silk quilts on her bed, threatening to cast herself from the window, or down the dark pit of the stairs, if Fenton left her. Frequently he was late to the office, not daring to put her threat to the test. Presently Olga would forget the emotional moment, but Fenton did not. At first he went about, in his eyes a look of bewilderment; and, when he looked at Hester, something beseeching and a little angry, as if somehow

301

there was some connection between that dependence upon Hester during the summer of cholera, and this business of being married to Olga. Then after a little, he became sneering in his attitude toward all women, and he drank too much.

The bachelors in the hong, off in the interior most of the time, were gay when they came back from their trips, snatching at companionship and love where they could find it.

In the Creightons' apartment, the pent-up energies of the boys—in all the crowded city there was no other place for them to play—at times threatened to burst bounds. There was a succession of servants. *Amahs* came and went, worn out in their efforts to get the twins to bed at night, out of bed in the morning, to protect Sister from the onslaught of her brothers. Then Creighton decided on a boy to do *"amah* pidgin," and things went better. But the hong rocked to the vibrations of velocipedes ridden at top speed round the Creighton dining table. Crowds of gaping coolies often gathered on the bund below the Creighton gallery to watch the twins vigorously performing on a trapeze. Heavy guffaws of laughter rose from them, as the boys hung over the rail chattering to them in their own language.

"I'm proud they are learning Chinese," said Mrs. Creighton to Hester. "All of their own accord. That's what the Montessori method does for them—leaves them free, and they want to learn."

That the twins spoke of marriage and birth with the lewd frankness which exists in a country where the chief concern of rich and poor, old and young, is birth, she did not guess. Or that they spoke the native oaths, epithets accusing a man of impotence, or curses bringing down barrenness upon his women. They never used these words before their father. Stephen heard, but said nothing to Creighton, feeling it was none of his business.

Now did the hong, indeed, look like the hotel worn with too much living, to which Hester once had compared it. The kitchens were blackened with the smoke of cooking. On the wall along the stairs were two gray lines, one where the servants' hands had rested, and below, narrower and darker, another where the children had placed theirs. The varnish had been worn from the Creightons' dining-room floor where the bicycles had circled the table, even the boards worn away in a groove. "The sawdust ring," Creighton called it. And here and there over the house, there were signs of white ants gnawing at beams and supports. The hong distressed Hester. No longer, even in her own apartment, could she achieve the look of luxury she desired.

Stephen had asked Shanghai to have the hong done over. He started work in his own apartment before the final word came, thinking he would pay for it himself, if Shanghai did not consent. Hester wanted the work finished by Christmas, for she was giving a big Christmas party.

Stephen felt that he had lost some touch with Hester since the summer of the cholera and the death of Dee-dee. She seemed restless nowadays, and preoccupied with her own activities. She had learned to play *mah jong* and she and her friends started their games before luncheon. When she returned, late in the afternoon, he often thought she looked tired, but she never refused an evening party. If he could not go, she went alone. On the rooms of their apartment, her clothes, she lavished the care of many servants. To think he had ever thought an *amah* would have little to do to tend his wife! *Amah* was the busiest servant in the family. The moment he left their room in the morning *amah* entered, tending Hester where she lay in the soft daintiness of her bed, brushing her hair to glossiness, performing mysterious rites upon Hester's body. At night she was again there. Sometimes

303

Stephen resented *amah's* yellow hands in their intimate touch upon her. At other times, *amah* bent over the frailest of soft undergarments, taking stitches so fine that only a people who counted human life as nothing could give themselves to such minute effort.

Stephen did not guess that Hester sought security, trying to build up her old sense of strength and position, once so powerfully felt, lost on the night of Dee-dee's death. She heightened the luxury around her. It gave her security for a little, then it was gone.

But if these things troubled Stephen, they did not Kin. He was at last delighted with his mistress. Now she was idle as a lady should be, a buyer of goods, a person of prestige, giving him prestige.

XIII

THE friendship of Stephen and Ho was threatened. Since that night in the launch when each let down the barrier of his own culture and entered into friendship, only once had they seriously misunderstood each other. That had been at the time of the death of the old *tai-tai,* when Stephen had seen there were ways in which he could not trust Ho. Now it was Ho who did not understand Stephen—and over the same matter.

The day before Christmas, Ho came to the hong with his gifts. There was nothing more important in the eyes of Ho than the proper gift for the proper occasion. Among his own people he kept the custom, and he was not a little proud that he understood the foreigners' custom which set the day of giving on the birthday of their god, rather than that day of greater rejoicing, the New Year. And he was not a little pleased, too, with his choice of gifts, especially with his gift for the *tong ja.*

With ceremony he entered Stephen's office, shaking his own hands in salutation, for he abhorred the Western custom of touching another man's hand, even the hand of his friend. A servant followed, his arms heaped with red-paper parcels.

Stephen rose to greet Ho, pleasure in his eyes. There was the customary formality between the two friends, then Ho motioned the servant to come forward. He took from the pile of gifts a long narrow package. Holding it in his two hands, he proffered it to Stephen—the gift of Ho to the *tong ja's* wife. Stephen, as he took it, knew by the shape and weight that there was silk within. Now the great Ho, injecting into his manner even greater ceremony, bowed gravely, and placed a second package in Stephen's two hands. The package was small and, Stephen hoped, not valuable, for an order had gone out from the main office forbidding Company men to accept gifts of value from the Chinese in their employ. Some of the presents given the men of late had smacked of bribery, they said.

As Stephen opened the little box, Ho spoke, "In token of our friendship." There before Stephen lay a gold ring. Without alloy, he knew, the gold was so yellow. And upon the top, cut into the gold was his name in Chinese characters, done in reverse for use as a seal.

It was a beautiful thing, and Stephen coveted the possession of it. He held it for a moment in the palm of his hand. Then he turned to Ho saying gravely, "You have made it difficult for me, friend. Do you not remember the letter from the Company that was sent to each of the agents two moons ago? I showed it to you, did I not?"

"*Ai,*" said Ho. "That is understood with the agents of the Keepers of Light. But between us, there is no Company standing. That I said long ago."

Stephen sought to explain that if he took the presents, all his men would feel free to do the same. And that he

305

must accept also the presents of the agents, setting the order of the Company at naught. At first Ho persisted, thinking it could not be that his friend refused his gift—it was only good form to demur before accepting. Then suddenly, he knew that Stephen would not accept the ring and he was angry. His cheeks glowed golden yellow.

"Throw it away then," he cried, "and the silk after it! I will not have them!" He flung his words about the room in great gusts of sound.

In Ho's eyes, Stephen realized, there was an implication in his refusal to accept the ring—a hidden insult. He had accused Ho of wanting to bribe him! Squeeze, he had accused his friend of it! All unaware, he had stumbled into this dilemma, and he must go farther; the ring and the silk must not stay in his keeping, or it would mean that he had accepted them by that indirect method so beloved by the Chinese. So he took the ring and the silk and performed the last ruthless act, thrusting them into the hands of his friend, in order that Ho might know beyond a doubt that he would not accept them.

Then, at the moment when he felt that their friendship was destroyed, a way out occurred to him. The barriers of their two ways of thought had erected themselves so suddenly, that he had forgotten there was a solution.

"Ho, my friend," he cried eagerly, "I can accept cigars, cigarettes! And I will accept, I will accept." Now it was Stephen who flung his words about with emotional stress. But Ho said nothing, only snorted like a great porpoise. Then he turned and went out so hastily that the skirt of his long gown blew out behind him.

Stephen was unhappy, unable to take satisfaction even in the jade bracelet, his Christmas gift for Hester, which he felt, a hard substance, in his pocket. Would the compromise he had suggested save Ho's face sufficiently to re-establish the relationship? Nothing, of course, could heal the disappointment of Ho over the ring—or his own

306

disappointment, for that matter. He would have liked to own the ring, to have worn it as a token of Ho's friendship.

That evening, as he went about his dressing in preparation for the Christmas party, his spirit was heavy. He could think only of the loss of his friend. Not wishing to talk, he hurriedly completed his dressing and went out, leaving Hester.

"Damn the Company's ruling," he said. "Why can't they trust us to decide for ourselves?"

Then Kin entered, presenting the card of Ho, and behind him, carrying a tray loaded high with cylindrical boxes of cigarettes, came the coolie. Behind him followed the office coolie, carrying a tray stacked with boxes of cigars. Behind him was the cook with another stack. And behind him, the outside coolie, with another.

Gravely, Stephen received these offerings, ordering one of the tables to be cleared, so all could be piled upon it. Then he gave Kin his card to send to Ho and, hastily, wrapping money in the remains of some red paper Hester had been using, he told Kin to give it to Ho's servants who had brought the gifts. Thus carefully did he keep the custom. But when Kin had gone, he burst into wild laughter, not at all like his own laughter. Creighton, hearing the unaccustomed noise from the Chase apartment, ran up the stairs, poking his nose in at the door.

"By golly," he exclaimed, "are you starting a cigar store? I'll lend you one of the boys for a Red Indian to stand outside."

"Go and see what you've got," said Stephen. "You'll need your own Red Indian."

He had seen at once what Ho was about; he had spent for cigars and cigarettes the amount of the two beautiful presents—only by spending as much as they cost, could he free himself from the implication of squeeze, only thus could he get back his face. But it was over the cheapness

307

of the cigars and cigarettes that Stephen had laughed. It was a bit of sardonic humor on Ho's part, putting bulk in place of quality, a hidden insult to the Company, an insult enjoyed even though the recipient did not know of it. "Perhaps a little of the insult is meant for me, too; an implication that I, like the Company, do not know how to appreciate quality," thought Stephen. He picked up a box of cigars, thinking ruefully how often he must smoke the awful things in the presence of Ho. "Well, let him have his triumph," he said to himself, "if in that way we may keep the friendship." He looked up happily from the table piled high with its offering, given half as a matter of friendship, half as a matter of offense, his eyes resting with delight on Hester who had just entered the room.

"You're so beautiful!" he cried, drawing her to him. And he kissed her suddenly and forcibly.

"Why, Stephen!" said Hester, with a happy little laugh. She added, "This is the dress Elsie sent me from Shanghai, the latest style."

From below came the sound of doors opened and shut, the murmur of voices, white man's laughter echoing along the halls.

"Listen! They're coming!"

"Merry Christmas!" Fenton leaned over the stair-rail of the second floor, calling down to those beneath.

"Merry Christmas!" they shouted.

"Now for the carols," somebody whispered. There was a muffled consultation. The sounding board of the hall picked up and carried their words to Stephen and Hester waiting to welcome their guests. "All ready now? Come on!"

"Hark the herald angels sing, glory to the new-born King . . ." Two by two, up the stairs came the members of the white community. "Peace on earth and mercy mild . . ."

Outside on the bund a crowd was gathering. *"Ai yah, ai yah!* In that window, look, a great tree! See, a tree that puts forth light instead of flowers!"

For many days, stiffness remained in Ho's manner; in fact, until China New Year, which fell in February this year. Then it appeared that he had forgotten the affair of the ring. Toward noon of the first day of celebration, Kin came in, announcing, "He comes." And Stephen knew that he meant Ho.

Soon there was the shuffle of cloth shoes on the stairs. Stephen, standing in the doorway of his drawing-room for the greeting, watched the figure of Ho emerge from the pit-like darkness of the staircase; first the red button of his black satin cap, then the cap fitting as close as a skull-cap above the high yellow forehead, sunken at the temples, the face narrowing below, the slanted, calm black eyes, the inscrutable mouth. Now Ho loomed before him in the glory of his six feet, behind him the two sons that Stephen knew—the profligate, the marks of the opium smoker in his face; the younger son, awkward and ungainly. After them, one by one, coming out of the darkness, boys of all ages, until Stephen stood surrounded by the Ho clan.

After they had gone, Stephen was pleased to remember how much easier Ho had been in the presence of Hester than he had ever been before. Respected her, no doubt, for her education and the teaching of his women, although they came no more. The son's wife had a man child now, it was explained. As to Shiao Pao, Ho had said only that he could not bother Stephen further, although his friend had assured him that Hester would be glad to continue teaching the girl. It was Kin who explained the matter. "It is only a foolish man who makes more valuable than necessary a possession to be parted with. And Ho is a wise man."

Hester asked Stephen what Kin meant.

"Well, I suppose that when Shiao Pao marries she belongs to another clan."

Hester often looked into the curtained windows of Ho's foreign dwelling. The windows of the third story were on a level with hers, and in the daytime when the shutters were open, she could see into the bare interior, the white walls hung with a few scrolls, two chairs and a table standing against each wall. Often there was a woman leaning out of the window, looking down into the street. A new thing to have happen in Ho's house. Hester wondered who the woman was. Strange, she thought, I know no more of Ho's family than before I taught his daughters. But Stephen knew. It was spoken openly in the Chinese office that the woman was Ho's latest concubine.

Through the winter, forced forward by the combined efforts of the staff, the sales climbed toward the four-million mark. The business was at its height in these winter months, when the gray rain brought darkness early into the windowless huts of the towns and cities. Then the desire for light grew. Men bought lamps and oil to push back the evil spirits lurking in the shadows. Shops bought lamps. The makers of firecrackers gave a lamp to each woman and girl working on the night shift; when the oil was burned out, then the stint of labor was done and the workers might creep home. The modern schools bought lamps for their students—boys and girls reading books from the West, reading the words of Rousseau and Marx. Patriarchal families bought lamps, and by their light girls like Shiao Pao read with flushed cheeks of individualism and even of women's rights.

It was spring, the moment of the Green Valley's greatest beauty. In the black mirrors of the flooded paddies, the young blades stood in serried lines of vivid green, in the morning and evening each blade throwing its thin shadow on the mirror of the paddy. The valley floor a succession of such mirrors, each framed with green dike paths.

It was after closing hours and Stephen was alone in his office. The only sound within the shell of chants of the city was the occasional swish of the coolie's brush as, bending low like a gleaner, he swept the floor of the outer offices. Stephen had just finished his records of work, preparatory to turning them over to Creighton, who was to be the new manager.

He had brought the line of his graph up to the desired total. Only two days before, the sales report had shown him he had reached the four-million mark. He sat now tipped back in his chair, his hands behind his head, thinking of these years in which he had been steadily moving nearer to that desire lying close in the secret recesses of every man's heart—success, the sweet wine of fulfillment. Memorable years, for he had lengthened the distance between himself and that haunting dread of all men—failure, that bitter, disintegrating acid he had seen at work in one form in his father, another in Jenkins, and still another in Burnham. He was waiting for Kin to return from the street where he had sent him to buy one of the primitive peanut oil lamps. He had a fancy to take one of them back with him to America. Show what trade had done. Ah, there was Kin!

"Master," said Kin, "I have been throughout the city. It cannot be bought. It is no longer desired by the people of the city. But they say they can send to some village, and get the master what he wishes."

The smoky lamps no longer even made in the city! Stephen continued to sit tipped back in his swivel chair, his hands behind his head. At that moment he looked very young—like the boy who had first come to China. His dreams, so long forgotten, covered up in the fierce

311

drive to make sales, all coming back. The dream of the little lamps, that beautiful ardor which had come to him the night he had tended Li Tsu's little mistress—dream of progress.

To complete this moment, there was Ho entering the room. Come for a last visit. But it seemed Ho had come on an important matter, and he would not sit down.

"Tong ja," he said, "for days there has been sickness in my house, a strange sickness, in the throat. Our doctors can do nothing. Perhaps the *tong ja's* doctor could help?"

"How many are sick?" asked Stephen.

"Two, *tong ja*. My youngest son and"—Ho hesitated a moment—"a granddaughter."

Stephen was gratified. Often he had tried to get Ho to accept this science of the West. He went to the telephone, asking the mission doctor to come to the great house which he, himself, had never entered.

It was nearly seven o'clock when, as Stephen was arranging the last paper, laying it neatly in the final bundle, the doctor hurried in.

"Why didn't you call me sooner?" he demanded. "It's diphtheria, and it's gone too long. The boy I can save, but the little girl, hardly a chance. It's a shame. According to my notion, more worth saving than the boy. He's a heavy loutish child. But this girl—about fourteen, I judge, but looks younger—she's got curly hair. You should see her. Strange how this race bears pain. She's got real spirit, this child. I've sent over to the hospital for serum. I'm going to save her if I can." And he hurried out.

Shiao Pao, Little Precious, she whom they had not seen for many months. So she was Ho's grandchild.

Stephen rang for Kin to carry his papers and walked slowly up the stairs, taking the way up the outside gallery, liking the spring air to touch his face. Earlier in the day they had been drying fish on the bund and the noisome odor had filled the hong, but now the men had

312

packed up their half-rotted fish and gone home. A little breeze had freshened the air. All the sounds of the bund and the city seemed intimate and dear to him, giving him the sense of belonging here. Only the news about Little Precious disturbed him.

He had but reached the apartment when the doctor called him over the telephone, telling him the girl was dead. Should he tell Hester? Not now, he thought. He sat at dinner, not hurrying, in order that Hester should not guess there was any trouble; but he wanted to send word to his friend Ho, placing the launch at his disposal in order that the family might go to the family burying-ground. At last he was free to slip down to his office to send the message. Quickly the word came back.

"It is not necessary. It is the girl child who died, not the boy, and all has been attended to."

Then Stephen knew that this pretty child was held cheap by the Ho clan, and had been buried without benefit of priest, maybe of coffin, a worthless thing.

Rudely shaken, Stephen saw the East again as aloof from all that was Western, and his friend Ho worlds away from him. Well, he would not tell Hester. No need for it now. Shiao Pao would never be mentioned, thought of, among the Chinese again. So the news would not reach Hester, to shock her. Let her think the child was as precious as her name.

It was the afternoon of their going. Hester and Stephen stood leaning against the rail of the steamer. The final farewells had been said, the last firecrackers were going off. At one side of the pontoon, stood the agents, the tall Ho in their midst, next to him fat cock-eyed Ting, the skirts of their pale silk gowns blowing in the wind. The little white community stood in a noisy waving group at the other end of the pontoon. There was Mrs. Creighton, holding up Little Sister, who was waving a tiny handkerchief. And there were the twins giving a last war-whoop.

The steamer turned and moved down-stream, the groups on the pontoon growing smaller. Then they were lost to sight, but the late sun striking the narrow white walls of the hong made it glow like a bar of silver, the last thing to be seen.

"I saw Ho go to our cabin just before he left the ship," said Hester. "Presents, of course. I hope it's that lovely new silk they are making. I hinted to Kin I'd like some. Perhaps he told Ho."

On the bunk in their cabin lay a long thin bundle and a small square one, familiar shapes to Stephen.

"It's the silk—a whole roll!" cried Hester, tearing away the careful wrappings of the long bundle.

When Stephen opened his package there lay the seal ring, the Chinese characters of his name cut in reverse in the heavy gold. He need not refuse it, now that he was no longer to work with Ho. Now the ring was a personal matter between them.

In the last light of the day, Hester and Stephen stood on the deck, gazing out at the valley floor, light green where the last rays of the sun touched the young rice, green black where the sun had left the paddy, mottled where a puff of wind ruffled the young rice blades.

"Green pastures beside still waters," said Hester.

Stephen did not answer. He was thinking of Ho and the ring, sign of Ho's friendship. The two overlapping sections clasped his finger tightly, and when he moved his hand he was conscious of the unaccustomed weight.

PART THREE

I

It was eight years before Stephen and Hester came again to the Green Valley. During that time, in one stricken community after another, the Company had used Stephen to rebuild a lost business. He had been sent to the valley of the river called China's Sorrow, after one of the ever-recurring famines. Slowly but surely, as the populace filtered back, he had reestablished the business. Later he had been sent to Honan to see what he could do with that bandit-devastated land; and, again, as the populace recuperated, he rebuilt the business.

The Company thought his ability to do this lay in his patience. In reality, it was the quality of the dreamer in him which saw in the business more than the mere selling of oil. In the people's struggle to rebuild their lives to whatever standard they had had before catastrophe overtook them, Stephen saw an unquenchable instinct to win back to civilization. It made him thrill to the first tiny up-springing of trade. Then he went to work with a dogged determination, learning poverty in all its manifestations.

Now he had come again to the Green Valley—China's storehouse of food—to bring back to full power of buying a great province on the lower river. No spectacular poverty confronted him here. It was a more insidious poverty which had undermined the people of this province. In the days before the coming of the republic, the great imperial potteries a little way up the valley had brought prosperity to the city. Now that the emperors were gone, and no longer any one required the beautiful procelains, only an inferior grade of rice bowls and wine jugs dribbled through this river port. The silk of the province once had brought splendid returns, but the greater share of the silk trade had gone to Japan. Huge cargoes of tea once had been exported, sent by junks on the Great River to Hankow, thence overland by caravan to Russia. But now Ceylon and India had gained the tea market.

Merchants from the West still came, saying, "There is no tea in flavor like the China tea. If you will improve your tea-fields, plant them less thickly, not let the harvest lie where rain and dampness destroy its flavor, we will again trade with you. Your silk, too, we will take, if you will destroy the diseased silk-worms that make the silk thread so uneven that it breaks in spinning."

But the people did not wish the hurry and excitement of competition, and the change of their customs. To minds dim lit by the twilight of under-nourishment, akin to the twilight of old age, such effort seemed impossible. The forces of life were running low. The deaths from starvation—which is not called starvation because so gradual is its process—were more and more numerous. And now each year the creeping paralysis of under-nourishment was being hastened by war—war that had semblance of vitality. Did not the wages given by the war-lords and the profits of looting fill the empty belly quickly?

On the bund in front of the hong, rapacious coolies such as those who met the steamer on the Chases' first entrance to the Green Valley, only fiercer now, fought for baggage, and by brute force secured more coppers in payment. The chair-men, the ricksha-men, also were more demanding than once they had been. The extra flow of money through the city was only for this little interim of summer heat, when the white people passed through to get to the hills. If then the belly was to be filled, a man must get all he could for the sweating, panting labor of running between shafts in the cruel heat.

316

The British concession in which the hong was situated seemed more of a fortress than a town to Hester. At the back and one side ran the wall of the native city. In front was the Great River. On the other side was a creek. The foreign hongs, the splendid house of the Keepers of Light one of the most important, were set close together as in a stockade, no gardens around them. The hong was of stone, its windows narrow and long. Hugged so close to the other buildings, there was no room for verandas at the sides; only in front where the hong faced the river. And even there only on the second and third floors. On the ground floor, the building was flush with the bund. An iron grill kept the crowds from pressing against the windows.

It was two months since they had come to this station. Hester had risen this afternoon from her siesta and was standing on the veranda of the third floor, the manager's apartment, looking idly upon the violent scene of a steamer's unloading, when she heard Stephen coming, two steps at a time, up the stairs. What, in the heat, would possess him to hurry so, she wondered, when he charged in upon her, looking young and excited.

"Hester, Kendall has just come in! You'll meet him at last! He's staying for dinner. We'll almost have a reunion of our classmen. Look got in an hour ago from the mountains where he left his family. We're going over to the club first."

When, later, the men entered the living-room, in the instant before Hester advanced to meet them she had a single vivid impression of Kendall. Before polite conversation cloaked his real nature, she saw him, a man consumed by his passion of ambition. Every one in the room—Stephen and Look walking on either side of him, herself—seemed to be swept up into his hand like chaff into a hopper. She felt herself drawing back.

Stephen was speaking, "Dave, this is my wife."

"We hardly need introduction, Stephen has so often told me about you," Hester was able to say. And in speaking, that intuitive impression was gone. As Kendall walked beside her into the dining-room she was conscious only of the affable dinner guest, Stephen's old friend.

"Here's glad to have you aboard," said Stephen. And he lifted his glass of champagne. Hester could see it was a great moment for him—having Kendall at his table.

"It's sixteen years since the three of us have been together," said Look.

"You talked pretty big in those days about just a short stay in the East, didn't you?" said Kendall.

"I was a kid then. What did I know about business out here?"

"What did any of us?" said Stephen. "And how invincible we felt."

"Look said he was only coming out for three years. I told him then he'd never get away once he came," Kendall explained, turning to Hester.

"Well, at that time I guess we all thought nothing in heaven or earth dictated to us very much," protested Look.

For a moment all three men fell silent, twirling their glasses by their stems, looking into them, as if they saw their youth in the sparkling golden liquid.

"Well," said Kendall, finally breaking the spell, "whatever we thought then, we know now that there is a lot that will dictate to us, unless we get ourselves into Shanghai out of the coming mess."

Thus did Kendall voice the common thought of Company people. The body corporate was again to undergo a change, as it had when Look and Stephen and Kendall had been given their managerships. But this time there was no excited talk of expansion. For some time no new sub-stations had been opened where young men could win their spurs. Men were becoming impatient of the slowness of their advance, for the only opportunity was not now in new fields, but in crowding upward in the organization. A few men holding key positions in Shanghai were nearing retirement age. Who would get their places? Ambition, and fear of the gathering chaos in the interior, made many a man tread relentlessly on the heels of the men ahead of him.

Kendall and Chase held the most important provinces in the Green Valley, as things stood just now, and it was generally believed they would get the Shanghai vacancies. They had earned them, most of the men acknowledged. Look was stationed in the city of the great Ho. Among the men that station was now considered a routine job. Business seemed to have reached the saturation point there, not one of the places any longer where the best men were sent, although the Company insisted that all its managerships were of equal importance. That Nathaniel Look, called "the Lummox," by the men, was stationed there only strengthened the general belief in its non-importance. Until recently his position had satisfied Look. His overfat body craved an easy job. But lately, with the growing danger in the interior————

Now, as Kendall voiced the common desire, Look broke out, "I'll say we need to get into Shanghai. Take my province. We've had four changes of government in as many months, and now there's talk of the New Order taking the city."

"Is something dreadful going to happen?" asked Hester, sensitive to the note of fright in Look's voice. But no one seemed to notice that she had spoken. Look was occupied with this latest threat to peace in his province, and Kendall had turned to Stephen.

"Steve, what do you think about it all? I've been mostly in the big cities—Mukden and Tientsin. Nobody knows the condition of the country better than you. What is going to happen? Laying aside their anti-foreign

319

talk, will this new movement among the students make things better?"

"Well," said Stephen, "the war-lords are pretty bad, and yet—it's strange—those fellows spring from the people, they seem to have an uncanny instinct that tells them just when to stop in their taxation. Haven't you found it so? They tax heavily, but they manage to leave just enough so that the community in time recuperates. Never quite kill the goose that lays their golden egg."

"Do you mean the New Order will?"

"Might," Stephen answered. "They're faced with a tremendous temptation. Many of them have been in America or England, for years, and they've learned a new way of living. They want the comforts of the West, and they're impatient to make their country as powerful as the countries they've lived in. To do it, they may bleed the people worse than the war-lords. Not necessarily because they will mean to, but because they aren't close to the people."

"Well, even so," said Kendall, "if they do away with squeeze . . . Those of the New Order talk of patriotism as a religion. Higher taxes, but less squeeze. Better government, more business. Isn't that all right?"

Hester felt uneasy as Kendall continued to probe into Stephen's views. For some reason she could not explain to herself, she wished Stephen wouldn't talk so freely. But he was expansive to-night in his pleasure over this companionship with his old friend.

"You know they won't do away with squeeze," Stephen was saying.

"Well, why not?" persisted Kendall.

"It's instinctive," answered Stephen. "For two thousand years, there's been a famine in some part of China. With their mothers' milk, they've taken in fear of want. Squeeze is deep-rooted in centuries of want.

"You know"—he was warming to his subject—"there's

something else about these young Chinese. They're breaking away from the median way of Confucianism. It's something like our breaking away from Puritanism. It's reaction from restraint; of course, not the same kind of restraint as Puritanism, but restraint. Suddenly released, the proportion isn't kept. They might—mind you, I don't say they will—but if they gain power, we might see such violence as we haven't yet seen. There are many signs pointing to it."

"Very interesting," said Kendall. "I've been wondering what you thought. However, the popular thing to say is that the New Order will bring in the millennium."

Just then the whistle of a steamer struck across the heated air.

"We must be off," said Look. "That's our boat."

"Wait a moment. There's time for a last drink together," urged their host. "No telling what will happen before we see one another again. Here's luck!"

As the men's steps died away on the stairs, Stephen turned eagerly to Hester. "Kendall has just been down to Shanghai, and Truesdale told him that when the assistant managers are retired, we are to be put in their places."

"Stephen," cried Hester, "we'll be safe!"

In a moment everything was transformed for her. The door of her cage was open. Escape from this British concession in which the hong was situated! Escape from this town that seemed more of a fortress than a town to her! What was she doing here? All her own world lost to her. She was thirty-six. Soon she would be old. Music! She wanted music and beauty. And the craving for children had come back. But now she would escape her cage.

Stephen watched her standing before him, clasping and unclasping her hands, her delight playing across her face. So it meant that much to her. How good it was to be able to do this thing for her. It was good to be forty, to be

321

reaping for Hester some of the fruits of his labor.

"Dave Kendall is fine, isn't he?" he said, going back to the pleasure of the evening. His old friend in his own house!

"Why did he ask you so many questions?" Hester countered.

"Oh, I don't know," said Stephen. "Just wanted to hear what I'd say. He's got a lot of mental curiosity. Of course he knows as much as I do about conditions, more, perhaps."

"I don't think he understands the Chinese as you do," persisted Hester. "You've got a peculiar understanding of the Chinese. It's almost a woman's intuition."

"You're partial," said Stephen. But across his sensitive face there was a momentary passage of light. "I don't know, I often think my success has been simply an ability to slog along. Kendall is more aggressive."

"Stephen, your belief in him is unreasonable."

"Well, it's not only I who think well of him!"

"That's just it," argued Hester. "It's that strange something that gets around about a man. It's queer how men get tabbed. They're given a rôle and made to play it. Why don't you do your own thinking, as you do about the Chinese! He impresses me as—well, as ruthless. I imagine he loves to break men, so that he can have power over them. And every one admits that he is hard on his men."

Suddenly Hester saw what she had done. "Oh, I'm sorry," she exclaimed. She had forgotten for a moment about Stephen's friendship for Kendall.

"It's you who aren't doing your own thinking, Hester. Lots of us, when we get to be managers, have the reputation of being hard on our men. It's said of me, too. Burnham for instance."

"That's not true," cried Hester. "You're like the boss. The last year we were in Manchuria, I thought he was hard. Every one said so. But I know now he was one of the kindest of men. And you, Stephen. You've been good to your men. Burnham, too. You never asked to have him transferred out of your territory, even though you knew he was disloyal to you. He's your assistant again. How do you know he'll be loyal? Kendall wouldn't put up with him."

Stephen looked troubled. "Hester, you wouldn't have me say anything now, surely? With another baby coming?"

"All of you top men seem to have two reputations. A bad and a good. It's as if the Company played up the one that was most useful to it. . . ." Hester's words trailed away. Stephen saw she was troubled.

"There's nothing to worry about," he said gently. "Burnham's all right." He felt invulnerable here, a mature man, trusted by his Company. Now for the best work he had ever put in, controlling that inferno of poverty and war!

II

THE New Order took shape quickly, more quickly than any one had foreseen. Up from the south came those who would make a new China, the idealists, the dreamers and the personally ambitious, young men and women, trained after the ways of the West. Up from the south they came, establishing themselves first in the province where Ho lived. On they swept over the valley floor, over the paddies, young revolutionists advancing to meet seasoned war-lords. Between the two lines of soldiers the peasants worked, harvesting their grain. Not one day could be lost, with hunger so close on the heels of production.

It was July when the first rumors came to Stephen that this new army was nearing the border of his territory. No one had thought the soldiers would come so soon. Stephen was worried, for his agent in that district had large credits outstanding. There seemed only one thing to do, to out-travel the advancing troops, reach the district first, collect the money and get it exchanged into good American gold, before the old currency was declared useless by the New Order. It was dangerous. He might get caught in the midst of battle or retreating troops, but he was going, for he could not afford to fail now. He'd leave Burnham in charge. And he'd send his youngest assistant, a man just out from home, in the opposite direction, to collect another indebtedness much overdue. He wished he had a more experienced man to send. But he was short of men and this griffin would be perfectly safe. So the two started, Stephen toward the fighting, the griffin away from it.

As so often happened, the rumor proved to be false. When Stephen reached the border everything was quiet, and his agent doing a good business. But he found the agent filled with excuses against paying his indebtedness. He was undoubtedly playing for time. Ordinarily Stephen would have let the matter go a little longer, as the agent's standing was good, but the threat of a changing order made him adamant. He stayed until the money was in his hands. It was on the morning he was leaving that another rumor reached him, the rumor that one of the generals of the war-lord had undercut him and taken a rich city for his own—the city to which he had sent the griffin.

Stephen hurried back to his office. Here the rumors were confirmed. But he could get no real news. Communication was cut off. Where was the griffin? As the days passed and the young man did not return, Stephen grew quieter, and his mouth more stern. The men in the office, watching him, thought he was callous, though Burnham knew otherwise. Chase had looked like that when he battled for the life of Dee-dee.

On the seventh day, as Stephen was talking to two Britishers who had dropped in, there was a cry along the bund, then commotion at the gates of the hong. Chair coolies set down their burden. The griffin, disheveled, dirty, entered the office, the men gathered around him.

"What happened?" urged one.

"My word, you need a bath!" cried another.

They chaffed him, hiding their emotions. But Stephen stood apart. Feeling made his voice flat when he spoke.

"How's the agent?"

"Crazy," said the griffin, falling into a listless silence.

"Not really?" said Burnham.

"Yes," said the griffin. And then he began talking and no one could stop him. "I guess I know more than you all do. All of you put together." He spoke with belligerent braggadocio. "I got caught right in the middle of them, but I went on as I was ordered. The boss here sent me into it, didn't he?" Lifting only the thumb of his hand resting on his knee, he pointed toward Stephen.

"It was in the night when I finally got there, and they were hunting the merchants. They were after their last cent and they pretty damn well got it. They made an example of our agent just to show what they could do. Want me to imitate his cries and their laughter? They tortured him, they . . ."

"You need not go into that," Stephen said. He had seen Hester in horrified silence at the door.

"They used our oil to do it." The griffin flung the words after Stephen as he moved away, intent on protecting Hester from the details of the story.

When Stephen was in his own living-room and had shut the door, his voice shook. "Hester, he thinks I knew there'd be fighting when I sent him there. He's too new in the country to understand how these things happen."

"Yes, I heard," said Hester. "But he's not quite right

just now. Didn't you notice how high and squeaky his voice was?"

"I didn't," said Stephen dully. "Wish I had the right to give him a vacation. Shanghai probably wouldn't approve of making an exception. There'll be hard things to meet from now on."

He went back to his office and after a while Burnham came to him.

"That youngster ought to get out of here for a bit. What he saw has knocked him out."

"I've no authority," answered Stephen. "You know that."

Then anger rose within him. He'd have been held responsible if this man had been killed.

"It's my treat," he said grimly. "I'll take the responsibility and ask permission afterward. There's a steamer leaving for Shanghai in half an hour. Tell him to get off. See that he has everything to make him comfortable and then send a telegram to Shanghai telling them why I've given him a vacation. Tend to it for me, will you? I've got to get into that district—see if anything can be done."

"You're a fool to try," said Burnham. "You take too many chances."

"Can't help it. I'm responsible for the money."

Sacked cities had become a common sight of late years. The shuttered shops, no light showing between the chinks, occasional skulking figures, were all familiar to Stephen. In fact, as he went through the city to the agent's shop, he felt there were no details of looting that could any longer shock him.

After many whisperings at the back door of the agent's place, the door was opened a crack. In the dim light of a lantern, he saw a middle-aged woman. With dignity she spoke.

"It is useless for you to come. Although for two centuries the business of this family has been conducted with honor, it is over now. Only my husband is left."

"Your sons?" asked Stephen.

"Not here," she whispered.

"And their families?"

"The young women taken by the soldiers."

"The head of this business house, your husband?"

"I, his unworthy wife, speak for him."

Was she protecting some hidden money? Stephen could not believe, even yet, that there would not be recuperation. He remembered cock-eyed Ting and his spirited bargaining after the looting in his territory. "I must see the agent himself," he urged.

"Come," said the woman. Without another word, she led the way to the inner courts. As they went, Stephen heard a babble of strange excited talk that curdled his blood. The woman lifted her lantern. In its light Stephen saw haunted eyes, a cowering, footless form, chained to the floor. It was the agent, a babbling madman, straining at his chains. Then Stephen was ashamed that he had doubted, and he pressed no further his claim that they pay for the consigned oil. All the Company could do was to make a claim against the government for foreign goods destroyed by soldiers. But Stephen knew it would be one of those hopeless claims never paid. Government? What government? Here to-day, gone to-morrow. Well, here then was his first big loss.

As he rode back, there came to him a definite conviction that the day for large credit was over. Looting was constantly increasing; governments shifting so rapidly that sometimes a new government, not holding itself responsible for the last, was in power before a claim could be made. And the very foundations of private credit were gone. In the social revolution which had

327

preceded the coming of the New Order, the solidarity of the family had been weakened. Now that he had left behind that insane merchant, who at the time had so aroused his pity that he had room in his thoughts for little else, another impression was taking shape. He realized that the attitude of the wife toward her husband's obligations was not the old attitude. She did not consider her sons responsible for the debts of their father. No longer was the honor of a man upheld by the family. Stephen remembered that payment by Lin's family when Lin had defaulted. He remembered how Ho had taken it for granted that the man's family would pay. That was the ethics by which the old patriarchal families lived. Now it was gone.

This thing he had envisioned when he had been a young man in Manchuria—this thing called progress—was upon China now. The hour had come. But progress arriving not in the way he had envisioned it, like the bright flame of a lamp illuminating darkness. More like some gigantic man seeking to be born, tearing and destroying the womb in the agony of birth.

It was the white man who had brought the East to this travail. The East hadn't wanted to change. The yellow man would hate the white man and strike out at him blindly. Never in all the years in Manchuria had Stephen felt so outside as he did this moment. His very knowledge making him more alien, showing him the two races alien at heart, and yet drawn down together into the struggle.

In his sudden realization, he clenched his fists and, as often of late, Ho's ring, the soft gold worn to a fine edge through the years, cut into his hand, reminding him of his friend.

But no catastrophe seemed great enough to stop Big Business. Like a mechanized Juggernaut, it took its unconcerned way over the torn ground of revolution and chaos. War even seemed to be a stimulus. More oil was being sold. Director Swaley was out from America, extending the organization a little farther into the interior. "Oil must be more accessible to the interior points," he was insisting. "All this war means that our business will be blocked if an enemy gets between our supplies and the people."

On a hot August morning Stephen was up early to meet one of the Company's river tankers, pulling into the dock. Aft, under a white awning, looking out over the Green Valley, sat Director Swaley and Mr. Truesdale.

"Hello there, Chase!" said Swaley, as Stephen joined the two men, the steamer already under way. "We've looked over your reports on the land you've found for the tank. According to the map, the last site is the best. Ocean-going tankers can pull in alongside. Oil a lot nearer your interior points, eh, Chase?"

Stephen stood at the deck rail, looking out over the valley, the green and luxuriant rice-paddies soaked in hot sunlight, and the distant clipped hills enveloped in quivering heat waves. He felt for a moment mesmerized by those shining shores that seemed torpid with productivity and peace. But he knew what lay under the surface. A day, two days, a week, the valley would be serene like this, then violence would shoot out of it, a violence that showed less and less restraint.

This made the scheme a bad one. But Stephen knew that the director wanted him to acquiesce. As he turned toward Swaley, silently appraising him, he saw the real man, a little pompous, a great deal of the bully in his determination to put his scheme over.

"Well," said the director, "what about it?"

"I've been wondering," said Stephen, speaking slowly, "if what you lose will be greater than what you gain?"

"How do you mean, lose? What kind of loss?"

"Well, there's the good-will of the province, for in-

329

stance. We need that, if we are to deliver the oil after we get it here. This building of a tank just now might be interpreted as aggressive. Suppose the New Order, these super-sensitive nationalists, come in? They're against foreigners owning land."

"Well, won't money fix that, as in the past?"

"Perhaps," answered Stephen. "It's not quite clear yet, the New Order's attitude on that. But, yes, I should think so. Still—well—it's an isolated spot up here. Pretty big risk to the men. My own feeling is that a white man won't be safe away from the bigger ports, if this anti-foreign propaganda continues."

"Ah," said Director Swaley with his most benign look. There was something almost ministerial about his expression, thought Stephen. "Of course, we always take care of our men. But aren't you exaggerating the danger?"

In Truesdale's face, Stephen saw relief. He realized, now that he came to study the man, that he looked old for his years and careworn. He remembered the rumor that Truesdale worried about the men up-country. He felt certain Truesdale, the general manager, was with him on the matter of the tank.

Swaley was thinking, "We've had a lot of good work out of this fellow, Chase, just as I prophesied when we selected him. Certainly he understands the Chinese. Wonder if he knows them too well. He can hardly be hoodwinked about them. In case we need to have the managers shut their eyes to danger. . . . Odd that rumor . . . something about sending that youngster, Denton, into the midst of fighting. Hmph . . . quite the other way I imagine. Too careful of his men, I should say. Suppose we should need to send men into places Chase felt dangerous, would he do it? Wish we were expanding just now. With his knowledge of the Chinese, he would certainly be a prize."

Back once more in the office, the director went over

330

Stephen's reports, saw the graph he was keeping and the black line ascending as usual in spite of the upheaval. And Chase was not a penny behind on outside credits, except for that loss of oil in the looted city. Could hardly be held responsible for that. For the rest of the afternoon Swaley talked over the affairs of the province with Stephen, a man-to-man attitude displacing his official manner.

After the director's departure a warm glow of individuality remained with Stephen. He had spoken freely, even when in opposition to the director's ideas. Certainly he did not "yes" him. And he felt sure the director had considered his opinion.

Evidently he was at the place in the Company where clerkship ended. The last thing Swaley had said to him was that there could be no set formula of procedure now. The managers would have to use their own judgment more than in the past. That feeling of frustration, so often with Stephen during the years, was gone. In the days that followed, he felt himself functioning as a whole man—rather than a cog in a machine. Even when against his judgment the Company decided on the new tank, the impression of participation in Company policies remained. Thus, although he did not believe in the plan, he set to work whole-heartedly to execute it.

He worked at top speed hurrying to get a high wall built around the site for the tank. "If there's opposition later over building the tank, we may be able to work if we have the wall," he thought. "If the village needs money, the head man may let the artizans work, provided there's a wall. Then, he can pretend he does not know what is happening inside."

OCTOBER came and, with it, a day of strange excitement. The golden haze of late autumn hung over the valley and the Great River. Where the steamers moved, long columns of gray smoke lay upon the golden haze, and high in the sky the wild geese flew northward in wedge-shaped lines of black. There was some sorcery in the day. No one was doing business in the city and the banks were closed, although the peasants worked in their fields. In the foreign hongs, many of the high stools in the accounting rooms were unoccupied, and the staff of interpreters was small. The younger men were especially noticeable by their absence.

For the second time in Hester's experience, the solidarity of the servants' quarters was broken. During the morning the *amah* sought her out, leaning over her mistress' chair, a bit of embroidery in her hand. Seemingly solicitous about this work, she whispered:

"Better that my lady look in the servants' quarters. The son of Kin is there."

"Yes," said Hester. There seemed nothing for *amah* to be concerned about. When Kin had joined them at this station, he had displayed to them his son Skee Sax—a Chinese version of "Skeezicks," their own name for this lad when he had been with them in Manchuria—grown now into a tall and handsome boy of sixteen, a stalwart and well built northerner.

The lad had been dressed, not in the long silk gown of the country, but in a suit much like Stephen's. In fact, Stephen had seen that Skee Sax was wearing an old suit of his own which he had missed since his return. The lad was taller than he, but the cuffs of the trousers had been turned down, a cuff cleverly simulated by a narrow fold pressed closely. When Stephen had addressed him in Chinese, the boy had replied in perfect English. Then

Kin's pride had seemed about to burst the bonds of propriety of attitude of servant to master.

"Master," had spoken Kin, "to a very good school I have sent him. Some day perhaps"—he had fallen into the few words of pidgin-English he had acquired of late—"master wanchee very good interpreter." The matter had been waived for the time. Skee Sax was attending school in the city, to learn "plenty fine English," said his father.

But now *amah* was whispering to Hester that it was "very dangerous" to have Kin's son here. "If the troops of the city begin looking for revolutionists—if they find him in our house———"

"Nonsense," said Hester, "he is a northerner."

"*Ai,* but a student!"

"What would you have me do?"

"Go, missie, to the servants' quarters. When you see him—for he is there, he does not go to school—speak with surprise. What, you, that are not my servant, are here? Then he will have to go away and we shall be safe."

Hester and Stephen, taking whispered counsel at noon in the bedroom, the door open so they could see if any servant approached, decided against such a step, remembering well that other experience when they had taken part in the affairs of Kin and his women.

"What is going to happen?" asked Hester.

"I don't know," her husband answered.

"If something does happen, will Kin be faithful?"

"I do not know."

To Hester, there seemed nothing real in the wild rumors that came in a little later that the generals of the great war-lord had been bought by the New Order. There was some sorcery of danger that kept her from realizing it.

In the early afternoon an agitated human mass began to move across the bund: richly dressed men, women, children, in rickshas, luggage piled high around them, urging the men in the shafts to all possible speed; chairs, the curtains drawn, the men under the yokes panting in their haste; plodding along on foot, men, women and children, in coolie blue, meager bundles upon their backs. Junks moved away crowded. Steamers going down-river went crowded. The Chinese stewards reaped a rich harvest, asking an exorbitant sum to be paid to them for accommodations, over and above the fare paid to the shipping company.

The great war-lord, governing three provinces, had met defeat at the border. With such a loss of face, what could they hope for from him? He would retreat; he might take shelter behind the wall of the city. There would be siege! There would be massacre! There would be rape! There would be starvation!

Hester watched the sun, a splendid ball of fire, sink below the close-clipped hills across the Great River. The human mass was thinning now. At last only a few stragglers, seeking frantically for sampans, or a chance junk. Then the bund was empty except for an old woman, hobbling along on her bound feet.

That night the settlement became a fortress, as Hester had once imagined it. A machine-gun was placed at the intersection of the two streets of the town, and men patrolled the foreshore of the creek, patrolled the bund, guarding the hongs. If the northerners retreated, they might try to loot the settlement.

As Stephen was preparing to take his watch Kin came, saying:

"Master, if the soldiers of the Old Order retreat to-night they will loot the Chinese, even the servants' quarters, but not the foreigner. I have money; if the master would let me place it in his care . . ."

"Many times Kin has consulted me," thought Stephen, "but never yet have I seen the money he talks about. Conditions must indeed be serious if he really brings me his money."

Kin left the room. Stephen went on with his preparations, buckling the holster of his revolver to his belt. And then to his astonishment, Kin returned, in his arms a great bundle of native cloth, oddly heavy for cloth—the weight dragging at his shoulders.

Stephen thought first to put Kin's bundle in the safe, but decided against it. The safe would be the place any one coming would look for money. In the drawers of his dresser, then. But the bundle was too high for the drawer, so he untied it, spreading it out. It was stitched carefully by hand into compartments just large enough for a Chinese silver dollar.

The last roll Kin brought had hundreds of oblong sections, padded soft with bills, of what denomination Stephen could only conjecture. Kin, his servant, receiving twenty native dollars a month in wages, and a rich man! Then Stephen knew he had at last seen squeeze in tangible form. Every transaction of the house through the years, leaving something behind in Kin's hand, was represented in those rolls. Nothing too minute: a *cash* squeezed here, a copper there, a dollar there. *Cash* accumulating into coppers, coppers into dollars, draining away Stephen's resources, each salary increase bringing an increased leakage.

Pacing his beat Stephen looked up at the tall hong. It appeared substantial enough, looming there above the low native city. Only an illusion though. How frail it would be against attack. He thought of Hester, lying up there, awake in the dark, waiting for him. He was thankful, then, for that pile of Kin's money in his keeping. Kin evidently was faithful. His precious money would not be committed to a place of danger.

At the end of a four-hour watch, Stephen was relieved by a young Englishman. Kin opened the door immediately to his ring. Stephen was gratified at this vigilance and fell asleep quickly, feeling all would be right with Kin on watch.

But under Stephen's own roof that night, the New Order paid money to a traitorous general of the provincial war-lord for possession of the city. In Kin's room, around the rude deal table, shining from the many sleeves which rubbed it, smooth from countless *mah jong* games, sat four Chinese: two southerners belonging to the New Order; two others, men of this province—generals in the provincial war-lord's army. All wore white gowns, the garb of Chinese house-boys. When they had entered the room, they had had the manner of servants, but they did not have it now. A bargain was going on between them. Money lay before one of the southerners and the faces of the four men were expressionless. Kin, in a black gown, obsequious in manner, went often around the table, a teapot in hand, filling the cups. In the corner of the room stood Kin's son. No mask over his features. His eyes glowed and his lips moved often as if repeating a prayer. The men at the table paid no attention to either Kin or the boy.

A small Cantonese, a man of the New Order, was talking now. "You are to be generals in our army and your soldiers are to be paid. Is that not enough?"

"Not enough," said one of the northerners. "The money you promised is too small for our services. The danger has been great, placing men of the New Order in the war-lord's army. Treason has been suspected, and many have been beheaded to-day by the lord of this province. Heads hang from every gate to-night. We must have more money for the extra danger."

Instantly the hand of the Cantonese went to his hip.

"Take care," spoke the northerner, "I still command the city, and around this house I have placed my men."

The second southerner, a man taller than either of the

336

northerners, who had until now bent over his cup, drawing in the hot tea through the aperture between bowl and lid with a loud sibilant sound, lifted his head and spoke:

"I, General Ho, will act as go-between in this matter, arranging the sum between the New Order and the Old."

He spoke in the dialect of his own province and the other men did not understand him. Even his associate, the Cantonese, did not wholly comprehend what he said, so then he spoke to Kin.

"Tell your countrymen from the north what I say. You are a northerner. You speak their speech, and, a little, you speak mine. Tell them that when your master was in my province, your household and ours were friends and you now speak for me. The price I, representative of the New Order, offer for turning the city over to us will be increased a third."

"Two-thirds," the general of the provincial war-lord insisted.

At last a half was agreed upon, and the money passed from the long delicate fingers of the small southerner into the long delicate fingers of the men of the province.

"And I," spoke Kin, "how much am I to be paid for the use of my master's house? Only here could all of you be safe, and it is my son who risked his life to carry the message into the very camp of the war-lord."

Each threw down a handful of bills. Kin's long thin hands closed greedily over them.

Now the four men, one by one, slipped stealthily from the room, were let out through the back gate by Kin and, unnoticed by the white guard of the settlement, gained the creek.

The first streak of light was in the room when Hester was awakened by countless horns playing the gay nursery song, *Frère Jacques,* and men's voices singing, putting

337

a strange Eastern cadence into the song. But the Eastern words she did not understand.

> Long live the revolution,
> Down with foreign trade.

At that moment Kin entered the room, carrying the tray with the morning tea, announcing proudly, "The New Party holds the city."

"Without fighting!" exclaimed Stephen.

"Very clever," said Kin. "A little money, I hear, and matters were arranged. The troops of the city now declare themselves for the New Order. How could the Great Lord of this province fight now?"

"No, of course," said Stephen. "To be without face is worse than to be without ammunition."

Stephen had hardly entered his office when a general, wearing the insignia of the New Order, forced his way past the gateman, his sword clanking as he walked up the steps. Without knocking, he opened the door into Stephen's room.

"The son of Ho!" exclaimed the white man, rising, recognizing the third son of Ho, the son with the facial contour of an aristocrat, and the heavy nose and mouth of a coolie. This man was tall like Ho, but he had not the conventional stoop that his father had. He was erect and soldierly. Stephen had been hearing of this General Ho among the revolutionists, but he had never connected him with the family of his friend.

"Thy father?" he asked, suddenly conscious of the ring on his finger.

"I know nothing of him. I belong to the revolution."

Stephen felt the foundations cut from beneath him. The favorite son of Ho speaking like this! He divined

338

that there had been a clash of wills, and that this favorite son had defied Ho.

General Ho sat at Stephen's side, as his father had so often sat, his knees far apart, his hands resting upon them.

"My affairs are many," he said. "It is my duty to see that this city is rid of the obstacles to progress."

Stephen was at a loss, not knowing what to reply. Had Ho's son come to make an example of him, send him from the city? There came back to his mind the lively tune he had heard that morning.

> Long live the revolution,
> Down with the foreigner!

Then General Ho took a card-case from an inside pocket of his smart uniform. He rose and, holding his card in his two hands, presented it to Stephen.

"There may be times," he said, "when it will be useful to the friend of my father."

He moved toward the door, his sword clanking. Then once more he addressed Stephen, speaking this time in English.

"Meeses Ho will call on Meeses Chase."

As soon as he was gone, Burnham rushed in.

"Look," he cried, "they're picketing the British hongs! They're not going to be allowed to do any business. A boycott until they give up this concession. Not even going to be allowed servants. Got it from Kin's son. Are they going to do anything to us? What did the general want?"

"The general called personally. He's Ho's son, don't you remember him?" said Stephen. "I don't know what they're going to do to us. I shouldn't be surprised if at least a partial boycott was started against us. None of the Chinese have come to the office, have they?"

"No, not a stool in the Chinese office is filled."

"Get the other men in, will you, Burnham?" Stephen asked.

When they had come, he said to them, "We must carry on as if all the Chinese were at their posts. We must not let the leaders think that we are paralyzed because the Chinese staff is not here. At all costs we must preserve the face of the Company, until the Company sees fit to withdraw us."

Every man turned now to the duties of the day, dividing the work of the Chinese staff among them.

It was late in the afternoon when the wife of General Ho came to the hong. Hester had been standing at the window, watching the British women and children under escort going down to the afternoon steamer. Coolies often blocked their way. Twice she saw the carrying coolies put down the women's luggage. Evidently they were demanding more money.

All at once there was a loud knocking on the door that led to the Chases' private quarters, and the sound on the stairs of men marching. Then Kin came, as on that day many years ago, saying, "The woman from the household of the great Ho comes." And Hester rose to greet the wife of Ho's favorite son, curious to know how Still-Water would appear in this new rôle.

For a moment, as Hester looked at the trim figure, she thought it was a soldier sent to announce the general's wife. Then she saw the figure was that of a woman, and she went forward eagerly to greet her, vividly recalling the day that Shiao Pao and Still-Water had first come to her. The sound of their tiny feet striking the floor with the clump, clump of padded sticks raised and lowered, was still sharp in her memory. What a change, this trim military figure approaching! Could this woman be the dull-eyed Still-Water? More like Shiao Pao, for her hair was short. And then she saw that the wife of the third son of Ho was a stranger, a young woman, little more than a girl.

"How do you do, Mrs. Chase," said the girl in perfect English.

There was something proud and scornful about her mouth which made Hester uncomfortable. "But she's so beautiful," she thought, "and so young."

They sat side by side on the couch, and again through the window came, as all day there had come, the gay song of the morning.

"It's my soldiers singing!" The girl lifted her eyes to Hester's.

"Are you a soldier too?" asked the white woman. "Do you really march?" she added curiously.

"Yes," answered Ho's daughter-in-law, a defiant lift to her head. "We believe in equality."

"And your family, don't they mind?" Hester remembered the closely guarded family of Ho, and wondered what had become of Still-Water and Shiao Pao. Shiao Pao would have liked to be thus attired, she felt sure.

"I have no father or mother," said the girl. "The State is my father and my mother."

"And your husband's father, the friend of my husband, how is he?"

"I do not know," the young woman answered. "We believe in the separate family. Man and wife. The old must go." She spoke vehemently, something of violence in her tone, then rising abruptly, she said good-by, going quickly across the floor, not turning to let Hester offer the old salutation, "Leave me slowly."

But Hester, watching her, saw that despite the splendid carriage of her shoulders and her military air, she walked with the stiff ankle of the Chinese woman whose feet have once been bound. She could hear her going away down the stairs, striking each step with a thud, as had all the women of China who had ever gone down Hester's stairs. Brave and beautiful as she was, she could not step quite free of the past.

The October day with its astonishing happenings was drawing to its close when Stephen thought it safe for them to go out.

"It's quiet in the city now," he said. "They've cleared it of the old régime. Let's walk to the edge of the settlement and see what's doing, Hester."

They went along the deserted streets until they reached the gate of the concession, where they stood for a moment. Although the shops were still closed, most of the people in hiding, the city had a gala appearance. Floating from every shop were the gay flags of the New Order, red, except for one corner, where a white sun reigned over a blue sky.

Stephen had the peculiar sensation of having seen all this before. Why, of course he had, in Manchuria, when the first revolution, not yet two decades old, had floated the five-colored flags of the first republic, signifying unity of all China. He remembered them, flying bravely, taking the place of the yellow dragon flag of monarchy. Now the flag of the New Order, signifying unity, was taking the place of the five-barred flag of the first democracy.

Stephen felt Hester clutching his arm, her eyes on the flags, and then he saw above them, raised on poles, a row of bloody heads.

"Dear, I shouldn't have brought you. I didn't realize. . . . I thought the Young Revolutionists . . ." His sentence trailed off.

Now he noticed right up to the gates of the concession, even on the gates of the concession, there were posters, bloody-looking things. The white man snatching away the rice of the Chinese coolie, the white man crushing coolies between stones until their life-blood ran away in a red stream. Pictures calculated to raise the passions of the people to violence.

Stephen thought uneasily of his men at sub-stations far off in the interior, and of the man and wife at the isolated fortress of oil below the city. "I'll telegraph the men in the interior to come in," he said to himself. "Down at the tanks they're safe, I think."

"Hester," he said suddenly, "I wonder if I should have got word to Riley. He's alone there working on the new tank. Perhaps he won't be prepared. Anyway he's living on the launch. If nothing happens before night, he's got a good getaway."

They were about to turn back when from a dark corner beyond the gate, a coolie stepped forth and spat full in the face of Hester.

"Oh-h-h . . . Give me your handkerchief, Stephen." As she wiped her face, first with his handkerchief, then with her own, she turned hurriedly, almost running down the street.

"Stop, Hester," whispered Stephen, catching up with her. "Don't let them think we're afraid. The game is up then."

Afraid? Not held aloft now above the sweating, panting throng, not carried on the laboring heart of the land. Pulled down into its violence. She could not cease wiping her face, but she schooled herself to the pace which Stephen insisted on. Once inside the hong, she leaned against the wall, panting as if she had been running and, suddenly, she was sobbing.

"Hester, I shouldn't have taken you out," Stephen kept saying with remorse, "but don't cry so. Why, sweet, you're not hurt."

She was leaning against him now, and as his arm encircled her, he was conscious of the slightness of her body. For years now her feminine fragility had been an

343

accustomed part of himself, but in this moment he was caught back into his first vivid impression of her lightly built form, her delicacy, intensifying his own heavier, more solid self, and he was filled with the instinct to protect her.

"Dear, there isn't any reason for you to stay here. I want you to go to Shanghai."

Hester lifted her head, looking at him, "Really, do you want me to go, Stephen?"

"No."

They stood there, his arm around her, the shouts and cries of the city coming faintly to them; and in that moment they realized their mutual dependence, not that sharp necessity of first love, but here in their middle age, a more sober need of each other. In the long succession of the years the strength of each woven into a combined strength, making a weakness in each when they were apart. Each fitted to the partnership.

"Stephen, I'm not going away."

"I shouldn't have said I don't want you to go. I haven't any right to keep you. You'll be the only woman."

"I know. Elsie isn't coming back to China until after the baby comes."

"Burnham says he wouldn't have her here, as things are," said Stephen. "He's right. But it's different with us. We have only each other."

"Only each other. . . ."

"Hester, I don't know that I can make you understand how I feel about your staying, because if you should want to go later, I'd understand. It would be all right. But, Hester, for a long time I've felt China's going down into some dark struggle. I used to think of the West coming to China as a light, illuminating darkness. It's not going to be like that. It's going to be hard travail to get the West born in the East, if it ever is. And we who helped bring the struggle will be drawn into it. Well, what we

344

shall make of ourselves, I don't know. But we'll make less without our women."

Stephen's embrace tightened, premonition taking hold of him that some day he would be forced to carry on without her.

IV

THE next morning the revolutionists began gathering on the water-front. Wharf coolies and ricksha-men, water-carriers and, lowliest of all, the carriers of night-soil, gathered around the revolutionists. A short way from the hong Hester saw Mrs. Ho standing on a platform, her soldiers grouped around her. They were singing *Onward Christian Soldiers.* Unfamiliar cadences pulsed through the Christian hymn, speaking to Hester of violence. Now that Stephen's arm was not around her, panic filled her. Once more she began to wipe her face, as if it could never again be clean of the coolie's spittle.

Out of the past of assured and ordered living came the thought of her violin. At last, breaking the inertia of years, she took it from its hiding-place. The feeling of the hard case against her hand was reassuring. She rested the beloved instrument in the hollow of her throat, laying her bow across the strings which quivered and twanged as her stiff and awkward wrist wrought in faltering uncertainty. Her spirit faltered too, moving out into the lofty space of music once familiar to her, now an austere and lonely region. She laid away the instrument and wandered uneasily through the hong.

Down in the office, Stephen's Chinese adviser was giving him the first news from the city. He spoke in a whisper:

"The merchants are afraid. There are rumors of a heavy tax. And unions of workers—at each mounting of the sun, one is born. And they say, going along the street, 'This shop shall be ours for headquarters,' and that one they take. The clerks and the apprentices have unions. They have told the merchants that the hours of work must be lessened and the wages more. Already the merchants eat bitterness. To pay the tax and increase wages—both they cannot do. And no man may send from his shop a worker. Neither may he close his shop because he has no money. That, too, he may not do. And every man must let his workers answer the call of their union to parade. Soon no one in the city will be working."

Stephen gave a start at the last words. Even with incessant toil, so many in the Green Valley lived on the borderland of want.

And now the first procession moved out of the city to the water-front, carrying their bright banners—"Higher wages, shorter hours. Plenty! Riches! Down with foreign trade and the foreigner! Rice then will be cheap as it was before they came." And when the first procession had moved back into the city, another came.

Day after day, the bund was a scene of color and life as the workers paraded. Clerks, apprentices of the weavers, the silversmiths. Farmers formed themselves into unions. Taoist monks paraded, dressed in their yellow gowns. In the bright autumn sunshine, their robes looked as yellow as gold. The gray-robed Buddhist monks and the nuns paraded, red banners stating their demands—"More incense. More offerings for the temples that they may sell more and increase their rice." And once a long procession of women and little girls, their lips redder with paint than the lips of any other women, their clothes more gorgeous of hue, their eyes seeking boldly among the men crowding the way—the prostitutes of the city. "More for our labor." All bearing banners, shouting their cries, "Freedom from poverty! Freedom from toil!"

Day after day, through the hong echoed the ecstatic

346

cries of men breaking through the mold of poverty in which they had dwelt, in which their fathers and their fathers' fathers had dwelt. Men under the imminent menace of famine beholding the vision of wealth untoiled for. And everywhere the leaders moved, ushering in "the good life," as they had seen it in the West.

Those in the hong had little to do but to watch the bright spectacle. That dreaded evil, a boycott, had fallen upon them. Not the drastic brand used against the British; only a partial boycott.

In some districts of Stephen's territory no one would buy oil, and the sales dribbled away to nothing. In some districts unaccountable accidents occurred. Junks transporting the oil caught fire or capsized. In some districts the more acquisitive merchants continued to do a clandestine back-door business with the townspeople, but they made their own interpretation of the boycott—withholding payments. At the new tank, accidents were continually occurring. Work was done wrong and had to be done over, and sometimes the men refused to work, though they demanded their pay. The office staff demanded higher wages, shorter hours. And none of them could be dismissed for incompetence.

Stephen, as other managers above him on the river, saw business grow less. But there were still enough stocks of oil in the interior, placed there in the summer, to make him apprehensive that he might have a great loss. Watching each district closely, gauging to a nicety where there was violence and where there was not, he managed without disaster to send his men out to visit one agent after another. Then, after some missionaries back in the interior were attacked and killed, he stopped sending them, and he called Riley in from the tank. Stephen knew he had been criticized when he sent his men into the interior, and that he was criticized now when he did not. The managers, when they were cautious, were called

347

panicky, yellow; when they took chances, fools and gamblers with human lives. As never before, criticism had reared its head among Company people, as the men pressed into the ever-narrowing bottle neck of the Company's contracting business.

Stephen would have liked to know what the Company really wanted done in the matter of traveling. No definite instructions were given out from the Shanghai office, but he got the impression that the manager who kept his men traveling was considered more efficient than the one who did not. He understood Kendall's men were traveling.

In the hong, the separate households were done away with, for the servants of white men were often ordered out on strike. The table in Hester's dining-room was now extended to accommodate all the Company people. Sometimes there would be a houseful of servants—a half-dozen coolies, boys, cooks—on duty at breakfast time, and by noon there would be none. On Thanksgiving Day Hester prepared dinner, Riley acting as her assistant.

"I tell you, Mrs. Chase," Riley said, as he helped her, "it's good to be at work again, even if it's only this sort of thing. There's my job to be done and here I sit idling. The Company won't keep me long if I can't get at that tank." Then, as if he found relief in it, with zest he lifted the great pails of river water on to the stove. He boiled and filtered the water, then filled enough bottles to supply the house for several days.

"It's just as well, Mrs. Chase, to have plenty. Any day the water coolies may go on strike, and then where'll we be?"

Such a day came. All the servants of the white community were called out in a general boycott of the foreign business community. The men waited until night, fearful that the pickets might stop them. Then in twos, they went along close to the compound walls, meeting other

348

silent figures from other hongs bent on the same errand. In bottles hidden beneath their coats, they brought back the water.

That was a gay evening in the hong. The men laid aside their idleness, taking on the activities of the servants. They enthroned Hester in the living-room, refusing to let her work. Riley was cook this time, the griffin said he'd be the little learn-pidgin-cook. Stephen took Kin's place, going about with a napkin over his arm in Kin's most approved style, and Burnham said he'd do coolie-pidgin. When at last they sat down to dinner, there was the good sense of comradeship.

But only now and then did fellowship break through like this, although every one seemed to feel the need of the physical presence of the others. They continually sought one another out, and yet there seemed no real fellowship. They chaffed one another a great deal, but the chaffing only thinly veiled a growing jealousy and strain.

"We're fine ornaments to the office," Riley kept reiterating. "Wonder how long the Company will feel it's worth it!"

"As I see it, one man could do it, the job here," said a middle-aged man recently transferred from a closed station.

"Not at all," answered Burnham. "It couldn't possibly be done without two."

Thus they talked endlessly.

Early in December a highway for automobiles was started—a road that the New Order planned should go all the way to their new capital which was to be established in the spring. The work moved forward swiftly. The wrecking of the one-storied shops and houses on the confiscated property along the right of way did not take long. The paving stones of the old alley-like street, put there centuries ago, made the center of the road, the hard-packed dirt floors of the many huts torn down, the sides.

And now the business of the Keepers of Light, curtailed by the trouble in the interior and the paralyzed business of the cities, took a sudden spurt in a new direction. The old kerosene business was well-nigh dead, killed as the New Order had intended it should be; but suddenly there was a demand for gasoline from the leaders of the New Order, for their cars and their motor-buses. The motor-buses, and expensive models of private cars, arrived almost before Stephen could get enough gasoline up from Shanghai, for on the oil tankers sailing up the Great River there was a go-slow strike. But there was no strike on the foreign ships chartered to bring the new cars, nor among the wharf coolies, conscripted by the soldiers for labor, when the cars arrived.

Down at the wharves the cranes swung out, lowering the tonneaus of the new cars, light green and blue. A hundred conscripted brown hands reached up to steady them and bring them to a safe resting-place on the wharf. They were on the bund now, the drivers taking their places in the buses, smartly dressed chauffeurs in the private cars. General Ho and his wife rode away in a fine, shining Packard, soldiers crowding the running board, the horn screeching, "Open the way, open the way!" Then the buses started, filled with soldiers laughing like children, crowding the seats. Off at full speed, slowing down neither for the uneven paving stones nor for a hole left by the road builders.

In the afternoon, those who had government charge of the new transportation appeared in the office of the Keepers of Light. Spare parts for the machines, they wanted, for the Company had decided to handle spare parts as an adjunct to their sales of gasoline.

The three men who had the matter in charge were young and handsome. They seemed to Stephen not to be closely allied with old China like General Ho, but wholly of the new. Their tweed suits were well cut, their stiff black hair stood away from their heads, accentuating their well-proportioned foreheads. They spoke English fluently. Altogether, they gave Stephen the sense of racial differences obliterated. The indirect maneuvering of past negotiations fell away from his manner. Swinging his swivel chair around facing them, he spoke in direct fashion as he would to his own countrymen.

"I'd like to call your attention," he began, "to the fact that your drivers aren't driving carefully enough for the unevenness of the new road. Your cars will soon be of no use to you."

There was a sudden stiffening in demeanor, that sudden stiffening which Stephen once had known so well, but which he had not experienced for years. The New Order had created a road over which to drive motor-buses as in the West, at forty, fifty miles an hour. In suggesting that they drive slower, he had implied that their road-building was faulty. The old question of face. But Stephen had distaste now in preserving it for them, for it meant assuming that their copy of the West was perfect. He must give admiration of an efficiency that did not exist. But the business of the Company depended upon his giving this admiration. Even life itself might depend upon saving the face of these three handsome young men who sat before him, their coats nonchalantly thrown back, their hands in their pockets. So he spoke to them of their splendid road.

The new business was quickly transacted. Business simple enough in itself, though often in the weeks that followed Stephen found himself at a loss with these men, never knowing when to speak to them as to men of the

351

West, and when as to men of the East. He was outside again.

Winter and the sun seemed to have gone for ever from the sky, and the rain fell day after day. Many shops closed. Merchants were fleeing in the dead of night, fearful that the government might demand money which they were no longer able to raise. The merchants were like candles burned at both ends. Strikes of their employees, and a succession of holidays, had curtailed the sale of goods in their shops; and high wages, taxes, forced contributions, had eaten up their ever-decreasing profits. But the government did not understand that they were burned out.

No longer did this and that union march in celebration with gay banners and gay songs. They had become little more than rabble, collecting here and there in the city streets, on the water-front; sometimes bent on plunder, sometimes merely idle, sitting in sheltered places, filled with the inertia of the underfed. But sometimes they were angry. Prosperity, where was it?

One way of bringing prosperity had not yet been tried. Rid the country of white men and rice will be cheap! Any moment now the empty belly might rouse the brain to do violence. Any moment the mob might move against the foreigners—rich men who squandered water, and fuel, and food. Above, on the river, violence had already broken out. Look's station had had to be given up; Stephen's station on one side of the river, and Kendall's on the other, were now the outposts of the Company in the Green Valley.

As the situation jumped from discomfort to real danger, the Company people were wrought to a high pitch of excitement which burned up the dark uncertainties of the last weeks; fear of the loss of their jobs, fear of failure. All in the hong seemed young, filled with some elixir

352

of youth. A current of newly acquired vitality flowed through them, as they took their turns guarding the tanks, as they made the necessary trips across the bund through the menacing crowd. Death hugging them close bound them into brotherhood.

Then in the midst of the crowded hong, Hester and Stephen were caught back into the eagerness of first love, with its sting of curiosity. Each, familiar and yet unfamiliar to the other, in this setting of danger. Death, so near, gave youth's immediacy to love. As spring drew on, Hester grew more and more certain that in this flare-up of youth the barren years were over. But she would not tell Stephen yet. He might think she should go away. She could not go. This wine of danger of which she had partaken for so long had intoxicated her. Hers a charmed life, held in the chalice of love, her body again tenanted.

The first hint of spring luring the city into a spurt of energy, the now vast army of the New Order cried, "South, south! Unify the country, so that prosperity may come! China for the Chinese!" On moved the army, leaving General Ho in command of the city. But there was rumor that dissension and strike threatened him. There was no money for government, and many fell away from the New Order. Danger increased.

The day had been unusually warm. It was evening now and the windows stood open. The old sounds and smells of a Chinese city entered the hong, lulling the occupants into a momentary sense of safety, when from out the city burst forth an angry roar. In a group, Hester in their midst, the men moved forward to the windows. Men were running, thousands sweeping forward, their cries echoing in the high room. No one spoke, each was certain that at last they were trapped. Then all at once they realized that no man looked toward the hong. Led by the flaring torches, men were carrying their gods in procession, as in the old days. Then they heard the high-pitched voices of young men, crying in unison, "You have obeyed not the mandate of the new government! You have not destroyed your images! Old things must go!"

From the mass of the people, a wail went up. "Spare the gods lest you bring disaster on the city!" In the light of the torches, the group at the window saw the young men lay the gods on the ground, raising their axes to behead them. "Spare Kuan Yin, Kuan Yin!" beseeched the crowd. "Because of her mercy we were born; because of her mercy, given sons."

The hacked-off head of Kuan Yin rolled on the ground, touching the bare legs of a coolie. Evil! Evil! The gods had singled him out, would take vengeance upon him. He and his family would be barren. "Hide, hide, I must hide!" The people trampled one another, frantic in their efforts to hide themselves. Hurry! Deep, deep in their houses! Far back where the evil spirits could not find them!

"Quiet, until the vengeance of the gods has passed," whispered Kin at Stephen's elbow.

Below, the band of executioners of the gods stood out clearly in the flare of their own torches. A moment before, Stephen had seen Kin's son among them. He hoped his father hadn't seen him. It would be terrible for Kin with his superstitions.

"On to the villages!" some one called. "The riddance of our country of superstition is only begun!" But the crowd of youths that moved on was smaller. Some of their number were frightened now, running as the crowd had run, seeking shelter from vengeance.

Kin's son ran along the street at the side of the hong, the evil spirits attending him in childhood at his heels. What terrible thing had he done? Faster, back to the

354

shelter of his father's room. Sobbing, he fell against the gate of the hong.

"Open, open, father!"

The voice of Kin, "Go!" as if he spoke to a dog. "Go, before I drive you forth!"

Skulking along the empty streets went the lad, his breath coming in sobbing gasps. Cast out by his father, pursued by the gods. No hiding-place, doors closed, bolted. Evil spirits filling the air. No light to drive them away. On he ran, his heart filling his chest, beating against his side. There, a lighted window! The house where he had come so often to learn of the New Order. He fell against the door. "Open! Give shelter!"

Light flooded the doorway. A voice, a human voice, "What is thy fear?"

Kin's son stumbled, all but fell over the high threshold, "The gods! They will take vengeance!"

A slender Chinese, clad in the garb of his own country, stood in the doorway. He looked gravely at the son of Kin in his foreign suit, chattering of gods and evil spirits.

"You are of the New Order. What then is your fear of evil spirits?"

The lighted room, the steady voice, broke into the panic of the boy's heart. "For a moment, that which my mother and my father taught me . . ."

The stranger filled a bowl with tea. Warmed by the drink, the lad told of the night's happenings, tumbling forth a mingling of adolescent pride and fear.

"I am an outcast," he ended, "sent from my father's house and from the New Order. I failed this night to do the work of the revolution. . . ."

"I, too, am an outcast from my father's house," said the stranger. "Me, too, the New Order has thrust forth. To-night I must escape. Come, then, with me. I am a teacher, and you, too, shall be a teacher." His thin aristocratic face had in it only humility. "We shall be brothers and we shall live without violence, and we shall teach the people.

"The country must be born again," he went on. "We have called our culture spiritual. Spiritual, when the nation is full of poverty, disease, ignorance! And the leaders, the new leaders, filled with corruption, too!

"We, the small group within the larger group of the New Order, are cast out because they say we have used ridicule against the leaders. Face! Still in the hour of crisis, the leaders talk of 'face'! We, who would purge the party, are called traitors because of our frankness. For the sake of face!" Bitterness and contempt filled his voice. "Our hope is in the people. But how slow! Four hundred million people to educate. But men like you. We must have many, many to serve."

"Let me be your servant," said the son of Kin.

Late that night Stephen was awakened by the whispering of Kin at his door. "Master, the son of thy friend Ho is here."

"All right, Kin." Stephen was on his feet and dressing in a moment. So General Ho was fleeing. The rumors were correct. He felt no surprise that the general had come to him for protection.

At the door of the butler's pantry, Kin stopped. "Here in the pantry. He is not safe in the servants' quarters."

Out of the darkness, some one spoke. "Prior-born, there is mutiny among my troops, a plot against my life. . . ."

The voice was thick with fear and Stephen did not recognize it, so he flashed his electric torch. Yes, it was General Ho, and he was alone.

Where, Stephen wondered, was the young wife? At the same time as he was thankful there was but one to care for. Where, in the crowded house, could he hide General Ho?

"Hurry, hurry," spoke the thick voice.

"In the attic," whispered Kin.

"Can it be managed?" Stephen was thinking of the ladder, hooked out of the way, that must be lowered— and all the sleeping household so near.

"It can be done," Kin murmured.

Like a cat he moved stealthily forward and Stephen directed the steps of Ho. There was no sound of the placing of the ladder. Stephen thrust his flash-light into the hand of the tall shadow at his side. "Use it when you get to the top."

The ladder creaked, but the sleeping house gave no sign of hearing.

Back in his room, lying tense in the darkness, Stephen made his plans. He counted on no disturbance in this change of generals. Probably the new general had money to pay General Ho's troops, and they would follow him without violence. It would be safe to keep Ho for a day. To-morrow night he could get him away in the Company sampan.

The morning brought no unusual stir in the city. The people did not seem interested in the change of generals. The crowds on the bund seemed no more dangerous than always, ready to be swayed suddenly into violence or laughter.

Burnham, watching them, was suddenly alert.

"Look here," he said. "It strikes me that group coming toward the hong means business. See, they're pointing this way."

"Oh, I don't know," said Stephen. "About as usual, hungry probably." There was a clutch at his heart. Suppose he had endangered all the household, because of his instinctive acquiescence to the Chinese idea that one should help the son of a friend.

A mob was gathering now around the front of the hong; a stone hit the window.

"What about Hester?" said Burnham. "Hadn't we better get her down here?"

"No," said Stephen. "Too dangerous. She'd have to go outside among the mob. Separate entrance." Listening, he thought he could hear her violin. He hoped to God she was playing. She wouldn't be listening then.

"What are they saying, Burnham?"

" 'Soon this house is ours,' " answered Burnham.

"They're not after General Ho, then," thought Stephen. Aloud he said, "I believe I can manage them. At least, I can try."

"You're mad," protested the men, gathering round him. "We'd much better stay here, fight them off if they try to break in." They had their hands on their revolvers.

"We can't afford to fight. At our first shot, they'd be reenforced. There aren't many here now. I think I can manage them, if they don't hit me first." Stephen put on his old sun helmet. "This will protect me for a moment. Shut the door quickly behind me," he commanded.

"Guess I'll come along, boss," said Riley. "Hold your hat for you if you get into a scrap."

Those left in the room watched the two walk across the veranda, seat themselves on the railing, seemingly indifferent to the stones flying around them.

Stephen spoke to the ringleader. "You and I know that the ways of these men around us are foolish. This house soon to be theirs, they say, and they are destroying it. Only stupid men break their own rice bowls, spilling the rice."

"Verily a warm snug house," echoed the coolie. Then a light of understanding broke across his face. "True, master, stupid to break one's rice bowl!"

He turned now, haranguing the crowd. The great man of the moment, he walked among them, knocking the stones from their hands, shouting, "Would you destroy that which is to be yours?"

The crowd fell away as if they had forgotten what they

358

had started to do. All but the ringleader, walking proudly back and forth as if on guard.

Stephen and Riley stepped back into the hong. "Well, I'll be damned!" said Burnham, a note of admiration in his tone.

That evening, just before dinner, Stephen slipped secretly from the house, reconnoitering to see if any soldiers lurked near. Rain was falling, bringing an early darkness, and wind was rising. "An ugly night to get a man away by sampan," he thought, "but I guess I can manage, with Riley to help me. Good in one way though. Few Chinese will be out on such a night."

Then he saw a Chinese figure skulking along the veranda, and was fearful that news had leaked out of Ho's hiding-place. Falling back into the shadows to watch, he recognized the coolie of the morning. The man had found an old broom and was sweeping away the mud and stones from the veranda. Stooping, he tried to peer between the cracks of the shutters Kin had had closed early. A gust of wind and rain whipped back the fellow's long ragged gown, and Stephen saw his naked yellow body beneath.

At dinner that night there was high excitement. In the afternoon the mail, uncertain in its arrival these days, had drifted in, bringing the long-looked-for letter. Stephen had been told to report to Shanghai, and Burnham was made manager.

Down the long table, Stephen's and Hester's eyes met often, exchanging their mutual delight. The stimulus of danger had already begun to pass from Hester. Soberly she realized the risk she had taken with the precious life within her.

Burnham sat erect, a new self-respect in his bearing. At last his chance, even if it was dangerous. And the younger men felt the thrill of the promotion, too, for each of them had stepped up one place, and all felt the stamp of approval put upon Stephen and Burnham by the Company. So they toasted one another, feeling that the experiences of the past winter had joined them together.

"Here's to the Company," said Stephen.

They rose and drank.

"And now to our very good selves. We've held this outpost."

As they seated themselves, Stephen took from his pocket the Company letter.

"I didn't have time this afternoon to read it to you. Mr. Truesdale thanks us all for carrying on this winter. He says the great thing has been that the Company has kept its footing. They believe progress is bound to come with the New Order, this wave of boycotts and exclusion a passing phase. The future is in gasoline. He says one very significant thing, I think. That they must go on a cash basis in business."

"What will that mean to us?" asked the griffin.

"It will mean," said Stephen, "another organization. For one thing, you won't need to know the language."

"Hurray!" cried one of the men.

"Which means," Stephen went on, "that you won't have to judge about the Chinese. It is now only a question of buying and selling over the counter."

He stopped, realizing that it was a man satisfied to act merely as a clerk that was needed here. He was thankful that Burnham did not see it.

They sat long about the table, loath to break up the charmed circle. But at last Stephen rose, knowing the work he had ahead of him that night. And as he did so, the elixir of wine, danger and the good news of his promotion, receded. He noticed that the men glanced fearfully over their shoulders—the sign, recognized among men in the interior, that one was near breaking under strain. When he got to Shanghai, he'd tell them these men needed a change.

Two hours later, as the sampan carrying General Ho put off in rain and darkness to some unknown port, Stephen and Riley turned back to the hong. Riley placed his hand on Stephen's shoulder. "Glad you're getting away, boss," he said. "You look too often over your shoulder."

Stephen had handed over his desk to Burnham. He wished that this once the Company had told him definitely what his position was to be. It would be a fine ending to his sixteen years in the interior. "Well, mustn't want too much." He went up the stairs two steps at a time. All he had to do now was to get the luggage to the steamer. And then Hester and Kin.

It was a slow and expensive business, as it had been to get the trunks away. They started—a little cavalcade of Company men carrying the hand-bags. They had just left the shelter of the compound wall when a picket gave a sharp whistle. A crowd of coolies appeared, jerking the bags from their hands.

Riley swore under his breath.

"Don't anger them," whispered Stephen.

"How much?"

"Five dollars," was the prompt response.

Again Riley swore.

"All the way to the dock for five dollars?" bargained Stephen, knowing that twenty cents was big pay.

"Hao la."

The fellows arranged their light loads carefully at the ends of their carrying poles and started off, the group of white men following, walking fast to keep up. Suddenly the coolies stopped.

"Ten dollars."

"But we arranged for five," protested Stephen.

"Ten is the bargain," they insisted, squatting on their haunches, one taking his half-consumed cigarette from behind his ear.

"There's nothing to do about it," said Burnham. "Better pay!"

The coolies did not pause again until they reached the wharf. But when Stephen paid them, they were indignant at the ten dollars.

"Fifteen," they roared.

"Clear out, take what I give you!" cried Stephen, his anger blinding him now to all caution.

"Look out!" cried Riley, as he caught the fellow's carrying pole just in time to ward off a blow on Stephen's head.

"Why did I get angry?" thought Stephen. Well, it was almost over now. Only Hester and Kin, and Kin's money still to get to the steamer. Poor old Kin! Something was wrong with him of late. And where was his son?

Hester, safe on the steamer. Now Kin and his money. The separate bundles were divided among the carrying coolies. Half-way to the dock, quite safely. Then the coolies stopped. "This is heavy. It is money," they cried and gave a sharp whistle. In an instant, a crowd fell upon them.

"Money. It is ours."

"It is not money of the foreign devils!" cried Kin. "Money of a son of China!"

"You are protecting the foreign devils. This money is ours." Then, seeing Kin's distress, they said, "It belongs to this son of China. Let us divide with him." So they took the good silver, handing Kin the now all but worthless paper money.

Some one bethought himself, "Enemy of the revolution! Capitalist!" he shouted.

They would have taken Kin and led him to the execution grounds without trial, but the white men took advantage of the moment of quarreling over the division of the silver, to get Kin aboard the steamer.

There was a hasty shaking of hands, "Good luck to you!"

"We must get back to the hong," said Burnham uneasily. "There may be trouble over this."

Darkness had already fallen and Hester and Stephen could see nothing of the men in their dash along the bund, but lights springing up suddenly in the hong gave them knowledge of the men's shelter within it.

V

THE hands of the clock in the new tower of the Custom House on the Shanghai bund pointed to three, as the Yangtse steamer made its way slowly up the Whangpo River between sea-going junks, river junks, and the gray hulls of foreign destroyers and steamers. Stephen and Hester, standing on the deck, watched with excitement as the tall buildings along the bund emerged from the mist of rain and smoke shut down over the city by the gray bowl of the sky. Although the day was mild, Hester drew the fur collar of her coat more closely around her, for the moisture-laden air had a penetrating chill.

"Shanghai's getting a sky-line," said Stephen. "You remember how it looked a few years ago."

The steamer turned now and was drawing near the wharf. There was a waving of handkerchiefs and many excited calls.

"Why, a lot of Company people!" exclaimed Stephen. "Men pretty high up come to meet us."

"Then it must be true about the promotion, if we're that important." Hester had spoken his thought.

Now they were on the gangplank. A coolie stepped forward, thrusting a note into Hester's hand. From Mrs.

Truesdale! Stephen was busy seeing about the baggage, talking with the men. She plucked at his sleeve, trying to get his attention. "Stephen, Mrs. Truesdale wants us to stay with her. She's sent her car."

"Yes, I know. The office coolie's had instructions about our baggage. I must get to the office before closing. Truesdale's sent word he wants to see me immediately."

Hester could get only the surface of his attention as he hurried her forward into the waiting car.

Riding in the big car, she had one fleeting glimpse of the funnels of the foreign steamers, the jumbled mass of junk masts, before they turned from the bund into Nanking Road. Her heart beat loudly. It must be true—Stephen's promotion. This city to live in. Safety! Now, at last, unaffrighted, she could rejoice in the coming of her child. To-night she would tell Stephen.

Through a haze of happiness, she looked on the swift passing panorama; ricksha- and motor-crowded streets, the endless stream of Chinese and Europeans moving along the narrow sidewalks under the gold signs. The streets broadened, "French Town," high walled gardens, the perfume of some flower. A sudden memory of Ho's garden with something in bloom each month.

Then the car passed through the wrought-iron gates guarding the Company house—this house greatest among all Company houses. A heavy oak door opened. The house-boy ushered her within, and Mrs. Truesdale, exquisitely dressed, advanced across the long living-room to meet her. "It's lovely to have you, my dear. Do sit down." The voice, so beautifully careless.

Hester sought to gather poise to meet it. It was difficult to assume all at once the casual suave manner of this sophisticated city, stepping so suddenly out of that tense world of danger where she had lived. Then the beauty and charm of the room caused her to speak impulsively.

"There's nothing like it anywhere else in the world,"

she exclaimed. "Your room, your lovely dwarf trees!" If she had studied her remark, it could not have been better. The trees were Mrs. Truesdale's pride.

"I'm glad you like them. I always think it is a shame you can't take such lovely things into America."

Hester's gaze wandered from one tree to another, placed here and there on low tables, their delicate flowering branches sharply outlined against the black paneling of the room. Her eyes rested on a foot-high pine, standing in an earth-brown jar on a high chest. It leaned slightly, all its branches thrust forth in one direction. So true were its proportions that it seemed a perfect replica in miniature of a sturdy tree which had continually resisted the north wind blowing upon it.

"It's a hundred years old," said Mrs. Truesdale. "Pure Art, isn't it? Dwarf trees are my hobby. I wish I could take them with me."

Was Mrs. Truesdale, then, going away? Hester felt that her hostess wanted her to ask, but uneasiness had come upon her, checking the question on her lips. She did not know her footing here with this woman whose life was so rich, so safe, that all her conversation lay in the region of polite convention. "A hundred years old!" she murmured absently, "no wonder it gives one the sense of strength."

Abruptly, Mrs. Truesdale moved across the room, as if she could no longer be bothered with intimacy. Hester, ascending the broad stairs, followed her to the guest-room, felt that she had missed some opportunity, that Mrs. Truesdale had intended to tell her something, had asked her here for that purpose.

She pulled a low chair before the open fire. It was a long time before dinner. As she sat there by herself, the impressions of the afternoon sorted themselves out. One dominant impression remained: every Company person she had seen seemed bent on some secret urgent business of his own. She had felt it in those who had met them at the dock, she had felt it in Mrs. Truesdale. What was it?

It was morbid of her to sit here in the dark, imagining things, wilfully destroying her own happiness. No doubt it was reaction from those weeks of danger. She got up, turned on the lights, hearing, to her relief, Stephen's voice in the hall below, speaking to Mrs. Truesdale. Now, as so often before, the quality of its tone steadied her. It gave her an almost physical sensation of leaning against some support.

"Tell me, Stephen," she spoke quickly as the door closed behind him. "Is it all arranged? Oh, do tell me!"

"I'm going to. Give me time." But he dropped into a chair, slouched down in his accustomed attitude when thinking. He seemed to have forgotten her.

"Oh, Stephen!"

"Hester, listen." His voice held a note of entreaty. "Truesdale has asked me to go back up-country, because he can trust me to handle a difficult situation. It doesn't look very big on the face of it, but it is."

"Where?" Hester hardly spoke above a whisper.

"They say I'm the only one who can get anything out of Ho," he answered. "You know he resigned a few years ago, but they think he'd work again with me."

"But that station is closed!"

"It has been," answered Stephen. "Truesdale said that, as late as yesterday, they planned to put both Kendall and me in the main office; but to-day, when they decided to see if they could get back on the upper river, my appointment was changed.

"You needn't think it's the little routine job that Look managed," he went on, a little defiantly Hester thought. "You see it's the very center of all the change. Only some one who understands the Chinese can be trusted to handle the situation."

"What you mean is, not bigger but more dangerous," Hester spoke at last, her tone hard and unnatural.

366

"Well, doesn't danger make a thing bigger?"

"And me?"

"They're not letting any women go. You'd have to stay here. But it's only for a little while. I'm to be there just to get it started. Then they're going to send some one else. Truesdale didn't command me. He asked me. You wouldn't have had me say no, would you? Isn't it the moment to stand by?"

"Stephen, it's all right to help Mr. Truesdale. But what about yourself? You might be forgotten up there. Are you looking after yourself?"

"I can't do anything else, if they've asked me, can I? Of course, if I do this for them, the Company won't let me down."

"How do you know? Suppose anything should happen to Mr. Truesdale?" Something was going to happen to Mr. Truesdale. That was what Mrs. Truesdale would have told her. For some reason the Truesdales were leaving. Who was going to take his place? Did Mrs. Truesdale want to put them on their guard? If she had only not been so afraid to ask, she might be able now to put some weapon in Stephen's hands. But yes, she had a weapon—the child!

"When do you have to decide, Stephen?"

There was a little pause. "It's decided."

"Without asking me?"

"Sweet, please understand."

He could not tell her that, although it was couched as a request, it was a command. It was strange, though. All the time, he had felt that Truesdale was speaking as a puppet would speak, that he was no longer master in his office. He was sure it was not Truesdale opening up this dangerous interior point. He, as well as Stephen, powerless before some newly introduced element.

Conflicting emotions held Hester. She felt her only weapon fall from her hands. There was no escape. The

Company was too big to oppose. It filled the earth; it controlled the earth. She stood silent. Now, after months when she and Stephen had been so much a part of each other, suddenly they had no means of communication. Hester would not tell him about the child. It would make it hard for him, starting on this dangerous trip. Stephen would not tell her his fears, he did not want to worry her.

The small steamer used in the last lap of Stephen's journey was nearing its destination. Stephen was the only passenger. He was standing on the upper deck beyond the boiler plate, placed there as protection against sniping from the shore.

They had crossed the border of the province now. Uneasiness grew within him. In paddy square after paddy square, last year's stubble stood in monotonous unrelief; in paddy square after paddy square, there was no sign of the green mustard or vegetable; no fields with the dredgings from canals or river heaped in them to be used in the perpetual process of fertilization; no water-leveled fields awaiting the spring rice. Surely there was no moment between crops when all the fields could be allowed to rest.

Stephen went forward to the captain of the steamer.

"Yes," said the captain, "the peasants have refused to till the land until the landlords give over the deeds."

Viewing the neglected fields, Stephen felt terribly alone. What did Shanghai know of this dark strife in the interior? How futile was his coming!

Late in the afternoon he saw the great gray tanks of the Company. After a little, as the steamer came in line with the city, he saw the four-storied hong, the Narrow House, rearing itself above the city. And suddenly he saw that Ho stood upon the pontoon, waiting for him. "Ho knew I was coming! The 'bamboo wireless' is still intact," he said to himself. Of a sudden his depression fled. It would be good to work with his old friend again.

How familiar the voice of Ho asking, "How is your honorable self?"

Stephen, following the old polite and distant formulas, felt the foundations steadying. China would not lose her unique self. She was only readjusting herself.

As they walked together the few steps across the bund to the hong, he felt the upbuilding that renewed faith in one's fellows always brings. It was no casual courtesy that had made Ho declare himself thus openly his friend. The crowd had closed in upon them. They spat upon Stephen and they hissed Ho. Ho's tall form reared itself above these smaller men as he walked forward in quiet dignity, his hands folded within his sleeves.

Kin followed close behind. Stephen felt he could go through anything with these two, his friends, for Kin had become more than servant to him. Two men could not have traveled together as he and Kin had, lain side by side on the *k'ang* beds, shared discomfort and danger, and not become more than that. The fact that Kin was here meant more, Kin assuming that where Stephen went, he went also.

As soon as they were within the old living-room, and Kin had closed the door, leaving them alone, Ho passed through a startling change. He no longer held to the traditional slow approach from impersonal dignity to intimacy. *"Tong ja,* why did you come here? It is not safe." He spoke half in anger, half in agitation.

"Why do you ask? You know. Because the Company sent me," answered Stephen.

"Because the Company sent you? Your consul is not here. It is not safe for any outside man."

Now that that outer control had relaxed a little, Stephen saw what ravages had been made in Ho's face.

369

Time alone would not have done this. The temples were sunken, the eyes deep in their sockets. Ho's whole expression was that of one who had had a view of hell. Now the news Stephen had heard of this province, and which the Company had discounted, he believed.

"Many moons ago," Ho went on, "I told you I did not care for this thing you call the Company. It offends the human relations. Now in this moment of my people's suffering, it is of no importance. But you, you are my friend. *Tong ja,* go away. Just now we are exhausted and it is quiet, but none of us knows what the night will bring forth."

"You know I cannot leave without an order," answered Stephen. "Surely this feeling against us has passed. It was hysteria. We need the trade, you need the trade. Those oil tanks standing down there untouched are proof of it. My people have not always done right. Neither have yours. But, teacher, I had nothing to do with that; you had nothing to do with it. That is political. We . . ."

The words died on his lips at the expression that had come into Ho's face. Ho, too! Stephen knew now that there was one subject which could never be discussed between them.

After a long silence, Ho spoke. "The *tong ja* will stay in the house for a few days? Here I can watch, and my heart will be at rest."

Stephen gave his promise. He must give Ho time to arrange matters. Only with Ho's cooperation could he hope to reopen the business; he would not hurry him, increasing the difficulties.

When Ho had gone, Stephen moved through the empty rooms that had once been his home, going back and forth over the building, remembering each tread of the stairs. Night had fallen. There was a bright moon shining through the cracks of the closed shutters and across the floors. How large the hong was! How strange that it had once seemed so cramped! Why, the building was huge. Through the long dusty corridors he paced, past the room where Dee-dee had once played. From his own apartment he turned back. Had Hester been here, even now the place would have been touched with home. A half-hour ago he had tried to pull chairs and tables into groups, commanding Kin to build a fire, but the room was desolate, even as he was desolate without her.

Up and down the stairs he tramped, looking out of the back windows into Ho's garden. Demolished now. One of the waves of revolution had swept over it. The tea-houses, the bridge across the artificial lake lay in ruins. The wall around the patriarchal dwelling torn away at one corner. He could see the sweet olive tree's gnarled branches, its great trunk. The foreign house stood shuttered and seemingly deserted. Somewhere within it was the fragment of the great family. Poverty was in evidence everywhere. Many times in the last months, Kin told him, Ho had had to buy his life.

Finally Stephen came to a halt at a side window, looking out on the remains of the American consulate. In one of the moments of improvement, it, with other buildings, had been partly pulled down to make room for the new roadway, planned on a grand scale, wide enough for eight motor-cars going abreast. One more day and the hong would have gone, too. What chance, Stephen wondered, had made them stop just there? But after all the road had not been built. The bricks and the refuse lay in great piles. Already the tracks of the rickshas had worn circular paths around them.

A week went by. Stephen, shut in the hong, felt utterly isolated. Kin told him there were two or three Britishers trying to carry on business for their firms. Of his own countrymen, there were several missionaries back in the city, but he had not seen them. Undoubtedly marooned, all of them, as he was. Down-river a little distance, a small British gunboat was anchored. He had received from the captain the plans for reaching the gunboat, in case there was an attack on the white people. Ho, he had not seen since their first meeting. He had hoped each day that Ho would come. He was growing impatient to get to the tanks to find out what the Chinese in charge was doing—the main thing the Company had wanted him to do. There were hours when the need to get to the tanks and do something became an obsession.

The seventh day came and, after luncheon, Stephen slept in his armchair. It was late when he woke and, as the farmer, almost before he wakes, senses a change in the weather, so he sensed that the temper of the city had changed. He opened the French window, pried the slats of the blind apart, and peered out. A crowd was gathering on the bund, every moment growing larger. There was shouting. Men were crowding forward from the alley and in their midst Stephen saw Ho, his shoulders, his great head, looming above the little men who were hurrying him along. Stephen rushed down the stairs two steps at a time, the clatter of his running resounding through the empty corridors; but to himself he seemed not to move forward, so paralyzed his limbs felt. At last he was in the lower hall, by his old office door, and finally the street door, tugging at the wooden bar nailed across it. Some one pulled him back. "Master, no."

"Get out of my way, Kin."

What he was going to do he had not thought, only that Ho was in trouble.

"Master, master, draw in your heart, draw in your heart. Their bellies are empty. The foreign devil has made the rice high. If you go among them . . ."

Then Stephen understood. To go out would only endanger his friend the more. Back up the stairs he went, to peer again from an upper window. A procession was forming, at the head Ho. Taller than ever now, almost a giant. Upon his head a four-foot-high dunce-cap. On his back and his chest, where the mandarin squares used to adorn the coats of officials, were large white placards with staring black characters, "This is the running dog of a foreign devil." The crowd laughing and jeering, pushing Ho along. Like a float he seemed, so immobile were his shoulders and his features.

"Because of me, because of me!" Stephen said over and over to himself. If only they did not kill him. He would make it up to Ho. Get him out of the city to-night. Kin squatted at his side, mumbling over and over again, *"Ai yah, ai yah."*

"Kin, stop it. I can't stand it."

"Ai yah, ai yah," moaned Kin, "he is destroyed. *Mei yu fatsu,* it cannot be helped."

"Anything can be helped!" shouted Stephen, shaking Kin. "Stop that racket, I say."

Kin paid no attention. "It cannot be helped, it cannot be helped, *mei yu fatsu,"* he groaned. "Will the master have his supper here?"

With the startling return of Kin to the remembrance of his duties, Stephen was brought also to composure. He stopped his agitated shaking of his servant.

The last cries of the mob died away. Kin came with his dinner, his composure intact now. But Stephen could not eat. He sat there, his head bowed in his hands; in imagination he was walking the streets with Ho. Again he heard Kin's soft footfalls in the room and his voice, "The great Ho has returned."

"How is he?" Stephen managed at last to ask, though his throat seemed too dry for speech.

"He will die."

"Did they beat him?"

"No," said Kin, and went out.

All night Stephen remained in his chair before the dead fire in dumb supplication for the life of Ho. He must have slept, for he realized suddenly that morning had come, since Kin had entered, bringing a newly filled, brightly burning lamp to take the place of the one sputtering now, about to go out. He thought he was alone, but hearing some one moving, he looked up. A figure in sackcloth, bowed nearly to the floor, shuffled across the room and fell at his feet. From him broke the death wail, "My father is dead."

"Stand up, son of Ho."

But the son of Ho did not rise, and Stephen stooped and raised him to his feet. It was like holding an uprooted tree in its place; the long thin body of Ho's son fell against him and he could hardly support it. But it was better for two men to stand erect when they talked, even if one was held so. Stephen looked into the face of Ho's son, swollen with weeping, the black hair disheveled.

"The wounds, they could not be healed?"

"They could not be healed."

Stephen knew then with a flash of insight that Ho had taken his own life. In the mystery of the dark night it had been done. Too great the humiliation, that walk through the city, its ridicule heaped upon him. A few weeks ago, Stephen knew, Ho had so highly prized his life that he had made himself poor to preserve it. And last night, because of that walk, it had become a worthless thing. He looked straight into Ho's heart now and saw that for him Ho had made this supreme gift. Tragic, that now in the moment of deepest realization of the friendship, Stephen stood with the veil of opposing thought hanging between them. He was unable to grasp to the full the bitterness of humiliation that lay for Ho in that ridicule, in wearing the dunce-cap, the placard—for a Chinese unbearable, complete loss of face. But one thing he did grasp. For him, Stephen Chase, despised white man, Ho had given his life.

The tide of violence that had been at ebb since Stephen's coming to the city swept forward now. The passing of Ho seemed to have broken some barrier of restraint. Cries and shouts echoed through the silent building. Every moment Stephen expected the mob to attack the hong. But just now hunger held them in the city, where the soldiers and peasants fought for possession of the last stores of rice. Kin said, "When night comes they will attack these foreign houses. We must get away."

As the hours of the day moved slowly by, more fixed in Stephen's mind became the thought of the safety of the tanks. If any good were to come out of the Company's futile attempt to force their way back into the province, the vast stores of oil must be saved. He did not know whether the Chinese in charge of the tanks could be relied upon. Stephen remembered how he had held back that other mob. Perhaps he could hold back this one. It was only a chance, he knew, but not until he had tried to save the oil could he feel warranted in leaving. He must get to the tanks.

He gathered together a few articles, stuffing them into his pockets. There was relief even in this simple activity. He laid his pistol and his flash-light out and then, through the quiet hong that was like a great shell, he went in search of Kin. He had not seen him for hours. Damn it! Where was Kin!

As he opened the door at the top of the stairs leading to the servants' quarters, he paused. There rose up to him many voices talking guttural Chinese. What was up? Were they going to attack him? He went down a few steps and peered into the dim recesses below. The room looked like an improvised food shop. And there was Kin selling the canned food Stephen had brought for himself.

Here now in the midst of such utter chaos, Kin was making money!

Perhaps he'd better slip off to the tanks without him. No, Kin had followed him up here. He must wait until Kin came with his dinner to tell him he was going.

"Master," begged Kin, "no man can tell what the night will bring forth. This foreign light . . . if it burns, it will burn. *Mei yu fatsu*. Master can not stop it. Better we go in the British boat."

But when Stephen refused, Kin answered, "Where master goes, I go."

"Quickly then, before the moon comes," said Stephen.

They slipped into the shadows of the ruined consulate, then in little spurts they advanced from building to building. At last they were in the country, following the dike paths. It had been many years since either had gone this way, and in the dark they lost their sense of direction. Suddenly they heard the long-drawn-out screech of the siren of the British gunboat. So the captain, too, feared an attack to-night. That was the order to the few white men in the city to get to the shore below the city, where sailors would pick them up. But doggedly, Stephen plodded on, Kin at his heels. He must save the tanks. He alone could save the tanks.

Looking back he saw a great light on the bund, there where the hongs stood. So the mob had begun their destruction. He and Kin were beyond the paddies now, circling the high wall of the compound, coming at last to the entrance on the river. Again the siren screeched its message. Two long blasts; that meant hurry. But Stephen had his work to do. He knocked on the iron gates. A voice answered quickly. Wang, the Chinese caretaker, was at his post. How glad Stephen was that he had come! Surely the white man should not be less faithful than the Chinese.

376

"Tong ja, tong ja," the man kept saying, "good, good that you came."

They took counsel, planning the defense. Only one thing they had to rely on—that inborn instinct of the Chinese to arbitrate.

In the distance, every moment growing louder, they could hear the roar of the mob, and above all that screeching siren of the British gunboat.

"If they start to batter down the gates, I will go out to them," said Stephen.

"Open! Open!" The butt of a rifle was driven against the iron gate.

"Not a large crowd yet. Perhaps I'd better try to pacify them now, before the crowd grows too big." Stephen thought. Still in his mind the hope of negotiation—the middle path so often trodden throughout the years in China.

Wang on one side, Kin on the other, he walked out, commanding the coolie to bar the gate behind them, to be ready to open it quickly if retreat were necessary.

"I come as friend!" he cried to those gathered outside. "Let us speak together."

For one moment, the note of authority in his voice laid silence on the crowd. Then a woman shrieked, "Foreign devil! He takes our rice!"

"Da! Da! Kill! Kill!"

No negotiations now. The extreme violence. The mob charged down upon Stephen. The gate behind him swung in, Wang and Kin pulling him back. The gate almost closed now, all three of them pressing against it to force it shut, to shut out the howling men pressing it in.

"Da! Da! Kill! Kill!" Only the thin iron of the gate between them and the fury of the mob.

From over the rice-fields came the cry, "Kill! Kill!" swelling the tumult. The opening was widening, the gate was slowly swinging back under the pressure from without.

Stephen, Wang, Kin were carried back with the gate. The mob swept into the compound, blood lust upon them. White man! Stranger! Enemy! Their violent hands were upon Stephen. No escape now.

Then a new cry burst forth. "The foreign light! Destroy! Destroy!"

The mob caught up the cry, swayed in an instant to a new hatred. Stephen was swept forward toward the tanks looming silent and black above the tumult.

Then the earth heaved itself up with a great roar, a geyser of oil shot up in a burst of flame, throwing the top of the tank high in the air like a huge hat tossed skyward. The cries of the mob turned to howls of fright. Forgetting the white man, they trampled one another to get away from the accursed spot. The evil spirit in the foreign light was taking vengeance, dropping angry tongues of fire upon them.

Stephen was caught, jostled, carried forward, dropped, sprayed with the burning oil. . . .

Red-hot light, agonizing light, then sudden merciful darkness.

VI

HESTER did not find her position in Shanghai unique. The city was crowded with the wives of men off in the interior, crowded too with idle men, men no longer needed in the Green Valley. Thousands of people were gay, reckless, morose, as they had been of late in the interior, the atmosphere charged with excitement, fear, failure.

Little concerns were going bankrupt; big ones curtailing. With kaleidoscopic rapidity, the Company changed. The Truesdales were transferred to the Near East, and Kendall jumped up into the general manager's place. Hester heard it from Creighton. One evening she was walking on the bund to escape from the crowded hotel where she was living. It was the fashionable dinner hour and there were not many, except Chinese, on the street. The familiar lounging figure of Creighton stood out among them. He was passing her, when she stopped him.

"Why, Tom Creighton, how do you happen to be here? I thought you were up-country."

"Would be, but just as I started the steamer canceled its sailing. Something's up," he said. "See here, you've no business to be out like this alone, the way things are in Shanghai now."

He turned and walked with her back toward the hotel. Hester looked at the gunboats of half the countries of the world, all alight on the river. A spotlight played on the dome of the new international bank. Light! There was light everywhere, it seemed to her, inside this safe city. But in the darkness beyond . . .

"Why don't they bring the men in?" she asked angrily. "It's so dangerous."

"Trade never stops for danger. You ought to know that by this time," answered Creighton. "Sometimes it's adventure that keeps it going, sometimes greed, sometimes necessity—a man's kids, you know."

He asked then, changing the subject, "Heard the news? Kendall has been made general manager."

"And Mr. Truesdale?"

"Transferred to the Near East. Not so big a job. Rumor is he kind of failed them of late. A little panicky, they said, about sending the men into places he felt were dangerous."

"His sending Stephen up-river wouldn't indicate it." Hester spoke bitterly.

"It's my opinion Truesdale didn't want to send him. Maybe that's what broke him."

"Well, who did then?"

"Ask the marines!"

Creighton left her at the hotel entrance. Hester sank down on the first chair in the lobby, oblivious to all but the tumult within her. For what purpose had Kendall been made manager? She saw him again as on that evening she had first met him—saw his shut hard face, felt again swept up like chaff into his hand.

A young British woman, leading two children, came and talked to her. That she did not know Hester seemed to make no difference. Strange for a Britisher.

"Your husband in the interior?"

Hester nodded.

"I'm worried about mine," said the woman. "He'll hang on to the last. It's his own business. We were prosperous a year ago, but now he's so in debt to the banks, that even if trade started again to-morrow, it would take him all his life to pay back what he owes."

She seemed eased a little, now that she had spoken, and left as suddenly as she had come.

A week later, as Hester came through the door of the dining-room, Creighton met her again.

"Office sent me," he said awkwardly. Then he blurted out his message. The foreigners had had to flee from Steve's station. Most of them were on the British gunboat, one killed. Stephen was missing. The hong had been destroyed. The tanks were on fire. If he were at the tanks, there was no hope.

Hester had but one idea, to get to Kendall's office. As she entered, she saw a flicker of pain pass over Kendall's face and, forgetting all her antagonism toward him, she remembered only that he was Stephen's friend.

"Oh, I'm so glad you're here," she said. "If any one can find Stephen, you can."

"It's as important to me as to you," he said. "If Steve's killed, I will be held responsible."

"Were you?"

"I might have telegraphed him yesterday to come in. I left it to him to decide. Steve knows as much about things as I do. He should have left when it got dangerous. That's why he was sent, because we thought him capable of judging."

He walked back and forth across the floor, pad, pad, like an animal caged. "If they spill a drop of his blood . . ." she heard him mumble.

Something mounted guard in her mind, holding back the thought of Stephen dead. Lowering and terrible, it crouched behind the guard. In front, her mind went busily picking up the tiniest details around her. The telephone was ringing.

"Yes. On the upper river?"

Hester sat tense. Some word. No, something else.

"So you'll withdraw your men, if I will?" she heard Kendall say. "Well, I won't. Not until I'm convinced there's no business they can do."

He slammed down the receiver. Men came and went with letters. Kendall signed them, did more telephoning. Business seemed to be going on as usual. A realization of how little any individual mattered to it swept over Hester. On, on, Big Business. Her mind made a picture of it like the great Juggernaut she had seen in India. The crowds cheering this, their god. The offerings of flowers transmuted to service and loyalty. Hers, Stephen's. Stephen thrown in front of it, passed over, forgotten. The Company moving on, on.

The telephone, men coming, Kendall going in and out. The telephone.

"Good," she heard Kendall say into the transmitter. "Picked him up below the city? Well, I never! By his white helmet!"

Hester clasped and unclasped her hands. It was Stephen. "Old Chinaman with him?"

That must be Kin! Yes, yes, they have found Stephen!

Kendall turned to her. "He's on the British gunboat, Mrs. Chase. Pretty badly burned, but nothing dangerous. Oil from the tank sprayed him. Haven't any more details. They're coming down now as fast as they can."

Hester felt the earth reeling in its course, and the terror long held back moved forward. She seemed in this moment of relief to feel Stephen dead. In the three weeks he had been away, a life without him had taken tangible shape, the richness of mind and body that was Stephen's masculinity no longer blended in her.

As she moved in a daze through the corridors, men crowded about her, coming out of every office, shaking her hand. Men she didn't know—the personnel man, assistant managers, accountants—insisting on shaking her hand. Strangers saying, "Chase is a hero." Friends saying, "Oughtn't to be anything in the Company too good for Steve." Something spontaneous, beautiful, growing up here in the house of Big Business, each man in the Company seeing himself in Stephen, for one good moment stepping free of the mold of expediency and conformity. When they heard that Kendall had been set forward into the place of manager, there had been envy mixed with congratulations. But now they themselves, without envy, lifted Chase up above the mass that was themselves. And as they did so, they recreated him for Hester.

It was then that Stephen's child for the first time moved within her. She was the proud bearer of his child.

The evening paper carried Chase's name in the headlines. The news was flashed to America.

It was a week later. The afternoon was fading into dusk. Hester stood with Kendall on the pontoon, wait-

382

ing with other wives and other heads of firms, most of them British. "The boat's late," some one said. "Ah, there she is!"

Presently Hester found herself going forward with Kendall through a lane made by the parting crowd. Four sailors came ashore, carrying a stretcher. She looked down at Stephen, a strange Stephen. Bandages swathed his face like a cowl. She was struggling against tears when all at once she found herself smiling. It was so just Stephen after all—his battered old sun helmet, a box of cigars on his chest.

Kendall reached out his hand and shook the ends of Stephen's fingers extending beyond the bandages bound around his right hand.

"Don't talk now. We'll settle everything later."

Then he vanished into the crowd. Hester was thankful he had left them. When they were alone, shut off to themselves in the clanging ambulance, Stephen spoke:

"It's all right now, isn't it? I've done this thing they asked me to do. I've made good. And I'm back soon, as I said I'd be."

"Oh, Stephen!" She fell on her knees at his side, pushing away the old sun helmet, stretching herself across him, taking renewed life from the warmth of his body. So she did not see the look in his eyes when he told her that Ho was dead.

VII

THE violence started that night in Ho's city spread down the river, and the Green Valley was all but closed to foreign trade. Shanghai was crowded to its capacity. The beautiful house of the Keepers of Light was no longer the exclusive residence of the general manager, but was filled with managers of provinces seeking shelter in

Shanghai, Kendall its host. Stephen and Hester, there too, when Stephen's burns had healed sufficiently, and a crutch had been secured for him.

But this number one house of the Company was not as Hester remembered it. She was conscious of its difference when, on the day of their arrival, they stood looking around the great hall. Now, without the Truesdales' fine furniture, bright hangings and dwarf trees, it seemed like a cavern. The black wainscoting reached to the ceiling, the black wood of the stairway made the room a mass of lurking shadows. "It's sinister," she cried. "I don't like being here."

Then she fell silent, ashamed of her fancifulness. The excuse she found for herself was that, at such a time as this, women were likely to be fanciful.

"It's evening, that's all," answered Stephen, as he laid his hand on her arm. "Help me up the stairs, dear. I think it's good to be here. It makes me a part of things, even if I can't go to the office just yet."

It was two weeks since that evening. Each day since they had been in this house, their position in the Company seemed to have dwindled, as if the house had absorbed it. The heroic figure of Stephen Chase the Company men had so spontaneously lifted up that day of his rescue, slowly but surely was disappearing. At first, the change was nothing. Half-friendly, half-humorous bantering, as if men felt a little ashamed of their first unchecked emotion. "How's that reckless husband of yours?" asked the personnel man, when Hester met him one day by chance. Then, all at once, it seemed as if every one was assuming that Stephen was reckless. As she went about, the women began asking her about a fire, oh, long ago, in Manchuria. Hadn't Stephen torn down a lot of buildings? Suddenly Stephen seemed to be the topic of conversation. Everything he had done in the Company

384

being rehearsed, as it would have been if he were a man of importance, only not credible things; things that raised a question. Shipped a lot of tin plate once without orders. Everybody seemed suddenly interested in a tale about a young griffin caught in the midst of fighting. Had Stephen risked his men? And wasn't there a loss of money at a time of looting? Something, too, about his attitude to the Chinese. In a tone here, a word there, the disparagement gradually took shape. It terrified Hester. So surely did each stroke destroy Stephen, the efficient man, that it seemed to her there was some guiding hand deliberately shaping him into an inefficient personality.

Until Kin came to Hester, saying he must leave, making the excuse that he was an old man, she had fought to make herself believe that her own sensitive condition was giving her this impression of Stephen's diminishing position. But she knew the reason for Kin's leaving was an excuse. Through all the troublous last months there had been no talk of leaving; and now, if they had been in a position of importance in Shanghai, Kin could not have been induced to leave. Yes, something was wrong with her husband's position.

She was in panic, feeling a lifetime of effort crumbling away. Did Stephen know? He seemed so remote, shut into his convalescence in the Great House. If only Kendall would give him the place which had been promised him in the Company! That would bring back dignity and security. This swinging in space, the position in the interior wiped out, no definitely assigned position here! Hester's mind went like a squirrel in its cage, scrambling about on its treadmill of fear. All good things flowing from the Company. Pension, insurance, binding them to the completion of their years of service. "Paternal in its attitude,"—where had she heard that? Their lives bound into the Company, the only business experience Stephen had had. And the baby coming! She could not tell

Stephen about the baby just now, adding that burden to his convalescence.

One afternoon she had escaped from the house, trying to elude something frightening that dwelt there. She was hurrying along, the tears burning behind her eyeballs, when she met Creighton.

"Why, Tom Creighton," she managed to say lightly, "your station closed, too?"

"It is, so far as I'm concerned."

"What do you mean?" asked Hester.

"I've resigned."

"But, but, the children! Why, you said . . ." Then she stopped. She had no right to tell him his duty to his family. But she had gone too far, so she went on apologetically, "You know you said trade was kept alive because of children's needs."

"Yes, I know. I won't let you think I'm a coward about being in the interior. I don't mind danger, it's not that. The Company's getting rid of its men, but it's living up to its reputation of never firing an old and reliable servant—lets you fire yourself. Cheaper, too, you know. Saves a lot of insurance. Fortunately, I can afford to do it. Just had a letter that that great-aunt of mine I used to tell you about has up and died. Left me a little. Not so much, but enough to tide me over, until I can get a start. That doesn't excuse the Company, just the same."

Hester wanted to ask him what he meant, but a certain loyalty to the Company held her back. Even in this hour of her own terror she mechanically reacted to the slogans of the Company, heard through the years. "Something wrong with a man when he talks against the Company." So she changed the subject, hastening to show her friendship.

"Do come to see Stephen," she begged. "You're his friend. It would mean a lot. I think it's all this inactivity," she hastened to add.

He looked at her sharply. "What's Steve got to worry about? I did think, when he went up-river, the Company was trying to shelve him. But after what he did up there, they've got to recognize that kind of loyal service. Kendall can break 'most anybody, but he can't break Steve. Wouldn't dare to, after what he's done. Besides, Kendall is an old friend, isn't he?"

Hester went away comforted, not knowing before how much she had needed comforting. Nevertheless, as she passed through the wrought-iron gates of the compound, and heard the heavy door shutting behind her, she said to herself, "I wish we could get away. This house has some sinister power. It's a vampire sucking out our hearts. If only we weren't in this house!"

In those first days, Stephen found his life good. It did not bother him that he was only a transient in this house where a man came at the pinnacle of his attainment. Not only had he no envy in his heart for Kendall; he rejoiced that so great an honor had come to his friend. For Stephen, Ho's friendship, with its ultimate sacrifice, had made all friendship more significant. Kendall was just the right man for this important position. Stephen felt he had reached his own pinnacle of attainment, and it pleased him to think that his special knowledge of China would aid Kendall.

Those first days when he sat resting were good days. After the work of the years, a man liked at a time like this to catch the savor of living. And before he put his deed of heroism from him, he wanted to have a moment to say to himself, "This is fine, this thing I did when I tried to hold back the mob from the tanks." To be physically brave—as a boy how often he had dreamed of it. And yet he had never been certain that in a crisis he would be wholly brave as a man should be. Not seeking danger in a spirit of bravado, but going straight up to it when it came in the path of duty. Well, now he had done just that, and it had been great. He could feel still the pulsing of his veins as he stood at the gate before the mob of hungry, desperate men, his arms locked with Kin and Wang. That moment of exaltation when he had thought he might turn the tide. Well, anyway, he had not quit while there was a chance of saving this storehouse of oil. He had kept some inner integrity that would have been outraged, if he had not tried.

In his brain, like forked lightning, still flared and flashed the events of that night. The terrific noise of the explosion, the great burst of flame shooting up. The hot spray of the oil; his clothes bursting out in jets of fire. Then the agony of his burning flesh when he had stood, the center of flame.

The rest had not yet become clear in his mind, whether he had led Kin away, or Kin had led him; how he had got rid of his burning clothes; why Kin wasn't burned as he was; how he came to have his sun helmet. But he remembered the first gray of morning, the uncared-for paddies lighted up as if by a huge lamp, and the soot falling around him like black snowflakes. His mind could not yet disassociate itself from the scene, as he sat in the great house waiting for the burns to heal. He still lived in the exaltation and the anguish of that experience.

Suddenly, he was ready for work. The events of those days receded, leaving his mind craving work; and each day of waiting for Kendall to say what he was to do was long and tiresome. Each day became a little more difficult than the one before, and the consciousness of his injury enhanced. Then began a slow disintegration of confidence in himself. This uncertain self incased in his injured body. Stephen had never had anything the matter with him before and he felt humiliated now by his inefficient body. The continued inaction, the uncertainty, added to the shock of the burns, now affected his whole system, and the burns, healing rapidly at first, were healing slowly now, for no reason the doctor could discern.

Over and over, Stephen's mind pursued its treadmill of thought. Surely to-day Kendall would make some mention of what his position was to be. Then it occurred to him that Kendall might be holding back, thinking that he was not well enough to work, wishing not to hurry him.

The next morning at breakfast, he said, "I think I could go back to work, Kendall. I'm all right except for a little clumsiness."

Kendall looked at him sharply.

"If you want to be busy, all right. But it's not necessary. The men are fairly falling over one another at the office."

"I've got to."

To Hester's ears, Stephen's words had a note of desperation. Did any one else notice it?

"Well, come on down then. I guess I can make a place for you."

Kendall gave him a desk in the large room next his private office, where the assistant managers had their desks. For a day it made Stephen feel like a new man, this tacit acknowledgement of his coming position, and the fact of having a desk in front of him. But the waiting began again; waiting for work to come to him over that desk, as work had come to him throughout the years; waiting for Kendall to call him into his office and assign him his duties. Then, when nothing happened, Stephen's happiness, his self-respect, as with most men, inextricably tied up with his work, began to evaporate.

But still some inner core of personal dignity remained untouched, withstood the awkwardness of sitting at the desk with nothing to do; withstood, too, remarks made by men who assumed that he was in the group who had no sympathy with the new aspirations of the young

Chinese. It was vain for Stephen to protest that he did believe in the ideals of the New Order, but that the changes could not be made in a year, or even in ten years, as he saw it. Some seemed to be lecturing him. "You see," they said, "we must make these young Chinese feel we believe in China." As if he would be the one to doubt the people of China, Stephen thought; he, who had had the gift of Ho's friendship! Other men whom he had known well seemed to be avoiding him. Still the kernel of self-respect held. There was this good service, this last act of loyal service to the Company— in his worst moments, it was something tangible which gave him back his faith in himself.

To Hester, black magic seemed at work in this bare house, unadapted to the personal uses of a family, only the atmosphere of the Company pervading it. Every time the members of the household gathered about the round table in the dining-room, each cast of features seemed accentuated—the hard ruthless lines of Kendall's face, the easy diplomacy of Look's, the uncertainty in the faces of Stephen and Mr. Chesterton. The younger men at the table, almost griffins in the Company—there to help Kendall, so he said, especially a young man named Thornton—at first were marked only by a nervous deference. Later they began to take on self-confidence, even as Stephen and Chesterton seemed to lose theirs. Until now, Hester hadn't seen Chesterton since that time they had come up-river together when Stephen had his first managership. Much older-looking—the only change in him, she thought. That conscientious look of his that she remembered so well, and a quiet dignity, were the dominant expressions in his face. But gradually, it seemed to her, uncertainty seemed to be blotting out everything else.

One evening Kendall left the dinner-table as soon as the meal was done. After the door closed behind him, Chesterton said quietly to the others, "I'm leaving in the morning. I've resigned." Nobody spoke. Outside the quiet room they could hear desultory firing—beyond the barb-wire encircling the foreign settlement, revolution and counter-revolution extending down the valley to the very gates of Shanghai. Then the door opened and Riley came walking briskly across the room.

"Hello, every one! Getting better, boss?" He wrung Stephen's left hand.

"Chesterton's resigned," said some one.

Riley whistled. "Paid you that compliment, did they? Just fired me. Perfectly all right. There is no work in my line. I've only been with the Company a year. They've got no obligation to me."

No one spoke. Some Company inhibition held them against speech, as Hester had been held when she talked to Creighton. Men still in the Company bound by loyalty to the Company, or by some fear of it, not taking sides with their fellows.

After a time, Stephen was left alone in the room. He was waiting for Kendall. He meant to find out what the Company's intentions were in regard to himself. He did not intend to go on in this anomalous position. Let them declare themselves. He felt he had a right to that consideration.

It was a strange meeting between the two—this the first time they had been alone with each other since Kendall had been made general manager. Stephen had taken it for granted that he would be speaking to a man secure in his position, free to consider the problems of his men. But as soon as Kendall had grasped the fact that Stephen was alone in the room, he had burst forth into speech, pouring out a torrent of disappointment, frustration. As if, with relief at last, in the presence of a friend, he spoke freely, crying out from the depths of his lonely power.

"You wouldn't envy me, Steve, if you knew where I stand! It isn't the job I thought it was going to be. I've known for months, ever since last summer, to be definite, that the Company was thinking of putting me here. I've planned what I'd do—make a big thing of it. I've always felt Truesdale was soft. If only I'd had his chance when things were expanding! It looked first as if I could keep the stations up-river open, but, well, you know all about that. But I'll open them again, don't you forget it—I've got to."

With wonder, Stephen listened to his outburst. Here Kendall was, pouring out his heart to him. And yet, ever since he had been in this house, Kendall had avoided speech with him! Stephen was conscious of but one thing—whatever had kept his friend away from him, Kendall trusted him enough to disclose his troubles to him. He forgot his own troubles for the moment, as he looked at the other man, sitting on the edge of a chair, his hands hanging limp between his knees, speaking in short phrases, long pauses between.

"But even then the job won't be the big thing it once was. I know now the cash business is here to stay. That doesn't make the big thing of the business it once was. This tank destruction proves that the Chinese have got to buy at big treaty ports and take the up-country risk. I wouldn't mind clearing away for a bigger thing. Well, maybe I can make it yet. A small tight organization first."

Suddenly some hard shell seemed to close over the man's heart. "Now as to you, Steve," he continued without giving Stephen a chance to speak, "I don't know anything about your situation. You were, as you know, slated for a position close to the top. Then Truesdale sent you to a small station."

"But," protested Stephen, "he told me it was to do a particularly delicate piece of work."

"I know nothing of what he said. Of course, there's this tank business—haven't had word from New York on that matter yet. But, see here, Steve, these burns of yours don't entitle you to hold the Company up. You told us first the doctor said they'd amount to little, and now you talk as if they might amount to a great deal."

Stephen drew back as if a whip had been lashed across his face.

"Surely, Dave . . ." He could get no further. Wild horses could not draw from him now any appeal to Kendall.

After Kendall left him, Stephen sat on in the desolate dining-room. He could not go up to Hester while this tumult raged within him. He could make no headway among his own conflicting emotions.

He wished he could have a friendly talk with Creighton, or Chesterton. Kendall called them dead wood. They weren't dead wood. He knew their work. Why were they leaving? If only there was more understanding between the men. But, as in the matter of salary raises, resignations and dismissals were always made a private matter with the Company. To talk about one's own relationship was not done. He must fight the thing out alone and his hands were tied. There was nothing to do but go on with his waiting.

VIII

A stir ran through the offices. The day before, a ship had got in from America, and the American mail had just arrived. Stephen could hear the bustle in Kendall's office and the men coming and going. Kendall's secretary went back and forth carrying letters to various desks.

Young Thornton had been called. The glass door had been shut, but now it was opening. Thornton coming, and Kendall with him.

"I'll show you your office," Kendall was saying. "Just a minute, though." He spoke to the roomful of men. "New York has appointed Thornton as my assistant."

Stephen sat very still. An hour ago, Look had been given the other vacant assistantship.

But here came Kendall's secretary, handing him a letter. Across the top in Kendall's handwriting was written, "Instruct Chase to carry out the wishes of the Company." Stephen opened the letter, his fingers trembling. It was from Director Swaley, written in the name of the Company, instructing the Shanghai office to issue formal thanks to all Chinese who had so valiantly defended Company property on that day of the burning of the tanks.

Stephen was surprised to hear himself laughing. Why, he felt gay—reckless. A man at a near-by desk looked up. Pity was written in his face. Pity was an effrontery to a man, took away his privacy, stripping him before his fellows. That was what an injured body did to one. Gave other men the right to pity you. He'd have no more of pity.

The man was speaking, "What's the matter, Chase? Can I help you? Want a glass of water?"

Stephen got to his feet, fumbled awkwardly for his hat. Confound it, he was a dub to be so clumsy. Somebody handing it to him. Damn the fellow. Just because he had a bandaged hand, every one wanted to help him. He didn't need help. Especially when he felt so happy.

He got outside. He wanted to get under cover, to hide. And yet he didn't get into a taxi, but stumbled along to the bus. The dust blew in clouds along the bund. He wished it would get thicker and hide him. Always so many people watching him, his bandaged arm, his grotesque, bandaged leg. There'd be that new house-boy of his. Damn the new boy! And there'd be Hester. Damn . . . Oh, what was he saying?

He made the side entrance to the house. Quietly now up the stairs. Thank God, Hester was out. People knowing his humiliation. He had failed Hester. Well, burns or no burns, he'd demand something of the Company. Because of his burns, he'd demand something of the Company. God damn fool to have pride in your work. Money, security—that was all that counted. Fodder in Big Business. Well, he'd been fodder long enough. Now he could see what a poor thing he was. All his life he'd been hampered with duty. Duty. Bah! He was a poor flattened-out thing. Pride in his work, poor stuff. Fodder for Big Business. He'd just work for the money hereafter, until he was retired. Why hadn't he seen that before? Jim was right. Little old pay envelope all that counted. He'd get Shanghai for Hester. She must not lose out because he had failed. His mind wandered in helpless bewilderment, trying to see why he had failed her. Well, he'd ask for a job in Shanghai. No matter how small it was. He'd not fail Hester, too.

Coming in at six, Hester wondered that Stephen was not home. "No, missie," said the boy. But when she opened the door to their room and switched on the light, she saw him sitting so erect, so pale, and his eyes . . . what had happened to make them like that—reckless and without pride?

Hester stood with her back against the door. Beyond the silent room, beyond the compound wall, she could hear the tinkling bells of the rickshas, the motor-car sirens, and still farther away, beyond the barbed-wire entanglement that encircled the settlement, intermittent shots, the constant pattern of danger woven about them; below in the garden, Kendall, working on his motor-car; and, occasionally, the ingratiating voice of Look as he helped him. She heard it all, each sound striking on her consciousness, as she looked at Stephen.

"Don't, Hester," Stephen was speaking. "You have no right to pity me. I don't need it. Leave me alone. Please go away."

Hester shut the door behind her. Surely, Kendall . . . if he understood. He could not mean to do this to Stephen. Why should he treat Stephen so? She, his wife, would speak for him. Say the things he could never say for himself. The child within her seemed not more her child than this man she loved. The depths of her love welled up within her, flooding her with an ineffable desire to protect him, shield him from all harm. More beautiful than passion, this hovering love. Down the long black stairs, out of the heavy oak door to the garden. Holding her breath, holding her heart, too—holding its beat down. She was afraid of Kendall. But Stephen's eyes . . . more afraid of them.

Hester creeping up the stairs as Stephen had crept up the stairs an hour ago. Not seeing any one. The words of Kendall. They were waiting until Stephen was well to bring him before them all in humiliation. Kendall said the Company felt that Stephen had done a spectacular, unnecessary thing in going to the tanks! Perhaps even inducing the destruction by his presence. She was panting with her distress.

They should not do that to Stephen. Stephen should never know about the way they looked at his courage. No, she'd never give them a chance to bring him up before them like that, like a wrongdoer. Somehow, without telling him, she must get him to resign.

All the lights were on in the room when Hester went in. Stephen had the radio going full strength. Noise! Light!

"I tell you," he said, "I've made up my mind. I'm going to ask for the cushiest job there is. Nice soft job. Got it all picked out. Here in Shanghai. The little old pay envelope is the only thing that counts. I'll not fail you, Hester. I'll get safety for you."

"If he'd only stop," she thought desperately. In all his life he had never rattled on like this. "Stephen, let's give it all up. Let's go home. Certainly there's a place for us in America."

"You're only a woman," her husband answered harshly. "What do you know about earning a living?"

Hester, who had been sitting upright on the edge of a chair, suddenly crumpled, leaning against Stephen, sobbing.

"Stephen, you can't stay. We've got to resign. I went and talked to him."

Two spots of bright color dyed Stephen's cheeks.

"You did what, Hester? I can manage my own affairs. You'd better tell me everything."

Hester sat up straight. Everything was crumbling, even their love. Stephen was angry with her.

"Stephen, you've got to resign!" she cried. "You're to be brought before them. He says you had no business to be at the tanks that night."

"They're going to do what?"

"Kendall says it was foolhardy. It did the Company harm. Oh, Stephen, " Hester cried in anguished entreaty, "were you?"

For one moment Stephen felt himself undergoing some physical pain that contracted every feature. Even Hester doubting him. A man was nothing except what the mob made him. Even Hester believed them. Then, suddenly, he felt himself falling back to some inviolable retreat within himself, beyond this humiliated driven person. That ignominious person he had taken for himself—that person who had crawled home from the office to hide—was not himself.

"Hester, dear," he said, "I had no orders to get out.

The situation was getting worse all over the valley. Why didn't Kendall wire me to leave? I'll tell you why. Because he thought maybe I could save things in a pinch. I'm not blaming him. I'd probably do the same. It was worth taking a chance—a lot was at stake. And, Hester, I'd turned that other mob—I might have turned this one, too. If I had it to do over again—even after what happened—I'd think there was a chance. Suppose I'd succeeded . . . ? What would Kendall say then?"

As he spoke, his sense of personal dignity returned. He had his own identity, of which no one could rob him. And he'd keep it. What was Stephen Chase to him, except as Stephen Chase who could respect himself? Gently he lifted Hester's head resting against him.

"You're right, dear. I'm going to resign. We'll have to begin over. I can do it. Where shall I find Kendall? Never mind, I'll find him."

Slowly he made his way down the stairs.

He found Kendall still working over his car. He did not look up, nor did Stephen speak. He stood watching Kendall, who, with an almost gentle look on his face, was filing delicately away at a tiny cog. Kendall loved machinery as Stephen did. When they had been in school together, they had always been tinkering on something. So familiar, that curve of Kendall's back, that intent look. Their friendship of so many years. That, the reality; these last days, the unreality.

"Dave," Stephen said at last. "I've come to resign."

Kendall went on with his work. "You're talking rot, Steve. Unless you've had a fortune left you. Then, of course, I've nothing to say."

"No, no fortune. But I'm resigning."

Kendall looked up now. "See here, you're too thin-skinned. It's only a question of being down and the pack baying. You can show them! Take this job I'll give you.

398

Haven't been able to speak until to-day. It isn't so much to start with . . ."

"Yes, take it," Stephen broke in, bitterness creeping into his tone. "And when the next emergency comes, and I leave instead of staying as I did this time, it will be much easier for you. You can call me yellow. No! I'll leave now, when you can only call me 'foolhardy.'"

Kendall was angry now. It wasn't his fault what was happening. Hadn't Swaley said last summer, "In the readjustment, you'll find we're top-heavy. It's at the top you've got to clear out." He had even raised a question about Steve. "Little too idealistic when it comes to sending men out when he thinks it's dangerous, don't you think, Kendall?" he had said.

Confound Steve, was he going to be stubborn? Had he gone too far with him? He couldn't have him leave the Company just now. "Burnham's and the young griffin's tales are believed now, but there's secret admiration for Steve in that tank business. If he resigns, it will burst out," he thought. It was up to him, Kendall, to persuade Steve to stay. But, by heck, after he'd got Steve to stay, he'd make him pay for this! He'd grill him on the tank business!

"Well, Steve," Kendall said at last, "I suppose you've considered what it means to get started at home. No business contacts, no experience in America. And you're over forty. Forty's the dead line there. Better reconsider, take a day to think it over. I'll not accept your resignation until tomorrow."

Kendall's eyes were on his work, but he knew Stephen had gone. He could hear the uneven rhythm of foot and crutch, foot and crutch, in the big house.

Hester, waiting in the quiet room, could hear their voices below, but not what they said. The minutes passed.

399

The fight ahead—could Stephen make it? America seemed so strange. Shabby struggle, ugly. Panic began settling over her.

What had she done? The habit of mind of years began to assert itself. Security. The child! In her concern for Stephen, she had ignored that. Now, suddenly, the instinct of the mother to protect her young seized her. Everything must be sacrificed for the child; that it might have comfort, that it might be spared all trouble, such as she and Stephen were passing through.

She looked up. There was Stephen, the old reliable Stephen to lean upon.

"Stephen, I must tell you something. If you hadn't been so absorbed," she cried out desperately, "you'd have known. It's what you've wanted, a child."

"A child!"

In that first moment, to Stephen it was as if the heavens had opened to bless them. Sorrow for the son he had prepared for burial so many years ago gave way to this living joy. Fatherhood, born in him so suddenly years ago and as suddenly thwarted, leaped again into life. He leaned over Hester, lifting her bowed head until he could look into her eyes.

"Oh, my dear!" He could say no more. As he gathered Hester into his embrace, like strong wings, he felt his tenderness closing round her to shelter her.

Shelter her? A man without a job? It was well that Hester had shut her eyes to feel the full bliss of his care —she must never know the sudden pain that contracted his features. A few moments before, he had felt himself free. Free to struggle to keep his self-respect. Now he knew that freedom was a luxury he could not afford. Forty! He was over the dead line. Hester must have security, and his child must have security. He was caught—the Company could work its will with him. He must accept the humiliation, take whatever they offered

400

him. And he must surrender Hester for an indefinite period. Since he had seen the terrible violence of the mob that night of the fire, he knew he could never again take Hester into the interior.

At last he spoke. "After all, dear, what does it matter? It's the money that counts." And, after a pause, "I'll have to go back into the interior. It's no place for women. The best thing is to have you go home. You'll have good doctors and good care."

Hester's clasp tightened. "I can't bear to have you go back alone. Is there no other way?"

"I can't see any."

In the night Hester woke. She was sitting up in bed, feeling that Stephen had called her, that for a long time he had been calling her, in dry hard sobs. She listened, but there was no sound. It seemed almost as if Stephen held his breath.

"Did you call me, Stephen?"

"No, dear."

Again the room was still.

THE END

BANTAM BOOKS

The famous mysteries, novels and books of fiction and non-fiction listed here are all available through the dealer from whom this Bantam book was purchased.

1. LIFE ON THE MISSISSIPPI, Mark Twain
2. THE GIFT HORSE, Frank Gruber
3. "NEVADA," Zane Grey
4. EVIDENCE OF THINGS SEEN, Elizabeth Daly
5. SCARAMOUCHE, Rafael Sabatini
6. A MURDER BY MARRIAGE, Robert George Dean
7. THE GRAPES OF WRATH, John Steinbeck
8. THE GREAT GATSBY, F. Scott Fitzgerald
9. ROGUE MALE, Geoffrey Household
10. SOUTH MOON UNDER, Marjorie Kinnan Rawlings
11. MR. AND MRS. CUGAT, Isabel Scott Rorick
12. THEN THERE WERE THREE, Geoffrey Homes
13. THE LAST TIME I SAW PARIS, Elliot Paul
14. WIND, SAND AND STARS, Antoine de Saint-Exupery
15. MEET ME IN ST. LOUIS, Sally Benson
16. THE TOWN CRIED MURDER, Leslie Ford
17. SEVENTEEN, Booth Tarkington
18. WHAT MAKES SAMMY RUN?, Budd Schulberg
19. ONE MORE SPRING, Robert Nathan
20. OIL FOR THE LAMPS OF CHINA, Alice Tisdale Hobart

Only 25¢ each

Bantam Books, Inc., 1107 Broadway, New York 10, N. Y.

palacios